CW00519992

Wire Pulling Sailors

robertbolumburu@protonmail.com

Wire Pulling Sailors

A Cornucopian Tale

Chapters

Acknowledgements

The author wishes to thank K. K. and A. B. A. for corrections and L. H., C. H., S. J., B. B. and S. K. L. for access to their correspondence.

These books are dedicated to Blind Boy Grunt, Bobby Allen and the Jack of Hearts.

—More of an outlaw than you ever were

Book Two: Phlegm

They are sleepy, saith Savonarola, dull, slow, cold, blockish, ass-like, asininam melancholiam, Melancthon calls it; "they are much given to weeping, and delight in waters, ponds, pools, rivers, fishing, fowling, etc." (Arnoldus, Breviar. I, cap. 18). They are pale of colour, slothful, apt to sleep, heavy; "much troubled with headache," continual meditation, and muttering to themselves; they dream of waters, that they are in danger of drowning, and fear such things (Rhasis)....If it be inveterate or violent, the symptoms are more evident, they plainly dote and are ridiculous to others, in all their gestures, actions, speeches; imagining impossibilities, as he in Christophorus à Vega, that thought he was a tun of wine, and that Siennois, that resolved within himself not to piss, for fear he should drown all the town.

Burton, Anatomy of Melancholy

1. The Unconvinced

It was a quiet street, *Stallburggasse*. Bjørn pointed down it, like a pointer pondering the game. He wore a fleece, chinos and small brown sneakers. The fleece he zipped to the top, breathing clouds. It was midday, but dark. The sky was full of snow.

He passed shining cars—silvers, blues, maroons. Past *Bräunerstraße* was an art gallery, black but bright-windowed. Next door was the *Bräunerhof*—close to the *Hofburg*, a skip from *Michaelerplatz*. Not difficult to find.

Bjørn was clutching a piece of paper. He was clutching it like a clamp, fingers concentred on one stressed area of paper. He wasn't aware that he was doing this. But he was. On the paper, a curious bystander—and such men existed—bending over on one side and dogging his steps, would have read the following words:

If, as the presence of this note folded about my door handle appears to indicate, I am not in fact here, I am, by inference, very probably there, which, curiously enough, is a euphemism for the Cafe Bräunerhof, which you will find on Stallburggasse in the *Innerestadt. If, Dumkopf that you are, you remain confounded, my advice would be to tap the Putzfrau, anglice, washerwoman. You might also inquire the way to the Bräunerhof.*

Jude.

The *Bräunerhof* had a plain, old-fashioned facade. Yellow walls, a mahogany-colour sign saying *CAFE BRÄUNERHOF*, over two large, chequered windows with window-boxes. Net-curtains hung in the lower portions of window. Above them Bjørn made out round lamps; beyond them, darker lights, like fires. You'd hardly have known it was day.

The door-glass was glazed, as if with rungs. Bjørn took a breath, pushing through it.

Waiters hurried to and fro. Tall waiters, stern waiters, waiters with strange moustaches. At the other end of the room was the bar, crammed in an angle, reflecting that angle with an angle of its own. There milled several more waiters, like particles in some heated experiment. Some perspired. Some swore. All frowned like the world depended on it. A traveller from a Utopian future, searching for the acme, or nadir, of the frown, might well have been directed to Vienna, perhaps, like Bjørn, to the *Bräunerhof*—by way of the washerwoman.

Between bar and door was a string quartet,

squeezing the spaces. Two violins, a viola and cello attenuated distance with Brahms and Beethoven. Now they were in the midst of a clamorous *allegro*. Strings flung fish-lines through the room, wayward, now returning. They were supreme masters, leather-gloved, blowing doves and canaries. The clientele were wound like clocks.

Bjørn's was naturally a long gaze. It wasn't always brought out, but when it was it went directly to the back of a room. Past tables and noticeboards it went, tangling awhile with moustaches, arriving at last at velvet, at curtain, at toilet. Curving round—like a central-defender with a wide turning-arc—it began a long return journey, querying coats, running sideboards, skipping through toast-racks. It was like Manet in there. Beige floors, beige seats it brushed. Pretty faces, in furs and mufflers, it found and fled from. Round squared inlets with the one-piece wall-seats, just like a peg in a hole. Getting in amongst 'em, hundred per-cent the full three-sixty, into row Z went the gaze, among lamps and plaster, smoke and rococo. It swung like *The Phantom* by oval mirrors, betrayed a space in self-reflection. What did that gaze see in itself, pausing in the mirror? A gaze: gazing backwards and forwards, for time immemorial. 'Ha!' thought a bysitter in the room. 'The Mirror meets the Gaze and relents, exhausted! Where's your *Jugendstil* now? Decadence decayed, secession all ceased.'

On travelled the gaze unawares, awkwardly negotiating, adjusting now to hatstands, now to music-stands. Hairs were tousled with, net-curtains buzzed in, skirting boards—invested with significance. The gaze was a very serious fly. Here a dessert-table, crammed with cakes. There, piles of newspapers, wood frames clamped along the fold. The gaze tripped on some bags, was becalmed in the window-booths. It studied a woman, as if there it might find what it was looking for. She was a fine woman. Golden-haired, strong nosed, middle-thirties; with a scarlet roll-neck, pearl necklace, jeans tight on the thigh. Her hair was tailed, or tossed on shoulders. She was looking at an older version of herself—money was on her mother—but she wasn't listening. Now and again her glance strayed beyond the booth.

Opposite the booth sat a fat man in a white suit and Homburg. It was hard to tell his age, but it was somewhere past seventy. He had large tinted glasses, pale skin, big red craters round the eyes. A soup-plate, roll and tea-cup were pushed from him. One hand held a book, the other a cigar. He was looking to his left whenever a newspaper rustled.

A newspaper was rustling quite frequently, because someone there was reading one. It was yesterday's *Guardian* and from behind it rolled slim, white fingers, and feminine. Bordering them, the sleeves of a long-sleeved t-shirt, one a little frayed. In front of the newspaper stood a tall espresso cup with a teaspoon placed across it. Next to the cup, a glass of water.

The gaze made out *all-stars* under the table.

The paper moved a fraction, an iota's more interest shown in its contents. Enough to reveal a blue forehead, a fall of ginger. There was a silence. Bjørn stepped to the table, stretching his arm.

'A Norweyan Lord,' said a voice of command. 'Surveying vantage. Flouting with his banners! Fanning our people cold.' The fat man adjusted his neckscarf. It was true, Bjørn had not closed the door properly; chill winds were sweeping the recesses. A waiter tutted hard, closed it softly. An expressive *adagio* began.

'Jude Harlow.'

'Bjorn Bjornsen.'

There were smiles and handshakes. More smiles. Almost a tear.

'Ridiculous. Ridiculous.'

'Ridiculous.'

Bjørn had a tight grin on his face. He was leaning over the tablecloth, shaking hands with a straight arm. The inverse of Muttiah Muralitharan, Bjørn's arm was always straight, even when it was bent. He almost forgot that he was still shaking hands. Jude didn't, though. He resumed his hold upon the paper. The fat man huffed.

'I saw you come in, surveying the room with a

Norwegian *gaze*. Norwegians may be born with skis on their feet—so you *say*, and I'm willing to believe it—but they are also born with long *gazes*. Which makes the birth more painful is a moot point among the crèches of Bergen and Bø.'

Bjørn chuckled, looking for an appropriate response. In the booth, the woman smiled.

'I supposed you would spot me eventually. Besides, I was reading this article about a certain *football manager*. A reasonable assessment of his tenure. *Turnarounds*, they talk of. *Steady progress*, they say.' Jude showed a glimpse of picture. The fat man pricked his ears.

'Ah, well, that's exactly what they SHOULD be saying.' Bjørn sniffed and drew out a chair. 'Because of course he IS making progress. And he HAS turned things round. What we've just got to realise is some other of these ordinary managers are just doing a job. For them, it's just a matter of OBLIGATION. But what we've got here is a man who just, when his working day is over at the football ground, he just GOES OUT and has dinner with some AGENTS, you know, establishing CONNECTIONS all over the place.'

'No, I appreciate—'

'NnnnHE'S ESTABLISHED all these, you know, conNECTions. He's always having dinner with an AGENT.'

'I believe it.'

‘Sometimes you find people are just not able to state the plain truth. The facts are just too obvious and, you know, their MINDS are just not able to deal with that. They have to start, you know, ah, sniffing outside the lines. What the media are not realising—although of course this article may be, er, quite reasonable—there may be one or two journalists who have some kind of DETACHMENT—but most of the media, they’re not INTERESTED in the truth, in some kind of obYECTive assessment.’ If Jude spoke in italics, Bjørn spoke the way he wrote, in capitals, lapsing occasionally into runes. ‘All they, er, NEED, is a story, just to run with anything. They don’t feel GUILT or REMORSE. That’s why I’m not reading the newspapers. I’m just not INTERESTED in what they have to say.’

‘He was just pointing out—’

‘Uh you know, you and I can just SIT here, just analysing the situation, and we’re gonna come up with all kinds of angles—all kinds of pointviews and insights which we’ve just, you know, DERIVED from the facts, and from the, uh, ANALYSIS of the large picture. We can sit here and we’re not needing the newspapers to add their penny in the POT (ah, is that what you say, er, penny in the pot?)’

Jude let him talk.

‘Because, you know, they’re pulling opinions

FROM THE AIR. Ahh, you're just gonna have to realise that the next time they lose, the same newspaper is gonna be running a story about, ah, you know, WASTING money and how it's all gonna be ending in some big DISASTER. I've been feeling, they're just into DISASTER SCENARIOS! I feel—you know, the media, all these journalists and people on the edges—you know, these vultures, hanging off the crumbs—'

As if by magic, a moustachioed waiter appeared. He looked as if he had always been standing there. Not that he was impassive; he looked highly irritable.

'*Er—ah—na ya—ein er—ein Kaffee*,' said Bjørn, flustered. He pointed to his chest. '*Für mich, ein Kaffee. Nur. Ja. Ja, das ist alles.*' He ruled a palmed hand and nodded. The waiter let him talk.

'*Ein große Schwarzer, und noch ein kleine,*' said Jude, lowering the newspaper.

The waiter span round. The fat man leaned sideways. Jude looked at Bjørn and turned a page. '*Kaffee* is too common,' he continued when the coast was clear. 'Here they drink *große Schwarzers*, a multi-kulti homoeroticism of the most *bourgeois* kind.'

The fat man eased back.

'But speaking of *disaster scenarios*—I take it you got here alright?'

'Uh, what? Oh no, I just came right here.

Incredible how—just how—EASY it was to find you, to just ah, make my way through, er, large SWATHS of Europe, and just turn up right HERE, completely ANONYMOUS, at this parTicular place. Suddenly there you are, Jude Harlow, just sitting there. With just a few simple directions.'

'Except that not only myself, but the whole of Vienna, has anticipated your arrival. No, a *huge military presence*—a veritable *encampment*, comprising living quarters, chinook helicopter gunships and hordes of nineteen-year-old conscripts with machine guns and live ammunition—is massing on *the Heldenplatz* as we speak. Right under the balcony from which Austria's favourite son gave his triumphant homecoming speech, circa, *ooooh*, nineteen-thirty-eight?'

'Na, wha?'

'Austria this is. Preparing for a *National Day* tomorrow. *Ohne* irony. Celebrating, with a display of naked aggression, the declaration of their permanent *neutrality*—nineteen-fifty-five—incidentally around the same time that, over in America, Vanessa McFly was attempting to seduce her own son and threatening to rupture the *space-time continuum*. I believe that's what they were calling it then.'

'Nnn, there's a LINK there somewhere.'

'No doubt Drake could spot it. But the obvious conclusion is that Austrian neutrality has been subconsciously, therefore consciously, constructed in Oedipal vocabulary, *i.e.* frustration at the dominance of the *Vaterland*—Germany—the drive to replace him, and the consequent creation of a *Mutterland* of milk and chocolate, sometimes both together, at whom to direct ostensibly fierce sexual urges, masquerading behind ostensibly Platonic—*philanthropic*, as The Man Who Would Be King might say—intentions, themselves masking the reality of post-war cultural and political *impotence*. All this in order to physic *themselves*, exorcising their own demons through auto-analysis, and instigate an orgy of self-congratulation—as well as verifying, by proxy, the methods and reputation of their adopted, *second-favourite* son.'

'Er, there's probably something IN that.'

'That's what the Austrians think too.'

'You know, AH, there are no MISTAKES in LIFE—SOME PEOPLE SAY! AND—ah—it's TRUE SOMETIMES. YOU CAN SEE IT THAT WAY!'

'Take themselves too seriously, they do. Thankful for being God's born Englishman, I am.'

'Nnnn, though you might laugh at this of course, but—I—I've got to say, I've been feeling QUITE good, ah, recently—about being NORWEGIAN.'

'Yes, I—'

'Ah, I've been travelling along here—just almost minding my BUSINESS. And, ah, I've got to say, often, as a NORWEGIAN, you seem, perhaps, to get more RESPECTT, than perhaps an Englishman, or a Frenchman could get, er, normally. Or a Russian perhaps. MmmM, there are ADVANTAGES of being SCANDINAVIAN, although of course normally we don't like to group ourselves with Swedes and Danes, and of course Finns, and Icelanders, although of course we get on much better with the Danes than with the Swedes, who we've always been regarding with, ah, some kind of suspicion. They've—they've been tending to think of themselves as—er, almost as—ABOVE we NORWEGIANS. AH, still feeling themselves to be KINGS of SCANDINAVIA! Er, but, OFTEN we Scandinavians are not perceived as a threat. We—we're thought of as a peaceful—er—RACE—er, even though we are several DIFFERENT races of course. AhhH, MYSELF, FOR INSTANCE! I have—probably have—ITALIAN blood, come up to BERGEN with the good old boxing sailors.' Bjørn pointed to his dark hair and grimaced.

'Oh yes, the *good old boxing sailors*.'

'But I've noticed that some Austrians—they're seeing some kind of conNECTION there—ah, even though, of course, their history is, ARGUABLY, greater than ours—er, all in all. ALTHOUGH, of course, we shouldn't FORGETT about Harald Hårfagre and the old Wiking explorers.'

‘As if we could.’

‘Na, but generally, they seem to see a, er, some kind of conNECTION with us—er, could be because we are both MOUNTAIN countries—’

‘Mutually benefitting from a dubious rock-and-snow trade.’

‘Er—’

‘Sending under-age immigrants up craggy peaks, in fluorescent *salopettes*, dawn till dusk, to scratch and *eke* a living. Having the gall to call it *tourism!*’ Jude raised a triumphant finger.

‘Ah, both always been under the threat of a greater power, or PERCEIVED greater power.’

‘The Faeroe Islands.’

‘AH—oh, huh—BUT, then, of course, every now and again, you just come across that famous, AUSTRIAN conservative—er—reservation.’

‘Mauthausen-Gusen?’

‘Ah, this kind of, er, uBIQuitous SUSPICION!’

‘No, exactly.’ Jude’s eye lit out to his left. ‘As opposed to Norwegian liberalism.’

‘NnnN, ALTHOUGH, of course, I have to say you find some real, ah, GOOD OLD souls too. Some kind of, er—though I wouldn’t perhaps go this far—but ANGEL figures—ready to just hold a helping hand.’

‘Hmm.’

‘Mm, ER, for instance! For instance! There’s that SERBIAN at the, er, *Studentenheim*—’

'Not an Austrian, then.'

'Ah, no, not an Austrian. But a VIENNESE, at least. Called, er, Darko I think—I think that's what he said his name was. And THERE I WAS! just, ah, just STANDING, just STANDING outside! Just waiting! Right under the RED TRIANGLE. Because, ah, I couldn't contact you and I didn't have a key of course. And he just LET ME IN, and just ah—you know—took me to his CONFIDENCE, showing me where is your room.'

'Really? No, Darko's brilliant. It's funny: that's exactly what happened to me, except it wasn't Darko.' Jude put down the newspaper, jabbing the air with the teaspoon. In the corner of his eye the fat man moved. 'There I stood, sir, in the pouring rain, in the eighth district, newly *lit* from a taxi—a taxi just come, that twenty minutes, from the *Südbahnhof,* also known as *Wien Mitte*, also known as *Stadt Mitte*, because they like to give you three chances in Vienna—and, like Peter, deny you thrice. And like the Apostle, too.' He tapped the spoon-handle on the table to indicate the stages of comprehension. 'I had just caught a coach, costing me handfuls of Österreichen Marks, to the *Südbahnhof* from the airport, where an unpardonably early flight had just brought me from *England.*' Here he raised his eyebrows, giving Bjørn to understand the import of the word *England.* Luckily, in Bjørn he had an audience susceptible to that import. 'So *early*, indeed, that I had to stay all night in the airport, where of course I begged, borrowed, nor *stole*, so much as a wink of the forty, but watched—merely *watched,* sir, and I would have you understand the *bleakness*—the cleaners and their wheelchairs go gliding athwart the floors. The *polished* floors, sir. The *phosphorescent*, *illimitable*, airport floors. An airport, by the way, to which, the previous evening, I had taken a train, costing more than *twenty* of my English pounds, from a train station to which I had *just taken* another train, costing *forty* of my English pounds. All this! Ha! Having just taken a flight from—where? I ask you. Where?'

Bjørn thought the question rhetorical.

'Come on, where?'

'No, I—I don't know.'

'*Vienna*.'

Bjørn frowned.

'To whose airport I had *just taken* a bus from whose *Südbahnhof,* to which I had just taken a taxi from whose abject, *accursed*, *Wohnungsvermittlung* near the *Staatsoper*, where I had been arguing for an hour about the *possibility*—in the broadest sense, understand—of a *room*, and then the potential *availability* of that possible room. Then the abstract practicability of a potentially-available possible room being *hypothetically* reserved for a *given*—*given*, mind—individual, at some *theoretical* future time. This, having just come from the *British Embassy*'—with a special emphasis—'account of having just come from, once again, the *Wohnungsvermittlung*'—again the spoon chopped the stages of the journey—'stopping in the meantime at a cashpoint, where, at the *third attempt*, my card was inexplicably seized, leaving me stony as a broke-down engine—'

'Nn, without any driving wheel.'

'I mean *ohne Geld*, sir—but for five, almost meaningless, Österreichen Marks, soon to be even more meaningless euros.'

Jude paused, placing the spoon like a chess piece. This was a gesture which pleased Bjørn, he knew not why. 'Alright, here it is, sir. I am *European*, and I am *sceptical*. Ergo, I am a Euro-*Sceptic*. I am not *convinced*. Of course I strode into the bank to get it back, and, of course, access was denied. Not thrice, but *once*. With *extreme* finality. Having therefore gone to the British Embassy, thinking hellfire, damnation, and maps coloured *entirely pink*, with a bit of blue around the edges. I stood outside that Embassy, sir. I stood outside that Embassy and I *froze*, before finally gaining admittance. Thereupon I pushed past crowds of immigrants and benefit-thieves-to-be, heading for the counter marked *British Citizens*, to demand some kind of *Reason*. Sure enough, I was escorted to a *small room*, accessible only by *two locked doors*, where I was left alone with a telephone to do *whatever it was I thought necessary*. And I did what I thought necessary, sir. I did it with *extreme prejudice*.'

The woman shifted her head. The fat man adjusted glasses. The book hadn't grabbed him yet.

'*Having*, I might point out, just come from the *Studentenheim—achten Bezirk*, and, believe me, I was close to it—where a relentlessly stupid man—and a blonde, mark you—called Stefan, who may be found three hours, one day of the seven (the exact time I happened to arrive), opening and closing the files of filing cabinets to hear their satisfying *click* in the pokey first-floor hole he calls an *Amt*—probably the only appropriate word for it—had barred my access, account of my not possessing a suitably stained document on which to wipe his Teutonic hind.'

'Crumbs.'

'Having, of course, just arrived in a taxi from the *Südbahnhof*—remember that?—otherwise known as the *Wien Mitte*, or *Stadt Mitte* if you are so inclined—and many here *are*—to which I had taken a bus from the *airport*, to which I had just that minute taken an early flight from an airport in *England*, to which, curiously, I had been driven—in a *limousine*—by a man called *Mike*—at the behest of the *British Government*.'

'Crumbs.'

'And there I stood in the pouring rain, a bunch of

bags in my grip, under a *red triangle*—near a phone box *stuffed with flowers*. A tear, sir, come to my eye. And, as I stood there, knowing not if I was coming or going—literally, *not knowing if I was coming or going*—actually moonwalking back and forth in front of the steps, wishing myself in a tunnel in the Glum—suddenly there appeared a washerwoman, scrubbing the door with a sponge. *Leering*.'

'Huh-huh.'

'I mean it. *Leering*. Actually *lolling* her tongue.'

'Actually, ah, now that you say that, I think I saw that, er, SAME woman. Ahh, doing the—ah VACUUM cleaning—at the end of your corridor.'

'Likely. Highly likely.'

'Ah well, I didn't SEE her vacuum cleaning.' Bjørn looked away and winced, drawing back his mouth. 'I only HEARD that.' His fingers played with his chin. 'But I saw someone—er—ah—PEERING round the corner. Just a head, PEERING ROUND.'

'An artificially blonde head?'

'—I think—'

'A fat artificial head, with piggy eyes?'

'—Could be—'

'Piggy, forty-something eyes, stripping you of your laundry? Eyes of the happy coincidence of work and leisure?'

The woman in the booth raised her face. She

looked like heaven. 'A highly exclusive, rigorously policed Aryan heaven, of course,' reflected Jude. 'A heaven of leather-clad seraphs, combing their *goldenes Haar*, drinking effortless *Weizenbiers* from sundry tuns and horns.' He looked back at Bjørn. 'So as I suspected: *heaven*.'

'Ah, I had the feeling—er, is she RUSSIAN?'

'Ha! It's a perfectly reasonable inference.' Jude looked sly. 'However, I'd wager her an *Österreich*, from two *related* habits. First, that of declaiming *Gruß Gott* at every turn, and, second, her incessant sexual innuendo devoid either of substance or charm. And very Austrian.'

At this point the waiter reappeared. You could not say *as if by magic* because you could see him coming from a way off, swinging past deserters and their coats like a sign in wind. Nevertheless, Jude turned a conspiratorial eye; and, as he was facing the room and Bjørn only the cream wall, the illusion of suddenness was maintained. An arm swung in front of Bjørn's nose, and at its end, a tray. On the tray, two cups of coffee on saucers, topped with two teaspoons. Next to them, two glasses of water. A precarious cargo, placed hastily on the table.

'Ah, *danke*,' said Bjørn. '*Danke*.' He waved. The waiter turned his back.

'A case in point,' said Jude.

'Ah, er, probably it was her. But, er, what we've

just got to REALISE,' resumed Bjørn, gathering his thoughts. 'Is that—that's the amazing thing about, er, travel, travelling JOURNEYS. It doesn't matter if you're going, you know, five miles or five thousand miles. You always arrive at a SPECIFIC point in time and space. It's enough to make you believe—ah well, if you could believe in that, huh-huh—in JUNG'S theories of the collective subconscious. It's almost like—although I've always, ahuh, been sceptical of that desigNATION—a DESTINY.'

'Certainly a destination.'

'Ah—you know—the idea that you could just turn out, up from the blue, and be somewhere—ah, HERE FOR EXAMPLE—just drinking coffee in the Cafe Bräunerhof.' Bjørn, with great synchronicity, stretched a straight arm for his cup.

'Outrageous.'

'Because of some, almost—er, what do you call it?—ah—SLIGHT HAND!' Jude's hand slipped down the paper to fold it. The quartet slipped into A-minor.

'I WONDER—' boomed the fat man suddenly. He had a voice like hellfire.

'UH, a phone-call HERE!' rejoined Bjørn, sensing threats to his theory, not as yet realising their source. 'Er—A NOTE—skillfully placed—OVER THERE!'

He produced another note and tossed it on the

table.

Bjorn.

If flying in, proceed to the front of the airport and take a coach to the Südbahnhof, otherwise known as Wien Mitte, or Stadt Mitte. Once there—or if arriving by other means—take a taxi to 8 Auerspergstraße 9 (the nine being the district). It's too far to walk with stuff and the driver shouldn't have any problem finding the building—it's right next to Josefstädter Straße. If necessary, use maps and/or secret charts to get you to the heart of this—and Other Matters. There's a big red triangle outside, and an English phone box used as a display cabinet for shoes and flowers. Pure cubism. Get someone to let you in, preferably a girl or a washerwoman, the blonde one. She won't be in the least surprised if you say who you're looking for—and she's very friendly. Room 210 is where it's at. Again, she will know this.

Jude.

They were smiling fiercely again. Jude, who had picked up the paper, put it down again. 'But, no, I feel, *thou knowst not* how strongly,'—he tapped the table with a forefinger—'the benefit to society, the very *world*, of the *skilful placing of notes*. I'm not talking about letters, mark you.' He took the *kleine Schwarzer* from the tray and placed it in front of him. 'And bureaucracy has nothing to do with it. On the contrary, that is exactly what the note disowns. Because clearly—and to this extent your bog-standard terrorist, who, after all, is nothing more than a man tired of filling in *forms*, is *entirely right*—clearly bureaucracy is a mangy Whore, straddling *nations*, sowing *wind*, reaping it *tenfold*. Exhausting the world of its revolutions. And the terrorist feels this, deeply, darkly, *shamefully! Lusting*, with a mad, puritanical hatred, for the end of bureaucracy. Pining away among his mountains for silence and whiteness. Thinking the only way to get it is explosion. *Huge* explosion. But you see, this is *exactly* where your terrorist gets it *all wrong*, persuading himself, like the Oxford-educated Wilde-reader that he is, that he is oh-so pathetically killing the thing he loves, whereas of course he is perpetuating it. Because if he really wished to kill the thing he loved, he wouldn't kill it at all. He would simply ignore it. Engage in the most perfunctory of dialogues, then amuse himself with something else. A crossword. A Rubik's Cube perhaps. All the while *completely undermining* the Whore by entering into an *entirely different* mode of communication, based entirely upon the skilful composition, and *even more skilful positioning*, of notes, missives, epistles. Until the whole Whore personification blew away in the sand.' Jude looked Bjørn curiously in the eye. 'Like some global, corporate *Ozymandias*. Like the idol of socialism,' he added. 'Or *fascism*, for that matter, which amounts to the *same*.' He looked out of the window. 'Which everyone *persists* in thinking were brought down by bombs and muscles and the heroic sacrifice of millions of human lives, whereas in fact they were magnificently *belittled*—by a note or two, judiciously—*unexpectedly*—placed. It's all about *apposition*. Poe would understand.'

The woman crossed, uncrossed her legs, like something from *Brave New World*. With a confident air, the portly man stubbed his cigar, looking for a moment like Quentin. 'I SAID I WONDER—' he barked with an American burr. Jude was momentarily pained. Why was it that no one was capable of normal speech? '—IF I COULD TROUBLE YOU FOR THAT NEWSPAPER?' The chatter seemed to fade. The quartet stopped halfway through his question. They picked up their bows and turned to B-flat major.

The newspaper was lying over the table. Jude still had a finger in a page.

'Just ten or fifteen minutes. I'll hand it over when I've finished,' said Jude, who was sometimes courteous to strangers. 'For the good it will do you.'

The quartet began the *Große Fuge*.

'AH, doesn't some of that stuff you've just said, there, just, ah, FEED INTO, er, what you're writing, here in Vienna?' said Bjørn, making concessions to Jude, eager to stay on track. He cradled the *Große Schwarzer* in his claw.

'I KNOW SOMETHING THAT CAN DO YOU SOME GOOD.'

'Apparently so—Oh really?'

'If ENGLISHMEN LIKE good things.' The old man lowered his voice. It was a hollow voice, opening under the strings.

'Possibly,' said Jude, half-smiles. The man was an American—that was at once a glaring error and a glorious success.

The American fingered his book, flicking through the pages. He seemed to take great delight in this. On the spine was the word *Fegefeuer*. The cover showed a boy in the foetal position, floating through a sketchy sort of cosmos.

Jude turned to Bjørn. 'But only *apparently*.'

'OH, just a club I know of.'

'Wha?—er—oh.'

'Kind of an exclusive place.'

Jude looked affable through the smoke. He looked like his mother.

'It's a dining room. Are you from London?'

'No. The *Cooley Valley*.'

'Is that near London?'

'No.'

'You won't find anywhere like this in London. Or anywhere in England, come to that.'

'I'm sure.'

'Not in the U.S. either.' The man was rustling another cigar.

'You find a lot of things in Vienna you won't find elsewhere.' Jude paused. 'The Viennese for example.' He chuckled. Bjørn didn't notice.

'You got THAT RIGHT,' said the man, easing back, seeing past the joke. 'But it's a place a—discerning gentleman enjoys.' Jude said nothing, smiling weakly over his *kleine Schwarzer*.

The American breathed through his nose. 'You go there—it's a backroom: candlelight and mirrors. The way they like it here.' He brushed some crumbs, took his time. 'A lot of brass and velvet. You sit there at the table—you can go there any time of the day, from lunchtime on; it's a good place to eat; good food; wine. You can get a martini—scotch—cocktail—whatever grabs you.' He ran a nail down the cigar wrapper. 'They don't make a fuss. Take a table; stay as long as you like.'

This was a peculiar conversation. Jude wasn't even sure it was a conversation.

'Get yourself a Bloody Mary.' The man laughed in his chins. His eyes were cast on the table. Now he looked up. 'They make a fine Bloody Mary.' He looked down again, removed the wrapper like it was air. 'I know the barman there. It's a pretty place. Kind of faded baroque interior. Smart furnishing; tassles and whatnot. Singers, jazz, Mozart—you name it.' He waved his hand behind him. With the other hand he turned a page of his book. 'You sit there at the table and the waitress comes over. You ask for a sausage. She's wearing—you know, I'm not talking about any kind of untoward ACTIVITY. Nice-looking girls in there. Well-bred girls. It's not a strip-joint.'

Jude folded his arms on table. Bjørn's body faced the other way, but his head was turned.

'Waitress is wearing a LOW-CUT BLOUSE. Nice figures they have. Well-rounded women. A pretty little mini-skirt.' He waved the cigar in the air. 'Austrian women. Czech women—Eastern European. Oriental. Negress.' He took out a box of matches from his suit-pocket. 'Mulatto.' He shook it inside a fist; rested the fist on the table. There was complacency in that voice, yet persistence. 'You ask her for a sausage. It's very sophisticated, very easy on the eye. It's not PROSTITUTION. It's not a BORDELLO.' The man was faintly smiling. But he was emphasising the wrong words. Where he should have grown quiet, he spoke up. 'It's a harmless procedure. You ask her for a sausage. She goes to the kitchen, you wait there at the table.' He placed the cigar between his lips. 'After about five minutes, she comes back with a sausage. The band stops.' He struck a match. 'She shows you the sausage. You ask how much it costs. She asks you what you'll give her for it. And you reply, "a smack on the bottom".' He held the match to the cigar-end, inhaling. He was watching them, waiting till the flame touched his fingers. 'Then she bends over, you give her a smack on the bottom and she gives you the sausage.' He waved the match in the air. 'It's a very civilised affair.'

The man took a puff. Jude's face was burning.

'If you want any more, you ask for another sausage. When she comes back, the price is two smacks. Want any more, it's three smacks. And so on.'

'An interesting concept.'

'It's not an interesting concept.' The man looked steadily at Jude. 'It's smacking a girl on the fuckin' ass.'

'Well'—Jude cleared his throat. He didn't know how far to take this. 'It smacks of the conceptual to me.'

'You're a Brit.'

'Ah—I'm a Norwegian!'

The man ignored Bjørn. 'You wouldn't raise a finger against a lady, would you?'

Jude warmed up a little. 'Whereas you spank them with a *whole hand*. It's the pioneer spirit, I suppose.'

'Your problem is EMBARRASSMENT. FRIEDRICH hit it.' The man pulled the word *Friedrich* from his chin. 'A race of Eunuchs, drowning in history.'

'Oh it's *Friedrich* now?' smiled Jude, who could pontificate with the best of them.

'Like the cow who forgets to say that he forgets.'

'Yet who, notwithstanding, crams you in a corner and forces you to make an improvised exit through a *hawthorn hedge*, wherein, amidst a mass of brambles, a barbed-wire lies cunningly concealed—witness my ribcage.' Jude pulled up his t-shirt, and witnessed a long red scratch on his side. The American didn't know what he was talking about. Jude was comfortable with this. 'But that's the thing about Nietzsche. He ceases to instruct when he begins to generalise—which is all the time. Reaching, when the *ballistas* and *mangonels* of argument have come apart, for that silly *Davidian* catapult, the *aphorism*. Of course choosing the target is everything. And since the target is an idiot Cyclops—not much more than a giant eye—a direct hit is practically inevitable.'

'That's what I like about Brits. They keep fighting—albeit in vain—to preserve their little fiction. After all, they can only bear a little reality.'

'While you can only bear a big concept.'

'Well, I'm like Pound. More of a natural European.'

‘Yes, you blend right in here. Must be the reserve.’

‘Hmh!’ The cigar was balanced on the ashtray. ‘Excuse me, gentlemen, while I go to the bathroom.’ The man shuffled out from the table. He wheezed and spread his mouth. ‘Oh,’ he said, checking himself. ‘Would you keep an eye on my book?’ He swaggered toward the toilets.

Jude raised brows at Bjørn. Bjørn’s mouth was flat and straight. He looked like a phone booth, devoid of flowers. There wasn’t any point in expressing surprise—far less outrage.

Jude finished the *kleine Schwarzer*. ‘Sorry—what was it you were saying?’ He turned to the *Arts* section of the newspaper.

‘Na, ya—er—what was all that about?’

The man disappeared behind a curtain. ‘I don’t know,’ said Jude, and he meant it. ‘A spot of tourism by the sound of it. You know the thing: rich Americans—European tours—looking for the Whitman in themselves.’

This touched a chord in Bjørn. ‘Ahm, no—er—I’ve got to say—er, Whitman didn’t need to do any—ah, EUROPEAN TOUR. Ah because—ah—every ATOM belonging to him as GOOD BELONGS TO YOU!’

‘Exactly. Sounds like recipe for imperialism.’ Jude went rapidly through the *Arts* section.

‘Oh no. Oh no. Ah—of course—there ARE—

er—GREAT Americans who have done European tours. Ah—of course—one of them you know already. But—ah—I'm also thinking of HENRY MILLER, for INSTANCE! NnnNHENRY MILLER—ah—is a writer I've been getting—I've been just—ah—WAITING! to get into for a while now. Ah right now, I'm just all PREPARING myself for—ah—probably the GREATEST of his works. THE ROSY CRUCIFIXION! Now he—HE—is a writer you've just got to be checking out! Ah, he of course, came right here to Vienna, although of course, he's probably more associated with Paris—ah, well, and of course, New York. But—especially—if you're writing about—well—actually, that's what I was asking you: what ARE you writing about exactly?'

'Well, ha!'

'Uhh, Poe! Edgar Allen POE, you were talking about?'

'No, it's a chaotic, I might say *inchoate*, thing at the moment.'

'But what is—ah—the TITLE? At least so far?'

Again Jude lowered the newspaper. '*Nationalism, Anti-Semitism, the Rise of Fascism in Fin-de-Siecle Austria*, something of that sort. It's not my title, I hasten to add—nor, in fact, is the whole project my idea—or it would have a few less *isms* and a lot less Austria, one might almost say *consequently*.'

'Nn—I'm sure there's ALL kinds of HIDDEN

DEPTHS to a project like this. Er—you KNOW—these people, they want you to just give them some kind of—er—tidy—TIDY kind of a SUMMARY of what's going on there. You know—they're just sitting there—ah, in their MANSIONS—just expecting some—you know—PERFECTED document to just drop on their desks, without any real kind of thought—you know, without any real kind of—er—COMPLEXITY. AH, because that's what they don't WANT! They're not WANTING that, these people! They're sitting around wanting SIMPLE answers—you know, simple overviews of things. And that's why they give you a title like that—so they can pack it all neatly and just hang it on the wall. They just want you to DANCE—ah—with who they TELL YOU TO.'

'A waltz, no doubt.' The *Arts* section was a bore. Jude went back to the football manager. A real-life story.

'And—but—ah, I'M sitting here as an ignorant. You've—you've got to tell me what it's all about. You've got to be going into some DETAIL. We've—you know, we've got plenty of time now. AH, I fully ADMIT! I don't know as much as I should about these topics. Of course, I've—you know my background's in science—and I can tell you all about the oestrogen receptors in Norwegian freshwater salmon. WHICH is useful in its own way—and I'm—I've got to be quite proud of being a scientist. You know that's a—that can be a label, some kind of name which gets put on you—er, to denigrate someone, and just put them DOWN. But of course, the greatest scientists and logicians were RENAISSANCE MEN! Nnn, look at Garry Kasparov, for instance!'—this thrown out to appeal to Jude. 'You know chess is almost the ULTIMATE—er—mixing ground—and really UNION of art and science—in which of course I include mathematics. You can just look at some of those great old chess players—ah, like the LEGENDARY Englishman'—sweeping straightly a generous arm—'HOWARD STAUNTON!—Ah, journalist, writer, SHAKESPEAREAN actor—and SCHOLAR! Er—in the days when London was—' looking to the ceiling—'probably—the chess CAPITAL of the WORLD. Who—er—died—er—at his desk—ah, STILL WORKING on his LAST—GREAT—'

'—Wickedness?'

'CHESS BOOKK!—er, that one's called Chess: Theory and Practice—and is buried—I think—in—er—Kensal—Rise, NO, GREEN! CEMETERY! Er—in London.'

'What, the chess book?' Jude saw the American coming back. Slowly, obviously—like a freezer in a meat shop.

'OR—uh—the GREAT—wha?—na ya—AUSTRIAN—ah, well, CZECH-Austrian—

VIENNESE JEW!—who YOU should probably KNOW ABOUT! I—I myself can probably—er—fill you up on a couple of details there.' A pause to renew lost emphasis. '*WILHELM STEINITZ*! The LAME! The ARTHRITIC! First official WORLD CHAMPION!'

'Direct correlations abounding.'

'AH, WHO, of course, studied—er—MATHS, I think it was—RIGHT HERE IN VIENNA! Er, before moving to England, and then of course, New York—ah, where he died—er, probably of syphilis, they say—a PAUPER! Buried now in the—ah—'

'CEMETARY of the EVERGREENS, Brooklyn, New York City,' said the American, rolling into his seat. 'Died of syphilis. He thought Jews were good at chess, because they had a PURE BREEDING!' The American chuckled. It sounded like an earthquake.

It took a lot for Bjørn to resist a chess discussion, but he managed it. Again Jude folded the paper. 'Well, he might have been onto something. Chess requires patience, God knows. And what is lineage but an extreme patience? In the face of which, the Holocaust becomes nothing more than a brattish tantrum. Hence my project, which, at the moment, revolves around a man who came to the conclusion that everyone bar the Germans—and certain *Scandinavians*'—an eyebrow arched—'is descended from a pygmy race of sub-humans kept as pets by the ancient *Egyptians* and bred as sex toys. The same pygmies, actually, who then raped Christ, created the Catholic Church, and went around suppressing all the high-priests of Teutonic paganism, forcing them underground. Where those same high-priests developed telepathic capabilities so as to by-pass the dangers of written language and, through ritual torture—updated as sado-masochism in nineteenth-century Vienna—achieved enlightenment through a process known as *gnosis*.'

The American licked a finger. He looked like a man with an appetite.

'Which is ridiculous, of course,' continued Jude. 'Everyone knows Scandinavians are descended from a pygmy race, kept as pets and bred as sex-toys.'

'Huh-huh, oh no. Oh no. Where do you get all this information?'

'Nicholas Goodrick-Clarke; his *The Occult Roots of Nazism; Secret aryan cults and their influence on Nazi ideology*. Robert B. Pynsent (ed.); his *Decadence and Innovation; Austro-Hungarian Life and Art at the Turn of the Century*. Peter *Gay*—like it or not; his *Schnitzler's Century; The making of middle class culture, 1815-1914*; and *The Cultivation of Hatred; The bourgeois experience, Victoria to Freud.* Pieter M. Judson; *Exclusive Revolutionaries; Liberal Politics, Social*

Experience and National Identity in the Austrian Empire, 1848-1914. Peter Pulzer; *The Rise of Political Anti-Semitism in Germany and Austria.* Robert Wistrich's *The Socialism of Fools.* William J. McGrath's *Dionysian Art and Populist Politics in Austria.* Malcolm Quinn's *The Swastika: Constructing the Symbol.* Chandak Sangoopta's *Otto Weininger; Sex, science and self in Imperial Vienna.* Goodrick-Clarke again; his *Hitler's Priestess; Savitri Devi, the Hindu-Aryan Myth, and Neo-Nazism.* Plus two or three *crises*—European thought, Reason, German Ideology; a bunch of unpublished theses, a few dozen sex-manuals; the whole history of fascism and sundry things in the *Ostdeutsche Rundschau* and elsewhere—*Götterdämmerung*; *Die Juden als Staat und Nation*; *Die Liebe in der Deutschen Mythologie*; *Schöne Frauen*; *Die Religion der Ario-Germanen—in ihrer Esoterik und Exoterik*, mark you; and the laughably titled *Die Hieroglyphik der Germanen.*'

'Crumbs.'

'Speaking of which, I woke up last night, in the *middle of the night*, realising I had to read *Mein Kampf.* I can't say for certain that the two are connected, but if anything becomes of it, it was not my fault.'

The American leaned over. 'I COULD SUPPLY YOU WITH A LITTLE READING MATERIAL.'

'Oh really.'

'You're wasting your TIME with Von List. Catholic self-FLAGGELATION.'

'Tell me about it.'

'MAYBE'—the American relaxed, drawing out the word—'I could interest you in a book of mine.'

'In another five minutes,' said Jude, but he leaned forward in his turn. He was half-smiles again, feeling the ground.

'Just what an ENGLISHMAN needs.'

Jude's wit dried up again. 'I see, I see,' he said, not seeing at all. 'What did you have in mind?'

'Oh just a pamphlet or two—a couple of books I've cooked up. I—er—run a small publishing company out of Virginia. We have—you might call them branches—in Wiesbaden; one in Amsterdam. It's not a profitable concern, but then I don't need the money. Its purpose is more—BENIGN.'

'You're from Virginia then?'

'I—originate—in Chicago. I operate out of Europe. Berlin, Paris, Amsterdam. Brussels last week. COSY little town. Quite the centre of the Union.'

'Quite.'

'Last month I was in the DEMOCRATIC'—he chuckled—'Republic of Congo. I had a meeting with the President. After that it was a tête-à-tête with the leader of the opposition in Burkina Faso.'

'Stopping off in Zimbabwe on your way?'

'Zimbabwe isn't on the way. But stop isn't how

I'd put it. I was a guest of honour. We have associates in Krung Thep—that's Bankok to you—Taipei, Manila, Ho Chi Minh. A growing interest in Mumbai—pardon me, Bombay. Believe it or not we're big in Bei-jing.'

'Most tourists *are*.'

'But I don't go there personally.' He chuckled. 'Gets a little HOT from time to time.'

The cigar was still burning in the ashtray. The man picked it up and drew in the smoke. His eyes were riotous under the shades. Circles stretched from the eyebrows to where cheek bone should have been. Jude bit his lip. It was all a boast. Yet something about the man was consistent. He didn't seem afraid of anything, not even death—and he was close to it. His mouth was black; teeth—yellow as leaves. So black was the mouth, sometimes the teeth were swallowed. And the voice came from the centre of that blackness, like a radio. In a strange way—like M. Valdemaar—he seemed already dead.

'Some kind of gnosis,' thought Jude. He tapped the frame of the paper. 'I see. What are you doing here then?'

'Kind of an ANNIVERSARY. I'm in Vienna to celebrate.'

Jude tilted his head. Bjørn stared at the table-top. They felt something coming.

'The *Endlosung*. "'Twas sixty years since."'

The man blew smoke rings. It was one of a few times in his life Jude lacked an appropriate response. Where was his father at a time like this? His response would have been dry and decisive. The response of a late twentieth-century liberal, a man of a certain standing, in whom elected councils put their faith. The kind of man the War had made inevitable, and not just because he had been born in it. Father of two, husband, husbandman. Lord of Time, Changer of the Course of Rivers, Polluter of the Moon and Stars. He would have known what to say.

'AND to distribute a little MATERIAL.'

'What kind of material?' Jude saw his continuance in the conversation as anthropological. But that wasn't all the story.

'*The Road to Recovery*. I think of that as a kind of *Long Work To Freedom*. You've got *Elites Known Only To The Inner Secrets*. A self-evident work. Then, a personal favourite, *The Economy of the Christian Science and other Penitentiary Writings*. Inspired by surroundings. And there's hundreds more where they came from. I've got something in mind on *The Infants of Lucifer: the Cultural Congress for Sexual Fascism*.'

'I see you value brevity in your titles.'

'Matter of FACT I've got something with me here. Little something on the HIV epidemic and the—er—cult of the Virgin—or should I say s—.

You know what I'd have done to that b—?'

Here the man said things beneath our interest.

He continued: 'you've heard that HIV came from the copulation of men with monkeys in the jungles of middle-Africa? It didn't. It was generated in the cess-pools of Belsen and Dauchau. Found a breeding ground in Israel, worked down through Egypt. Jewish survivors brought it to America.'

'A scientific view then.'

'Trouble is, Jews have proved resistant so far. They carry but they're rarely affected. Has to do with the monkey gene.' Bjørn was getting up to leave. 'Oh you're leaving. Here—take my card.' Jude stood up, took the card, selected his scarf from the hatstand.

'Yes, we're leaving,' he said, slipping on his parka. 'In our own good time.' The card went to the inside pocket. 'Some colourful theories you've pro*pounded*. But, you know—I can't help *thinking*.' He flipped up the hood, choosing his words carefully. 'You're a *little* man—in a manner of speaking, obviously.' He paused. 'Doomed for a *certain term*—five or ten years, judging by your complexion—to walk the halls of Viennese tea-rooms, dispensing cards to the disinterested, name-checking the President of *Equatorial Guinea*, implying a critical role in spreading the global fascist *manifesto*.' Through heroic lashes Jude cast his eyes on the American's critical roll. 'And justly so,' he meditated. 'A more global role you couldn't wish for. And you are nothing if not *manifest.*'

Bjørn was at the door. Jude strode halfway down the room, nodding to the waiter. The heavenly woman had gone. So had her mother.

'I'LL BE AT THE *CASANOVA* TONIGHT,' barked the American into his chins. He was pushing ashtray, roll and soup plate further from him. 'DOWN THE ROAD.' It sounded like a final gambit, but it didn't look like one. He wasn't even watching Jude. 'I can introduce you to a couple of people.' The voice was like cancer.

Jude turned. 'Haven't you been watching too much of *The Third Man?*'

The man seemed to feel Jude's barbs not at all. He smiled, as if at his own little joke.

'The OTHER PLACE, you'll need an INTRODUCTION. Kind of an EXCLUSIVE CLUB—private. Members only.'

'I'm not convinced by *privacy.* I suspect privacy of *lying.*'

'You'll be right at home.'

'Only insofar as home consists almost exclusively of little cliques of grandly-deluded, desperately self-exiling American visionaries, whose idea of *doing* Europe consists of rubbing mutual thumbs at imitation-marble tables in the red-light districts of Hamburg and Bratislava, briefcases spilling over with stick-on aphorisms, indiscriminately referencing Henry Miller, misquoting Eliot, appropriating Pound, all the while *obsessed*—ha!'—and he pointed at the copy of *Fegefeuer* on the table—'with Anthony Hopkins! Which, while it paints a pretty accurate picture of the Glum Valley, is a far cry from *The Yew Lawn*, Dimly, Piers obviously excepted. No, I suspect your so-called *totalitarianism*: a flabbily transparent euphemism for a smug *punctilio*. I'm not convinced your crashing fascism isn't actually a fussy, fuddy-duddy fetishism, in furtive fancy-dress, rooting among the closets of old Europe for stained copies of Percy "*Inky*" Stephensen and *Elsa* von *Freytag*-Loring*hoven*. A less total notion you couldn't find. Your papery aspirations, merely an excuse for the sapless cabals which supposedly realise them. In many ways, you're the least Machiavellian man I've met. Never was it so well applied, as to your pubescent political posturing, that the *means justified the ends*.'

'Careful young man. You don't want to COME DOWN with a DISEASE.'

Jude crowded Bjørn through the open door. The quartet put down their bows. The American reached across, lifting *The Guardian* from the table. The last they saw of him, he was tucking into cake behind the tints.[1]

*

'What a faggot.'

'Ah, I can't—I don't wanna start reacting to that. I've just got to be feeling that someone like that is showing OFF in some way.'

'It's the authentic *European* experience. Sit in some popular cafe, threatening revolution—two thousand years of history massaging your temples. And two thousand years of temples massaging your history. No, your American mistakes history for novelty, and novelty for glamour. Not that Europe isn't glamourous. It is! But the glamour is in the *anonymity*, the matter-of-*course*.'

'Nnn, that's exactly what HENRY MILLER is saying! Ah, you've just got to go and BUY some HENRY MILLER! In—er—*TROPIC OF CANCER*—he's just pointing out—he's seeing Americans being interested in—just FAME and

---

[1] It turned out later that he was L— L—, famous anti-semite, fascist propagandist, cult-supremo, presidential campaigner, and probable inciter and accessory to the murder of British student, Jeremiah Duggan, who wandered onto a Wiesbaden Bundestrasse one early morning, in 2003. It would be gratifying if the relevant authorities could conduct a competent inquest, before anyone else falls inexplicably in front of a speeding car.

MONEY, and always everything BIGGER.'

'Fame, like fascism, is *passé*: a thing of the 30s and 40s. A man can't walk out the door without tripping over a celebrity. A person—if ever there was one—of whom it could be said: *You're in the wrong place my friend.* Constantly appearing in newspapers, a whole rancid stream of them, parading from party to premiere, like—yes, exactly like *water*—filling up a *container*.'

They were walking by the *Stefansdom*.

'I stood next to a famous person in the airport the other day,' continued Jude. ''Ee looked at I, I looked at 'ee—jiggered if not only did I *know* that he knew that I knew *exactly* who he was, but if the only legitimate reaction wasn't *pity*. Fame is a second class citizen. He has given up the grandeur of anonymity.' Jude put forth a flat stomach. He would not have changed his grandeur for a throne.

'Whereas he's saying European people—ah, perhaps French people, but I think he means Europeans in general—ah, he's quite a EUROPHILE. He seems to be saying that Europeans, they—they are just—more CONTENT with ANONYMITY, even in POVERTY—also TO DIE!' The day was turning cold. Hunger was setting in.

'Yes, even the poverty is glamorous. It's *old* poverty; *revolutionary* poverty. Poverty with a novel in it, though hardly a novelty. Heirs to invisible welfare, a kind of cultural dole dispensed from the *Reichstag* and *Palais de la Justice*.' The voice went slow and sly. 'And that's *true*. But it's a kind of Hades; it extorts silence. *You got to be born on my side, sweetheart*.' There was an excited chuckle. 'Of course, silence itself—like America—is a romantic fallacy, implying *dichotomy*. But then, at a certain point—unlike America—you have to take it seriously.'

'Nnnn, that's—TRUE—that Americans—European writers, for instance, they know the MEANING of—er—real slowness and silences.' There was the pause of gathering thought. 'They can often just say things with a HINT.'

'I hate a hint. Your writer drops hints like a dog, expecting Benjamin Kepperly-Lie will clear up after it.' They stared at pastries in the windows.

'Ah, but British writers, for instance, they will be much more particular, describing the details.'

'Description, sir, is most *passé* of all.' The word was pushed through a shredder. 'Constantly *describing*, and *being described*. I'm fed up with people *describing* things.' A mouth minced. 'The whole world is obsessed with *description*.'

Bjørn shifted tack. 'Ah, but the BRITISH, they are able of taking a—almost quite a MACHIAVELLIAN view of the world there—without too much—er—morality talk. Ah, that can—that can be a weakness of Americans, is that they're always thinking of the LARGE PICTURE. They can be getting lost in DREAMS—emphasising the VISIONARY aspectss. Ah, of course, Americans can be more straightforward and down to the earth, too! They like to call a spade.'

'So I've heard.'

'But very often they're just talking and improvising, throwing a whole load of CRAPP at the wall, hoping something sticks. Whereas the British are distrusting—er—LANGUAGE—in some way—Americans seem to INVEST in communication.'

'To mask an even deeper distrust of language.'

They stopped outside what appeared to be a record shop. Then again, it might have been an office. It had posters, flyers and record sleeves on a noticeboard in the window—some European, mostly American music. Skip James was there, Billy Holiday. The door was strongly barred—*portcullised* would be more accurate—to prevent desperados from breaking in. Jude turned away. Bjørn was studying a sleeve in the window. *Mississippi Sheiks*, it read. *Stop and Listen*. Bjørn stopped and listened. A wind was blowing off the *Donaukanal*. All the whiteness of the afternoon invaded him. Bjørn continued stopping and listening, ignorant of the cold. At his delicate nose a drip formed.

'Wha?' he said, waking up. The window filled

him with courage. 'Nnn, LOOK at all these great records. This great MUSIC, just EMANATING—to the heart of classical Europe!' he exclaimed joyfully. 'But, hold on—we can have all these little objections. Ah, but I've got to say I—I LIKE Americans. I'm—I'm FASCINATED by America! That's—you know—an inCREDibly old continent, with all kinds of magnetic fields and MINERALS and ANCIENT TREES! Most of these people who sit around criticising America, half of the stuff they listen to and watch and read—that's all coming from over there. I've got to feel there's a certain JEALOUSY there.'

'Yes, one might suspect them of as banal a motive as *jealousy*.' Jude plucked an upbeat air. 'No, Americans are intellectual, bellicose, opinionated, full of bombast—childish in what they don't know. The Americans have the Open Mouth and the Loud Vowel. Death to the English consonant! Death to the Irish *brogue!* sludging through the bog.'

This was a particularly pitiful word, suggested by a poster of Joyce in the window of *Freud and Friends*. They were in a stone-paved side-street, narrowing like a womb. It was a dark day; but the sky was lighter than the street; the buildings grew paler as the eye went up. At the end, a flight of stairs fled to the *Kanal*.

'The problem with brevity is its self-consciousness,' continued Jude. 'Ironically, the problem with *verbosity* is also self-consciousness, making anyone who swears by either an obnoxious companion.' He stared at a box of books on a stool. 'No, British Islanders are a nasty, narrow, small-dealing people,' he declared. A smaller stool stood beside, with another box of books and leaflets. The windows and shutters of the shop-front were filled with books, dust-jackets, posters and announcements. '—Sentimental as Brighton Beach.' He tossed aside copies of *To The Lighthouse*, *Portrait of the Artist as a Young Man*. 'And your so-called *moderns* the worst of the lot. Spavined nags, self-saddled, ridden with *ambition*.' Bjørn was fingering a magazine rack, carrying *Time*, *Spectator*, *Vogue* and *Rolling Stone*. There was a *Sunday Times* stuck at the bottom. A sign, like an inn-sign, hung above, bearing a bad portrait of the bearded Freud. The whole was lit from above by a single bulb, plus a general light from the windows. Bjørn looked like a ruler in the halflight. He pushed through the door and a bell tinkled.

'To that extent the Fascist is right,' continued Jude, far too loudly for the context of the shop. 'Marx underestimated the sentiment—*embarrassment*—of the workers. They work because they feel sorry for their employers, just as they feel sorry for the famous. Pathetic specimens, both. Embarrassment is their engine, engendering both their peace and war.'

It was a long room. Like the street, it narrowed at the back. Along the wall of the bottleneck was a desk, and the woman sitting there lifted head and eyebrows simultaneously. She was hawk-like—high-blue eyes behind glasses. Steel-grey hair draped to a pony-tail. It was a young look for an old woman.

'Ah, that's just—Marx would be seeing that as just an economic condition.'

'A convenient explanation.'

'But when the BOOM fades, there's gonna be a scrapping for bread.'

'Who needs bread when you have *humiliation?* Because that's the thing. Man can live *by humiliation alone*, distributed *piecemeal* to each *grasping* palm.'

'Huh-huh, ah, nya, perhaps you're right. They DO SAY Marx is generalising too much, seeing everything from his narrow ECONOMIC VIEWPOINT. That's what people like us now, at our point in time, we've just got to be learning from and avoiding. Er, so that history DOESN'T repeat itself. We've just got to be STEERING AWAY from these GENERALISATIONS!'

Jude begged to differ—though difference was never less beggarly. 'On the *contrary*,' he said, hands pocketed, swinging his inquiry wide and high. 'Everything we've ever *achieved* has been via *vast generalisation.*' It wasn't quite clear what Jude had achieved, but it was clear it was significant. 'Just don't mistake it for *policy*. That's the trouble with your Teuton. Forever mistaking a generalisation for policy. It's called *imperialism*.'

The lady put a pondering finger to her chin.

'Your Teuton thinks too much and lives too little. Nietzsche was right—and *wrong*. Ha! Because he was Nietzsche! Aaah!' he suddenly rumbled, 'look at Fred! *Compromised!*' He chuckled to himself, swept back to the Glum.

Bjørn didn't follow. 'Ah, I've got to say I find those Nietzchean—er—APHORISMS quite profound.'

Jude flapped at a poster proclaiming *The Wit of Wilde*. 'There's your aphorism, sir, albeit of the tawdriest kind. Throw together a couple of concepts, add an unusual adjective: *eh voila!* An aphorism!'

The lady eased back in a swivel-chair, took off her glasses, lit a cigarette.

'Your Teuton'—continued Jude, flicking at a copy of *The Sorrows of Young Werther*. '—Is the spoiled blonde child in the sweetshop of the world, grabbing grubbily everything round him, shouting *MEIN!* And occasionally *HERR!* Adolf *Loos* implied as much. Everything so violently typified as Teutonic, the rest of the world has already comprehended and exhausted. And everything violently typified as as *Ausland*, the Teuton is intent on comprehending and exhausting.' He tickled at an advert by the door. 'Speaking of which, Mister *Edward Said*, his bonnet, and, zounds! his *bee—all three* will be offering their *two American-sponsored cents* to an impoverished *Schwarzenberg Platz* this evening. I wonder, can one buy custard-pies in Vienna?'

'Say, was you ever bit by a bee?' said Bjørn, *apropros* of nothing. He pointed and swayed like a boxer. Jude's attention was drawn to a flyer on the door. *Jules Arles*, it read—

is a jazz-musician and actor from New Orleans. Failing to make it on the stage, and several times to the stages, he began playing music halls and bawdy houses, cut a couple of records and enjoyed a seventies heyday, before disappearing from public view, to surface sometime later in Eastern Europe where he remains inexplicably popular. He operates out of Vienna.

There was a close-up of a cracked, hat-topped face, scrutinising the camera. Underneath it was written, *9 pm, Casanova*, and the date.

'On the other hand, this could be more interesting.' He said it innocuously.

'Nnn,' said Bjørn, coming over. He looked

sideways at Jude. 'Isn't that where that Fascist said he was going?'

'He obviously likes music-hall. Mind you, that was obvious already.'

'Nn, we seem to have—er—the SPECTRE of FASCISM hanging over us!'

'Well, I'm comforted by the Spectre of Fascism. Because, if there's *one* thing about the Spectre of Fascism, it's not Fascism. It's the *Spectre* of Fascism. It sits around in cafes drinking tea, saying, "Sorry, have you finished with that *Guardian?*" The Spectre of Fascism,' concluded Jude triumphantly, 'is a *Guardian* reader!'

'What Spectre's this?' asked the woman, projecting her voice. It was a husky, theatrical voice, mixing German and American. You could imagine it doing Medea.

Both young men spun around. Jude, still triumphing, hit the ground running.

'Oh, just the Spectre of Fascism. He's harmless enough.'

'You ever seen a spectre?'

'All the time. That's the thing about your Spectre. He will insist on *apparition*. You'd almost think it defined him.'

'I see what you mean about aphorism.' The woman took a drag. 'Just wait till you see one before you get comfortable.'

'An aphorism?'

The woman drawled: 'Just keep your wits about you.'

Jude seemed to invite concourse with strangers, Bjørn was thinking. That wasn't Bjørn's talent, but he was keen to acquire it. Nevertheless, he wasn't sure to what extent the exchange was metaphoric. He had to tread a fine line. 'Nnn, you think,' he began, 'we—might have a NEED to be NERVOUS?'

The woman had crossed her legs and swung her chair to face them. Now her hand snaked behind a computer, returning with a bottle of beer. This was a new development.

'I see no reason to be self-satisfied. Particularly if you're British. Particularly now.'

Bjørn jabbed his chest, smiling grimly. 'I'M Norwegian.'

'Did you come to buy books or just to chat? We don't have any fascist propaganda I'm afraid.'

'Well, there's plenty to be had at the *Bräunerhof*,' said Jude, unbowed. 'Besides!' he cried, waving a hand at any amount of fascist propaganda, 'Melville was a hearty democrat, I suppose; Wordsworth, a man of the people—friend to reapers and leechers!' A waft demolished the *Children's* section. 'To say nothing of Potter, Blyton and *J. M. Barrie*, those pillars of a liberal education.'

'I see.' She poured the beer into a glass. 'I need a

present for my niece's birthday,' she said, with some of Jude's innocuousness. 'What would *you* say was appropriate for children—entering, of course, upon a *liberal education*?'

'How old will she be?'

'Nine.'

Jude pondered. '*Dr Jekyll and Mr. Hyde*,' he said solemnly. He was looking round the shop in slow circles. It gave the impression of autumn, looked like a Gauguin, thought Bjørn—or Van Gogh, depending on the light source. No, said Jude—depending on the number of naked Philippinos browsing the shelves, in search of a liberal education. Bookshelves climbed to high ceilings. Roll-wheeled wood-ladders scaled them. They leaned askew, as if the wheels had ceased to fit. Posters, portraits, adverts and flyers bedevilled every gap. 'You'd have thought there was a lot going on here,' he mused. 'And so there is. But it's all so determinedly *clandestine*: *Großehaus* this, *Kleinegasse* that; bring a *turnip* with you. Which inevitably leads to the conclusion that it's a whole heap of nothing: Viennese *hot air*, amply perfumed. You stare at bare baroque and watercolour walls—none the wiser. Go beyond the doors, you'll find an orgy. Lift up the orgy, you'll find afternoon tea.'

Bjørn absently rotated a book-cabinet. He wasn't sure this was polite. The woman sighed, putting down the glass. The free hand she folded on her bicep; the other held the cigarette like a specimen. She was an attractive woman; aging now, but in her prime—well worth the trouble. The nose was high-ridged and hooked; teeth sloped inward. She had an appealing horsiness. Jude respected horses. Then there was the mane. He had a history with bobbed kittens of kinds; but long hair on an old woman—this was a teaser. Hers was not voluminous, but coquettish enough, right down to the thumb-size tail. Stray traces fell on a white roll-neck, tight round the breast, like a small swell on the ocean—or, more aptly, a dull ripple in a tarn, stirred up, perhaps, by some sort of punter's pole. There was nothing insulting about this. A small swell on the ocean was a known quantity. But what could be more terrifying than a dull ripple—a pulse even—in a lonely, brackish tarn, no matter how many times you'd seen one (and Jude had seen more than he cared to remember).

'Don't you have enough excitement at home?' Her eyes looked down. She sounded suddenly weary.

'Certainly.'

'Go back.'

'I can't. I've got a *gang injunction.*'

'That sounds like jargon. I suppose you're going to tell us what it means.'

'It's a banning order.'

'Oh, oh,' said Bjørn, forgetting etiquette. 'I didn't

REALISE that! How—where did they BAN you?'

'No, this is the strange thing. *It only comes into effect if I go home.* Apparently my father, at the suggestion of *A Man Known Only As The Man Who Would Be King*, who besides being a local philanthropist and councillor, may or may not work for the MOD, traded official exile for unofficial exile, under the guise of studying Jewish history in *fin-de-siecle* Vienna, "until," as he so sanctimoniously put it, "It All Blows Over".'

'Why Vienna?' snapped the woman.

Jude thought about it. 'I'd be tempted to say,' he said, 'that, to a student of Viennese Jewish history, as much as to a Viennese Jew, Vienna is a necessary evil. Were it not for the fact that all evil is *entirely unnecessary*. As was the *fin-de-siecle* come to that.'

'But what was their JUSTIFICATION?' said Bjørn to the whole shop.

'Ha! I can't imagine! You'd have to ask the Viennese.'

'Na, of course I mean these COUNCILLORS.'

'Oh, I was *Horatio* in the play.'

'Wha? Oh, that can't be all.'

'No, you're right. I also went over a *stile* (pretty much taboo nowadays), and, what's more, was made to *account* for it. The pleasure of stealing lightly, and *generally*, over a forbidden lawn was wont to be self-evident. Now it wilts under the floodlight of *accountability.*'

'Nnn, they must have THOUGHT you were some kind of THREAT!'

'I daresay—and I am.'

'But what did they SAY? How did they JUSTIFY themselves?'

'It's all about *diversion*, apparently. Diverting us, not only from each other, but, simultaneously, from both crime *and* the criminal justice system. Completely failing to notice that they *are* the criminal justice system.'

The woman looked sceptical. 'And you were diverted here. A pleasant sort of diversion.'

'Oh, three punishments they conceived for my person. The first: to imprison me. The second: to throw me in the lake with lead-weights tied to my feet. Believe me, this was mooted. The third was to extort from me *academic research*, on pain of the previous two. Proof positive, if any were needed, that education is not something you *cultivate* but something you *suffer.*' In his mind's eye, he touched again *The Sorrows of Young Werther*—and dashed it to the floor.

Bjørn watched the dialogue. It looked well over the metaphoric line. 'Nnn, Harper said something about putting on *HAMLET*! I was to be FORTINBRAS!'

'You'll have to wait a while. Besides being banned six months from the valleys *Glum* and

Cooley, and in particular (on pain of further penalties) the reservoirs Glum and Bullish, any Water Board property, and the farms *Fourpoints* and *Freely-Lowe*; besides being prohibited from sporting any of the following costumes: The Grim Reaper, The Crocodile Head, The Invisible Worm That Flies In The Night In The Howling Storm, or any other Gothic or—and I quote—*creepy* costume or the several individual appurtenances and appendages thereof, we've also been banned from performing any Shakespeare play for the same period, and Hamlet for a full two years, or indeed—and again—even sporting the costume, make-up, or other habiliments, of any of its *dramatis personae*, but in particular, Hamlet, Horatio, Marcellus, Gertrude and the Ghost of King Hamlet. Breach of any of which incurs a two year jail sentence. Ha! Completely brilliant! We are allowed, however, after the elapse of the initial six months, to apply to stage, film, or otherwise represent, *other* Shakespeare plays, pending approval of the regulatory committee (comedies and late plays preferred).'

'Two YEARS. No. It's not possible.'

'Not that it would have made any difference to you. Bearing in mind we still haven't *wrapped* Scene One, it would have taken Harper about two years to get to Fortinbras.'

'That would be fanTAStic,' continued Bjørn

roaming, pausing, pointing, licking his lip. Two years was nothing to him. He could easily spend that two years just reading that magnificent play and GETTING INTO CHARACTER. Intending to do just that, he began looking for *Hamlet*. The further he roamed, the more he was forced to consider the layout of the shop. This was an inconvenience, but his consciousness made room for it. In the middle, bookcases and a table made a horseshoe, open to the door. The bottom of the horseshoe had a cash-desk attached. Beyond that was the bottleneck where the woman sat. Beyond her—curving round the back—

'—Go on through!' barked the woman, 'but you won't find any Shakespeare.'

This perplexed Bjørn. Should he go through? No, there wasn't any point; yet the invitation had been made. He looked like a weather vane. Eventually he turned back, defeated.

'In the corner,' said the woman, pointing near the door. She was watching Jude who had picked up an English copy of *The Man Without Qualities*. He was standing astride, feet planted, like a man whose qualities are assured. Bjørn wandered back past him, found a copy of *Hamlet*, tossed it about, weighed it in his palm, shook it with great success, grinning, and then put it back on the shelf. He looked around. There didn't seem to be any other customers. He disappeared up the bottleneck to the back-room.

'Sounds like cavaliers and roundheads all over again!' said the woman, standing up with the bottle. She stubbed out the cigarette on the desktop. 'Puritans running amok, persecuting anything that moves.' With each clause she took a step closer. 'Kings—actors—*anarchists!*' She said *anarchists* as if summoning saliva. She was watching him.

'Actors, certainly. *Anarchists*'—Jude gave it an emphasis to match—'don't tend to visit the Glum and Cooley Valleys much, it being a trifle too anarchic for them. They prefer to gad about town—ironically, where they exiled Marcellus.' He returned her gaze.

'What's ironic about it?'

Jude could smell beer. 'Well you don't know Marcellus,' he smiled. 'Furthermore, you don't know *Harper*, who purports to play him.'

The woman raised her arms. She removed the elastic round the pony-tail, pulled the hair back and replaced it. All the while she looked out of the door.

'Marcellus, *aka* Harper,' continued Jude, '—absurdly perceived as a *potent threat to the state*—is, you must know, a deeply *conservative* man. Underneath, though—*underneath*—he is *MAD! MAD!*'

'And the irony?'

'They have planted him *exactly* where he may

become a *potent threat to the state.*'

'Indeed.' She narrowed her eyes. 'And the King—'

'—Got away.'

'Who was the King?'

'A man of sorrows.'

'A spectre after all.'

She placed a hand athwart *The Sorrows of Young Werther*. A tartan skirt ceased above the knee. Green tights shone toward slip-ons. It was a tidy look, and *tidiness* was the dark secret of feminine charm.

'But he is *mortal*, this spectre of ours,' said Jude thoughtfully. 'And likely to remain so.'

Back came Bjørn with a book. He was tapping the cover and grinning. That was the thing about Bjørn, thought Jude: his ambitions were immaculate. They never involved real harm, only *harrassment*. Their deadliest weapon was an interminable barrage of enthusiasm—a grievous harm, admittedly, but cursedly forgiveable. How to betray a man like that? Bjørn's vices were only ever exposed during competitive sports: namely, chess and football. That would be the time then. Bjørn could turn a lost game to a time-win without trace of guilt. He could shove you face-first into a trellis fence and talk about fifty-fifty challenges. Other than that, chuckled Jude to himself, he was perfect.

'Nnn, THIS is the one I've been LOOKING for!

SEXUS! The *ROSY CRUCIFIXION!* HENRY *MILLER* at his BEST! Ah—so I've heard.'

The woman turned to Bjørn. 'Are you buying, or just celebrating?'

'Oh, I'm BUYING,' said Bjørn good-humouredly.

'And you?' She started back to the counter.

'I suppose it has to be done,' said Jude, weighing in his hand *Mein Kampf* and *The Man Without Qualities*.

'A noble sentiment.'

'A few pages should suffice.'

'—And a British one.'

'It's not *what* you know. But it's not *who* you know either. It's ensuring *nobody* knows.'

'A nice excuse,' said the woman offhand, ringing the books through the till. Bjørn had been sidetracked by the rotating cabinet. He had *Sexus* in one hand and *Metamorphoses* in the other. 'You should be a spy,' she continued.

'The only difference between a spy and a pervert,' pondered Jude, 'is *pornography*.' And he burst out chuckling.

'I was thinking Marlowe, or Sidney. A *gentleman adventurer*.'

Jude handed over his money. 'Who just *happened* to be writers,' he said. But he liked the sound of it.

'*Genau*. Talk much and do little.' She gave Jude the books. It was a precise transaction. Jude liked precise transactions. 'You look like a Hamish,' she said.

'Jude.' There was a connection of eyes. Four large, sentimental eyes, two blue, two green.

'Rosa,' she said. 'You should be a Hamish—or a Fergus. You've got a Jacobite look.'

Bjørn followed busily to the counter, Van Gogh's *Letters* in his pile. He looked highly satisfied. 'You should go into that BACK-ROOM,' he declared. 'FanTAStic things in there.'

'Really?'

'FanTAStic. Nnn, you've just got to GO in there.' Bjørn paid for his books, finding, to his surprise that he had exactly the right money.

Jude looked down the bottleneck. 'No,' he said slowly, turning for the door. 'No, I think not.' He tapped *The Secret Agent*. 'Nothing reveals a man like his curiosity. I rest unrevealed, not because I cultivate *identity*, but because I am fundamentally—maddeningly—*incurious*.' He glanced archly at Rosa, pushing through the door to the tinkling bell.

*

The air was cold. Evening was falling. What time was it now? Since they were going to the show, opined Jude, going home would only give them a few hours there before they had to come straight back again. And what could you possibly accomplish in a few hours? Even if they weren't *sure* of the show, he conceded, wasn't it presumptuous to rule it out? No, there was no point in going home.

In the heart of Bjørn such logic found an ally. Neither reasoned why. The wind flapped up the steps from the *Kanal* and they headed into it.

'Nnn, what was that about curiosity?'

Silence.

'Uh?'

'Ha! I'm like a cow who can't be bothered to explain that he can't be bothered.'

Bjørn jumped straight past. 'Ah, I've got to say, I feel IDENTITY is a powerful force. Er! that doesn't mean it always has to be fixed and AUTENTIC. It can twist and—er—reSHAPE itself—er like a SNAKE or a SHAMAN. Ah, the old Irish MYTHOLOGY—'. Bjørn pointed at Jude. They were edging the *Kanal*.

'I fear thee, *Ancyent Marinere*. I fear thy *skinny hand*.'

'YOU for instance! You—you've got a STRONG identity! Er—in a certain sense. You—you just seem to attract these CHARACTERS. Look at today, for instance, you—you get into conversation with a Fascist—'

'The *Spectre* of Fascism.'

'—And then that woman in there. She was a

REAL character!'

'Character is overrated. I'm not convinced character is anything more than *atrophied neurosis*. Far better to have no character at all.'

'Oh no,' said Bjørn. 'Oh no, you don't believe that.'

'I don't believe it, I observe it.—*Belief*,' said Jude into the wind, 'is the spawn of *character*.'

They came to a waste of white buildings, large, soulless, stretching for miles.

'It's *character* puts up these,' said Jude, waftily. '*Character* spanks arse for sausage. *Character* which *conceives solutions to the Jewish problem of Europe*.'

'Character drinking BEER in her BOOKSHOP. CHARACTER charging forty Marks for books worth forty-seven, because she could see that's all I had! CHARACTER which has, round the BACK there, walls filled with letters, notes, photos of all kinds. From writers, artists, ACTORS that she's KNOWN.'

'So we're agreed on that.'

They walked back along the *Kanal*. Night had set in.

'—JUST an INCREDIBLY interesting woman. Nyah, I'll bet—I'm willing to bet she's seen things in her time. She's—ah, she's a real old timer, whose been AROUND, probably seen the high and the low life. A HAND in every PIE!'

‘No, that’s probably the Spectre.’

They were swept off the *Kanal* into the side-streets. Bjørn was sidetracked by stonework. He threw angles with his arms, talking about nooks and crannies. Then he remembered his theme.

‘That bookshop—that BOOKSHOP—seemed like a place you could spend HOURS and HOURS. That’s the kind of place that seems to have been there forever. She’s most probably seen everything happening outside that bookshop.’

‘Certainly little seems to happen *inside* it. Except for alcoholism.’

‘Oh no, in there, everything goes by an older order—of Rilke, Rimbaud and Percy BYSSHE Shelley! That’s a different way of seeing the world. You don’t really measure by CLOCK and CALENDAR. You measure with events—encounters! You just go so involved in something, time gets attached to things—like PIPE smoke! DRIFTING in books and ladders. I could even imagine just SITTING DOWN in that, er, amazing BACK ROOM at the back there, one snowy afternoon, with a good old copy of MARCEL PROUST in your lap, and, ah, SUDDENLY WAKING UP! Realising you’d actually DROPPED OUT for several hours!’

They stopped for chestnuts at a charcoal-bin, standing in the smoke for warmth. At some point you had to concede to hunger. Jude munched purposeful, pronouncing satisfaction; Bjørn picked eager among the bag. Smoke billowed like sea-mist. They were facing downhill—upwind—where the city was darker, as if watching where they'd been. Behind was all lights and shop-windows.

'I've got to feel bookshops—they're a bit like those SIXTY-FOUR SQUARES,' said Bjørn, returning to his favourite subject. 'Once you've just stared at them for a while, you lose all CONCEPT of time. You're starting to see them in exaggerated DIMENSIONS. And you don't want to leave that world—ah, I'd have to admit, sometimes that can be BAD. You see some of these chess characters, and you feel they'd just be better throwing over the board.'

'Well, if they will travel by sea.'

'Ah, well—it's a bit LIKE being at sea!' pursued Bjørn, riding a wave. 'Surrounded by waves of SQUARES. You easily get DISORIENTATED, rising and falling with the flow of the game. Think you're facing east when it's west. You start DRIFTING, er, too FAR from SHORE. Bishops and KNIGHTS circle—like SHARKS! A pawn like an albatross—free on the *H* file.' Bjørn blushed. He saw the termination of his voyage. 'Suddenly a QUEEN barges in!' he trumpeted. 'The WHALE has sunk you!'

Jude looked on the lights of the *Kanal*, distant now. Bjørn was talking like Magnus. Where was

Magnus—in what wild barn, what fiery flood, under which leaky roof—on a night like this? What bough his bivouac, what cold ground his groundsheet? They passed silent through the *Judenplatz*, sidling by the Holocaust memorial. It was a block representing a gas-chamber, looking like wordlessness. Jude wished it were. A blanket silence would have been alright, but the constant chatter about it, the putting up morbid little memorial blocks to celebrate our insufficiency, that left him cold. He shivered. Only Bjørn's footsteps sounded on the flagstones. Perhaps the Glum was kinder tonight than the Pannonian plains. How could it not be? The Glum had nooks, yes, and crannies too, such as Vienna, with all her Goth and Baroque, never knew. Ditch and drainage, hut and hideout. A pump-house here, a stable there. Magnus would be alright. He was loving every minute.

What was Bjørn talking about? The bookshop woman. Jude examined his *all-stars*. 'Whale is a little unfair—seahorse perhaps.' He reflected. 'But a queen, no doubt—and a catch in her prime, though it's questionable who was reeling who.'

Swiftly through *Minoritensplatz*. Bjørn stopped to admire some more stonework. 'I've got to feel,' he said, 'she had some kind of INTEREST in you. Ah, there's something about you that FASCINATES people. I, oh I don't have that. And that's—that's not something I'm jealous about. Myself, I'm not really going around looking for that. Ah, of course, I'm not saying you're looking for that either, but you just naturally—er—INTRIGUE people. The same with the SPECTRE—hah hah—of FASCISM. He just—er—he seemed to ATTACH himself just to you.'

'Well, it takes one to know one.'

'THAT'S HARD on yourself.'

'Well they think I've got all the answers. Which I have of course—because *everything* is *already known*. The only difference is, I shamelessly repeat them, while others only dither.'

Past the *Staatsoper*, under the *Lorelei*. Bjørn stopped to buy salted potatoes. 'I feel that's a bit FATALISTIC for me,' he said, licking four fingers. They stood in the ship's-funnel smoke again.

'On the contrary. Knowing does not preclude *doing*. The excuse for indolence has ever been the air of *mystery*.'

To the *Belvedere* and back with a wind on their tails. 'Nnn, I don't know,' continued Bjørn, coming upon the *Donner Brunnen*. 'Ah, look right HERE!' he cried, pointing at the fountain. 'HERE we've got Providence—er, FORESIGHT—who, of course, knows EVERYTHING—just like a kind of—er—autoriTARIAN government.' It was definitely Bjørn's moment. 'And she's just sitting there—and they're all just sitting round her, comPLACENTLY catching on a fish there—like Roman SENATORS with the BARBARIANS at their door.'

Jude had a gander. There they were: *Providentia* and Danube's desultory tributes—lime-stained, as if Danube herself had just washed over them. It was true, there was a listlessness about them, tridents aimed glibly at the water. Providence herself was of a certain age; boy's hair, a faraway face, one breast exposed to the night. She still had it though; it just needed coaxing.

'I suppose you'll be for dressing them, like Maria Theresa.' Jude had read his guide-book too.

'Oh no. Oh no. But I feel the world is MYSTERIOUS. That's why we're curious, we want to SHAPE all the VAGUENESS.'

Bjørn was a shape in the vagueness, back down the streets and alleys. It was funny—they'd hung around waiting, now they'd overshot the show. It was nine-thirty—cold. High time to be inside. Might as well be the *Casanova* then. 'Ah, it's the same with WOMEN!' cried Bjørn, inspired. 'That's probably what lies behind all this POLITICS—ah like some HELEN of TROY! They are the SIGN of that mystery.' Swinging down *Dorotheergasse*, right in front of them—exactly where they thought it would be—was a red strip saying *CASANOVA*. Between the *N* and *O*, a tease draped a leg. Next to it a sign said *Girls Girls Girls*.

Jude stretched up a finger. 'We asked for signs,'

he said. 'The signs were *sent*. What all politicians are continually, *desperately* ignoring—and deep down they know it—is the fact that there is *no hope whatever*. The world is *doomed*; the gift horse, looked in the *mouth*.' They looked the club in the mouth. The doomed state of the universe suited them nicely.

They leaned on stiff metal doors, confronted by curtain. They brushed through stiff black curtain, confronted by bouncer: a big wide man of uncertain dimensions, uncertain character; nothing particular about him except spiky hair. Past the bouncer, through more curtains, harsh, heavy and scarlet. They might have hung there for sixty years, polishing faces like medallions—worn in their turn by a thousand backs, two thousand shoulders, till no-one knew whether they were coming or going.

Suddenly they were in the club. It was as if they had always been there. Darks and scarlets coupled. Smoke drifted. Thick carpet wound like a staircase; the walls were the stairwell it climbed in. They too were thick, canvassing opinion from booths and crescent-benches. A handful of figures sat in shadows, with all the grace of furniture in awnings.

To the left was the bar. In the middle of the room, drawing the attention down it, was a black floor-space, where a girl was poised to dance. She was a big girl but the floor looked too big for her. Above was a wide round lamp and in the corner, a raised rostrum. There, amid a clutter of instruments, a band was conversing.

A voice asked for thirty *Österreichen Marks*. They fumbled in pockets, pushing through books, aware, to one side, of a dark opening, piles of quiet coats. Everywhere you went were grey legions of coats, like Napoleon's army still sleeping. Overlaying the dark was a girl's long face, black as water. She was high on a stool, in a silver dress, sliced into straps over belly and shoulder, and the back-line implied a plunge. A marvellous garment. '*Sie können mit euros bezahlen, wenn Sie wollen*,' she added.

'*Aber wollen wir* nicht,' countered Jude, but his palms were sweating. There was a lot of water around. The band struck up and he realised how quiet it had been. '*Here's a greasy rackety shiffle-shaffle blues*,' leered the singer over an even-stepped descending riff. That must be Arles. He was leaning into the mic, bongos round his neck. Guitar and tuba ground and descended. 'Introductions: a bad sign,' said Jude, fishing out the money. But Arles jumped in, tapping boots on the linoleum:

Shoeshine Joe
Where d'you up and go?

Bjørn wasn't sure. He handed over his reluctant

Marks.

Shoeshine Joe
Plenty more than six feet below

The girl stowed them at a counter, descending the stool with incredible care. It was hot in there but her dress left breezes. Or were they perfumes? The dress was an inconstant thing. Thrown in the air, it might just turn to rain. With a soft disdain she eased their coats from them. If she touched a flank here, a wrist there, she didn't mind—the disdain was maternal. Jude stood like Christ on the cross, frayed sleeve plain to see. It was possibly the most erotic thing he had ever experienced.

She carried his parka to the darkened room. Joy to that parka in its darkened room. She emerged, black from black, like Echo from the cave. Bjørn was more resistant. His own brown leather jacket he half-shed himself, like Barabbas, unwilling to die. But she got it off him in the end. Even the books were checked in. Two of them. *Metamorphoses* he smuggled inside, by virtue of a back pocket. He sniffed, satisfied again. You never knew when you might need reading material. Then again—and he swung a mental arm—what was all this if not reading material? Lights hit his eye and the environs dimmed. There was too much to take in. A perfect anthropological opportunity. He wanted to stand there all evening, or find a nook, perhaps, where he could see and not be seen. Jude didn't care about this. He was content to assume the world's expectations, because those expectations, so unfounded, were so easily-swayed. There was no vanity in it, nor martyrdom; the world longed for an air of certainty, and Jude supplied it.

Shoeshine Joe
You're gon' wear out that leather though
Why don't you polish more slow
Shoeshine Joe?

'But if they can't deal with it—no skin off my chin,' said Jude, strolling to the nearest free booth. Bjørn sat down, back to the stage but at an angle to see it. Jude faced the stage, but if he glanced to the right—and he frequently did—he could make out the cloakroom in its cavey glory.

The stripper was a prancing pony; tall, Russian-looking, in lingerie and heels. 'It's the French cut,' said Bjørn admiring her slip like a connoisseur. Blondeness flew, heels clacked out of rhythm. The band cranked up to the bridge and, quicker than consistent, she slipped off the *brassiere*:

Took out your toothbrush, spit upon a star
Why d'ya have to wipe that jet black car
Straight through the snow

Shoeshine Joe?

What, did he swallow a helium balloon,
Laughing all over the street?
What, did he want to float straight up to the moon
With the earth caked about his feet?

The song was a drunken brawl, the voice a chorus of bullfrogs from the swamp—all trade and industry. It was gruff and cut-glass—half-English accents, strong on elocution. He might have been doing Shakespeare. But the voice wasn't everything: the whole man was a theatre; thorough, mechanical, extravagant. He was surefire: a slashed greedy mouth, like a shark in a swimming-pool. Judge and executioner—with an appetite, he could have hung fire on the walls. But he was all control: black slacks, lined; wine-red waistcoat; fedora pushed high. He looked in the Lent of his artistic year, goose-stepping the stage and pummelling. The hair, once fair, was curling, colourless; nose long and beaten-looking; eyes were narrow, with a wash of eye-shadow. He was fifty if a day—but like a goat on a mountain, seen a hundred years.

Next to him the stripper looked lost. She had abandoned her heels like the Witch of the West, put her round rump to the wheel. 'Aroint thee,' thought Jude, munching a remnant chestnut. 'If there's *doing* to be done, I'll do it—and drain thee dry as hay.' His glance went to and from the entrance. 'But it's a witch all the same, and a windy one too.' The garters broke like smoke-rings.

Shoeshine Joe
Sleeping with a string attached to his toe
Tied with a ribbon bow
Shoeshine Joe

Take the wrong end of the tether
Put your lips together
And blow,
Shoeshine Joe

As if responding to a need, over came the coat-check girl. Not that she looked grateful; it was all one to her to embody a need. She looked South-American. It was a long way to wind up here. She was slinky—*petite* even. Jude liked it that way. Age—thirty or so. He liked it that way too. '*Etwas zu trinken?*' she asked.

You won't try any of those moves no more,
That old soft shoe
Figure somebody just opened up the door
And walked all over you

Lacquered that leather down to the sole

Lacquered a little more
Didn't ever stop till he lacquered a hole
Right straight through the floor

'Na ya—er—*ZWEI SCOTCH*,' said Bjørn, unexpectedly taking control. He held up two Churchillian fingers. Jude raised eyebrows, looked at Bjørn, at the girl, conceded with a hand.

'*On the rocks?*' She blinked slowly, looking away.

'*Ja.*'

'*Haben Sie Laphroaig*?' said Jude weightily.

'*Weiß ich nicht. Warten Sie bitte.*' She went away.

'Nn, she does TWO THINGS,' said Bjørn, grinning slyly.

'Well, there are *two ways*. One must needs do two *things*.' They laughed at their private joke; stuttering machine-gun laughs which, like the pump at the heart of the Glum, went on much longer than you'd credit.

Shoeshine Joe
One man went to mow
Shoeshine Joe
Way out where the cornflowers grow

Bjørn smoothed hands over the table, looking from Arles to the stripper. Bjørn had a thing for dark complexions—but you couldn't rule out a blonde. He'd been away from home a while. 'Under certain conditions,' surmised Jude, also staring, 'in particular *circumstances*, your blonde—even your loose and lank variety—is so *blatant* as to make centuries of nationalist bravura almost forgiveable. I speak of the female, obviously,' he advised Bjørn. 'The blonde *man* is a thing not to be tolerated. For that silken fop, 'twere better to have never been born—ripp'd untimely from the womb. If he be loose-haired too, it is worst of all. Let grave reject him and name be expunged from record. Filthy slave! His moral laxity clear for all to see, sliding from his pate like buttered salmon.' He meditated. 'But your blonde *cunt*,' he continued suddenly, 'is different field: just when you think they're forgotten, up one pops and almost *surprises*.' He fell into blonde hypotheses. What cared a blonde if life was short? A blonde was brash and silly; a blonde too long in the sun. A blonde could perplex a man; damage his paradigm. Not a thin, slide-rule blonde: a sheafed full-blooded blonde, tumbled in the hay. He thought about Fran Peters. Where was she now? On a stage, probably, surprising with a body-swerve. A girl has to make a living.

The stripper did a body-swerve of her own. The stakes were upped and all her cards on the table. Arles glanced over to see what she was up to. He didn't break stride. Sweat and spit leapt from him.

Bass and tuba pumped away. In reality they paid her scant attention. It was a sly song. Bjørn could hear Louis Armstrong doing it. Perhaps he had. 'He's making it come ALIVE!' he grinned, tapping his foot, and back came the bridge:

I don't care to leave a trace
Make it shine so I can see my face
Whaddaya know?
It's Shoeshine Joe

Who's that looking in the mirror?
Thought I heard an echo
Someone's footsteps followed me here.
Should have known it would be Shoeshine Joe

Shoeshine Joe
With a mouth just like an O
Hammer in that nail
Like so

Shoeshine Joe
Was he expecting the wind to blow?
Oh no,
Shoeshine Joe

Song and stripper played themselves out. The girl collected her items from the floor. '*Gonna take a short break*,' croaked the singer and he ambled to the bar. Back came the girl with whiskey and water. They sipped away and eyes took in the room. Instinctively Bjørn looked to the right of him—at the wall. It was like a Bacon: intense scarlets—like seats, like floor—covered with a print like leaves. He swallowed down. Or were they candle-flames? Any rate, they climbed round the room to high places. The ceiling was dark. Lights were low. They were thrown from the walls in closed spheres, like gems. A real flame browsed at a wick on the table.

Instinctively Jude looked to the right: the long gloom of the club; the bar over his shoulder, a blaze of glass and bottle. The waitress was mopping the bar, black handles rising like rifles. The whole thing was a shooting range; one of those weird ones where you shoot your own reflection. She watched him for a second, enough to kill coyness in the bud—then went back to the mopping. Hair fell in braids about her shoulders. A sapphire fell between breasts: fish in a bear paw.

This could not go on for long. That nose could smell a look at fifty paces. Jude swung back, and cloakroom, toilets, stage swung with him. The band were changing instruments. Bjørn appeared to be studying the wall, one finger resting on his glass. He looked to be in a paradisal reverie. If he felt any discomfort at being in a seedy old dive, he didn't show it. He looked pleased to be in a site of special historic interest. And of course he was right. All that red-light was restful for the eyes; the girls—pleasant disturbance on the rim. It was an honest transaction. You paid your moneys—*Österreichen Marks*, if you will—and you got your eyeful.

Jude's restful eyes fondled the audience. The near booth he couldn't see into, but, in the next, a pinstriped man was licking a roll-up and grinning. Hanging on his arms were two girls, brunette and laughing blonde, and he was ogling the blonde's ample breasts. Jude couldn't hold that against him. He was tired and lined, looked like he'd seen it all. Jude couldn't hold that against him either. The trouble was, neither could the brunette, eyeing him under strain, long neck carelessly erect. She looked like a violin, had a fretted, wooden grace, but strayed from her century. Next was a booth overspilling with laughter; probably some girls night out. Or were they fellow dancers? The lines were blurring. Further along a man resembling Bill Clinton was enjoying the show. And over there—shabby and squinting, in a booth by the rostrum—wasn't that Columbo? The man squinted and puffed at a cigar. Perhaps it was Peter Falk, *playing* Columbo.

Suddenly Jude caught sight of the Spectre. He was in the far corner—opposite the rostrum, one booth back from Columbo—in suit and hat, as before. From the wall of his booth, smoke was detaching, drifting toward the lights. It looked like a trench in Flanders.

'My God, there he is.'

Bjørn's eyes roved over the ceiling, took in the bar, the returning Arles, came to rest, side-on, with the impatient Jude. 'Hmm, wha?' he said, curving round like a nutmegged defender. 'Oh, oh no,' he said feebly, but there was no pretending ignorance. He was silent.

'A man of his word.'

Bjørn sniffed long. 'Well, we can just IGNORE him. He's—he's making a BIG ERROR if he thinks we're here for him.'

'When clearly we're here for the girls.'

'Exactly!' said Bjørn, chuckling. It was nice to confess a truth while correcting an error. Jude wasn't so sure. Was the Spectre staring at him? Hard to tell through smoke and tinted glass. Certainly he was looking this way. Perhaps he was short-sighted—perhaps drunk; that would make things easier. Jude held his own glass to his nose. The odour was insidious. Taking a pencil to his brain he made a mental note: in correcting an error, it was easy to imagine you had confessed a truth.

Arles put down a double-bourbon, started a *Mojo Blues*: a bleak lament to the tune of *Another man done gone. Threw the dog a bone*, he sang, slapping a guitar. A big bronze girl about to hit the stage decided to wait a while. Jude took a gulp, smoke drifting past his eyes. Who cared if the Spectre was watching? He could watch away, now the dog had gone. He turned instead a full hundred and seventy over his shoulder. Bah, what good was his convenient seat if the girl—under the influence of the *two ways*—was going to go right out and do *two things*? What, indeed, was his convenient seat if not itself a subscription to that tired dichotomy, the *ways*? Was he, too, not entitled to *two things* he thought, easing back around. He stared right at the Spectre, daring him to restrict individual liberties. What the Spectre didn't realise was that he was caught in liberty's totalitarian web. Nothing he could devise that had not been dared him.

Bjørn kept a determined back to the business. The sight of the Spectre had sent a jolt through him—or was it the note of drama in Jude's voice? *Must have cut my mo* repeated Arles, crooning and growling. Tuba and tambourine weighed in on a sudden. He was gone *where the water flowed.* Throw his mojo *overboard.* For a moment Bjørn questioned their coming here—to the lion's den, so to speak. What kind of fatalism was that? What perversion of motive? Unlike Jude, Bjørn did not belittle the lion. Old and toothless, perhaps—there was a kill in him yet. But Jude's platitudes put him at ease. Whatever their motives, they were over, now that reality bit. Bjørn set his mouth, built a high striding wall, said no more about it. Of course, it was peach and plum they were here for—globe and hourglass. He flicked his own glass complacently. Bjørn could tell you all about oestrogen receptors, should you be so inclined.

The song stopped abruptly and Arles turned to the band. *Here's a lullaby*, he rasped. *Kind of like a cradle song*. He took up the bongos, waiting for the bass. 'Where's the bathroom?' said Bjørn, finishing his drink. He tripped along the carpet, spied the big bronze girl, slipped through the second *exit*. She smiled like an angel. '*Skal på skal*,' he reflected more than thought.

Alone at the booth, Jude felt suddenly approachable—thrillingly so. His eyes wandered once more along the room. Clinton was clapping, Columbo lighting up. The girls were still spilling from the booth. They seemed to be pushing one another. Come to think of it, didn't he recognise one—the pusher in chief—from the *Studentenheim*? Surely there wasn't another mouth like that in Vienna? It was a sly mouth—flexible lips—Spanish gums o'erarching. A cruel, laughing mouth—magnificent! A mouth to twist the knife.

He was just thinking that approachability took many forms when, with unerring instinct, the waitress brushed by, bent a touch and delivered a drink to the Spectre's table. 'THANK YOU MY DEAR,' said that familiar voice, eating up the room. What did the Spectre do to be served in such a way? Enslaved mothers and devoured their children. But he was an obsolete fur-trapper. A panther like her would scorn his snares. Back past Jude she sauntered, a trail of scent in her wake. He shivered. What was the meaning of all this to-ing and fro-ing? The *brush-by* and the *saunter-back*? He'd saunter her back—buy her brush too, if needs be. This he spoke mentally to Harper and, lifting whiskey over water, drank it down.

He was still congratulating himself when the waitress leaned beside his shoulder, placed two full tumblers before him. Jude thought nothing of this until after she'd gone. He was still saying *Danke*, she was still flashing a grin. The whitest teeth you'd ever seen. A bust to sink a plumb-line. He let fall his eyelashes as Arles began pummelling the skins. *And we're all at sea*, he murmured, when the bass was found. *And we're all at sea.* The band joined the refrain, halting, dissonant, until it became a fracturing wave, mantra and shanty together. *And we're all at sea. And we're all at sea.* Jude girded his loins. Everything was turning uncanny. Had Bjørn ordered more drinks? It was unusually liberal of him. The girls must have addled his mind. Still there was no reason why Jude should not profit from his folly. He picked up the tumbler, as, picking up the rhythm, the dancer decided to chance it.

And we're keeping our eyes on
The sleeping horizon
The sun—relies on
The sea
And the waters leaven
And the bread of heaven
Breaks on us
Deafeningly

And we're all at sea
And we're all at sea
And the moistures stand
Out on our hand
The manacles land
On the sea
The hand it shakes,
The manacle breaks
And makes it
All milkily

No sooner had he gone, than back skipped Bjørn with an air of complaisance. Like Jude, Bjørn was not a man on whom the refectory requirements of nature appeared to exert much influence. In fact, Jude—who had once fasted for a full five days, without even really meaning to, on the grounds that food, although necessary, was nevertheless *overrated*—was annoyed to find himself outgunned on his own territory. But then his was a *vegan* abstinence, while Bjørn's was a blasted carnivorous one, supported with *wurst* and seafood. A vegan malnutrition was more susceptible to alcohol. Jude put down the tumbler.

'I see your little game, Bjornsen.'

'Nn—er—wha?'

'Trying to drink me under the table.'

'Mmm, or rather I SEE YOUR GAME!'

There was a pause.

'What's my game?'

'Trying to drink ME under the table!'

Jude glanced side to side. He sensed the shadow of the Interminable, like a palm tree over the shoulder. He looked at the tumblers. Maybe they were a hint from the waitress. Maybe they just gave them away. Arles, on the other hand, was doing no such thing. The song was a storm of near-rhymes: *sundown* and *London* and *drowned on* the sea.

'Let's understand ourselves,' said Jude, chopping a pale hand. 'Who's drinking who under the table?'

'Oh no! I just came back from the toilet!'

'And where did this come from?'

'Er—oh, you've lost me now.'

And we're all at sea. And we're all at sea.

'Alright,' said Jude. '*Everything*—just needs to—*stop repeating itself.*' He looked to the band and back, then back to the band.

Securing the bales

Folding the sails
A somnolence pales
The sea
Quiet conversing
While we're rehearsing
The work of the
Mercenary

And we're all at sea
And we're all at sea
And a slow fog, and thickly,
Yellowly, sickly,
Trammelling quickly
The sea
And if it were done,
Having been done,
Best it were
Consequently

'This is GOOD STUFF.'

'And the music?'

Bjørn rolled his eyebrows all the way up. 'Er, THIS is good stuff too,' he chuckled, savouring the Scotch. 'But THIS'—jabbing at the band—'THIS is EXCELLENT GOOD.' Once again he stopped and listened. Arles was raising his voice, racheting up the tension. It was hard for the dancer to live with.

And we're all at sea
And we're all at sea
And a stir in the air
Manoeuvres our hair
Who goes over there
On the sea?
But it's just that seadog
With a hunger for grog
And a penchant for
Pornography

And we're all at sea
And we're all at sea
Mein Irisches Kind
I fear ve have sinned
Ze ship is destined
For ze sea
But he augurs awry
Who says we shall die
Besides, we defy
Augury!

'It's *atmospheric.*' Jude pouted.

'I, I have to say—I'm sometimes UP for a bit of ATMOSPHERE.'

'A clear, remote atmosphere is one thing. A thin, weightless *exosphere*, if you like, *minding its own business.*' Jude glanced significantly at Bjørn, and was unnerved by a completely comprehending gaze. 'But as soon as an atmosphere gets *too close*,' he continued, watching the bronze girl, awkwardly defrocking to the bongo, 'lowering breathily into your stratospheres and *tropospheres*, it becomes a *vile invasion*.'

And we're all at sea
And we're all at sea
Lo siento, Señor,
Mi scusi! Alors!
Je vous implore
Le mercy!
But they're all of 'em traitors,
Slaves and placaters
Who crave a dictator's
Decree

And we're all at sea
And we're all at sea
O Cap'n, my Cap'n!
The sky is misshapen
But worse things happen
At sea!
The climate is rough
But we'll find that our stuff
Pays more than
Sufficiently!

'You know what's too close?' came a voice over

his shoulder. 'You. Your head's in the lion's mouth.' The voice came from the booth behind, accompanied by a swathe of smoke.

Jude's broad back was all hackles. 'Hello?' he said, turning slowly. There was anger in his voice. Conspiracy was for losers.

'I was starting to think you wouldn't show.' It was a hoarse voice, theatrical, familiar. 'For an *incurious* fish you bait easily.'

'I see. What bait is this exactly?'

'Insiderism. Membership. *Anschluss*.' It was Rosa again, leaning beside his shoulder. The world was closing in, unaware how ludicrous it looked. As for Rosa, she was looking fine: black beret and jumper, grey-wool skirt, white tights. She disappeared as she went down. 'Cults and cabals. The usual youthful fantasy,' she barked, squeezing next to Bjørn. Bjørn hardly noticed. He was listening to Arles, eyes searching the ceiling. Arles was sharing the spoils—herpes and boils—which he got from gargoyles in Quang Tri.

'I'd be a member in that youthful fantasy.' Jude nodded toward the bronze beauty shedding a negligee. It lay on the floor like cannon fodder.

'I suppose that's why you came?'

'Absolutely.'

'AH, I've got to say I'm QUITE INTERESTED in this band right here.'

And we're all at sea
And we're all at sea
And the thunder is muttering
Lightning is shuttling
Shuffling its coils
In the sea
And the face of the earth
Is the picture of wrath
And she's throwing out the bath
With baby

And we're all at sea
And we're all at sea
And she's starting to poop
And the pea in our soup
Has gone to regroup
With the sea
And the bottle is empty
And it's hands to the pump—see
You pump her
Peremptorily!

'Derivative.' Rosa hailed the waitress, pointing to the tumblers on the table.

'So you came for the girls too.'

And we're all at sea. And we're all at sea.

'I heard there were drinks on the house.' She spread long-nailed fingers, cigarette between middle and fore. Breasts were heaving, bones were cleaving, clothes were receiving the sea. On top of that, Arles was roaring:

It's so ridiculous
How they bullshitted us!
And fitted us
Up for the sea!
The same moneygrabbers
Who pulled down Barabbas
And stabbed Jesus
Christ on the tree!

And we're all at sea
And we're all at sea
And the waves are a-shelving
Vallies are delving
And we're pissing ourselves in
The sea
And all these effluvias
Rise like Vesuvius
So
Insalubriously!

And we're all at sea
And we're all at sea
Haul on the bowline
We sing while we're rollin'
Deep down below in
The sea

We hauled on it and
It came off in our hand
So sadly abandoned
Were we

'So it seems.' Jude sniffed the glass. 'Peaty. *Floral* even.'

Bjørn dipped a finger in his. What was Arles driving at? An extended metaphor? A *sow's arse* and a *silk purse*, and something disbursed on the sea. Swimming in decks and cashing the checks, up to their necks in money. After that, an *uproar* and a *downpour*, but what was the *furore* to Arles? All he recalled was the rise and the fall, as if he had been all at sea. *And we're all at sea, and we're all at sea, and we're all at sea.* The band tapered off and called for water.

'Didn't mother tell you not to take men's *gifts?*'

'Well she took them, as I am testimony.' Jude looked at her. Her blue eyes were calm. Perfect lines ran in segments from the corners, like strata in rock. The long mouth smiled fractionally at the edges. 'She also told me not to look gift horses in the mouth, stitches in time save nine and that—*mysteriously* mind—there was *many a slip*.' He smiled, watching the dancer gather her garments. 'All of which torpid augury turns out to be true—as today has made strange proof.' He tasted from the glass. 'Still, since Bjorn is not gasping for the antidote, I assume the gift benign, though, by definition, the intention *poisonous*.'

The waitress crossed the dancer with a tray of bourbon. Rosa took Bjørn's glass and sampled.

'It's good.'

'EXCELLENT good.' Bjørn ran a finger along his eyebrow, still chuckling. He seemed to have become a law unto himself.

'Anyway'—it was Jude's turn to run a finger, down his glass—'what makes you think it was a man?'

'How often do women send drinks to your table?'

'How would I know if they didn't admit it?'

'Because you would ask for WATER and they would bring you GASOLINE.' Bjørn took another sip and held the glass to the lamp. It slung a band of gold over his eyes.

'The girls admit everything here,' said Rosa. She watched the bronze girl wading to the bar. 'Even when there's nothing to admit. I suppose that's why you like it. You can get excited about concealment.'

'On the contrary. I forgot more than girls ever knew about *concealment*.'

'After all, there are *two ways*,' she pursued.

'In a *manner of speaking*.'

Rosa looked unconvinced.

'If you're going to eavesdrop,' conceded Jude, 'I have, at least, recourse to *ambiguity*. Covering, of course, a multitude of sins.'

'Though not indifference. For all your affectation.' She stubbed the cigarette.

'No, just a multitude of sins. But you're right. A man gets tired of pretending a girl has something to hide.'

'Nn, hiding what they don't KNOW to BEGIN WITH.'

'You're on a hiding to nothing!' snapped Rosa. Arles had gone to the piano. Slurping the bourbon he introduced a song for old friends.

'Did the waitress forget your drink?' asked Jude, reminded.

'I'm sure if I wait someone will send one over.'

'*Kind of a drinking song, owes a little something to Walter Scott*,' said Arles, playing nobly with the keys. He snorted. '*Less and less each time.*'

'Allow me.' Jude made as if to rise but the chivalrous Bjørn was up like a shot. 'Allow ME!' he asserted, passing from the booth as if Rosa were not between. He stepped towards the bar, wonderful in his ephemerality. Then he stopped.

'Oh—er—what WILL you drink?'

'Oh, whatever you're drinking.'

Bjørn wasn't sure what he was drinking. He felt for his wallet then took off decisively. Certainly someone would know.

Speechlessness like a buoy floated in his wake. Then the ballad came riding the waves.

Well it's many a year since we dropped anchor here,
Where are the young rovers to stand us a round?

Jude minced another mouthful. The voice was rough and rowdy. Arles sounded seven times the sailor. 'Maybe you should find out,' said Rosa at last.

'I'm fairly sure it's the same as before.'

They're making 'em merry in the cemetery,
Drinking six feet underground

Even so, he looked round to get Bjørn's take. Bjørn reached the bar and hovered. There was no one there but the bronze beauty and she was on the wrong side. Or was she? The waitress was serving Pinstripes. '*Mayte!*' hissed Rosa as she returned, and signalled again for a drink. Mayte folded her eyes, complicitly. They were big, wide-lidded eyes, and the lashes long. They folded Jude's heart, shading his loins in the streams.

And drink to their healths—drink 'em in claret,
Give us partic'lars and lend us a pound,
All our old friends were thieves and were fiends
But they always did stand us a round

'You don't strike me as the shy type,' said Rosa.

Jude put down the glass. He swallowed. 'In the game of *Dungeon Quest*,' he began, as if it would take a while, 'on the encountering an *enemy*, you must choose of options *three*.' He showed three white digits in the gloom. 'Firstly there is *Attack*, wherein what you lose in guile you gain in momentum.' Three became one. 'Next is *Flee*, wherein you gain in distance what you lose in observation.' Became two. 'The third—and *last*—option is to *Wait and See*, which partakes in smaller measure the consequences of the other two.' Became three slim fingers. 'I *ever inclined* toward *Option Three*.'

'How liberal.'

'Yet *radical*. And *vegan*, what is more. I might add, treasure or no, I invariably escaped the dungeon before sundown, while my procrastinate companions perished in their greed.'

That charming chemise who sailed the high seas,
Real raconteur we called Swashbuckle Bill?
—Caught a disease from a cheap Cantonese
In the Hotel Maison De Ville

'So I see.' She shook the cigarette packet. 'Lucky for you.'

Jude lifted his chin. 'In a *manner of speaking*.'

'Some are more equal I suppose.'

'Even equals get lucky.'

And a drink to the braggart—drink him in claret
At least he weren't ignomin'ously drowned,
The smile of the pirate was twenty-four carat
And he always would stand us a round

Mayte brought the drink, ignoring Jude completely. Watching her leave, Jude saw Bjørn ensconced with the stripper, whose substantial haunch spread over the stool. She was Turkish-looking: pearl smile, curls and brown-skin. Bjørn loved her just the same. He ordered more drinks. It didn't seem worth going back for the other. He was establishing that everyone's opinion was worthwhile in its own right.

'Not tonight perhaps.'

'The night is young.'

'And for the unlucky?'

Jude examined a theatrical nail. '*Purgatory.*'

That avuncular jester, the Abbot of Leicester
—How come the Abbot don't answer the phone?

'Where you abandon them.'

'Where I observe them, which is as much as you can ask from a friend. Besides they have their wounds to treasure.'

The Abbot of Leicester turned out a molester
As the autopsies have shown

She took a sip, swilled it in her mouth. 'Which *are?*'

'Martyrdom: that excellent scar, looking nobler than it feels.'

'More reason to reward it.'

'It has had its pay.' Jude took a long draught. It was perfectly warm in the room. For the dancers, he supposed. That made sense: you had to look after the dancers. Everything flowed from there.

And a drink to his health—drink it in claret
Until some proof more conclusive be found
The crook of the Abbot was pure eighteen carat
And he always did stand us a round

'And what's become of these companions—since we're drinking healths?'

He eased forward. 'These are long stories—and tall ones too.' They drank to that and Arles commenced an instrumental. While Rosa ordered more, Jude checked on Bjørn's position—two inches closer to the Infidel Turk. 'Where to start?' he smiled slyly, reclining in the cushions.

'With the first watch.' She gave him a cigarette.

'That would be Marcellus.'

'*Aka* Harper.'

'As ambivalent as his name.'

'The madman.'

'*Raving.*' He tapped his temple; drinks came to the table. 'A bird's nest in his hair! Like all cowards, he will die for an idea. His big idea being to film a version of *Hamlet* without the Dane—at the Glum Valley Reservoir, which, as the Glum Valley Reservoir just happens to contain a *very small village*, is exactly the kind of obvious pun for which Harper, like Shakespeare, *loses the world.* Certainly the Glum Valley. For six months at least.' Now he tapped the cigarette. 'No, Harper is a skinny, begrudging Sisyphus, gone both to seed and town, fallen on hard times, living in an immigrants' home, condemned to Taskforce Apprenticeship Community Service Schemes, kicking a pebble up the concrete valley of the *Blacklock Road.* More *specifically,*' he demurred, jabbing this time, 'he is like Sisyphus in *Ulysses in the 31st Century*, waiting for a shard-metal ball to rumble down the beating desert and balance on the rim of the *Pit*, into which his job is to lever it—lunching, if he can get it, on hallucinogenic fungi, springing from the floor.' He chuckled. 'Then repeat the process, ad infinitum, occasionally crying *Will this never end?* while, *simultaneously*, brooding on the mechanism of the Gods and the deceits he will play on Ulysses—when he finally arrives to swap forever their existences.' He drank and was solemn.

‘Harper in a concrete valley,’ he said brusquely: ‘a *mythe de Sisyphe, sans Sisyphe, sans mythe.*’

‘Mythic indeed.’

‘Then there’s the whole tawdry troupe. Saint: a fool; Drake: a ham, and Quentin hardly counts,’ he continued. ‘But the Lie, now. The *Lie* is a genius.’

‘Whose is this unfortunate name?’

That extravagant tailor, styled Vlad the Impaler

‘No one really knows. But a man of high degree.’

Vlad must be sitting on top of a pile?
Vlad the Impaler was stabbed by a sailor
In his own bell-bottom style

Rosa lifted the candle. It was a big wheel of wax, fixed on a lead dish. She carried the flame to the cigarette and watched him through the fireworks.

And a drink for the faggot—drink him in claret
Nevermore will he the public astound
The pin in his cravat was a dozen gold carat
And he always did stand us a round

‘You mentioned a *man of sorrows*.’ The butt-end looked like a smelting works. Her hollows were dark, nostrils exaggerated. It took Jude back to a tunnel in the Glum—Magnus—his waterproof torch, its tiny wind-up device.

Poor Prance of Padworth, so full of such mad mirth?
And old Nom-de-Plume—what the hell was his name?
Prance-a-lot Padworth fell into the sad earth
The other fell victim to fame

'That was just an apparition. *Epiphany* if you will.'

'How religious you are.' She spoke from the corner of her mouth.

'You sound like Red Riding Hood.' Jude was quiet with disdain.

'I suppose you think you're the wolf.'

'Well *yes*. A wolf tired of being interrogated about the size of his religious beliefs.'

'Oh, a wolf with beliefs?'

'—Bored above all with the affectation of *doubt*.' Jude looked out of the booth.

And drink to their names—drink 'em in claret
Long may they loudly in Padworth resound
The plume of the parrot was dipped in six carat
And they always did stand us a round

'Everyone's religious,' he said at length, gazing at the cruel-mouthed girl. Was she Spanish or Sicilian? Their eyes had met in the *Studentenheim*, over the spaces of an interminable corridor. Her mouth was a pump now. She gyred on the seat like the worm had got her. 'Everyone's bound by vows. Every time they open their mouths.' He dropped crumbs in the ashtray, and the subject went there too.

And it's drink every braggart, and drink 'em in claret!
May they forever with laurel be crowned!
Ah, my dear friends, we will give dividends
If you only will stand us a round, and a round,
If you only will stand us a round

'And the King?' said Rosa. Smoke fountained from her mouth. She passed the candle.

'Ah, the King!' Jude raised both globe and sceptre. 'Banned from both valleys—*Glum* and *Cooley*—for a full two years. By now, assuming he hasn't given himself up, he's probably looking at a two year prison sentence, minimum. Was last seen rowing—on a lake of diminishing returns.' The flame grew tall around the paper. 'Always one to bring high places low.' He exhaled slowly. 'No doubt hiding in some oak tree now, going by the name of Magnus.'

'There's your martyr then.'

'Oh there's more. Not only are we banned a variety of roles and disguises. We are banned a whole host of *associations*, take it as liminally as you like. Specifically, we are selectively banned from associating with *certain among us*. Obviously Harper, Magnus and myself are banned from associating with each other, inclusively. But—and *further*—Harper is allowed to associate with Quentin, but not with Saint. Saint can associate with Drake but not with Quentin. And I can associate with Saint but not with Drake. Quentin I wouldn't want to associate with anyway, so that wasn't an issue—and ha! believe me, I made that quite clear in court. To Quentin's loud amusement.'

And it's drink to their mem'ries—drink 'em in claret
Wherever they're buying is where we are bound
Our oldest of friends were all treacherous fiends
But they always did stand us a round, and a round,
And they always did stand us a round

'And Magnus?'

'Prohibited from associating with *anyone at all.* Which, you'd have to think, will make catching him tricky.'

'So fox found a hole, bird a nest, but what will become of the Son of Man?'

'He shall have spring.'

'On a lake of diminishing returns.'

'*A-haugh, I got a little preamble here*,' sighed

Arles to the microphone, still laughing. He slid along to a marimba by the piano. '*Lorelei's a big bluff on the Rhine, place called Sankt Goarshausen.*' He fiddled with the beaters. '*Hundred and twenty meters high. I passed it on my way from Germany. It's the narrowest part of the Rhine, and a COMBINATION of rocks and currents have taken a historical TOLL on wayfaring SAILORS.*' Now he began tinkering with the keys. '*Lorelei means "murmuring rock", because the rock acts as a kind of AMPLIFIER to the sound of the water. That's what they SAY. But they ALSO say the sound is the Lorelei herself, a maiden—unhappy in love—who committed SUICIDE jumping from the rock and now lures men to their DEATHS. She appeared in the 1801 novel, Das steinerne Bild der Mutter by Clemens Brentano I think it was, who, they say, was influenced by the Echo-Narcissus myth.*' Bing-bong when the marimba. He was locating an accompaniment. '*She also crops up—time to time—in folk and POPULAR culture—there's a handful of songs about her, and—I BELIEVE—Lorelei was the name of Marilyn MONROE's character, in Gentlemen Prefer Blondes.*

Okaay, that's the Rhine. Noow, the Danube stretches from the Black Forest to the Black Sea—sounds like the Styx, don't it? Over one thousand seven hundred miles, flowing through ten countries and touching another nine with her DRAINAGE BASIN, she's the longest river in Europe, unless you count the Volga—but we won't QUIBBLE over terms. She also formed an old natural border of the Roman Empire. Apparently the name ultimately derives from Celtic—danu, to flow—finding equivalance in the Welsh, Donwy.

'SHE'S navigable by ocean ships into Romania and small crafts right up to Ulm in Germany. Partly CANALISED, in Germany she has five locks and in Austria ten. There are two double Iron Gate Locks—big mothers—between Serbia and Romania. Named one of ten Pan-European transport CORRIDORS—the SEVENTH as a matter of fact—in 1994, she forms part of a trans-European waterway stretching from Rotterdam to Sulina on the Black Sea. Transports over a hundred million tons of goods each year and she's the source of drinking-water for ten millions of people.

'She's a lot more, let's call her EXPERIENCED, than the Rhine; but the two rivers compete for water in the Southern-German CATCHMENT.' He had found the accompaniment now, such as it was, and the cello fed in. *'Before the last ice-age, the Alps used to feed the original Danube, but, after the Upper Rhine valley was eroded, the Rhine stole its waters away—carried 'em north. Some kind of Anschluss—not sure the Austrians got over it.'* He chuckled. *'You can still see the now-waterless*

canyons on the Swabian Alb plateau in Germany. But—did you KNOW—that because the Rhine has lower levels, and because Swabian limestone is so porous, VIA the subterranean rivers it's still stealing 'em today? MOREOVER, there are two locations where, in summertime, the Danube's emptying into underground channels is ACTUALLY AUDIBLE.' He spoke every syllable of the last two words. '*These locations are known as the DonauverSICKERUNG, or Danube Sink. And because these subterranean waterways are eroding the limestone, experts predict that in the future the upper Danube will COMPLETELY DISAPPEAR, ceded to the Rhine in a transaction known as STREAM-CAPTURING.*'

He paused. '*I used to date a tour-guide, I dunno.*' The oboe dropped by. '*I'm not sure if it's real relevant. I guess that stuff filters through your brain.*'

Rosa had craned her neck to listen. It was a formidable neck. Lines like hawsers strained it, but none of that hen-chin. 'I've known Jules a long time,' she said, turning back.

'A camp character.'

'Not a bit of it.'

'Just a dash, you understand. That's the thing about your *dash of camp*: a warped smile. A flagrant hand. The soul of power.'

'Matter of fact he's married to the waitress.'

Jude's world fell apart for a minute. Prompt with the oboe Arles embarked:

I pulled lovely Lorelei
From the river weeds
And wherever go my love and I
The river leads

'I would have married him myself once. Lucky I didn't really. We didn't stop fighting.'

Jude smiled awkwardly. This was a peculiar turn.

All the honour I had gained
By the wearing of the blue
Blew off upon the wind
At the sight of you

'What happened?' he said, dropping ash on the table.

'Syphilis. That was the end of that. I consoled myself by firing rounds into cardboard cut-outs of Gunther Grass.'

'Oh really?'

'I lived in an ex-warehouse in Berlin, eighty metres wall to wall. Not much in the way of furniture. Sort of became a shooting-range. It was a long time ago.'

'He moved away?' Jude took another swill. The marimba was the current and oboe a dying swan.

You were my pledge and my treasure
I don't think the boys understood.
I tied us to the world forever,
Said goodbye for good

'He was always moving, touring. In the end it was me who moved—down here—and Jules followed. He didn't admit it, he just knocked on my door one evening. Nineteen seventy eight, April nineteenth—I remember because the next day was Hitler's birthday.'

'And *mine.*' Jude took his time, nodding a fraction, fingering his trump. 'Not the anniversary. The *actual day.*' He blew smoke, like one who cannot lose.

Rosa looked stumped, for all her eyebrows. She hummed, merely, then dismissed him. 'Jules wanted to mark the occasion—on the midnight—by climbing on the Neue Burg balcony with accordion and horn, and singing "Brother, Can You Spare A Dime".'

'So did my father.' Jude smiled. 'Why didn't he?'

'Have you tried climbing the Neue Burg?' This was enough; she had recovered her poise.

Jude persisted though. 'I'm sure Bjorn has. At least in his *head*—which is almost as hard.'

'Jules was an artist, an actor—maybe too good an actor. He didn't deal in life. He could mime murder—show him the point of a gun, he'd run a mile.'

'Eighty-five metres ought to have done it.'

'You don't talk like a coward.'

He leaned in. 'But I talk.' In the circumstances, it was about the most flirtatious response he could have given.

I gave a rod to shoulder
You gave a ring to shine
Shine when the sun grew colder
On the hollow line

Rosa smoothed her skirt. 'He's very elusive.'

'A contemptible quality.'

'Almost made it big back in the day, but they couldn't pin it on him.'

'Perhaps he was wearing body-armour.' Jude looked out from the booth. Rosa reached for the candle and looked at him looking.

'My, you're a wounded animal. Like Byron—straight for the kill.'

Jude blushed for pleasure.

'Growling back to the jungle.' She lit up again.

'Well, better a jungle than an Alpine *gorge*,' said Jude, keen to fix the impression. 'Positively *oozing* with the Romantic sublime.'

'You're oozing the Romantic sublime. Out of your ears.'

'Must be the cholera.'

The line fell on your eye
And the sun was white,
Not surrenderin' to the sky
What it held so tight

'In any case,' she said, 'you take it or leave it.'
'Cholera?'
'—And he left it.' She finished the whiskey. 'He's not into control, just the work itself. Runs a tight ship.'
Jude responded in kind. 'So I see.' His eye rolled over the waitress, whose dress reflected in the tilted glass. The accompaniment stepped to the chorus:

You're my pledge and my treasure
I don't think the boys understand
I have begun to measure
The hour by the sand

They were really keening now: marimba was tugging and cello threading through. Rosa reached over the table.
'Let me see that sleeve.'
Jude offered it up. 'It's an old favourite,' he said.
'You need mothering.'
'So say the mothers. It's an incestuous industry.'
'You're young. You need to find a woman who

thinks as violently as yourself.'

'Impossible. Just as women don't recognise a man's brilliance, so they don't recognise his badness. Rank *badness*. Which is why they're always to be seen with some idiot any man could see through instantly. And not only is the idiot stupid, as of course he is, but he is sinister. And not only is he sinister, but he is undeserving. Which is why women are the very *type* of mercy, because mercy is blind as knives.'

We set a course for waters
Many went before
A sextant and a star have brought us
To the ocean floor

Arles was tight to the microphone, voice all agriculture and fisheries. Another two whiskeys swam to the table.

'Men are stupid, wild, competitive creatures,' continued Jude, oblivious. 'Take him for instance.' He steered his glass at the Spectre, who was entertaining the blonde stripper. 'I don't mean wild in any titillating sense. I mean bestial.' The Spectre steered his glass in kind. 'Women: sane, clear-eyed beings, calm in the eye, civilised. Aware of fashions—of the people round them—tuned to gossip—in towns and cities contented.' He relit his civilised cigarette. 'A woman's worst imagining cannot hold a candle to the trite, Alpine abysses of the male mind, whose Alpine triteness, of course, is precisely why they are dangerous. No, men are *fundamentally*, and I mean funda-*mentally*, unqualified for women.' Jude tapped his temple.

Rosa let him talk. 'I was wrong, you're not a Byron,' she reflected. 'You're a Shelley.' She whispered something to the waitress. 'And the tiger is your problem, as Lawrence says. You want life in terms of the lamb.'

'*Incorrect*,' said Jude, unexpectedly quoting the flower-man. 'Although certainly partial to the fox, I have no objection to life in terms of the tiger, an *infinitely* preferable animal to the lion. But a tiger who, having long since established his primacy in the Indian jungle—and *constantly aware* that, amidst a crowd of curry-eating, cricket-loving elephants, primacy means very little—has consciously, *audaciously*, gone vegan, much to the secret disappointment of various kinds of touring Norwegian elk who were hoping to pique themselves upon their Western self-restraint—yet who shows no compunction at all in mauling the occasional *homo sapien*—albeit no morsel of the species passes his lips.'

'Except our waitress, perhaps.'

'Unfortunately, the tiger and panther (speaking now of its *jaguar* expression) are continents apart. Besides, I respect marriage—not only because adultery is so self-important—but because nothing else so well preserves a man and woman's essential difference.'

'That's eloquent. A lie, but an eloquent one.'

'By definition—as Magnus would say.'

'You're a good liar,' she continued.

'Well, if you're going to be a liar, you might as well be good. Then again, if you're going to *lie*, you might as well just tell the truth.'

The world was just an oyster.
Discovery was done.
I bid the boys to
Go but they were gone

The song ended. Again, Jude checked Bjørn's position. Bjørn was moving onto the importance of an open mind, drawing your own conclusions—or no conclusions at all. The Infidel was smiling sweetly, one forearm resting on the bar, fingers not an inch from his. It was a smooth brown forearm, pale on the inside. The smile could while away a day: front teeth protrusive, resting also on the lip. She was young, barely twenty. She didn't seem to mind her job. It was all in a day's work. Her legs were tight-crossed on the stool and a hollow ran down the thigh, like aerodynamics on a jet-wing. Large legs, sculpted ankles. Black heels rested on a crossbar. Everything about her spoke present rest.

She was a sleeping breeze, which roused could wreck you.

They clinked fresh glasses, toasting an open economy. Bjørn glanced over at Jude, who was leaning forward, ensconced in conversation. There was no telling with Jude, Bjørn was thinking. He didn't mind the mature type once in a while, but Jude might be going too far. A lot of attention, but he didn't know how to use it. Women intimidated him. Perhaps he was—but it couldn't be.

Arles reached for the bourbon and went back to the piano. '*Once again it's that time of the evening when you gotta run*,' he said, playing odd chords. The strippers had given up now, filtering out into the room. He watched them go. '*Woow, I'm all finished*,' he added. '*Maybe I'll feel better after a dance.*'

'*Ja, weil—ich fühlte mich einsam in der Türkei*,' said the girl sadly. She was still smiling.

'*Oh nein. Oh nein, das musst du dich NIEMALS fühlen*,' said Bjørn, pointing aggressively. His hair fell lank on his forehead. '*Weil, in einer Weise, könnte man sagen, daß wir NIEMALS allein sind!*'

'*I've been dancin' all day but I, I, er—*'

'*Fühlst du dich nicht alleine?*' Her forefinger moved and rested on the bar.

'*Oh nein, oh nein. Ich habe viele große Freunden.*'

'That's Bjorn. As honest an elk as ever shoved

you into a fence and call it a *fifty-fifty*, or won a chess match by boring you to death.' Jude became confidential. 'He has worked at a mental hospital for the last year—*night* shifts, mind—on the edge of a *lonely fjord*. His only conversations have been with people who believe they are God's own mouthpieces, extrapolating His plans for the world from the lyrics of *Blind Lemon Jefferson*. After translating them into Norwegian, obviously.' Jude's smile was above all laughter. 'He's also had some good talks with the patients at the hospital.' There was no end to this kind of thing.

'*But I might have a final song in me.*' A cheer. Chords became a current. The voice was all internal affairs.

'*Das ist Jude*,' Bjørn was saying. '*Er—er ist fanTAStisch. Ich bleibe mit ihm.*'

'*Hast du kein eigenes Zimmer?*'

'*Naah, in diesem Moment nicht! Aber ich bin frei! Ich kann kommen und gehen, wann ich WILL.*'

'Why is he here?'

'No reason at all. The sole excuse he can offer is that last refuge of a scoundrel, *the experience*. And spending as much time in sleazy Hungarian chess-cafes as he can muster. And, since it runs so slowly, it will muster indeed.' Jude accepted a cigarette. 'No, he is brilliant. I don't know what I'd do without him.' He jabbed it in the table. 'But if he expounds to me one more time how he has no need for possessions, money or ambitions, I'll drive a stake through his ambitious heart.'

'You'll need the last, to do without the others.'

'And it's the last thing I'd care for. No, money and possessions may not satisfy the spirit, but at least they placate the body. Absence of money and possessions, on the other hand, satisfies, in the most sensual possible manner, an *idea*: some paltry miscarriage of that lamest of faculties, the *mind*. A mind *utterly crippled* by the day-to-day betrayals which money and possessions take for granted. Man*i*acally intent on taking the play out of everything. Pitifully busy with stringing up Trespass for a Traitor. "Traitor to what?" Trespass will protest. "The idea!" cries the mind. "Go fuck yourself," replies Trespass, wearily summoning its confessor.'

'*Another booze ballad. Kind of a-poca-LYPtic valediction.*'

'Looking nobler than it feels.'

'On the contrary, betrayal is the authentic expression of love. If any man come to *me* and hate not his father and mother and all his family, he cannot be my disciple. There, it's not so hard.'

'And *his own life too*.'

'Well, *ecce homo*, you might say. I wouldn't obviously.'

'A coward, then.'

'You sound like him,' said Jude, indicating the

Spectre. 'No, you don't deserve the title of friend if you can't betray the one you love. Only Magnus understands this. Saint devotes, Bjorn is too loyal, Harper: a man who carries courtesy like shopping, not knowing what to do with it. He is intent on giving everyone the rub of the green—crack of the whip—benefit of the doubt, the benefit of which, since he doubts everything, is highly dubious—not to say *dilute*. He would die before offer an insult: blown up in front of the cannon, with the word on his lips. This of course makes him angry: deeply, cleanly angry. *Everyone*, you see, is not so courteous as himself.'

'His anger springs from his courtesy.'

Jude considered. 'Yees, and *yet*—and here's the irony,' he said, leaning in. 'Behind that—*beneath* that—is his *anger* again. Detached. Imageless. *Harper*,' he declared, 'has no love for life. Poor sod, a whiteness will seize him; a shroud trailing in his face—like clouds of *glory* cut adrift.'

Let's all get sentimental—

Rosa drank off her drink. 'Well, it's time for you to show some courtesy.' She nodded at the empty glasses.

'Yes yes.'

Don't forget the good-bye.

'You should thank your benefactor.'

This was too insistent. 'That would make me *beneficiary*: a ridiculous role.'

'I think you've had the benefit, doubt or not—and nothing *dilute* about it.' She folded her gloves in her handbag. 'It's time for grace.'

Once we've repent all our sins and sent all our friends
To the devil we'll die

The beret was peaked, tobacco stowed away. Rosa was becoming a bother. Moreover, she was spoiling an acceptable evening—the worst of crimes. Bjørn slipped by for a pen and paper, hinting he might have somewhere else to sleep. Jude supplied him, cursed his profligacy. Everyone was so keen to give themselves away. The good which fell in their laps, they spent in someone else's. Far from immoral, it was slovenly. He strained round for alternatives, but there were no alternatives. He fished in the glass. He watched Rosa's eyes for a moment only.

'Perhaps I should say *thank-you.*'

'That would be courteous.'

'It's all about courtship isn't it?'

'That's how it starts.'

'I suspect that's where it *ends.*' He was annoyed by now. The conversation had gone on too long. He had permitted too many liberties.

'After the blood is spilt.'

'The ultimate act of courtship.'

'So spill away.'

The early riser leaves no one the wiser,
Virtue is so incidental,

'Fine.' Jude rose from his seat. The room span. There—Bjørn with the Infidel, so *entwined*. Mayte over there, a hat-check girl again—handing a hat to the Blonde. Who was that if not the Band, commanding from the stern? And what, but the fat, flat hand of the Spectre, rising to greet him, in a military salute? 'Yes, yes,' he repeated to himself. 'Follow the world's weary rigmarole. Shake Murder by the hand and thank it for the drink. Then back to his place for *Wurst* and world-domination.'

Bid it be welcome—we see it so seldom
But let's all get sentimental

He stared round like a zeppelin. Pinstripes was soothing the brunette. Columbo was on his third beer. A quiet held the girls' booth: the calm before a storm. He drained his glass, and started for the Spectre.

Everything from this moment happens in slow-motion. He makes it half way across the room when out flies the Sicilian from her booth on the end of an almighty push, breaking against his broad shoulder. Enraged and afraid, attacked on all sides, he cocks a cold white fist. He looks like a cherished member of the proletariat: mouth-wracked, tight-biceped, arm angled to the strike. He remains there for aeons. Slowly he notices the clownish face of his aggressor. It is burrowed in his side, mouth wobbling, body slipping like soap. Briefly she reminds him of a mouse—a curvacious, mischief-making mouse. A mouse which is actually a Dragon in disguise. Rasping through her teeth, grabbing hold his nooks, and even crannies, she raises and extracts herself. The piano bestrides the scene. Trumpet blows a dirge. Turning, she launches a foul silent invective at her friends and they fall silent a-laughing. Let's all get sentimental, goes the song. The cup is brimming with blood. Still watching that silent laughter, Jude slips himself, grabs a cardigan, winds up with arms around the Sicilian Dragon. The women have torn all their hair and borne all their babies down on the flood. 'Don't show yourself up,' says Rosa from her booth. She looks exactly like a sea-horse. 'Dance.' And they begin to dance: a slow waltz-like movement. The vagabond leaves with the sun on his sleeves. The pan depends on the handle. Bjørn's belle gets the message; the elk is led to water. Slowly—like animals coming to drink—the inhabitants of the booths arise and take the floor. We that are left are we are bereft. The mice come out to play and pair together. Clinton like an owl with one in his talons. He doesn't even look like

Clinton any more. Here is the zebra; the bruised brunette, a violin in his neck. So let's all get sentimental. There, the lion, the pony stiff above him. And, over there, Columbo, offered the hand of the panther. He rises to his feet, transforms into elegance, and they are dancing, light as gazelles. Let's all get sentimental, my friends. The excrement's hitting the fan. The tiger is the worse for wear. He almost falls for alcohol. The ways that we went, all the money we spent, all have left us where we began. The Dragon holds him in her arms and a tear wets his cheek. Seeing that tear, the lion weeps also. Little boy blonde, he fell in the pond, angling with his utensil. The lights dim. Bears, cats and trappers fall away. The curtain falls on this strange scene, dancers crowding and fading like flowers, none whose face is not wet for shame. He caught him a fish he could not relinquish. But for the serene Columbo, smiling on nothing. So let's all get sentimental. Let's all get sentimental, my dear—let's all get sentimental. It's too late now to leave anyhow so let's all get sentimental.

2. Stream-Capturing

Here came Orson Welles again, rolling down the Wurstelprater like a pin without the nine: pinned in the Russian Sector; exiled from pretty much everywhere. No doubt there was something ridiculous in this. Rolling and stopping as if he didn't realise; as if it wasn't an act. Absolutely nothing like a ghost. Then it was old man this and indigestion that and the weary rigmarole all over. Gah, the worst thing in the film. And yet one had to admit it was disturbing, almost scary—like a car in a darkened lane, a long-expected, over-rehearsed apparition. Ghosts didn't ride only by night. They marched cheery through the day, among bright carousels, chuckling and chirruping and congratulating themselves.

Jude could take it no longer. 'Not con-*VINCED*!' he roared, flinging his pillow. Bjørn's arms flew like hammers. 'Wha?' he gasped. 'Nn.'

Jude stormed to the sink, clicked the mirror-light. Not that the room had been dark. On the blue curtain, an exterior lamp made a yellowy blur. He cursed the blur, ran the water, cupped hand and drank. He splashed his face and stared. From inside a sleeping-bag, Bjørn checked the clock. Twenty past three. What was Jude doing? Applying shaving cream, apparently. Was he mad? Certainly he had no respect for the sleeping. Then again, Bjørn should be the last to complain about that. Jude reached for the razor. Bjørn burrowed in the bag.

Two minutes passed. Bjørn was lying there, thinking Jude would see sense. But no, he was going through with it. The cream, the scratching, the cursing. Bjørn heaved a sigh and rolled over. Of course, it was Jude's room, he could do what he liked. But this was a bridge too far. Bjørn was going to have to find a room of his own. That blonde bureaucrat, Stefan, would have to be consulted. Or would he? Perhaps he could be bypassed altogether.

The next twenty minutes passed more slowly than a slow opening move—the kind where they spend half an hour deciding whether to play *d* or *e4.* Then again, Bjørn was content to see them run down their clocks. The rules were the rules. What, to Jude, was a petty *end* was always, for Bjørn, a legitimate MEANS; there was always a time for such a word. Bjørn was comfortable with the last syllable of recorded time. Sometimes, when he got talking, it seemed his to speak.

Here, though, was little comfort. Jude scraped and churned and wallowed. He stomped and he stormed. *Clink* went the glass, and *gurgle* the water.

He filled the sink again, a drainage basin if ever he'd seen one. Steam broke on the mirror, passed the sleeping-bag in a sad cloud. The bag looked like a windsock. The room was a temperate zone; a microclimate; a corner of some Eastern-bloc block that was forever England (and Norway). It was neat, minimal: no pictures, figurines, icons. It was rectangular too, with fitted cupboards, bedside table and bed. Brown ribbed carpet rolled under a desk, where a bent note lay discarded. A boat-like note, floating with intent. A remnant craft, holed for a handle, carven with curious runes:

REUBEN RANZO,

BETTER STOP TURNING THAT DOOR KNOB NOW, OR THERE'S GONNA BE SPOOKS AROUND YOUR BED. FEEL ROUND FOR YOUR WALKIN' SHOES AND DROP THROUGH AT THE CAFE MUSEUM, COS THAT'S WHERE I'M GONNA BE TONIGHT, SOMEWHERE AMONG THE SIXTY-FOUR SQUARES, DRINKING ME A COUPLE CUPS OF STEAMING HOT JOE—MAYBE A MALTED MILK—TO EASE THESE OL' WRITIN' PAPER BLUES.

CATCH YOU LATER.

RAILROAD BILL.

P.S. I'VE GOT YOUR KEY.

Jude turned the tap tight shut. Left of the desk, a window looked onto an inner courtyard, where no one ever set foot, except for Pilar Santana Artale, who had set Jude's boot there (a surrogate sort of foot, as far as he was concerned) by dropping it from the fourth floor kitchen. Not that Jude had stood for it. A man's boot was his crown, which Pilar Santana Artale had been humbled into retrieving, via the common room window. Near the desk was the sink: engine of interior weather. Right now, it was low-pressure belts and a north-northwesterly, *alto cyrrus* and *alto stratus*.

'Might be a few *alto-clumulus* in there, rolling away,' mumbled Bjørn to himself. Whatever they were, their hair was the lanker for them. Bjørn rolled away like he was flattening pastry. Jude and Harper had scarce rolled as much on the earthworks and burial-mounds of ancient Britain—and they had rolled down a good many of them. At last, with many a huff, and the occasional puff, Jude finished. Bjørn sighed again. The other boot had fallen, metaphorically speaking; and the advantage of metaphor, Bjørn intuited, was that there was no requisitioning to be done. Jude might have disagreed, but then, Bjørn congratulated himself, Jude wasn't aware of Bjørn's semi-conscious intuitions. Or was he? Bjørn waited. He peered into his bag. Still the light strained through. What was Jude *doing?* He was looking at himself in the mirror, thinking how lazy Bjørn was. Something was wrong. Bjørn checked the clock again; perhaps he had been mistaken. No. Quarter to four. This was intolerable. Soon the dawn would come. Jude flapped into his trousers, clinked his low-pressure belt. On went the long-sleeved t-shirt, hands pushed through sleeves. Then he picked up his *all-stars*, stepped over Bjørn and left the room.

How long was Bjørn to lie there? Five minutes? Ten? At what point could he conclude that Jude had gone, it was safe to turn off the light? Why had he left it on anyway? Wasn't that what, if Bjørn or Quentin had done it, Jude would have called an *unforgiveable oversight?* He waited. He could hear the buzzing of the mirror-light, the slam of faraway doors. When ten minutes had passed he rose ghostly from the bag, stealing to the light as to a purse. Off it went and he was back in the bag, rolling, churning, fiercely fighting. The clock ticked. The room was the wake of a bomb. He was still baffled when he dropped out.

There was Vienna again, after the war, bombed about a bit. Where an amateur fell by the wayside, floated in the Donau Kanal. Divided into Zones, and the centre International. They could hardly communicate, poor devils, how could they stop the bootleggers? Besides, some of 'em made pretty good stuff. Bjørn scoffed excited in his sleep.

Jude was away down the corridors, floors, landings. Past lift-shafts, showers, all kinds of cubicles. Down a level, slapping with bare feet the linoleum. Aimless past offices, broom-cupboards, kitchens. In the rear stairwell, shallow-stepped, wide-windowed. Re-enter the halls, past lavatories, dormitories, depositories. Was there no one in this godforsaken *Heim?* He tapped round a corner, pushed through a door to an iron fire-escape, black and ringing, emerging in a common-room. Past table-football, table-tennis, tables of leaflets. Past shut reception-desk, into lobby, sneaking a look in the television room. The television gleamed like treefall in a forest. The door clicked shut.

He pushed the adjacent one. It creaked heavily. Inside were eight computers along the window. At the last computer, Rico, the Azabaijanian, looked sleepily round. On the screen twenty boxes showed twenty different pudendas, stretching, yawning, laughing. Sleepy ones, shabby ones, ones with no discernible character. Jude joined him, leaning over the chair. 'A perfect illustration,' he observed, 'of choice sliding helplessly into sameness.' Rico spoke little English but he grinned and sniggered with the best of them. He also stank, and after a while Jude took the first computer, as far from Rico as possible.

He switched it on, went through the usual rigmarole. Something was waiting in the email bucket. Not from the Embassy though. It was a message from Harper; a short one for once:

Sir,

Can't be long, because the Auld Cause has just come in, wanting to 'check his emails', and 'peek a wee while at the GURRRLLLS,' and he's muttering and fuming—and stinking—in the doorway. Some understanding between him and Garfield, apparently.

Time, then, merely, to acquaint you with my DREAM.

We were at a house, on the edge of moors. A low wall ran round the garden. We saw a wolf loping over that garden, disappearing over the wall. Then we saw lions, and bears, stealing from the side, gently into the precincts, potent, yielding.

I went round the side of the house, alone. There was a bear there but it was a man, with a vast nose (about three yards deep and long) and a great lower jaw (of the same dimensions). Behind the face, more like an animal. He was almost all face though, and he leaned that face over the garden wall, between lovely and murderous. I was standing by the wall and he took my arm in his jaw and started to crush it, slowly, like a bully exploiting the essential ambivalence of friendship. It was unclear if he was organism or machine. He started crushing my arm, but by keeping it there and pressing down hard, so that he couldn't close his jaw, I prevented him from hurting me. And in this strange position, with my arm pressing down inside his mouth, and his large eyes looking at me either side of that nose, he began to laugh. It was a slow, heavy laugh, a laugh from the chest, together with a heaving. And, in the tension, struggling, in the face of his laugh, I began to laugh too—a lot, even against my will.

I woke with a huge goofy laugh on my face, unable to control the sobbing.

And you should know these things.

Harper.

Jude laughed himself, drily, like one who could stop laughing very quickly. He scrolled down the correspondence, into a veritable abyss. A sprawling map of the subconscious, leading direct to the Origin.

Sir

I am being given a seriously lascivious eye by a gaggle of attractive girls sitting not three feet in front of me. More to my right. It is enough to give one ideas. Wrong ideas. About cuticles. And emerging from straight seams. And now there is another one standing at the computer opposite, legs to her hips. Look not to left nor right, they say, but then they just stand in front of you. And only this morning I was enjoying coffee with a closet communist and bookseller, both at the same time, who is only too keen to open up her closet and show you around, perhaps sell you a couple of the contents. Freud and Friends is the closet's preposterous name, and Rosa (its owner's) was telling me about her years as an anarchist in Berlin, and the gun she used to fire at life-size models of Gunther Grass. Where was she sitting? Genau to the left of me. As Magnus (and Hegel—and Roger Moore) would say (seriously, the three of them—in unison!), Where shall I turn me not to view my bonds? Certainly not to Vienna's freezing, bleak Red Light District, through which, yesterday evening, I accompanied Bjorn to the Hungarian chess cafe, actually no cafe at all but a dark backroom in some kind of—I can think of no other word for them—PREMISES, where ageing fat Hungars plied me with cheap Hungarian wine and cigars while I read about Bobby Fischer and roared with laughter. After several hours, and I might say the worse for wear had I not been surrounded by a throng of greasy oiks, no doubt itching to throw off their clothes and stand around in vests and Y-fronts, I could take it no longer and declared I was leaving, whereupon an extremely reluctant, not to say retarded, Bjorn was extracted from his table saying 'nd' and 'kl'. A man ENTIRELY devoid of vowels. Nevertheless, we pounded back through the Red Light District—the strip-clubs, porn palaces, torn-velvet brothels—where whores in huge furs called from the doorways: big whores, fat whores, old whores, but a finer sort of whore all round. It's the edge of Eastern Europe and that cultural night. We plunged through lights of windows. In one, a sad negress reclined. In another, a slavic vulture, giving me the eye. And over there!—in another! crowded with tinsel and little flashing bulbs—Bill Clinton! blowing his saxophone!

That night all I could dream about was the sad

negress. I woke still thinking on her. Anyone would have thought I hadn't slept. I became immediately enraged by the nightlight, imposing on my room. What was to be done? Something, sir. Something. And a concrete thing too. I got up, went straight for the broom cupboard and found the instrument in question. Then—brilliantly—and with a hitherto unsuspected pragmatism—I placed a shoe box on the end of it, projected it out of the window, and proceeded to shuffle that shoe box onto the nightlight. And it worked what my mother would call (hideously) a treat. Magnus Kroner, eat your heart out. Go on—eat it! Ventricle by ventricle.

Left without breakfast and stormed through various world-heritage sites, including Neue Burg, Stefansdom and, at pace, the Kunsthistoriches Gallery, sneering at Dutch Masters, cocking snooks at all kinds of Impressionism and straight to Renaissance Italy. Then, applying what I'd learnt, I went back to the Studentenheim, dressed up in a sheet, and chased the girls around the corridors, seizing every possible opportunity to stare up their trouser legs. For hours. And they loved it, sir, they loved it. Mark me, they will take to wearing flares. And so spoil everything.

Notwithstanding,

Jude.

>
>

Sir,

I woke to a knocking at the door. It was Garfield. Rain was on the window but my mouth was dry. He curled by the radiator for a chat, started asking about my friends, wanted to know what happened to you. 'Difficult to say,' says I. 'We can't speak without the phone cutting out. The only thing we know for sure about Jude Harlow, apart from the fact that his name IS Jude Harlow, is that he's in exile, in Vienna of all places, patronised by some fearful symmetry of those philanthropical Britishers, Messrs Embassy, Academy and Council, amidst darts of Socratic compliments and showers of Erasmian praise (with occasional obsequies to the European Commission), by whom, under the guise of researching nationalism and anti-semitism in fin-de-siecle Vienna, he is encouraged, almost obliged, to go a-browsing in bookshops, moping in museums, frequenting burlesque chess-clubs, where the Kings and Queens (and Bishops) of obsolete politics attempt to twist his English Opening into all manner of Reverse Sicilians, Hedgehog Defences, and Halibut Gambits.' 'Quite right too,' he agrees, sentimentally. His eye glistens. Picture if you will a bald collection of arms and legs with big ears and a pontificate air. Picture his regard for youth, his obvious, obviously-masked, despair. Picture again that glistening eye, large with nostalgia, obligation, shame. 'We have to get it right this time,' he continues, holding his chin in the air. I ignore him. He tilts just a fraction to measure my response, then back. Rain draws crowns on the window, confirming his stance. The chin protrudes, but the eye still fluttereth. 'What we need now is ethnic cleansing,' he murmurs, loud enough not to mistake. Of course, this is the greatest of burdens. He is sad this moral obligation has fallen to such a man of genius; all he ever wanted to do was paint, etc. He is pitiful, sir. All enemies are. But they are wilfully, stubbornly, pitiful and this makes them dangerous. So to you I say BEWARE of the pitiful man, the masochist, the grubber in the dustbin of conviction. He will concentrate his powers, slither up determined, and stab you in the KIBE. We don't die at impact. It's a long slow haemorrhage gets us in the end.

So I muttered something about milk and honey, left him in my room. What did I do then, sir? I went to the kitchen, drank milk with honey. Naturally my thoughts turned to Harriet Morris, Alicia Long, though I blush to say it, Ruth Murphy et al. Ruth Murphy, long ignored, pining plumply in her sex. The one we thought not of. Our thighs touched under the table; we thought it all a game. Cows crowded our windows and she brought us butter. Forgive us, fat Ruth Murphy. If we meet again at Compt, I'll love thee till the cows come home.

Donned a hat and baggy trousers. Went to the park to keep up a ball in the rain. It must be in the rain, mind. Have become EXTREMELY PROFICIENT at this. There I was, sir, on the edge of an almost-deserted park, evening falling, somewhere in the mid-hundreds, kneeing it, necking it, toeing it higher and higher, and what to my peripheral vision should appear? but movements, sir, in the bushes. A parting of branches. A pair of red eyes. Naturally I ignore it. Another blasted molester of some sort, thinks I. He can take a lesson in keepie-uppie, also learn how to juggle a football. I carry on a bit more. I stop. I start again. I hear a shuffle, a shiffle-shaffle, a sigh. I see a pair of blue suede shoes. There I am, ploughing into the double-ton, darkness coming on and sweats outnumbering the rain, when I catch it on my neck and the voyeur can take no more. Out he rages from the bushes, crying 'Och there, Auld Bomber!' I turn about, still balancing, and if it isn't the same tramp accosted me on my first evening here. Like all his ilk, the erratic nature of his appearances is specifically designed to mystify. As always with mystification, it is the last weapon left to him, and the closest to hand. 'I knew Shankly!' he starts. 'Trained with 'im up in Glasgee!' 'Crumbs,' says I. 'Did you?' 'Jus' fuckin' said so!' he growls. 'Ah, the auld Glasgee days!' he reminisces. 'It was schoolin' all day, footy all evenin' an' drink the Auld Cause all night! Aaaah, aul' Glasgee! One o' these days I'll hop the train an' go home.' He tugs his wet beard. 'They say where ye were born, ye should go to die. Don't they? Don't they, son?' 'Do they?' I ask. He looks disgusted. 'Got ta knaw ye're born first,' he mutters. 'Some o' these youngsters. Wouldn't knaw a Cause if it stood before ye and fuckin' took Effect. Heh!' He starts jabbing his finger to the ground again, as if he has some treasure down there. 'But seein' ye there, ye put me in mind of meself,' he explains. His voice gets husky. 'The touch. The vision.' The rain begins to pour. 'I've seen a few pleeyers in me time!' he shouts. 'Seen 'em come, seen 'em go by. Fall by the fuckin' wayside!' Up comes the finger and it points at me. 'But YOU lad! YOU can make the ball TALK!' Of course, I couldn't help thinking he was right. 'I can get ya a trial,' he continued. 'I know a few people. Few o' the Auld Causers. I can get ya a trial.' 'Can you?' says I, riding the wave. 'I can!' 'You should!' 'I shall!' We shook diseased hands. I told him where I live. Naturally the whole thing was an outrageous lie, but, as with the Bomber Harris story, pursued with a mixture of irony and obstinacy until it could be called, like all lies most tenacious, a hobby. He limped off under the railway bridge, with all the pride and bitterness of his kind, wonderfully pleased with his lies. And there I remained, walloping the ball sixty feet in the air, continuing to juggle it when it came down, hardly discernible from the rain, and, though brilliant and incredible, somehow flat and pointless and not worth a brass farthing. Damn him, sir. Literally. Not a coal less from Hell to warm his earthly life.

Started walking home—in the rain, mind. Almost there when I had to pass the laundry.

And there she was, swaying her body, sensuous, forgetful, in the lighted room. It was getting dark. My coat-zip was broken and I had to wrap it round. End of October winds, whirling leaves and newspapers, and, inside, the silent washerwoman, floating to imaginary music. No one around—it was warm and full of costumes. Because everyone is in Fancy Dress. Always. Her hair was braided and beaded, back was lithe. A pot-belly of kinds, maybe a rice one. Not pocked white and fleshly—brown round and smooth. There she was, in the hospitable shop, facing away, swaying down the floor's middle, no debate about her Nymphomyiidean branch. There was I, gazing like an urchin, snub-nosed for chocolates. I passed on—how naively!—like a large mating swarm. For, worse, far worse, between laundry and door—the newsagent. And in the newsagent, an exquisite Indian, in full Navratri regalia: tall, long-haired, with white, perfect teeth and all your vaunted symmetry of face. Married with two children. It maketh a man to weep. To lie down by still waters. Like the shadow that declineth. Like a menhir in a valley of rocks. Africk and Ind: a two-edged sword, of Damocles. Park Lane and Mayfair, with hotels on each. Take your flat-iron or terrier, shake your dice and clickety-clack. Ruined. And so close to GO. The wind slapped about. I closed my door behind me, passed into a half-sleep of wash-machines, bright influences of bright essences, and anything of nothing increate.

AND NOW someone is banging on this door (it's not locked), ORDERING the 'occupant' (me), in a heavy Russian accent, to 'EXIT THE PRRREMISES!'

With which I have a notion—strangely, disarmingly—

to COMPLY.

Being

Harper.

>
>

Gentlemen,

Research reveals that the gnat, along with the midge, is the colloquial term given to various insects of the Dipteran order, more specifically the Nematoceran suborder, among whom we include crane-flies, hair-flies, black-flies and mosquitoes, though there is some debate as to the classification of the Nymphomyiidean branch. Nematocera can be recognised by their filamentous, multi-segmented antennae, plumose in some males and the pupae are orthorrhaphous, meaning that adults emerge from a straight seam in the pupal cuticle. Feeding on plants, gnats and midges are typically found near water, the males often roaming at dusk in large mating swarms called 'ghosts'.

I will communicate when I can. Meantime, continue to state business and location.

T.

>
>

Sir,

A pity the phone cut out last night. Bjorn assures me he is going to buy phone cards for everyone today, so I might well effect another call this evening.

Vienna has gotten cold, and I am glad of a moustache to keep my lip from freezing. That said, what good did it do Scott when he saw icicles descend from his? Amundsen, History records, was clean shaven. Similarly the Turk, though momentarily blessed with a thousand years of civilisation (only to see it washed up and broken against the rocks of Civilisation), knows in his crescent-shaped heart of hearts that his moustache is just a forlorn archaism, anachronistic to survival. Wont to collect all manner of humus, the GOZLEM, the 'pide.' Falafel, too—the mark of a degenerate. What shall he do? Shave it off? And be—a European? As Dr Johnson would say, No sir.

As for Bjorn's intentions—honourable, I think. He should find out today whether he's got a room in our building—he should—and he intends to stay at least till Christmas. If he can get a job he'll stay longer, but as to how easy that is we don't yet know. As for what he's doing here, well, not much. I think he just spends his days in my room, reading, or exploring the city, getting to know first its nooks (sounds like some kind of racial slur, I'd say), then its crannies (which sounds totally vulgar, but you know Bjorn).

Myself, I'll storm off to the Neue Berg round about morning and sit there sweating and ogling a while, before, about three in the afternoon, I'll adjourn to either the Cafe Hawelka or, more likely, Braunerhof, for a large, black coffee, with two lumps o' sugar. Then back to the library till some time in the evening. When I get offa work, I might meet Bjorn at the Cafe Museum, where he plays chess. Already Bjorn has a reputation at the Cafe Museum for playing reeeeally slowly and boringly. Tonight he's going to a chess club in another cafe owned by a sleazy Hungarian. All Hungarians—certainly all the male ones, as far as I can ascertain—are sleazy. Meanwhile I sit and read for three or four hours, exchanging looks with all and sundry. I drink mineral water, all fizzed up 'cos that's how they like it here. When we return, we'll cook up a broccoli or rustle up a soya yoghurt and have us a slap-up meal in the kitchen, where we are joined by various national stereotypes. The hostel is a place you spend hours unintentionally—and sometimes intentionally—roaming, on account of its three staircases—mainstairs, backstairs and a fire-escape running down an open-air shaft between buildings. The back 'un is a wide, light, useless affair, with those low steps you hardly notice. The window is some kind of art-deco stained-glass occasion, and the morning light is a thing to behold, sir—and more important, be beheld by. You enter it by double-doors, via a kind of closed airlock, and if I were a pious man—and God knows I were—I'd say it were like stepping into heaven. The fire-escape, though, is a dingy plunge, dark in its shaft and bracing. Sometimes I take this, sometimes I take that—if only to better appreciate this. Naturally, all of this upper-lower, interior-exterior malarky were too strong a polarity, but the mainstairs puts paid to that, by providing what, if you were a VILE, RISIBLE politician, you might call a 'middle way'. A man can spend his whole day in these adventures, going up and down and in and out of staircases, corridors, identical kitchens and different (though identical) toilets (something which has been a pressing requirement recently—though pressing has not itself been necessary), sometimes meeting the odd person along the way, possibly even a girl for whom one has a passing interest, sometimes not a soul. It's tedious stuff, but you can indulge it for hours, days, weeks at a time. Then there's the added complication of the lift-shaft, which, needless to say all the girls use continually, even if they are only going to the first floor, so that if one is perchance looking, or lurking, for any of the aforementioned girls, one has to take into account not only possible routes, chance-meetings and near-misses (and non-encounters too)—but the twin problem of which end they entered, and at which end they may be exiting, and exciting, though, like the girls, it comes to the same thing.

Then there are your computer rooms, tables football and tennis in the cold ground floor, large youth-rooms to grow old passing through, a television room that one knows one will never use, but might look for someone in—perhaps a Norweyan Lord, trying to catch the highlights of some minor sporting event in which Norway might have, or once have had, an interest—and then the floors themselves, which are U-shaped, except that the bottom line of the U is the very long corridor, and the the other two are shorter. Then there are people like Cornelius Barry to encounter, possibly avoid, who if encountered will certainly sigh and speak gently and friendlily, and invite one to his room for coffee. All of this and more. Even now, Bjorn has just entered the computer room. An extraordinary, and entirely predictable, coincidence. This is what happens when you house your considerable features in a featureless socialist-era apartment block. We bound up and down staircases, grinning; slide along polished corridors in our socks; dress up in sheets and pretend to be ghosts. I did this last night and was barged so hard by Bjorn that I banged my head on a fire-extinguisher, fell over and was dragged by a gaggle of Spanish girls, kicking and screaming, down the corridor and, deposited outside someone's door (an American called Jesse as it turned out). They knocked on the door and ran off, leaving me to explain it all. Which I did. Brilliantly.

Then, coming back from a late night session at the Cafe Museum, Bjorn and I decided to race each other, he via the mainstairs, I via the backstairs, to then converge upon the (equidistant) fire-escape to gain the last floor. For a very specific reason, the architects of the building (socialists to the bone—and, let's face it, what socialist worth his salt is anything more than bone?) decided to award access to the last floor (and so to the roof) only to the fire-escape, as if to even things out, so, as is invariably the case, cloaking elitism in an air of equality. 'Weeell, the luck evens itself out over the course of a season,' is how they justified it to themselves, calculating, correctly, that a cold, black, tremendous fire-escape would be very little traversed, except in case of fire. And what is fire but elitism?

Undermining, then, a neurotic Teutonic logic

with conscious English idiosyncrasy, I challenged Bjorn to the aforesaid race, up six floors, through the fire-escape to the seventh, and so to the door to the roof. Naturally Bjorn became INCREDIBLY excited by the idea, rubbing his rocky hands and grinning his icy teeth and saying 'NnnnNN!' and 'Na ya!' So the marks were to, and the sets were got, and there we stood at opposite ends of the building, separated by hall, reception, and vast youth-room, all with the doors swung open, ready for the Word. A moment, sir, a breathless moment, clock striking twelve, swallowed by immensities. Then we were off—flying, soaring, virtually bodiless, up the eternal stairs, EXACTLY like something from M. C. Escher, only a lot less twee. Hooting we heard from far-away wells—a screech, a strangled cry, through corridors, doors, dormitories, through tomes and reams of sleepers. Who could know where the other one was, what unforeseen short-cuts he might take? It was a race built solidly on trust. And fear.

Naturally I won. But, for once, that's not the point, sir. A hundred yards apart, upwards we poured at our various gradients, two arch antagonists, linked by that most insidious of claims—an Invisible Bond. Flight after flight, floor after floor, level after endless level, till we met, on our way to the fire escape, myself a full foot ahead. Inside, outside, pounding the heartless metal, through heavy doors and inside again, breathing hard, screeching, laughing, up the final stairs, where stands (in this, the block's highest building) the door to both roof and World. And there, on the very top step, sitting all alone, as if all that World were implicated—a turd.

Jude.

>
>

Sir,

The Putzfrau, eh? It must be something about washing: warm liquids, circular rhythms, etc. Because I've got my eye on a washerwoman of my own, in a laundry on the Blacklock Road. An Ethiope, sir, whom I suspect of concealing a rich jewel—in her ear! She a small thing, sir, with the body of a woman well-endowed. She high for'ead, green teeth, wiry hair, looks like Derartu Tulu, of whom she and I had a short conversation, not so much to hide as to eloquently express the fact that I wanted her to throw me in the wash-tub, scrub me up proper, polish my new pin, etc. Instead, or therefore, she lends me a copy of Athletics Weekly—which I shall read, sir, cover to cover!

Talked some more to the landlord, a rich, bald manic-depressive ex-barrister called Garfield and anything but dear (though an expensive lawyer, I gather). He curls on my bed, lectures me for an hour on immigration, politics, religion. 'We are gnats on the rump of the universe,' he says. He says it many times. It seems to be his favourite expression, though it sounds microbiologically unlikely. Maybe you should ask Bjorn. He insults the lodgers here, calls them scabs and wasters but adores them, spends untold thousands on their welfare. Immigration is the source of our ills, he claims; we should round them up, put them out to sea. He only houses them for the money. He says the country has gone to the dogs, that the government has no feeling for people. He wants tougher social laws, longer sentences, capital punishment. He says we should nuke whatever threatens our existence. That is, I say, if we can stop adoring it. He's a socialist, he says. Religion is the opiate of the masses. 'There's this Man you should meet,' I tell him, 'and he Would Be King.' 'Ah, dear boy,' says he (he calls me 'dear boy'), 'I would be King when I was your age. What a thing is youth, hmhah!' and he chuckles as if dreamily to himself but for my benefit entirely. He is lost in projecting the projecting of a lost image of himself, and hovers a while twixt the idiotic and endearing. Only a while though. I usher him out of the room, on the pretence of sleep. When was it anything more?

Woke nevertheless to a hopeless, yet insistent—and no doubt insistent because hopeless, or, worse! hopeless BECAUSE insistent—knocking at the door, and who should enter but Kostas Krippopolous, the Greek. I don't know why he's an immigrant but he's the loneliest human being anyone ever heard crash in the silent Athenian forests (a big bone of contention with Kostas). His maw sinks from his cheeks, as if his very real mythological punishment is to carry between his teeth for an eternity an invisible bucket of water to put out an eternal inferno (in the silent Athenian forests) neither spilling nor drinking a drop. He stood near the bed in a thick quilt jacket, a yard or so into the room, saying nothing. 'How are you?' said I.

There was a silence.

'...I am...FIIINE' replied Kostas after a little,

drawing back his lips and vibrating the vowel. I didn't stare at him. You have to make Kostas feel comfortable, though it mean hours of sly assessment. I slyly assessed him. His front teeth are round and so are the edges of his descending mouth, bent like a boomerang. It is the kind of mouth that would bite through bread and find an iron file. From that desolation of mouth hangs a brush of brown goatee, without even moustache to depend from. Desolation is neither his friend nor enemy. It is an inconstant escort, a scout scoping the ground, now behind, now before, but ever and anon returning, with that silent bearing that says 'no news is good news'; a rarified level of consciousness, befalling him of an evening, reminding him who he is. Desolation, I say, eventually caught him up and familiarised itself with the room. This is usually Kostas' cue to say something profound. On this occasion he let air escape from one side of his mouth, kept his heavy fingers by his side, and said:

'I...cannot...find the words...to CHAAARACTERISE myself.'

Five minutes elapsed before the explanation:

'I have...no SPOOON.'

Then there are two Bulgarian teenagers, with whom I have sat up nights playing Poker, drinking Frascati and reciting Shelley. They can't get enough of this kind of thing. Then we laugh and swill and call each other's bluff, and then do it all over again, but this time behind each other's back, my friend. They are both in love with a Columbian girl on the floor above, name of Carlotta, whose presence here is likewise inexplicable, though heartening (though disheartening). They all seem to have got caught in the middle of student exchanges. Add to the mix some tall, positively aloof, Pole with three or four illegal jobs and that's the corridor.

So Bjorn is there. What's he doing? More important, what is he intending?

I have a phone. Some kind of oversized mobile device Kostas didn't want any more. The number is: 0044 7891 629 780. Vorsicht, though, 'cos it'll cost ya. I'm cutting Tantalus, Quentin, Saint and the Lizard in on this, in case they have access.

I am,

till death robs me of my face,

Harper.

>
>

Sir,

Strange that you have come to exactly the same conclusion as I about food, and at exactly the same time. It's an on-going thing, of course, and can probably be traced back to the Kellogg company's attempt at a subtle change—a cost-cutting measure, no doubt—in the shape, texture and taste of their most especial cereal. I resent food. It irritates me enormously that I end up spending about 90 OS on it every week. The best thing about being vegan is that I am compelled to spitefully reject almost all common foodstuffs, in favour of new, purer, blander ones that no one likes, although they are TEN TIMES more expensive. In this respect, however, I laugh at vegan food calling my bluff, taking things to their logical extreme.

Moreover, and I won't say there's a link, I also have been finding myself waking up in bizarre positions, not to say SITUATIONS, half-draped in sheets, unaware I ever went to sleep, a pool of dribble coagulating upon whatever surface I happen to be forming an almost imperceptible angle to. And dreams, sir—what dreams! Only last night, for example, I dreamt I was sitting in the Österreichische Bibliothek reading that Friedrich Nietzsche was NOT born in 1977, in Bullish, of plump parentage. His name, therefore, was BY NO MEANS Nemmins NOR was that of Immanuel Kant, Hole, the fact of which both Nemmins and Hole were only too painfully aware, though their cries for epistemological assistance went entirely unrecognised by all but Mad Jenny. She, however, was so fundamentally opposed to Nemmins' belief that God was dead (so brilliantly, albeit cryptically, enunciated in one his earliest works, 'Tractors on Glum Greater High Street,' posthumously re-christened 'There Is No Knowledge Of The Intelligible World') that she ignored them entirely. This led to a brief split between Nemmins and Hole, with the former retreating to the Mount Mary's Arms, and ending tragically drunk on Dry Blackthorn and covered in dung, in the arms of Sal Porter. Somewhat more sympathy was accorded to Hole, in whose dictum 'Act in such a way that you always treat tractors, whether your own or the possession of another, never simply as a means, but always at the same time as an end' it was possible to detect the influence of the neo-Platonists and their immediate successor, Mr. 'Godders' Godfrey. Mad Jenny, in fact, with the approval of The Man Who Would Be King, who saw in her plan an excuse to mis-use the word 'deconstruction' and to say 'hmmm...hochay!' was on the brink of attempting to implement a radical rehabilitation programme involving Hole, when he suddenly veered towards another philosophical school entirely, and thus beyond even her sphere of influence. This group, comprising primarily young, avant-garde thinkers from such diverse locales as Woorish, Chancery Fog and certain council estates in Backward Mass, quickly developed its own systems (heavily redolent of Nemmins') and identity. Most prominent were Messrs. Moore, Walsh, Hatchard, Church and Swerves, although Stan, Turner, Nailer, Browne and Streaghan formed a tenacious, if unlikely, sub-system. Sometime members included (briefly, somewhat bizarrely, perhaps) Giles Pilcher—who, on presentation of a doctor's note was excused from most meetings—and Laurence Finch, who was expelled. The group would meet between the hours of 4-5pm during the winter months, whilst preferring some time between

8.30 and 10pm during the spring and summer. As a result local types, gathered to witness the intellectual warfare which ensued, referred to them as the 'Idles of the Twilight,' at the same time coining the phrase 'Don't be tight, Nailer.'

I would accuse myself of some kind of dementia were it not that I observe the same phenomena in Bjorn Bjornsen, who, having dropped off biochemistry, drops out wherever he finds a floor. What he dreams, though, as he shudders his legs and waves arms like knives, one can only imagine. Perhaps he is skilfully scaling the various probosces, protuberances and proclivities of every statue and facade he insists on examining. Perhaps he is wreaking revenge on the pawns and queens—and the chess pieces too—that attack him on all sides every evening in the Cafe Museum while he frowns and grins and loses and I sit around for hours, reading, drinking mineral water, and doing not a jot of work. He's been sleeping on my floor for a week now, and with any luck should have the room next to mine as of this evening. He sits in the kitchen, staring so intently at chess-books that you can announce that Bergen is presently sliding into the North Sea on a freak tectonic plate and he won't bat a wooden eyelid. Ten minutes later he will lift his head and mutter 'kn...bj...ø...?' with a far-away look in his eyes. Tonight we are going to see Tarkovsky's 'Stalker' which should be right up his alley.

For the rest, well, there's Darko the Yugoslav, Rico, the smelly, grinning Azerbaijanian, Marcel the earnest Slovene, Kara the Austrian, Brad the American, his sister Tennessee, and Cornelius Barry, the Englishman, who, to the utter mortification of anyone who happens to have been born within a few hundred miles of him (including the French), sticks out like a SORE THUMB, not least because he is plump and red. Then you have Tomas, a Swede of all things, who sometimes comes down to use our kitchen because his own is swarming with Turks, and whose father, rumour has it, works for the UN in charge of Tropical Diseases—an orgy of intrigue and subterfuge which he modestly (yet unobjectionably) reduces to the word 'research'. After that there's a WHOLE BUNCH of Spanish girls. We're talking Pilar Santana Artale (hot), Laura Barbosa Escribano (ugly), Olivia Ruiz Fernandez (cute), Magdalena Jesus Maria de Carmen something (I'd do 'er) and Maria Garcia Garcia (tiny—but I'd do 'er too, if only for novelty value). Finally there's the Putzfrau, and aptly named. By your paranoid standards, she too must be spying on me, although more for pleasure than profit—as is probably the case with your landlord. Like him, she cannot see me without winking, which, as she sees me all the time, throws her into something of a spastic paradox. Moreover she will insist on entering my room without knocking, though knocking is her only thought, to find me sprawled a-bed, naked, dragged backwards through some latest dream. What can we do but laugh and keep on polishing? It's a good crowd, and many evenings have been spent sitting around the kitchen table laughing at, not with, one another, as one does when one is with foreigners. Vienna is good. Overwhelmingly pretentious and precious, but good. If it weren't for the Germanic majority and their total lack of style (which includes their language, though I converse in't), I could probably...

live...

here...(?)

I don't have a phone number, but I'll try to call you from a phone box.

I am

Jude Harlow

and my address is:

Zimmer 210
9 Auerspergstrasse,
1080,
Wien.

P.S. As for the Indian, the answer is simple. Keep getting sacked. It doesn't matter how you do it. Kill, burn, even stamp, so long as it has the desired effect. Eventually she will relent. She will assume that, as you are obviously a. eloquent and b. doomed, you must be a genius. Carried away with her generosity, she will have only one service left to offer.

>
>

Sir,

The rain it raineth every day. Literally—every day. I wake to wet wheels. I sleep to the same. The Blacklock Road is some kind of heart-valve or dialysis machine. The blood keeps pace to it.

I am suspicious of my stomach, sir. Every

evening I roam to the communal kitchen, boil up pasta or rice and spoon it down my gullet, perhaps to the tune of some tomato or courgette concoction. Occasionally a cabbage soup will lighten the tone. And thus I keep from dying. It is a treaty worthy of betrayal.

Speaking of which, if I ever get back to that valley I'm going to commit mighty acts of trespass and be the kind of person that likes it too. I'm going to scrump apples, plunge wells, and plough through fields to my heart's content. Because, as if six months' community service, cleaning toilets in town, and an injunction out, forbidding me from going within ten miles of the Glum Valley reservoir, were not enough, it seems I am being spied on, if only by the landlord. How else to explain the fact that he constantly barges in on me, always on the point of discharging some great secret? He can't speak but hint. It's wink this and nod that, and the flower of our youth over there. If so, he will be disappointed, because nine times out of ten he finds me asleep, dreaming about corridors, staircases, sentences—anything long and monotonous.

Speaking of which, I went to the Community Service office and waited an age. In the office was the most beautiful woman I have ever seen, sorting waifs and strays into wheat and chaff (aka builders and cleaners). Indian-origin of course: heavy eyelids, blue grey eyes that could slide in a second and never come back. A fine nose, blue-black hair, large soft breasts, mouth like a blade, or the tear it makes. Silk and steel. I wasn't even in her world. She gave me some service, though. Cleaning toilets in various nondescript council buildings. Lest I forgot I was

Harper.

>
>

Sir,

It sounds more like a corridor of certainty. And what are you supposed to be doing there? Community Service? What does it mean? It is a rotten, not to say tedious, society that confuses service with punishment. But I pity the poor immigrant—and the emigrant too—if only because, even when he uses all his power to do evil, he is never, ever, EVER LEFT ALONE. And as I sit in the Österreichische Nationalbibliothek, totally alone, using all my power to do evil (putting books back on the wrong shelf, flicking bogies under the table, etc), I pity the more bitterly—having been compelled here by a mixture of the usual threats (exile, infanticide, frogs and boils) and usual shames (patriotism, family, frogs and boils) to produce—what?—some kind of report on fascism and anti-semitism in turn-of-the-century Austria (oddly enough, and as coincidence would have it, a story of exile, infanticide, patriotism, family, and frogs and boils), as if history were destined to repeat itself and academia to stand knowledgeably by and watch it happen, what time I find Bjorn Bjornsen threatening to arrive, to much fanfare and trumpeting in Norway, causing me to struggle against the thought that whether or not he will actually hinder my progress, he will nevertheless BE IN MY WAY, and this will, ashamedly, cause me to resent him and force me into a flying, if suppressed, RAGE. Rioting, looting. The city on fire. The burning flesh of men. And yet...Bjorn Bjornsen...fantastic. A tear...a tear...creepeth on my cheek.

As, I confess, it did, when, JUST before I left, when my bags were all PACKED, shoes SHOD and teeth positively CHAMPING at the BIT, my mother, suddenly! and yet slowly, and all as it were by stealth, kissed my newshaven cheek and, sotto-like, said: 'Don't forget who you are'.

As if

Jude.

>
>

Sir,

Not sure if this will reach you, because recent emails have been sent back with the advice that addresses have not been, or have refused to be, or I am not allowed to know whether or not they have been, recognised, and that no such person may possibly be allowed to/known to/known to be allowed to exist, and can't or won't imply whether said person is to be contacted via the Embassy, British Council, University or Wohnungsvermittlung. Plus I'm writing this on the (only) computer in the Immigrant Home basement, which is not only incredibly difficult to access, account of all the Armenians buzzing about it, but/and is almost certainly bugged. For all these reasons, unsure about destination/audience of this apostrophe.

Anyway, I took that bus to Laughton, via Woorish hill, whence I could see right to the Levels, widening on the far air. Drifting over them: smokes of the fires of burning animals; mountains of cattle, electric red in distance, billows of smoke like lava. Just your mutt and jeff, common or garden, foot and mouth massacres, limbs spitting in the sundown. Thence a train to town, past factories, refineries, slag and scrap-heaps, ware and storehouses—the fences, freight yards, tyre-hills, sleeper-piles and sidings standing in sun, till it felt the heart would fail. The sun was failing too, pale over the angles. Verticals were sinking, simultaneously erecting chimneys, poles, lines of flawless ambition. We descended through first suburbs, endless estates, miles of limbo peripheries, finally arriving at the upside-down Satan of the city centre, munching like a mechanism on the Betrayer.

In town, I took a bus. Everything was peeling, everything unworkable, all things sliding from construction to decay. I realise I have to hone my awareness of infrastructure. I have to get in with the builders, roadworkers, furbishers of all kinds. Cleaners and electricians, plumbers and mechanics. These people know how the country works. Unacknowledged legislators, comprising together an unstoppable force. Not that you'd have known it watching the streets, their scattered masses. Woe, I murmured, to the scattered mass, climbing the steps of the municipal buildings, falling like leaves to graves. Never has so few been done by so much to so many. And, yes, it's a question of number. Through the window where I cast these words—like so many petals, paper boats, names writ in water—I watched the skeletal churches, crooks of signposts, flocks of pamphlets, losing themselves on the cemented slopes. I saw nests in the heads of buildings, futons falling from windows, eggshells on the cemetery tar. A dead dog lay at the cemetery gate. Ah, was it digging on a grave? No sir, not even burying a bone. Burial, it seems, is impossible here. Finally I came to my lodgings, a bricked, ex-nursing-home on the junction of Gut Street and the Blacklock Road. I got a key from the landlord, opened the door to my cell. I put down my bags and the sullen tear started to my ee.

I didn't go to bed. Spent the evening roaming the wind. The wind held disparate streets, the shards and ends of streets,—wind without wind, world without end, bottles blown and rolling bins, draining street into street, where even vanishing is partial. There was nowhere to go. Hours, sir, hours. Down to the docks, the freight yards, watched flotsam knock at nothing. Over lonely roads, through sudden estates, back up the hill, past the arts college, where a Scottish bum was entertaining a crowd. Pleased with the sudden masses, I stopped and listened. He was sprawled on a bench, slicked-back hair and a growth of beard, throwing out Shakespeare via Robert Burns. He seemed to have it down. He would raise a finger, stop mid-sentence, start again somewhere else, and all of it strangely coherent. He had quite a range, from the declamation to the whinge. A light rain came on. I walked on and sat in a Turkish cafe, staring from the window, eating hummus. All of a sudden the same man limps inside, saying 'Sorry to disturb, ladies and gen'lemen, I'm lookin' to raise enough money t' find something decent to eat, get mahself in a shelter for the night'. He turns up collar against storms in the eye. 'An' ah was wonderin' if you'd be kind enough to spare a li'l change? Toss an old soldier a bone,' he whines, tailing up beautifully.

I gave him twenty, sir, of your English pence, and was about to think no more of it, till he started staring at me, jabbing down his finger, as if the living Hell were six feet beneath, and much readier than anyone suspected to burst into the general world. 'That's a fine head of hair,' he says. He nodded and pointed down. 'That's a fine bushy beard,' says I. 'D'ya, d'ya, d'ya know who my grandfather was?' he asks, raising his nostrils. The clientele look alarmed. 'B—d, d, d—Bomber Harris!' he stutters. He looks around for a reaction, is disappointed with none. He's not much younger than Bomber Harris. 'That's BARON Bomber Harris to you!' he roars at a couple of Arab girls, one of whom I have been eyeing. 'You know what the Baron's solution was to Palestine Arabs. A five hundred pound bomb on every rebel village! Hah, yeh.' They study the table and he turns back to I. 'Ah,' says I, with surprising elan, lucky enough to anticipate him. 'What I couldn't tell you about Bomber Harris.' This confuses him a little. 'What ya couldn't...?' he raged. 'What I couldna tell you! He was bombing tribesmen in India when the Germans were still tryin' ta get their fuckin' act together! Weimar fuckin' Republic, yeh, Nazi fuckin' party, Rosa Luxemburg! Old Bomber! He cut holes in the noses of Vickers Vernons, dropped bombs in MesopoTEEMia! Fuckin' Baldwin, Chamberlain—fuckin' MacDonald, should ha trusted to Bomber! Saturation bombing—that was his idea! Bombed Dresden to smith'reens! Smith'reens! Not even a medal for the Bomber Command.' Well this was all too much for the proprietors and out comes a HUGE black man with a moustache, and asks him extremely politely to stop bothering the customers. 'Bothering—bothering—' mutters the man, anticipant himself, already wading away like a Baird's tapir. 'You're bothering ME!' He bustles out of the door, pretending great offence. Cold, still-starved, I returned at twelve to the immigrant home. It starts to rain again. A girl is sitting in the doorway in her pyjamas: 'Alright Mister?' she says. Then to her brother, 'Move out the way of the Man!' The quarters are vast and draughty, inside and out. Large rooms indicate former prosperity. Mine, though, is some kind of broom-cupboard, like a corridor—of uncertainty, say I,

Which is,

Harper.

Jude sighed, looked at Rico, looked back again. Then he looked at Rico. Rico was blinking at three writhing blondes. He looked chastened. It didn't seem so much fun after a while. Where could one go from here? Tits and arse, they all kept coming.

Rico couldn't connect; didn't know how to make it work for him. All those pixels and nothing to show for it. Why did it always rain on Rico? He gave away all the good things which fell in his lap.

But he kept watching. Too late to turn back now, Rico was in for the long haul. Jude clicked the *reply* sign and typed:

Sir,

Funny you should say so. I dreamt this night there was a cull at the Studentenheim. Call it a November clearout. Stefan was calling people's names out and, curiously, everyone was passing (myself included). Everyone except for Rico. Rico ran to the dressing room, crying. I tried to comfort him, telling him it was unfair, that he was one of the most skilful residents they had ever had, but he burst to further tears. He couldn't accept that he had to leave, not after his early season form. He felt he deserved another crack of the whip. Eight or ten people gathered, including Rosa from Freud and Friends. The Man Who Would Be King put his arm around Rico. 'Alone again,' he said, and he smiled, implying Humanism. At which everybody cheered up, except me, who woke up. I was sweating all over, the blanket had a diamond shaped hole in and the window was open wide. Only then did I realise I was ENRAGED. Moreover my pillow was giving me grief, both in its qualitative and quantitive capacities.

My second thought (best thought) was Pilar Santana Artale, which, given the circumstances, should (and did) come as no surprise. And this is the worst of all. I think she likes me though, which is fantastic of her. The other night, for example, we were in the kitchen boiling a broccoli with Jesse, who was minding his own business, cap over eyes, when all at once Tomas sidled in and a bottle sidled with him. Pretty soon we were smashing glasses and roaring. Bjorn was coming over all pacific, Tomas all Anglophile and Jesse was arranging teapots, toast-racks and cracks in the table to explain Sharpsburg, Vicksburg, Gettysburg—all the burgs. Bjorn's pious pacifism makes a man want to sign up to fire semi-automatics. Not only does he offer no solution, he offers no explanation how his puttering, pussyfooting peace differs from war. He merely speaks of hearts, yea, and MINDS, and exudes an air of both. Shock and awe, say I. Start war with Austria while we're about it. Evil faux-liberalism! Naturally, the blood will fly up to heaven—also cry from the ground (being capable of both), but leastwise won't pave hell. Aggressive as you like, enter more pacifist wasters in the shape (shapely), not to say sign (signally), of four Espanolas-cum-Catalans-cum-Basques, who seem, in their enthusiastic en-masse German-exchanging to have tolerantly forgotten the Condor legion, Teutons all, who bombed Guernica to horse-flesh-ridden pieces while Franco laid siege to Madrid. We're talking Pilar (whose name is actually Maria), Barbosa, Olivia Ruiz Fernandez and Maria Garcia Garcia, who appears not to know she has been the victim of a private joke, commonly known as inbreeding. Well pretty soon it all got down and dirty as we talked Barcelona F.C. (Barbosa), Veterinary Science, B.Sc. (Garcia) and Eliot T.S. (Pilar). Ruiz Fernandez doesn't speak a word of English and only a smattering—say it, sir, a SMATTERING—of German, so it seemed the culturally-sensitive thing to do to ostracise her completely (this being Ostria). Barbosa is a sleepy, heavy-eyed thing with an underbite (a national trait, it seems, forming a strange confederacy with perfect teeth). She will come over all sensitive, make an incongruous gesture and mumble various banal things in what can only be described as, and reproduced in, stray haiku, viz:

Although I don't think capitalism
Is the best solution
It's the only one I have in here.

Politicians make me not to believe,
State terrorism, oil in the ocean
Well, it's better not to talk.

She is an architect, sir, dealing in designs, extending them to Bjorn it seems. And this is right, as a man closer resembling an architectural design you will not find. Garcia Garcia is a mouse-like thing with pins for eyes. She is inhibited in all manner of ways, giving one to hope, unreasonably, that she may be lured into savagery. And then there is Santana Artale, the Sicilian Dragon, whom, rumour has it, one night at the Casanova, I very nearly assaulted, before immediately converting my attempted assault into a drunken dance. Incredible, sir. Incredible. Half-Spanish-Basque, half-Sicilian, to be precise, all line and length, hip that wiggle, mouth that snarl and surl. Beware her, boys, BEWARE HER! She studies literature, if you'll credit that, and goes around putting a piquant nose into BOOKS, sir, BOOKS, with the greatest of gall (Asterix books). Well, up she sidles asking if I have a lighter, and, incredibly, I do—Saint's as it turns out, which Hole slipped me at the Freely-Lowe Farm, and which I could not return to Saint on account of the fact that I went out of my way to avoid him, consciously avoiding the crowded Marching thoroughfares, until the time came to leave for Vienna. A butt or two later (usually Bjorn, though I much prefer Artale's) and we were egregiously into Organised Religion, Barbosa was discussing the Ins-and-Outs of Neue Styl with Bjorn, who is always up for ins-and-outs wherever he can get 'em, and Garcia Garcia was listening intently while Jesse outlined with great care the dangers of Retreat in Pitched-Battle. Meanwhile Tomas, who has a girlfriend in Sweden, spoke an elegant Spanish to Olivia, like the confounded gentleman he is, until the Spanish took it upon themselves to actually confound him, by buzzing about his midriff, punching and shouting 'Tomas!' which one can only put down to a young democracy. At least that's how they explain it. I was pleased at this show of bravado, but deeply irritated at the same time that Artale had been wrenched from me by the glory and the nothing of a name.

Pretty soon the lot of them buzzed right off and I was left holding the baby, not the lighter—which should come as no surprise, the baby in question (Bjorn by name) having spent the whole evening tearing stiffly and efficiently into silent forests of broccoli—because the same lazy, sponging, terrifyingly autodidactic baby, curse his tight Scandinavian soul, has still not managed to secure himself a room in the Studentenheim. Admittedly he has twice been to Stefan, the blonde pen-pusher (at once the least and worst of his crimes) who haunts occasional lower corridors, to inquire, and twice been given all kinds of unreassuring reassurances that the thing in question might conceivably be a possibility, before, upon the point of leaving, being stopped by the same nervous nelly, and asked in return where exactly he was staying now, since he was inside the Heim, only to answer in his turn that he was 'nn...wh...?...oh no, oh no...' and to beat a shifty and very un-American retreat through various doors and corridors. He is now considering bypassing Stefan entirely, but only considering mind, because in his tight Scandinavian soul, deeply impressed in its turn by the paranoiac Germanic soul, he wants deeply to play it by the rules. So he'll be on my floor another month then and I don't know how it looks to other people but I'm sleeping right next to him every night. This would be more bearable were he to rise and shine at tol'able times, but he is either up immorally—and immortally—early, to be found reading Ovid of a six in the kitchen morning, and declaring it too, or else, as today, rolling and shuddering all over my floor, when a man is trying to shave and prepare. Either way, he is a lazy lob. Albeit a brilliant one. I'm meeting him at the library this evening, and it's off to the Cafe Museum, then maybe The Third Man—midnight showing. For The Third Time in Three Weeks.

The British Council still have not written to me. They're supposed to be giving me details: papers, deadlines, directions, to facilitate my work. Some kind of reciprocal brief and pump affair, but the only briefs I've seen are those of the numerous Turks and Slavs who, as soon as they get home waste no time in pulling off trousers, walking round proudly in pants and vests and slapping each other, as if homoeroticism were engrained in their cultures.

Oh, hang on...

Then there's the Putzfrau who hints at briefs every chance she gets, but so far stops at garters, not, mind you, that she can see them for guts. As for pump action, unfortunately, the last time I saw any they arrested us for trespass, called it subversive activity and sent us into exile. Trouble is, I have a taste for it now. What are they going to do? Exile me back again? As Barbosa would say, 'deep voices of football were complaining.'

I am

Conspicuously,

Concupiscently,

Jude.

Jude signed out, shut the web. He looked at Rico, thinking of other things. Rico was asleep, nodding ever closer to the keyboard. The room was stuffy, the light oppressive. Jude could smell Rico from here. He slung hold of his satchel, tied on his *all-stars* and slouched out. Rico bowed low. Above him, a huge cunt floated like a sign.

On the way out Jude met the *Putzfrau*.

'*Und was machen Sie um diese Zeit hier?*' she leered. '*Nicht Mädels im Computer anschauen?*'

'*Nein. Rico vielleicht.*'

'*Ah, Rico. Aber wo gehen Sie jetzt hin, mein Herr?*' She looked like a tub of ice-cream.

'*Oh, hinaus, meine Dame, hinaus.*' She giggled.

'*Um zu sehen, ob es ein lebende Seele in dem ganz verdammten Stadt gibt.*'

She patted her hair. '*Kann sein, dass Sie lebenden Körper suchen, als zu Hause für diese Seele, oder ned?*'

Jude showed his teeth. '*Kann sein. Kann sein.*'

'*Und warum nicht, so eine lustige Jugend?*' She did some token swabbing.

'*Genau.*'

'*Kann sein, daß ich weiß, wo Sie ein oder zwei lebende Körper finden können.*'

'Crumbs. *In der Friedhof?*'

'*Nein, nein. Hmmf. Hähä. Es...es gibt ein Club, den ich kenne. Wo...wenn Sie nach Wurst fragen—*'

'*Müssen Sie die Kellnerin ein Slap auf dem Arsch geben. Ja, ich weiß.*'

'Oh, *wie dreckig!*' She made as if to mop him. '*Nein, ich meine, daß sie dann fragt, "Warum wollen Sie Wurst, mein Herr?" Und dann müssen Sie gleich ein Plastikobst herausnehmen—aber Vorsicht, eh, es muss Plastik sein—und sofort antworten, "Weil ich dieses Obst nicht essen kann!"*'

Jude looked aside.

'*Alle werden dann lachen,*' she continued, '*und wenn sie fertig sind, wird die Kellnerin Sie zum Tisch einer Frau scheuchen, die dasselbe Obst hat, und wo Sie zusammen essen müssen!*'

'*Wirklich?*'

'Hähä. Und flirten müssen.'

'Wie gefährlich sind die Österreicher!'

'Es gibt viele schöne Frauen da.'

'Ja?'

'Wie Lady Diana. Wunderschön.'

'Crumbs. Es ist *der Friedhof.'*

'Oh, das werd' ich mir nicht anhören. Das will ich nicht...Ich weiß, dass Sie ein besserer Mensch sind, dass Sie mich schockieren wollen! Oh, die unglückliche Prinzessin!' She menaced him with the mop; he parried and calmed her.

'Natürlich, natürlich. Ein Witz nur. Nein, sicherlich werde ich sofort gehen, um ein Plastikobst zu suchen.'

'Oh ja, das wäre besser.' She dried her eyes. *'Auf jeden Fall, um die Mädels zu treffen.'* She grumbled a laugh.

'Ich freue mich darauf.'

'Ach, was für Schande, dass ich nicht so jung wie früher bin, sonst wäre ich genau dort, mit Körbchen voll Obst jeder Sorte!'

'Ha-ha. *Nicht ein schlechte Idee.'* Jude nodded as if to leave.

'Oder kann sein, daß ich sogar jetzt ein bisserl Obst zu bieten hab'.' She lifted her hem to her thigh. A gold tooth showed one side.

'Kann sein,' said Jude slyly. He pushed from the door, swung down *Auerspergstrasse* to the *Folksteater* and *historisches Museums*, *Natur* and

Kunst. You could say that again. He swept over the empty road, fell like a wolf upon the *Heldenplatz* before stopping at the *Neue Berg* doors. They were closed. There was no one around. In fact he hadn't seen anyone on the streets. Cretins. Where were they all? It was cold, no sort of weather to wait on. He took *Reitschulgasse*, *Stallburggasse*, all the *gasses*. Had no one noticed the correlation? The *Braünerhof* was shut. Then it was *Braünerstraße*, *Graben*, *Stock-im-Eisen*. The *Stefansplatz* was empty; lamps were still on. Night still reigned on the *Donau*, taking an age, longer than he thought. Through the *Stefansdom* door, a priest was lighting candles, moving like milk. Would he accept confession? Jude cursed his barbarian homeland, exiled from Rome. After that exile was no other. What was the point of going home? But then what was the point of staying? Jude was free in the world. They had nothing on him. He didn't need no stinking passport; could go to the Black Sea, Caspian Sea, all the seas. The Embassy itself knew this. The threat of the irrelative—borderless, godless—was their last great wickedness; what kept people like Harper grasping at conspiracy. What was exile in comparison to that? Jude spun on a cold cobble. The spire boned above like the beanstalk. Six bells banged the hour. He punched and blew at shadows, ran up ramping walls, watched furs in windows. He retraced steps, *Stock-*

im-Eisen and *Graben*. He passed the silent *Casanova*, *Hawelka* and stopped at the *Jüdisches Museum*. What was that? A *clink*, a *churn*, a curtain of curls. He passed the arch and pushed through the door, blessing the chosen people. Warmth and coffee hit him at once. Hard on its heels were the massed black curls, a smile like civilisation.

'*Grüß Gott*,' said the smile.

'*Grüß Gott*.' He stood there on the doormat, looking about. It was clean and comfortable. There were tables, chairs, stools, an empty glass counter. Greys and greens, information on the walls, some kind of buzz in the background. Behind the counter was a kitchen; behind that, a storeroom, cluttered with boxes, books, what looked like a sleeping-bag. It could have been any cafe in any museum, except the *Cafe Museum*, but just now it felt like a haven.

'*Was darf's sein?*'

'Orangensaft.' Jude dropped his hood, looking mighty pleased with life. The girl stared back at him, sipping coffee. She was tidy and odd-looking; nose like hook and hair like chains, just how Harper liked them. But Harper wasn't here. Jude was here. He met her gaze with a gaze of his own; sceptical, charming.

'Orangensaft,' she said, putting down the mug.

'*Und ein Bagel. Genau.*'

'Setzen Sie sich bitte.'

Jude scuffed his feet. *'Es müss Ferien sein,'* he

said. '*Es gibt niemand hier in der Nähe.*'

'*Es ist früh.*'

'*Wieviel Uhr ist es?*'

'*Sechs, ein bisschen danach.*'

'*Sechs.*'

She nodded. Jude fell back through time, reappraised the day. Something was wrong with his body-clock. Days were peeping and hiding, like puppets on a hand. Each took an arm, a bow, a curtsy—fled in the foggy dew. How long could he keep up the charade? Sooner or later someone would find him. It wasn't difficult to do, even Bjørn could do it. Someone would discover he was wasting their time, take him to task, charge exile with escapism. They would thrust back his passport, turn his words against him, talk of storms in teacups, blanks and duds, like the *VF—121 BEST BOMBER*. The market would call and the bells bang the hour. Then again, at least Bjørn was with him. If there was one thing you could rely on with Bjørn, it was that his sense of time was more elastic than yours, if only because the rest of him was so rigid. Of course, had it stretched to escapism, Jude would have cut it down. But Bjørn didn't even notice he was wasting your time. He was a genius, was Bjørn. Jude sat happily at his table, toasting Bjørn over a large glass of orange juice. The waitress brought the avocado and walnut bagel and he eased into a copy of *The Jewish*

Chronicle. It was bad news mostly. Trouble in Gaza, trouble in Russia. Trouble in the water and air. He went all the way to the other side of the page and found a pointy-chinned Ezra Pound. *Pound*, it said underneath his picture: *crayfish*. He flipped it up and here was Wilhelm Reich. *Reich*, read the caption: *vegetable life*. Reich had had a sad time of it. His mother had committed suicide by swallowing a bottle of cleaning products, a slow and painful death. His father followed soon after. He went fishing in a pond, only not fishing but standing. He stood there for hours, contracted pneumonia and tuberculosis and died a slow, painful death.

Using sexology as a segue, the article leapt nimbly to Ernest Bornemann, the eminent sexual scientist, who had worked at Reich's clinic in Berlin. He had gone into exile in 1933, making it to London by disguising membership of the Communist Party as membership of Hitler Youth—and then disguising both of them as involvement in a student exchange. Ha! It was more than plausible. Once in London, he scribbled crime fiction, dabbled in jazz, and skimble-skambled at the British Museum. The British weren't having it though. Using the war as a pretext, they shipped him to Canada, via Huyton, Liverpool. But Bornemann was undeterred. Back he came with a handful of screenplays, novels, operas, and the like—even ghost-wrote a few episodes of the BBC's *Lives of Harry Lime*, for Orson Welles of all people. The ghost of a ghost, of a ghost, so to speak. Of course, it couldn't last. In the end he produced a groundbreaking study on patriarchy, settled into Austrian sexological respectability, and, in 1990, received the Magnus Hirschfeld Medal for services in his field. Then he topped himself, at eighty. Too little, too late, in Jude's estimation. Evidently sexology and suicide were inseparable bedfellows, and of the most decrepit kind—bearing the most putrid of fruit.

Jude flicked a wrist, dispensed with Ernest Bornemann. What else was *los*? A lot of explosions, exploitations, exculpations, based on nation, race, genetics. Pharmaceutical excuses, chemical imbalances, biological criteria. How did the newspapers expect to be believable? Like madness, race was an excuse. People wanted to get in the newspapers. There they all were, killing, burning and stamping, desperate for attention. Small armies followed the camera-crews, chanting in their faces, burning effigies. Jude wiped his fingers delicately of avocado, polished the orange-juice. 'What's happening in the world?' asked the girl coming over.

Jude paused. 'The killing, the stamping, the sexual repression.'

'In reverse order?'

'Er. *No*. The stamping is key. The other two are merely means to that end.'

The girl coloured, taking the glass. Jude jabbed the paper. 'Wilhelm *Reich*. He was expelled by the German communist party, subsequently outlawed by the Nazis, for stating, *in The Mass Psychology of Fascism*, what everyone already knew—that fascism was concomitant with sexual repression. *Ironically*—ha!—he fled Germany dressed as a ski-tourist. A brilliant disguise! as fascist and sexually-repressive as you'll find.'

'You're not a skier then.'

It was Jude's turn to colour. 'Of course, he ended up in Norway.' He looked up. 'No. Table-tennis, table-football, anything involving tables.'

'Try the *Casanova*.' She pointed down the street.

'Already been.'

'What are you doing in Vienna?'

'Um, losing track of time.'

'Good place for that.'

'*Yes*. Could I have a coffee?'

She set down the glass. 'What time did you think it was?'

'I just assumed it was day.'

'You assumed too much.' She went to pour the coffee.

Jude looked sly. This was the kind of remark he himself would make.

'As always,' he said.

'Well, history repeats itself.'

'Yes. As does an *old adage*. The difference being that *History* is rather embarrassed by repetition, whereas an *Old Adage* positively wallows in it.'

She smiled again, tightly. 'Didn't you wonder why everything was shut?'

'You were open.'

'Actually not.'

'Oh?'

'We open at ten.'

'In four hours?'

She shrugged. 'I have a key.'

'Yes, I suppose that is a reason.'

'I like it here in the morning.'

Jude leaned on the chair-back, looked through big windows behind. 'Me too.' He turned back slowly, sidling with eyes, but it was hard to focus in the gloom.

She said: 'in that case come back, at ten next time.' She brought the mug of coffee.

'I prefer it at six.'

'I won't be here.'

'You are now.'

'I've got stuff to do.' She swept up the plate with the glass. Big teeth bounced back the windows, then the curtain fell.

Jude turned back to the paper, and if it wasn't Joseph Conrad, looking stern under Wilhelm Reich. *Conrad*, read the caption: *tiger*. '*Anticipated*,' said

Jude. Conrad was exiled too, at four. What was it about exile? It seemed a ludicrously elaborate solution. You had belongings to pack, papers to stamp, trains to catch, passports to confiscate. A constant watch had to be maintained to make sure you didn't get the hump and sneak back in. Autocrats who trusted to exile were gluttons for punishment. Napoleon, Lenin. All an exile had to do was wait for the moment, take a fast-train home. Conrad's family were sent to the Styx for conspiring against Russian annexers. He was orphaned at eleven, shot himself at twenty—and missed. No doubt this was ridiculous. It was enough to make a man taciturn, create modernist classics of anticlimax and displacement.

Speaking of anticlimax, Jude checked the sports pages. Nothing doing. Hardly any pretence of it. What about the obituaries? It was the same story there. Where could he turn for climax? With great relish Jude settled into the weather, poring over the information, guessing at temperatures (minimum, maximum and average) in the Major Cities of the World. Charts and diagrams he studied. Conclusions he drew. High pressure ridges in the North Atlantic. A bar of gold at his back. Jude drained the coffee, realised the sun was up. The girl was sitting across the room, pencil-sketching, and the subject seemed to be himself.

'I hope you don't mind,' she said.

'Not at all.' On reflection it seemed a reasonable subject.

'Carry on reading.'

'I'm pretty much done.'

'I'll make you another bagel. On the house.'

Jude thought about it. Here was a new thing. Oddly beautiful girls making him bagels, wanting to draw him all hours of the morning, and all on the house. Did he like it? He wasn't sure he didn't. On the other hand *on the house* was an obligation. And being observed had a way of putting a man off his paper, let alone his bagel. Wasn't this a compromise too far? There would be awkward bits of food falling, grabbings with the mouth. The whole thing could make a fool of him.

Jude arched an eyebrow, considered the cold, the library, the prospects of eating again that day. A man didn't just spurn a bagel in the sunlight. Hadn't he already had a stolen breakfast, courtesy of Kara Kundera? And wasn't he about to get a second one in? He turned about; a rummage discovered *The Herald Tribune.* This was the clincher. Back he eased for another round of news. He could read about the major event in London, England, which offence-kicker shot the strike, and which wide-middle receiver made the vital assist. He could also catch the soccer news. Over came an orange juice and a carrot and apple bagel, declaring inner victory; and so he whiled away the morning.

Strange things are happening, sir.

LIKE NEVER BEFORE.

It was this morning. Plunging the last blocked toilet, and fixing the last flush, I clocked off for the day, and went to get some lunch. There was a breeze off the river but it wasn't raining for once. Autumn sun swung through cloud, just like a hanging basket, sir, all trail and geranium. I watched a sycamore's yellow leaves fall. The city is a puzzle, crumbled and unassemblable. The component parts—people, buildings, streets—remain but the frame is gone. The infrastructure is just structure. A place for the wind to blow in. For everything they put up—and they are continually putting things up—another falls down. The sycamore was falling down, it looked like an applause. Leaves were bronze globes, balanced on fence and drain—artificial fish, awaiting impalement on the Great Gilded Lure. Blackbirds and robins hopped on the stones. Such activity, yet such constancy. Yet not so much of that either. By the time I got to Llewellyn Square, the day had changed, cold now and darkening. A drear draining of the light. It started to rain. On a whim, I headed for The Pomp and Prestige.

Closer it hove, till it tottered above, like the House of Usher in a concrete tarn. The Pomp and Prestige stands in a wasteland, swinging its auspicious name over a painted gallant ship. It looks as if a bomb had hit it, which is probably exactly what happened. On one side, the toilet's scabrous walls open to the world; you piss on one of three. Yellowed, peeling, water-on-the-lungs; it is the shabbiest place, too scanty to destroy.

A red-faced man came out as I went in. I moved to the centre like a—not THE, mark you—lizard, half-illumined. There was only one person at the bar, and two bar-maids, bottle-blonde. Nevertheless, I found it difficult to get myself served. The short one occupied herself with rinsing, wiping a surface, looking at various things from nails to stains. A blank thing, in the divorced forties. After a minute or so, she brought me within the span of her attention. 'Yeh?' she said. It was a question which sounded like an answer. I hesitated. She went to the other side of the bar to move a glass. I looked at the other man, expecting to see the smile of mockery, but he was miles away in the midst of a sentence. Round the corner, another man was folded in redfaced gloom, miles away too—with the television news. They were talking about a water shortage, and the man was into it. He looked like he'd never touched the stuff in his life, but obviously it was important to go down the pub, catch up on all the water. 'What'll it be, love?' says the barmaid, finally sidling over. Love in the sense of hatred, obviously, violent and icy. 'Water,' says I. 'Cool, clear water.' She poured a small glass, from a jug of pure Scorn. 'A pound,' says she. A round English pound. Is it me (or her) or is water becoming expensive? What could I do? I reached over the counter, spilt six of water and half a dozen of money, and, turning a ridiculous crimson, set about sponging it up, while the barmaid poured another measure of Scorn. It turned out everyone here was just embarrassed. The man next to me opened his mouth in what might have been a toothy smile and nodded his head, appearing to say '—y y you...er...'. He had half-closed eyes, but his smile was shuddering like a star. He looked as if he was about to say, 'Prodigious!' but the barmaid got in first. 'Two pounds, love,' she says. 'Two?' says I. 'Two,' says she. 'Prices are rising.' The man next to me wound up his conversation with the other barmaid, a callous crone, all tall and scrawn, unmistakably single. 'S s see you...' said the man to just about everyone. He was a caveman, large, stooping, hair steel-grey and greasy, looking from the side of eyes, carrying a pint like a club he hadn't found a use for. Over he sloped to an adjoining room, where two men conversed in the corner. He limped as he went, as if one leg were shorter than the other. The tall blonde watched me. She was a goose of a woman: pinched little eyes and a silly long neck; a different pinch, however, from the genial half-closure of the man. It was a drawn look. The years—in particular the hours—had contrived to pull down her mouth, wearing a valley in that neck. I paid up, took my glass of Scorn, and drew to a nook in the adjoining room, where I was forced to eavesdrop on the men's conversation, the conversation being at all times shrill, booming or resonant, according to the speaker. The topic was that favourite theme of mankind's conversation, the French Revolution.

'—W w was asked if if if he thought the French Revolution was a success...and and replied that we couldn't couldn't say yet, huh huh huh...' said the caveman, whose voice was the resonant part of the trio. He moved a palm over his cheek. It wasn't sure if it was rubbing or just hovering there, for want of anywhere to go. 'Diff...diff different conception of t t time, time,'

he laughed, looking at his companions from hooded eyes. A slight man in his sixties watched him beadily, either side of a large beak. 'Oh, well that's the Chinese,' he opined, looking away with disgust. 'I don't like the Chinese. Not at all like the Japanese' he scoffed, 'whom in some ways I admire. Nasty flipping communists. Not of bead of religious feeling to be squeezed from the lot of them.' He scoffed again—an amused sort of exhalation. The man believed in opinion, but his eyes were smiling. The third man gobbled at his food, bent over his plate as if life were a matter of survival. He was built like the second man and was about the same age, but his face was the very chapter and verse of time. Character and wrinkles bespread it like volcanic rock, from fairbrown curls, down deep brow to slippery nose. I was struck for a second, as if a rupture had occurred in the space-time continuum. 'UUMMMMMMMM,' he bellowed, with a pipesmoker's hum. 'AH THINK AH AGREEEEEEEE.' His voice ran the dramatic gamut from gurgle and thrum to the trill and sly. A 'YES, UUUMMMMMM,' restored it to its foundations, whereupon the hawkish one took up the strain. 'At all costs we mustn't allow them leverage,' says he. 'Buying up our debt, and so on. Absolute bloody disaster. I'm sorry but I get quite emotional about it. Give them a sniff and it'll be Marx here and Trotsky there and flipping Mao all over. Picks and sickles and God knows what for icons. It'll be Spain all over again.' 'A a a apparently there there's a kind of pro proletarian summit down at the Strongarm Rooms tomorrow evening. A r rallying, rallying call.' The big man rustled cigar-paper. 'Of course there is,' replied the Beak, 'dredging up that morally bankrupt system, the Left, from the bottom of the estuary to try if she still hammers. Hideous! Hideous! But inevitable!'.

At that moment, in shuffles the Auld Cause himself, head-to-toe in holes, with his blasted scabs and killer hair, slumping beside me as if shot in the gut. 'Hm,' says I easing round, 'what brings you here?' 'Och,' says he. 'What brings YE here, Bomber? What brings YE here?' He sat there champing at the lips, looking from floor to ceiling. The clarity had gone right out of the day 'Aren't you drinkin'?' he asked, eventually. 'I am,' says I. 'If that's a drink, ah'm Joseph fuckin' Livesey!' says he, choking on his joke. 'Fuckin' cheese-eatin' Baptist Lancastrian scum!' he spluttered, banging the table. 'Nothin' I hate more than a philanthropist!' He leers in, squeezing the folds of my neck. 'Let me tell ya how ta drink Baptist-

style, ma boy,' says he. 'Look ya lisp, and weer strange suits; be oot of love with your Nativity, and chide God for makin' you that countenance you are. Else I shall sceerce believe ya e'er spurned communion wine. Heh. Hmm. Hchmm.' He made to cough, but nothing came out. 'I'll say it again,' he resumes, 'since ye're not drinkin' what the fuck are ye here for? A man o' talent as ye are, slummin' it with the likes o' me, in the likes of the fuckin' Prestige? Prestige!' he scoffs. 'Ah've seen more prestigious brothels. On fuckin' Stamp Street, if ye want to know. Come on, son, if you ain't got a story ta tell, ah'm Oliver fuckin' Cromwell, that shrivelled up sourface cunt of a butcher's bitch. An' while ye're tellin' it, we'll raise a toast o' wine to the King o'er the Water.' He knocked on the bar behind him. 'Oot with it! Ah doont have all dee!'

'My story?' says I. 'Too right yer fuckin' story! I doont want a goodnight kiss!' 'I'm in exile,' says I, 'banned, under a restraining order, from going within ten miles of the Glum Valley. So they sent me here, to clean toilets, in the name of Community Service.' 'For what, exactly?' says he, nodding, as if he understood all about it. 'Sabotage,' says I. 'Arson. Trespass. You name it.' 'Sabotage,' he nods. 'What did ye

sabotage, lad?' 'Nothing,' says I. 'Arson's a serious crime,' says he. 'I suppose so,' says I. 'Play with fire, do ye?' 'No.' He nods again. 'I suppose ye didna trespass either?' 'I loped over a few fields,' says I, 'and hung around a reservoir, putting on a play.' 'Did ye, indeed! That's trespass enough, heh heh. Which play?' 'Hamlet.' 'Heh, heh, Hamlet, he says. 'Ah played Horatio once. Fuck Hamlet, son. Hamlet prances aboot, gazin' at his naval. It's Horatio ye've ta depend on. Did ye have a Horatio?' I did,' says I. 'I did. He's in exile too. In Vienna. Seducing washerwomen and watching The Third Man.' He nodded again, as if this were to be expected. 'Horatio,' he said. 'Washerwomen,' he agreed. 'The Third Man. Aye. Ah could tell ye a story aboot The Third Man.' 'Really?' says I. 'Mebbe,' says he. 'Though ye'd ne'er credit it.' 'Try me,' I says. 'Hamlet!' he coughs. 'That's a good one. Heh heh. Och, yer the man fer me, as Sidney fuckin' Greenstreet would say. Now that's a fuckin' story! But I'd expect as much, from a fellow Thesp.' Suddenly, 'NAY, AN THOU'LT MOUTH, I'LL RANT AS WELL AS THOU!' he roars, half-rising, brandishing his fists. The other men pay him no attention at all, wisecracking, gossiping, prophesying, but the bar-maid brings him a bottle of Montepulciano and unscrews the cork. 'Alright Artie,' she says. 'Artie?' says I, 'it's all coming out now.' 'Thanks Jill, alright Bomber,' he replies, recovering. 'Ye can call me Artie.' 'But what's your name?' says I. 'Arthur,' he says. 'Arthur what?' 'Arthur fuckin' McBride!' he growls. 'So you're an actor,' says I. 'Actually I could have guessed. I saw you doing your thing, on the bench, outside the College there.' Artie recovers breath, gets closer so I can smell it, and thrusts a glass in my face. 'I'm a bum,' he confides. 'A wino, freebooter, moonshiner, tramp, blacklegger, alley-cat, CUR.' He jabs the glass a final time, slumps back in his chair, growling, 'I'm hoping to make it big!' I examine my own glass. He has already filled it. A butane heater is burning in the corner and I spy it through the wine. 'Yeah,' he ruminates. 'Ah've trod the boards. Done many things fer a livin'.' He nestles into his seat. 'Some more legal than others.' 'Such as?' I ask. He wags a finger. 'Ye know, ye're like me, in some ways. We're outlaws, ye an' I. Cannee help it. Awnly have to get oot o' bed an' we're on the wrong side o' the law. Motive's got naught ta do with it. It's nature. Jus' mother fuckin' nature. We were born like that, me an' you.' 'What did you do?' says I. 'Ye want to hear ma story?!' he chuckles. This agrees greatly with him. 'Okay,'

I says. 'The concise version.' 'Och, what I could tell, son!' says he, suddenly secretive. 'Go on then,' says I. 'What I could tell,' he repeats, as if he won't. He begins to whistle, orders up toasted sandwiches and another bottle of red, scoffing 'drinkin' fuckin' water' in his beard. I listen to the men opposite. 'Flippin' twentieth-century,' says the Beak. 'Good for flippin' nothing, except comedy.' He folds both eyes and argument. 'Except comedy,' he repeats, looking more than solemn. You would think he were praying. Over comes the bottle. An old woman, hitherto unnoticed, shuffles in slippers to a kitchen behind the heater, to prepare sandwiches. I watch her go. 'Yes, Stanley Laurel!' continues the Beak. 'Flippin' genius!' and he holds his thumb in the air like a beacon. 'All his soul within the thumb!' he chatters. These were mental-leaps I couldn't follow. The man had it all down, a position on almost everything. On the other hand, he also knew when he didn't, when it was time to fold cards and eyes. This was the condition he chattered on, the silence that bought his conversation.

No such condition existed for Artie. Silence ate him. He refilled my glass, whistled, drummed his fingers, itched for the prompt. Eventually, 'Ah've been many things in ma time, mon,' he continues. 'There's a story'd take all night an' up the followin' morning.' 'Get on with it, then,' says I, and this time he didn't pass up the chance. 'Och, if you're insistin',' he said, slapping the table. He touched the glass, smoothed his hair, pointed a finger at the kitchen as if checking on the sandwiches. Then he hushed and pushed off.

'Before ye get my history, you feerst have to know ma father's.' He touched the glass again. 'What's our story, without that of our fathers', ye ken?' He looked rosily at some humorous hunting cartoons. 'Dad was a Scot, like meself, and his father before him. Ma grandmother—Dad's ma—was Russian. They met in Glasgee, before the Great War, which grandfather died in. Grandma snuffed it, too, when Dad was ten, and he was sent to a cousin in London. Man called Toldov. Mebbe ye've heerd o' him.' 'No,' says I, not realising it was a BRILLIANT JOKE. Artie snuffed a few times through his nose, looked at me as if I was an idiot, and continued. 'Toldov kept him in London till he was fifteen. Talkin' late twenties. Lived in a Greenwich attic, read Shakespeare in the evenings. Och, he studied poor—he wanted to tread the boards, see, jus' like me. He was workin' backstage in theatres, fifteen years old. Toldov, ye ken, was

exiled from the Soviet Union. Och, the stories Dad TOLD OF *him! Heh. Heh heh. Fuck. Anywee, he wrote pamphlets against the fuckin' Commies. Travelled all of Russia—disguised!—as a children's fuckin' clown! passing leaflets on the sly. His base was a two-room flat in Leningrad, overlookin' a cemetery. Had his awn printing press an' all. Used to type away at night, watching the sun set on the Neva—Neva, Neva, Neva, Neva, as ye might say, heh—watchin' traffic crawlin' in snow,'—he flurried an arm—'flights of birds o'er graves, hammerin' out his pamphlets—naught but shackles to him. Once, on a night train to Moscow—a lonely route, with the firs flying by, a solitary bloody cottage every twenty, thirty miles—two Kommandants searched him in the carriage. Scared the daylights from 'im. Only thing they didn't search was the Shakespeare lying on the seat. Big fuckin' tome. That's where Toldov kept his pamphlets. Anywee, that put the jessies in 'im. Heah. He didna stop at Moscow. Took a boat to England and there 'ee stayed, opened his bookshop, sold poems an' propaganda an' suchlike. Hated the Commies, did Toldov. His brother was killed during the Terror. Heh, I'll give 'em fuckin' Terror! But he found a way to fight 'em. England was his promised fuckin' land. All that free market balls, an' cradle of crap, ye ken. No one told 'im it was a fuckin' wasps' nest. One day ma Dad found him surrounded by a pile of books, proppin' up a bookcase—bullet in his head. KGB, wasn't it, or GPU, or NKVD, or whatever it was then. I'll gi' em fuckin' VD! Anyway, the Brits turned blind eyes. The cradle of democracy fucked Toldov in the arse, put up a free fuckin' super-market, just where his shop was. See, they doont have the balls to kill ye ootright. Leave that ta the fuckin' terrorist. Na, they jus' set the scene, sit back, wait to take advantage. All that liberal piss, an' corporate fuckin' shit. Got ta be bigger, newer, shinier, ye ken? Endless fuckin' ejaculations. Where's the fuckin' foreplay? Where's the fuckin' foreplay? They took yer history, son, yours an' mine, put it in a mass grave, plastered over the top with polystyrene and fuckin' foam rubber. Gone to the dogs! We'll be lucky. Dogs won't dig so deep! It's a fuckin' sewer oot there, an' we're wadin' through it. You an' me, son. You an' me.' He burps, patting my arm as an afterthought. 'But I believe in ye, kid,' he continues, quietly. 'You're the man fer me, son. I can see that in your ee.' 'Yes, I'm hopeful!' cried the barnstormer suddenly, from across the room. 'I believe in progress! Things generally get better as we go along!' The caveman chuckled. The craggy-face one was eating faster than before. Artie drank again. 'All that was later though. Dad turned eighteen, got a break and was doin' nicely thank you. Fer a wee while there, whatever he touched turned ta fuckin' gold. Life was a whirl, ye might say, of stars an' footlights, entrance an' exits, curtains op'nin' and closin'. Same with the women—fuckin' openin' and closin'! Yeah! Like father, like fuckin' son!' He did a couple of pelvic thrusts on the bench. 'Fuckin' Banquo, Hotspur, you name it. He was toastin' his Horatio with a wee drink—a spot champagne, ye ken, regalin' the air, when he heerd the War was on. 'Course, he signed up, at last, as 'ee was 'bliged, and that was the end o' his dramatic career, fer a while. Not fer aye, though. He did 'is bit, o' course, fer the war effort. Did a wee spot espionage as well, sendin' reports an' whatnot, 'count o' his Russian. Anywee, the war tails off, as wars tend te do, and where does he end up? Where?' 'I don't know,' says I. 'Rhodesia?' 'Vienna! ye cretin! Vienna! Just like YER AWN Horatio! Heh! Fuck! Heh?' He tried to drum up some surprise. I tarried with my wine glass. 'Och,' he said, as if unimpressed himself, 'So there he was, in Vienna, on the communication wing, talkin' to the Russ quarter, doin' a spot trafficking on the side. Black market, an' whatnot. Used to help run tobacco. Wasnae much more than a wee bribe an' turn a blind eye. Anywee, that tailed off too, Dad left the forces, an' decided to stick aboot. He liked Vienna, did ma Dad. Ta cut a story short, he was still there, scratchin' oot a livin' teachin' English and so on, winter 1948, an' a cold one too, and what turns up on his fuckin' doorstep, heh, so te speak, but The Third fuckin' Man!'* He grips my hand, paternally, on the table, as if we are in this together. *'The whole fuckin' crew!'* he whistles. *'Well, Dad being Dad, with his past an' all, he hovered round, hopin' to pick up work, as an extra, or whatnot. And he got some too. Ye can actually see him, in the crowd scene, when that fuckin' brat is singlin' out whatsisface—Martins. Always fuckin' hated that brat, no fuckin' beating was too good fer him. He was actually instrumental in gettin' Orson fuckin' Welles to work. Not the brat, my Dad. See, Welles was cooped up in his hotel room, beheevin', actually like that spoiled fuckin' brat, to be exact. Didna want to work, did he, 'count on some contractual fuckin' shenanigans. Big fuckin' prima donna. But the thing is, that Welles loved his magic. Magic tricks, ye ken. An' ma Dad had picked up a few tricks from Toldov as a kid. So fuck me if they doont get Dad to do his tricks outside the hotel room, and fuckin' coax Welles to come out the door! Ah-hah-haaaah, that was Dad. A real fuckin' card, whichever way ye turned him. Anyway, that's where Dad met Ma. She was from Wroclaw, Poland, wanderin' around, lookin' fer work, just like him. Te be honest, ah wouldn't be surprised if Carol—Carol Reed, that's what they called him, jes' plain Carol—he was another with a "silly name" wasn' he? Nothin' fuckin' sensible aboot that! Heeeeh!' He roared, spluttered, choked. I had to slap him on the back. It is an unfortunate fact that a story needs a narrator. And needs him alive. 'She was a bit like Alida, was Ma. Alida Valli, ye ken? That's what they called her, "Alida". Anywee, Ma hung around the cameras—into photography she was—doin' different things, behind the scenes, ye ken—organisational, errands an' whatnot—and she fell in love with this jobbing chancer, sa to call him. Ah think it was the magic tricks. When filming was over, they stayed in Vienna. But Ma got pregnant—with yours fuckin' truly—and Dad got broke, an' they decided to head fer home. Dad got with a contact o' his, some fuckin' folk-music enthusiast from the traffickin' days, an' he said he'd give him passage hawm, an' a sizeable pay off too, if he'd take a package with him. Dad didna ask questions. They went doon through Italy, to Naples. One night they left the moony bay o' Naples, went out through the Mediterranean, rounded Spain to Vigo. From there, a contact took 'em to Britain. A chug-a-chug boat took 'em up the estuary to Truro, and they docked. Someone was s'posed to pick 'em up, but no one materialised. They stood there in the freezing fog, took an inn fer the night, Ma three months pregnant, an' the next dee they started fer here. Dad was supposed to meet someone here, te exchange the package, ye ken. Well, he got here an' looked aboot, asked some pertinent questions an' the like, but ne'er a contact could he find. So he buried the package an' headed te Glasgee, te look up his kin.' He wiped his mouth. 'No,' cried the man across the room. 'I'm Catholic, Northern and British—in that order! But I'm definitely British. I adore Italy, but I live in Britain kind of thing. Like Manfred, a mix of Southern and Northern mythologies!' 'Yes...yes...' said the caveman, nodding, blowing copious smoke. The craggy one puffed his pipe. You'd almost have thought they were eavesdropping.*

'And there they stayed fifteen fuckin' years. Course, he missed the stage, but that was over fer him. 'Ee actually became a school teacher,

if ye can credit that. English fuckin' literature. Ah was born and raised there. But me ma died, and Dad's dead too, last year, in a fuckin' nursing home. It's like Soren fuckin' Kierkegaard, ain't it? "In the end Lazarus died like everyone". He folded his arms, beard splayed on his collar, wincing into space—towards the conversationalists, as if inquiring if they were ghosts or men. 'Amazing,' said I. 'What was in the package?' 'That's jes it, son,' said he, as if through water. 'Dad never looked. Didna want to knaw.' He bares his teeth, as if guarding the past. 'He told you all this?' says I. 'Heh,' says he. 'Sometimes life's too simple, ain't it? There we go, an' here we are, emergin' through smoke, fallin' through trapdoors, an' all we want's resistance. Ain't it, son? Resistance.' He drank off his glass, red faced, staring through red eyes, purple folds beneath them, like plums in apples. He wanted me to get it. He wanted me to see the significance. 'All we want's to know we're fuckin' here,' he continued. 'Flesh an' fuckin' blood, not ghosts of fuckin' Christmases past, shiv'rin' in the fire.' He is about to refill when, 'Yeu!' he shouts suddenly, jabbing at me. 'Get yerself a fuckin' career, or cleanin' crap'll be the best of it!' Now he leans right in; I smell breath, body, wine, all mingled. 'Where's ye fuckin' dignity?

They've put you in a fuckin' home! Fuckin' asylum! In yer own country! Ye know what they say, 'boot a prophet an' his country. Take it from an old ham, son, an' an older soak. Smoke an' trapdoors won't do it fer ya. Aye, resistance. Ta punch the wall an' not put yer fuckin' fist through it.' He lapsed again. 'What about your story?' I said. Finally he answered, flat, apathetic, staring away. 'Me, ah trod the boards too, did ma stints, in Glasgee, Birmingham, Dublin, you name it. Spent a long while here, made a wee name for meself at the All and Sundry, on Joy Street there.' He closed his eyes, flipped a disparaging palm. 'Bloody great Richard, I made. But, ah don't know—one thing and another, the roles stopped comin' and I took ta tipple. Now ya find me in a fuckin' bush, drenched in piss an' wine, mouthin' Caliban. Sad, innit? Fuckin' tragicomic.'

He stopped. One hand still gripped my wrist, the other was placid on his lap. His head was slumped on his chest, as if asleep. I took a breath and a piss. The wine was almost gone, the toasties—grease and crumbs. After a while he woke up a bit, drank the last of the wine, renewed the grip on my wrist. 'Bomber!' he rasps. 'Ah could get you an audition! Ah knew Reedy, meself!' He looks at me significantly.

'From ma Kings Cross days.' 'Pity he's dead then,' says I. 'Pity!' he says, incredulous. 'Ah knew fuckin' Hitchcock an' all. Stick close to me, lad, an' I'll bend ye an ear at the All and Sundry, see if I fuckin' doont.' 'Alright, alright,' say I. 'Doont "alright" me,' he breathes. 'Doont ye fuckin' "alriiiight" me,' and he almost pokes me in the eye. 'Ah'm a secret fuckin' agent, son! Ah could have ya killed like that,' and he clicks the fingers he almost poked me with. 'Want te join the resistance? Think ye've the balls fer revolution?' I am about to go when he grabs my bicep, beard tickling my neck, and, enunciating like his life depends on it, actually tonguing my ear, whispers as only those whisper who cannot whisper at all: 'SAILOR'S CHURCH! NINE O CLOCK, TONIGHT.' He looked hard a moment, then a change swept him. 'Elysium Street,' he harrumphed as he got to his feet. 'Big fuckin' wasteland. As Elysian as you'll see.' He laughed and spluttered again, and was tripping forward on his feet, waving at the wall, leaving me to pay.

The plot, as B. K. Lie would say, thickens. And for once Sarah Kent has nothing to do with it.

I assume

Harper.

Jude huffed wearily. It wasn't so much a problem of taking it all seriously as caring a jot. Harper would lose the world, and Cleopatra too, for a long, drawn-out, thoroughly fragmented narrative. Much more of this and he'd think he had a story on his hands. Jude wouldn't be picking up the pieces. Clicking the *reply* sign, *Did I*, he wrote

hear someone

TELL A LIE?

Lust for public validation, like belief in a deity, is the legitimate means to an invalid end. Why invalid? Because it cannot be validated. No, come on, who does guard the guards? As for that secret agent of yours, let him do his secrecy—and agency—in private. Just because he's a secret agent, doesn't mean he's not a molester. Just because he's a molester, doesn't mean he's not a bore. What is it but a chain of signification, endless and pointless? Where's the validity, tell me, in a practitioner of that discredited format, barrel-bottom and last clutched straw, the LAYER, and its subtle accomplice, the LEVEL (he of the 'it works on many levels,' etc), the Russian dolls and Chinese boxes of our fetishist Victorian playrooms? I mean, what could be more pre-Raphaelite? A dirty old man dressed as a radical cabalist dressed as a ham actor, with a store of Shakespeare against any occasion. Skal por skal, as Bjorn would say (and frequently does, God rot him). No, no, it's bluff and bluff again, and I can tell that from here. That's the thing about your spy. It never occurs to him—not that you don't mind being spied on (because you're a law-abiding citizen, etc, happy so long as you're safe)—but that you might not actually CARE. Spy on, spy on, Voltaire, Rousseau. The joke is always—ALWAYS—on the spy.

Speaking of Russian dolls, and Layers, there is one over there, and I would. But speaking, more specifically, of Russian dolls dressed, with great patience and craftsmanship, as Russian spies, in a last longwinded bid to surprise and completely-implausibly delight you with their multiple wooden layers (and God knows I would NOT), I seem to have acquired one of my own, in the prurient, somewhat amorphous form of the Putzfrau, whom I encountered only this morning, before dawn as it turned out, a-lurking and a-loitering outside the computer room, with the half-baked muddle-headed intent of finding out what I had been doing on, with, and in front of, the computers (all eight of them), and suggesting, as an alternative, a very exclusive club she, like everyone else it seems, just happens to know, where the sweaty, seamy, deeply insalubrious business of flirtation is reduced to the rote-learning of official innuendos, and the ritual exchange of artificial fruit. An artificial fruit, sir, which one can only imagine they view as some kind of versatile symbolic amenity, easily cashed into the common coin (euro) of sexual vantage, and, AT THE SAME TIME, sir, and ON ANOTHER LEVEL, which they know only too well is a sadly necessary compensation for their utterly sexless existences. And all because they cannot deal with the repulsive, unguent obstinacy of the symbol, signifying nothing beyond itself. Unable to physically force it into their gagging brains that a peach and a fig are ACTUALLY a peach and a fig, in all their oozy glory. No, sir, much as it pains me to say it, your tramp was right. Where's the fucking foreplay?

Speaking of which, I've been spending time in the Prunksaal again, and its multiple checkpoints and security zones, permitted to enter only on the condition that the guards (no, come on, REALLY—I want ANSWERS) are impressed by the display of my voluptuous CARD, satisfied I have left my bag in a padlocked chest, and, like Bjorn, positively aroused by the fact that I have walked into the room with (nothing more than) a pencil in my hand. Yes yes, I know, built in the 18th C. and all that, but that makes it younger than my house. Last time I entered my house I carried an enormous scythe.

Which is what I'll take to the nightlight soon, because someone has removed my shoe-box. Which, also, is what I'll take to the British Council (the scythe, of course, but also—insidiously—the shoe-box, ready to place over all kinds of lights) if they don't get their act together and tell me what I'm supposed to be doing. Because as yet, they've told me, and I've done, pretty much Jack. Which means that I'm pretty much done here for today. Bjorn is sitting next to me, catching up on the runic news, deleting various injunctions to join the Norwegian Army. And, oh, that girl, what's she doing, over there, grubbing about in the Philosophy section, fingering Kant? I'll critique her pure reason any time she likes. As for that man there, he keeps looking at me, wondering why I'm always looking around, as if he were not looking at me looking, etc. Everyone in here is either a geek or a freak. I seriously doubt whether the majority of them tied their own shoelaces themselves before the left the house this morning. Now they've all come undone, and that explains why none of them can walk properly, which in turn explains why they are all so fat, so four eyed, so old, so Opera-loving, and so stuck here on a beautiful winter's day.

I am

Off.

Before he had the chance another mail dropped in.

Hello Harper,

Gnats are useful for trout fishing. They hover above the water and they're a tasty morsel for a trout. A bit like Sarah Kent. A black gnat fly is a good one to use, throughout trout season, but especially in the mayfly period—what you might call the 'business end' of the season. The famous Griffeth Gnat is a good one, created by George Griffeth. You can use wet or dry gnats for fly-fishing. Wet and dry flies of the black gnat variety are an essential part any trouter's fly box. You have to work the silk down the shank of the hook, thread in the poly yarn and the black cock hackle and tie off behind the eye. And then there's fishing...

As for Jude, we all know what that lusty widow is up to in Austria.

Österreich indeed.

Benjamin.

Jude smiled but he meant it, he was off. It was good to know the Lie was still ridiculous, but he could be ridiculous on someone else's time. He poked Bjørn who was indeed busy deleting a summons from the Norwegian army to complete national service. Bjørn had been dodging national service for seven or eight years. An artless dodger, thought Jude, but a dodger nonetheless. Among all the strange jobs Bjørn had taken in his surprisingly precise stride—right up there with the mental-asylum-nightshift-attendant, school-children's chess instructor, robot-armed-malt-sack-remover, fax-machine-troubleshooter-telephonist, and porcelain-factory-tour-guide—was the job he had held in Stockholm, of all unlikely places, where, in a windowless room—a room *within* a room—of a persistent Swedish evening, he had spent weeks reading entire biology text books for eight hours at a sitting (two small breaks permitted) into some form of recording equipment, for the use of the visually-impaired, or those who preferred audio-stimuli for their educational aids. Incredibly—always assuming, of course, that it was not all some meticulous practical joke, played on Bjørn by the entire Swedish nation, with the taxpayer's gleeful consent—Bjørn had come through a not so much arduous as slow selection process to emerge as the company's preferred, albeit only, candidate. An inspired piece of casting! No man better suited. Choosing his own hours. Arriving sometime in the afternoon. Pulling out his keys. Letting himself in. Conducting himself through corridors. Selecting another key. Introducing himself into an empty room. Behind him, the waft of door-brush on frame. The door's satisfying click. A final key selected. *Inducting* himself, sweatily now, to a room within a room. The waft, the click, the faint hum. The setting up apparatus. The adjusting the chair. The gurgle from the water-dispenser. Then spreading out the book, murmuring internally, 'now where were we?'. Clearing his throat, activating the machine. Begin. And all the while having met a sum total of nobody. *Nobody.* In the entire building. Astonishing. Astonishing. Inevitably, this sent Jude into dark reflections about what kind of—and *how many—a.* lackadaisical, or *b.* blind, Swedish students were staying up many a long nocturne, burning the aurora borealis, listening to

Bjørn—Bjørn *himself*—saying (in Swedish): 'Ah, er, osMOSIS! is the process, ah, by which molecules move across a MEMBRANE!' or, 'Nn, ah, the HUMAN BODY is roughly SIXTY PER CENT WATER!' Or—subversively now, in the dead of night, when he thought no one was listening—'Mm, er, Norwegian SALMON have the highest capacity of oestrogen receptivity of ALL SCANDINAVIAN SALMON! Twenty per cent more than Danish salmon and an AMAZING FORTY THREE PER CENT higher than SWEDISH salmon!' Who knew, Jude considered; they may still be listening now.

He huffed, but the Russian girl slipped him a glance. Perhaps he could stay a little longer after all. No, that was her parting shot. She was leaving. She left. Jude blew more narrowly this time. The gaggle was still giggling, but something too much of this. He poked Bjørn in the ribs. 'Wh—y—oh ya,' said Bjørn, who had become suddenly absorbed by *Dag Bladet*. 'You know the disquieting—although hissily, bum-shufflingly quiet—thing about all *this*,' commenced Jude, indicating, with a toss of his nose, the entire library, its putrid occupants and their festering *research,* 'is that significant *motions*, on major national and international *issues*, constantly overflowing into sewers and cesspools of global and interplanetary *concern*—are apparently dependent upon scholarly lubricants like mine.' He was stalking away now, and Bjørn's body was following. 'Hence this air of stuffy industry. This army of prissy, pussyfooting swots. Apparently *influential*. Apparently, *on the case*. Deciding America's future from *Amsterdam* to *Paris*.' Bjørn lightly chuckled, still distracted. 'No, ask an academic question,' railed Jude, 'get a smarmy answer, smeared with theory, positively padded with footnotes—truly the *ski-wear* of your talking world. Goons, sir. Goons that *gibber*. In the most determinedly ambiguous manner.' He swung through the exit, exhibiting his pencil. They collected bags from lockers, descended steps to the entrance, where a small crowd dithered at the door. Jude took advantage of their hesitation by striding through first. 'It's a dog eat dog world,' he explained.

They hit the square. 'The whole thing works perfectly,' cried Jude, not giving it up. 'Because, of course, through its fussily-cultivated unintelligibility, the academy has become so awesomely indispensable, that it can be dispensed with altogether. Government is free to act exactly as it *lusts*, secretly—though rightly—satisfied that, not having ever actually *done* anything—*anything*—in their *entire lives*—except glut themselves on *brie* and *gruyere*, the academics cannot of course *know* anything. In the most carnal possible sense. Hence, of course, their sweaty insistence on the carnal.' Jude looked round, at the rotting, sputtering corpses nervously negotiating the door. He saw them, in his mind, having great trouble mounting the staircase. Which of these virgins had gathered their rosebuds? Which had ever fallen heavily, got up with their seaman's papers? Twas chatt'ring, grinning, mouthing, jabb'ring all. Jude scorned, turned, with a white hand consigned the library to rubble.

It was cold. The air was thin as yarn behind the eye. Light dangled like fish from its ends, slipped among the cobbles. It puzzled them to look down. The sun was setting and they had hardly seen it. Now they set to wandering. There were chestnuts, cakes and coffee to get. Jude was thinking of visiting Rosa and that was alright with Bjørn. He was all worked up about Dante, wanted to descend all those seven circles. They whirled through crowds, lights, arches, watching girls and windows alike. Again they stopped by the record shop. *GEBR. PLACHT*, it said over the door, *SEIT 1816*. There were the same posters, flyers, record sleeves. It still had the advert for the *Jules Arles* show.

It wasn't portcullised this time; Bjørn pawed at the door and it gave. Warm air blew from above and they stood in it, looking round. The place was filled with odd utensils: on the floor, empty crates and cardboard boxes; to the left, a large cabinet; on its lower shelf, a three-tiered display cone, like a wedding-cake stand. The tiers were filled with plastic fruit, priced by sticker. They were selling two for an Austrian Mark. It wasn't clear if the stand came separately. At the back was a further room. Stacks of records could be made out. Behind the counter were musical instruments on the walls. A worried man looked over spectacles. He looked as if he had been there since 1816.

'*Ja, Gruß Gott*,' said the man.

They shuffled feet. Bjørn looked like a weather vane.

'*Nein, nein, wir suchen, na ja, etwas. Nichts*,' said Bjørn. '*Wir wollen gucken, nur*.'

The man looked displeased.

'*Ah, aber, VIELLEICHT, wir wollen etwas kaufen auch*,' added Bjørn, digging himself a hole.

They browsed the front room, which effectively meant turning neat circles, gazing at ukeleles, occasionally spinning on a fivepence to handle a plastic banana. The man was fixed at the counter. There was only a certain amount of time this could go on. Edging between two boxes, leaning halfway over one, Bjørn peered exaggeratedly into the back-room. It was a smaller and darker place. With Norwegian eagle eyes, he could read the sleeves that Jude, with his contacts, could not. *The Complete Big Mama Thornton* said one. *Memphis Minnie: Me and my Chauffeur Blues* said another. Bjørn's gaze lit on a box-set, edged with what looked firelight. It was the *Smithsonian Folkways Collection.* To Bjørn this was birthday and Christmas at the same time. He gestured to Jude, leaning over the boxes at an angle that didn't look possible.

'*NnnN, können wir in diesem Zimmer gehen?*' he asked the man.

The man looked as if he was being pulled through time. Austerlitz, Vormarz, Franz Joseph, Bruckner, both World Wars, fire in the Hofburg and entry in the EU went by him in about five seconds.

He said: '*Nein.*'

Bjørn looked blank. He turned back to the room, tongue curling onto his chin. Somehow he must have misunderstood.

'*Uh, können wir*'—he faced the man again, swinging a finger at Jude and himself—'*können wir gehen*—er—*HINEIN.*' This was a risky move. '*In diesem Zimmer hier.*'

The man rearranged some papers on the counter. He was slight-built, old hairs around the dome. '*Nein nein,*' he said—with a tremolo. He was white as death.

Bjørn raised his eyebrows. Jude was beginning to fidget. On top of the cabinet some lampshades seemed to be for sale. Then again, it wasn't clear. One of them had a tag dangling and Jude was trying to reach it without pulling it on top of him. He kept waggling a forefinger, but the tag stayed out of reach. Bjørn turned a full circle between the boxes, pretending to interest himself in a tray of baby-clothes. He waited a full half-minute. The tension became unbearable.

'*NnnNKÖNNENWIR IN DIESEN ZIMMER HIER GEHEN?*' he burst out. '*Nah die Schallplatten und CDs zu sehen?*'

'*Oh, ja ja,*' said the man, pretending to take no notice. He started filling a plastic pencil holder with paper flowers. This was a strange development. Another man might easily have been undermined, but Bjørn was not one to haggle over delicacies. He held firm, tiptoed gracefully round the boxes and was gone inside. Jude followed, pushing at the boxes with his *all-stars*. It was a different sort of haven from the cafe at the *Jüdisches Museum* but a haven all the same. It wasn't much bigger than a small boat. A lamp swung overhead. On the floor, crates and cardboard-boxes stuffed with goods. Before them, and left: deep shelves of records and CDs. To the right, the roof sloped down, as if under a staircase, and an electric fire glowed from the gloom. Behind it, you could just make out more box-flaps, an unused lampstand. Jude could hardly imagine a better place to hide; hunker down if the *Gestapo* came. Or if no one came, come to that. Hunkering down was every man's right, every woman's too, if the *Jüdisches Museum* was anything to go by. What did the *Gestapo* have to do with it? Nobody needed their sanction. The old man came to the doorway, put one hand on the frame and watched them. Electric brands slept in his glasses. He was a convict awaiting sentence. There was no getting round it: he wanted to make sure they didn't steal his records. But it was more than that. He was absolutely vulnerable. By giving them permission to enter the backroom, by acceding to a thrice repeated question, which was nothing more than his obligation, he had given himself away. What could he do if they did steal his records, smash his shop, break his age in two? The police? That was hardly the point. The man gazed on a floor he could barely see; its brown lines relaxed and rose. In his mind he was gone, like a snowdrop in summer. Experience was no match for youth.

Jude sensed this. He cast glances over the stacks, touching Big Mama Thornton with an expert finger. 'Crumbs,' he said. '*Complete* is the word.' Bjørn was already juggling the *Smithsonian Folkways Collection* in his vice, smirking as if possession were nine-tenths of the law. The man saw them as if backwards through a telescope. Here, the brash one, with the superior air, whose hair the fire didn't tint but intensify, robbed of its heat. There, the tall one, in the dark, weighing balances. Their power, their assumptions, were immense. The man put hands on hips; for a moment his eyes closed over. If they only knew their strength. What deference stopped them from gathering his goods like chestnuts from the grill; such a slow brown harvest, such a painstaking account, cleaning out his world? They could even go out and come back for more. He would sit on the boxes and watch.

He did sit on a box, just beside the doorway, watching as, over the course of time, like the faces of a medal slowly turning, the two sank and expanded, so that at last, as if it had always been, it was Bjørn flipping stacks and Jude standing by the fire with the *Smithsonian Folkways Collection* in his hand. How did this exchange take place? Jude thought it was one of his greatest triumphs, but it was one of Bjørn's. There was no way he was going to be able to buy all the things he needed. But if he could persuade Jude that the *Smithsonian Folkways Collection* was SIMPLY an ESSENTIAL purchase, why then he was freed up to buy *The Mississippi Sheiks: Stop and Listen; Hank Williams: the Luke the Drifter Recordings; Charley Patton: The Masked Marvel; The Folk Songs of John Jacob Niles;* and *Leadbelly: The Remaining Library of Congress Recordings, Vol. 5 1938-1942.* 'Ah, LOOK at these TITLES!' he agitated. 'When your WAY gets DARK! SCREAMIN' and HOLLERIN' the blues! Must I be CARRIED to the SKY on FLOWERED BEDS of EASE?' Nn, that's poetry right THERE!' He tapped them the way a cardsharp trims the pack. 'Yes yes,' said Jude, contemplating how it would feel to be a mole in the ground. Then again, he didn't need to contemplate. He'd done enough scrabbling, in hedge, ditch and drain, to know perfectly well how it felt. Fantastic. Nevertheless, wishing to be one was a different thing. Only a man who had not been, to all intents and purposes, a mole in the ground would wish to be one. He stared at the red bars. A man who had known the glory and the nothing of being a mole in the ground, would know it didn't really solve anything. Above ground, below ground, six feet here or there; it was all the same to him. Five foot eleven even.

He was on the threshold of pointing this out to Bjørn when Bjørn got his retaliation in first. 'Dark was the NIGHT! COLD! was the GROUND!' he cried, waving round Blind Willie Johnson. 'GOD! MOVES! on the WATER!' He narrowed eyes for emphasis. Jude was cast back to the Glum. Just as before, he wondered where Magnus was, what hole he had for refuge.

'I'm gonna RUN! to the city of REFUGE!'

What was he *doing*, in the Glum Valley, in the mud and sludge? Surely Magnus had bigger fish to fry. It was impossible that he feared to leave. It was equally impossible that he *enjoyed* it. Joy, if one could credit such a thing, resided in anomaly. Magnus was a walking decision, turning all anomalies swiftly to conventions. No, if there was any pleasure in it, for Magnus, it was on condition, on a bond, one no one knew but himself.

'You'll need SOMEBODY on your BOND!'

Jude said: 'You can say that again,' and it was odd that Bjørn didn't. He was taken up with his treasures. He only jabbed at Jude and said, 'but, er, on the other hand, YOU'VE got, er, the *SMITHSONIAN FOLKWAYS COLLECTION*, right there! That's the biggest TREASURE of the LOTT!' His finger hammered. Anyone would have thought he was drilling for oil.

'You've made your bed, you lie in it, Bjornsen. You're looking at the incumbent. Nine-tenths of the law, and all that.' Jude looked at the shopkeeper, as if inviting confrontation.

As arch as Bjørn could be, he stepped absent-minded between boxes, a wad of music in his hand. The old man followed meekly, skewed around the side and appeared before him, adjusting his glasses. Jude made the rear. Six titles Bjørn rapped upon the counter and Jude brought his box to bear. Bjørn turned, excited.

'Nn, I can't help THINKING you've got the BEST of the DEAL.'

'It's a question of priorities,' said Jude, but something was amiss. Bjørn looked too smug with his purchase, the man too doomed. Not to be outdone, Jude picked up a plastic avocado and added it to the pile. 'And...*this*,' he said. He regarded Bjørn superciliously. 'Technically a fruit,' he added. 'As I'm sure you know.'

Bjørn chuckled. He looked at the man.

The man didn't move. But he didn't say anything either. He just continued staring at the counter.

Jude's eyes wandered.

'*Was...ja...*' said the man.

'Mmm?' said Jude.

'*Na...ah.*'

'Ahah!'

'*Ja...ja....*' The man braced arms on the counter. '*Ich glaube so.*' He wrapped it in a sheet of tracing-paper, slid it in a bag with the *Smithsonian Folkways Collection*. They trawled to the door and touched it, hit by the blast of heat. The last they saw of him, he was in the same place precisely, braced against the counter, staring at a box of baby-clothes as if a crevice had opened before him and the moles were blinking in the day.

Jude and Bjørn were blinded by dusk, exhaled in the east by the Danube. The sun had hit the ground running, leaving a stray blue in the west. The rest was grey. Shops were doing roaring trades around them and music came from the thresholds. Only the music shop was quiet. Pouring into the crowds, they headed for *Freud and Friends*, hungry and exultant. It was shut. They veered back round without breaking stride, heading for the *Cafe Museum*. On a rounded corner a fat boy in a tie-dye t-shirt was performing karate. He was all alone, chopping and kicking and clothes-lining the wall, crying *yah!* and *hiyah!* Jude roared with laughter and Bjørn caught up the strain. Here was an intransigent fact. They actually had to go around him, merely to continue, and they were doing just that when the boy began sniggering too, as if in on the joke. This was annoying. The boy's redeeming feature was that he was being laughed *at*. To laugh *with* someone was no fun at all. It was positively incriminating. Any minute now he would run after them, crying *Papa!* and all hell would break loose. *Ha!* cried Jude and swept off down the street. Harper's old Beak was mistaken about humour. If the world was desperate for conspiracy (which it *was*), it was especially so in its so-called humour. And this, of course, was a social malaise. Either something was funny or it wasn't. Society and conspiracy were different.

The boy was still windmilling when they rounded the corner. For his part, Bjørn was tapping his bag, pointing at Jude's, implying success all round. He was thinking, hadn't they won a magnificent victory back there in the record-shop—weren't they about to enjoy more at the chess board? And, finally, weren't they intending to crown their glories with a visit to *The Third Man* this evening? Life was rich. 'Millions—millions!' he exulted, 'could not buy you the QUALITY of LIFE we're just enjoying RIGHT HERE. For the drop of a dime!' A more exuberant man might have pirouetted on his heel. Bjørn contented himself with a fierce point and a fiercer smile, which, in truth, contained more passion than any pirouette. Jude saw that smile, flecked with saliva, against old Vienna's upper floors, daring all kinds of Baroque exteriors. It flashed in windows, filled with furs, climbed old gas-lamps, dropped dimes from its pockets as it went. There was one thing undeniable about Bjørn: his money was where his mouth was. Perhaps that was because he had no money and was sponging off everyone. Yet none so persistent, none so unperturbed. This was a peculiar contradiction in Bjørn. Yet perhaps not so much of one either. His persistence was not egoism. It was sheer monomania. And his absolute calm in the face of all kinds of superficially demoralising situations was merely an extension of his monomania. He simply wasn't thinking about the demoralising situations. They were merely a means—to an end so different it remained wholly unblemished by them; *indifferent*, in fact. Bjørn was a marvel. In many ways he was not unlike Holly Martins who right now was persisting unreasonably in the face of a superficially demoralising sewer. For a start they both had ridiculous names. Damn that Martins! Nothing seemed to shake him much. He just went around writing bad novels, saying goodbyes all over. A man like that could end up making a success of himself, never mind a nuisance. He shouldn't be too difficult to dispose of. Hit that ground, no one'd look for a bullet. The streetlights were bullets, fired through manholes. Bjørn and Martins would traverse them unhindered, ducks through water, into the backroom of the Cafe Museum. They would peer through pipesmoke, drink their wine, studiously refuse the false gods of their time. Then the squares would spin round, and before they knew it, it was through the curtain, cold night air, and the clock striking twelve; down *Operngasse*, up the *Bergring*, and there were Bjørn and Jude, in the dark of the cinema, clearing throats, focusing, whispering, with many a consonantal prompt, that *sometime, very SOON, on next FRIDAY NIGHT, for example, Friday NIGHT would be an EXCELLENT night for it, when people would LEAST expect it, and LEAST pay attention, they, he, Bjørn, and you, Jude, just GOT TO BE exploring those old Viennese sewers, entering by an entrance SPECIALLY revealed to him by CERTAIN PEOPLE IN THE KNOW, until we've just investigated every NOOK and CRANNY of glorious Vienna's DARK UNDERSIDE.* Then, quietly, hesitantly, there would be a sniggering in the back row, foreshortened, however, as if thought better of. And there they were still, Bjørn and Jude, looking left, looking right, looking straight ahead, staring at each other among empty graves, *and Martins still standing in the Friedhof and Alida Valli still coming down the road.*

Sir,

I'm back, at the home, in the middle of the night, writing these notes under conditions very far from ideal, though I might well take a bath.

Here's for why. I left the pub, intent on killing time. The sun set, the rain set in. I met Kostas at the Turkish cafe, a dressing of hummus on his brush, and invited him to the Church. He said he miiiiight come, but first he had some important thiiiiiiings to do, which involved, as far as I could see, sitting in the cafe for hours, with a cup of coffee in front of him, watching rain trouble the windowpanes. I left him there, walked round for hours—HOURS! in the rain and—worse—the wind, turning, turning to them sir, and what choice did I have? None, except but for to go. So I went. Right down to the docklands. It grew oily on the river. I walked half an hour downriver, toward the sea. Docks gave to the hard walkway, the tar path, the running wall, buildings, fencings, railings—and always the wind, gusting from the sea like laughs from a mouth. Across the river, Pratsend lights ranged in the night, real enough. On this side, security lights. Driftwood hit the river-walls, flotsam, sir, and jetsam to boot (at least two pairs)—poles, bottles, bollards, clothes, even flowers. All on a sudden a strong blow blew and my hat flew off on the waves! My fishing hat sir. How do you measure a loss like that?

Now I begin to see sultry smokes, and it isn't Sarah Kent. It's fire. In fact it's a warehouse, quietly burning. I stand there like Thomas De Quincey, only not so self-satisfied. And like S. T. C., only not so fat. The rain floats above it. All kinds of crates and poles surround it, up against the walls. Firemen are spraying the flames, and there's a small crowd, on whom the fire is having its encouraging effect. No one wants to desert it. I see a fireman, 'ee sees me, and jiggered if I don't ask the first question and he come over all defensive. 'What happened here?' said I. 'I advise you to go back the way you came, son!' he barks like a man who resents being typecast. I scarper like a scally, away from the fire, the rain, the river-mouth. I walk by the railings, head down. I'm a forlorn figure, sir, to anyone watching. But no one is watching, and I'm not half as forlorn as I should be, all things considered. I rummage with my eyes among the flotsam, thinking perhaps my hat rode its luck, washed up along the walls. The warehouses throw inexpert light. A flight of stone steps dive to the water, and the glare hits the half of it. I peer down in. A ball, a crate, a pole knock nonchalant at the bottom. And there's my hat, miching and mulching at the wall. I go down the steps and try to fish it in, but just as I touch it, a wave bounces it away and it drifts downstream.

By then it was nine of the clock—and so still at the dock! I heard something like a foghorn miles away. So I pounded down the tar, crossed the wide deserted road, turned up Elysium Street. There was the Sailor's Church—the SCANDINAVIAN Sailor's Church, to be precise (and how could it not be?), all bricked and Victorian in a wasteland of cement and advertising hoardings. The entrance was right on the pavement, almost on the road. No room for hesitation. Two yellow doors, one of which gave. I poked my head in. No one was around. I was just closing the door when Artie poked his in, with grunts of greeting. Then he hung around in the hall as if waiting for me. It was a small hall with doors to left and right, both closed. A wood staircase climbed in front. I was unsure which direction to go in, when Artie motioned up the stairs. Going up, I could hear the chatter of voices. On the first floor a landing opened to a large wooden hall, where a crowd of about forty or so took tea and waffles. I pushed my way through to some tables, with Artie hanging to my coat-tails. This then was his plot to make the ruling classes tremble. Here, the seat of proletariat power; here, in big metal urns embrowned the revolving ferment. And blamed, sir, if presiding over the refection wasn't one of the loveliest women on the revolutionary globe. There she was, high-cheekboned, strawberry-blonde curled, and the smile that pities the admirer. If there are angels in Heaven, they serve tea in such a way, such haloes of steam round their ears. I become aware that I am staring, so I look down—and what to my wondering eyes does appear? A priest's robe, sir. For she is a Priestess. And the funny little man to her right, bobbing about in attendance and staring round through kind spectacles—with the dog-collar and balletic leaps, the brown bowl cut, boyish face, slight but honed of limb—must be her priest of a husband. As hard an Anarch as ever lit votive candles. I just stood there staring at that big old house as bright as any sun. Finally I introduced myself and Artie, who bowed low, took the funny man aside and, cupping a hand to his ear, grunted into it, with many a glance at me. Then I took my tea and waffles, and sat down, Artie in tow, with an extra large helping of waffles. I noticed Kostas in a nook. Someone had shown him what waffles were all about, and he appreciated that. He stood there, in a huge puffy jacket, next to a blasting radiator, shivering with cold, stony-blue eyed, long-lashed, with a grin broadening to a bite, shovelling it in.

With a FORK.

'In Greece,' he was saying, to no one in particular, 'are more cats, perrr caaapita, than other world countries.' He looked innocent a minute, almost perplexed. 'Only rival: Turkey.' He waited for this to sink in, also in himself, then grew the broadest grin in the whole Aegean and all Asia Minor. His teeth protruded, slowly, forcefully, like buds pushing blossoms. There seemed no end to its life-force. But, of course, there was. Eventually, like the Macedonian, Roman, Ottoman Empires, it discovered the limits of expansion. Life became shelf life. The teeth froze, appended to the lip, staying around like a snowman after thaw. From here, there was only one way to go. Slowly, painfully, and, again, just like the

Macedonian, Roman, Ottoman Empires, the lips relaxed, contracted, withdrew to their natural extent, folding away the teeth like so many jewels and watches they have spent the day selling—the way an archimage conceals a book of spells.

Anyway, what with one thing and another, the conversation went on like that for an hour or more, interspersed with casual talk of peaceful marches and laborious strikes, when who, of all erotic religious visions, as I am sneaking up for one last waffle, should sidle beside me saying I must have got wet coming here, should take something to warm up, perhaps a sauna in the basement, that's right, a sauna in the basement?

No seriously.

Go on down, she says. You'll find out how it works.

So I take a coffee, perchance a waffle, and when all are ensconced in armchairs, murmuring sleepily of peace and land, perchance a morsel of bread, I slide down the original stairs and take the right, now left, hand door. Through rooms of papers, stoves, boots, I reach a sign saying SAUNA. It points down another staircase. Down I go, into semi-darkness, hesitant, fearful. A flame burns in a window. The smell of eucalyptus. Beyond is a small changing room, almost wholly dark. I find wood-pegs on the walls and a bench to sit on. Jiggered if I don't have a peg of my own. What if the Priestess joined me in that sauna? She could join me in the sauna any time she liked. What about the husband? Maybe she had his blessing. I touch the bench, slap a foot on the floor. I'm silent as possible. Then a moment of weakness. I don't know what to do about my clothes. Remove all, or leave the boxers? This is a peculiar problem in a black basement, lit by the smear of flame on a window. I wished I had Bjorn to advise me, although strong heterosexual insistences no doubt muddy his understanding of Scandinavian sauna-related mores. I remove them all. I slip whitely through the chamber and approach the door. All I can see is the smear; the flame gazing from the past, like a clairvoyant. I pull the handle and the heat hits me. I walk through it, closing the door, thinking, they shouldn't leave it burning so hot, when something else hits me, harder than the heat. I actually cry for fear, shuddering to the door. Someone else is in there. You can hardly see them it's so dark, but definitely a someone, seated at the top in the pitchiest corner, feet on the seat below. It's the feet I see first—as good as any reason to panic. They're small. I catch a glimpse of white hairless shins, but they slip inside a towelling dressing-gown, the kind boxers wear, with a big hood draping the face.

It's an embarrassing situation, you understand. I have just screeched and collapsed against the door. 'Sorry,' I say, 'you gave me a fright. I didn't see you there.' The person says nothing, then: 'you're going to need more balls to be useful.' The voice is husky, almost inaudible, stopped amid towelling. I jam up on the near side, conscious of those balls. The person has both feet planted. He looks slim, medium-height, though it's hard to tell in the towel. In the upper gloom I make out a bowl he is sniffing from. The eucalyptus is heavy. Along the wall is a stove full of coals. The embers hold the eye, enlarge on the sight. They look like lava—now blurred, now relieved, and the black spots stand out. They look like Hell, in fact, all landscaped as Hell would be. Beside the stove, on the door-side, is a coal-scuttle and prongs. Beside that, a tin bucket half-full, puddles on the floor. There's a round thermometer, like a ship's compass near the door. I'm calmer now, accustomed to the conditions. 'Who are you?' I say. He plants his hands either side of him, athwart the seat. They are slender, expressive hands. 'Call me X,' he says. I note the smell of waffle beyond the eucalyptus. I say: 'I'm not sure I'll be useful anyway.'

He sniffs from the bowl. 'Not an option,' he whispers. The accent is hard to place. If it is Artie—which it probably is—he's going for the foreigner—perhaps Russian—well schooled in American. 'Why's that?' say I, sweeping sawdust, establishing myself. 'You've seen our den,' says he. I lean my head against the wall. After a while I say, 'I didn't ask to.' The person, (whom we will humour with ambiguity) touches inside the hood what might be a nose. 'You came anyway,' he says. 'You knew the risks.' I waft a sweaty palm. 'Maybe I just don't take any of it seriously,' I say. 'Maybe I suspect your revolution of self-content.' I point upstairs, although on reflection he probably can't see me, his hood is so low. He understands anyway. 'Pigs in clover,' he scoffs. 'Toothless, guileless. But their resources are useful.' 'I suppose,' I say looking around, wondering if there is a way to cool the place. 'It doesn't matter what you suppose!' he snorts. Then his voice drops again. 'You think they couldn't have put a bullet through you? Snooping round state facilities!

They reeled you on a piece of silk. You could have been gutted right there on the bank but they throw you back like small fry. You're spying, and you don't even know it. Don't tell me no one baited you here.' 'Well,' I say, seizing my opportunity. 'There was this lazy old tramp. Artie, I think his name was. Told a lot of tall stories, though you might have called them lies.' He sniffs long. 'Artie doesn't know his arse from his elbow,' he says. He sounds like he means it. 'They can squeeze you,' says he suddenly, leaning forward a fraction, and squeezing with his fist. 'Till yer bone fuckin' dry!' I am discomfited somewhat, thinking Artie may be dangerously insane. I look down. 'What was all that trouble, on the wharf there?' I say.

'You saw that,' he says. He sniffs, seems satisfied. 'Put some water on,' he whispered, 'got a bad cold.' His voice is like sandpaper. 'Have to sweat it out.' He took some more sniffs and I sloshed on the water, let the stove take over. It hissed and calmed. I returned to the lower seat. It was hot. Whole sheets of sweat were dragging down me, like the glass-wiper drags. On the wall the thermometer was climbing into red. 'Yeah, that was me,' he continued in a while. He falls silent, fishing for questions. I give him what he wants. 'Really?' I

say. 'How did you pull that off?'

At that he reaches in his robe and pulls out, of all things difficult to credit—a plastic lemon. Admittedly, it is smeared with waffle and jam, but a plastic lemon nevertheless. Yes, I know. But credit it.

Naturally I am affected by this—visibly. He might have pulled almost anything from that pocket—rabbits, conkers, pieces of string—and I had been unmoved. But a lemon obtrudes on a man, especially one which touches on a parallel life. He handed it to me and a moment I touched dexterous fingers. I brought it near the light, examined it. It was about the size of my hand, smelled of almond. A poor imitation lemon if I saw one. He must see this, because he says, 'what's the matter? Seen a ghost?' 'A friend of mine,' says I. He lowers the bowl, places it on the bench. 'Who's this friend?' says he. 'No nothing,' I say, willing it over with. I give him back the lemon and he pockets it. 'He's in Vienna. They keep talking to him about artificial fruit.' He nods again, as if confirmed in something. He wants to know what you're doing there. 'Oh, writing a dissertation,' say I. 'On the roots of Nazism, I think.' 'Dissertation,' he scoffs. Sweat drips from under the towel. It is as though he can't speak; as though he were suffering. 'What is it—drugs?' I say. He waits, sniffs from the bowl. 'Nobel 808,' he says. 'Plastique. Plastic explosives. An old concoction but effective. Semtex is better but you can't get the chemicals.' Now he chuckles. 'You know who invented dynamite? Alfred Nobel. He developed a taste for explosives, studying chemistry in St. Petersburg. They didn't agree with his brother. He died in an explosion at the factory—along with a bunch of others. Didn't stop Alfred though. He got rich on it. 30 million kronor or so. Then, in 1888, an obituary comes out in France. It said: Le Marchand de la mort est mort. But they were wrong. Nobel wasn't dead. He had a Damascus moment, left all his money to his prizes. Still, it was a woman—his secretary—talked him into the peace prize.' He chuckles again. 'Funny thing is, he was a Shelleyan. Wrote a play about incest called Nemesis—after The Cenci.' He pauses. 'I don't think it's been published.'

There is a silence; all that is heard is the crumble of coal. By this time I was fed up. I didn't try to make a stab, but I might have if I had had a knife. I excused myself and pushed through the door, relieved. 'See you next week,' he rattled. 'Same time, same place!' I shut the door, and breathed all the way to the cloakroom. Then I took a shower, dressed, trod down the mat toward the smear. The door was half ajar. The smear was becoming a bruise, as if someone had punched the clairvoyant—an understandable reaction.

Upstairs I found Kostas. He was still in his puffy jacket, eating waffles through an interminable smile and demonstrating a finely nuanced dance step involving the brushing of shoe or tsarouhi against the back of trousers (bourazana), to an audience of one. In fact he was enjoying himself so much that he decided to stay on for the Swedish folk-song recitals. 'Are you sure you don't want to come?' I asked, patting him on the back. 'Naaoo,' he said. 'I...

I...

Will...

STAAAY...'

And, looking away, he blinked—slowly—like a number changing on a manual scoreboard.

Harper.

Jude snorted, glared at Rico who was shuffling in. What time was it? *Halb drei*. Jude didn't feel well. It occurred to him, he had hardly eaten all day, unless you counted a couple of bagels at the *Jüdisches Museum*, a sandwich at the *Cafe Museum*, and a few Brazil nuts. What was it about cafes and museums anyway? The antithesis, presumably. Nothing piqued the appetite like *preservation*. He shut off the screen, stalked up the mainstairs, three floors, all the vast spaces of the *Studentenheim*, through corridors to darkened kitchen. It was a large square kitchen: two fridges, two sinks, two ovens, and cupboards all round. Otherwise there was nothing to suggest it was a kitchen.

Of all people in the world, Bjørn was there, rustling in the fridge, a copy of *The Divine Comedy* tented on the table. He had forgotten to turn the light on—or perhaps it was a conscious decision. The hall light cut through the door; otherwise the strong moon served, and the outlight in the courtyard slugged you from an angle. 'I'm thinking vegan pasta,' said Jude sitting down. He spread his arms on the table—a big, wide affair, six tables together.

'Ah, we DON'T have any onion,' said Bjørn, engrossed in the fridge.

'Are you sure? There's usually an onion somewhere, lurking behind some aluminium foil.'

'Nn, ah, no.'

'You're *not* sure?'

'Er, no, I'm SURE.'

Jude tutted, blamed Bjørn entirely. 'Hmmm,' was all he huffed. 'How about broccoli, sir?'

'I could eat BROCCOLI.'

'You should find one in *that cupboard.*' Jude indicated one of the many cupboards over the fridge. Bjørn found it, removed some leaves and dunked it in a pan of water. He added a touch of salt, put the water to boil.

'EXcellent!' he said, rubbing his hands. Bjørn was irrepressible. He was the kind of person completely capable of staying in town at someone else's expense, his only concession the promise of some kind of lecture on the Modern Novel, a lecture which he would perform singularly badly, utterly devoid of insight or interest, yet the public reaction to which, culminating in a mass desertion of the premises, he would not in the slightest take to heart. That was Bjørn. He took nothing to heart. Sometimes Jude wasn't sure if he had a heart; just a jumble of crags. Still, a jumble of crags was a heart of kinds. Easier to get in than out. A place of rare communings. You could trap someone there, forbidding them to roll.

Rolling into the kitchen came Kara Kundera, like a milkmaid from the cow. She knew not to turn on the light. She was young, plump and pretty, sheathed in wool. Her face beamed, come from a concert party. She rummaged in her pantry, handing cutlery to Bjørn. Bjørn and Jude didn't have a lot of food on the table—but they didn't have a lot of forks and knives either. They were always borrowing Kara's. Bjørn was thinking she could rummage in her pantry, hand him cutlery any time she liked. Kara disappeared but he continued standing there with cutlery in his hand while the broccoli boiled over and splashed on the stove. Jude was in no mood to move. Eventually Bjørn turned, said 'oh' and lowered the fire. Even then it wasn't sure it had registered with him. He might have been considering the spheres of heaven. Kara re-entered, tutted and smiled. Jude ignored them. Kara could enter and re-enter as she pleased; it was all the same to him. Certainly it was all the same to Bjørn. There she went again, to be replaced by a mournful Jesse, turquoise iroquois-eyed, straw hair about the brows. He was wearing cap, zipper-top and t-shirt, on which showed the letters *EAHAW*. He was well-built, middle-height, looked a million dollars down on its luck. He was shielding his eyes. He couldn't sleep, expecting a ghost at his door. A real giggle fell from him—almost a bray. A silence fell immediately after. He scratched at the table, organising toast. Bjørn hardly noticed: he was deep in boiling water. How long the quiet continued no one registered. It was measured rather in movements: the endless spiral stirrings of the water; the sporadic scraping of knife on toast; the occasional strained sigh, fidget of hand on table. After that it was the draining of the saucepan, the expression of steam, the partition of broccoli into two equal halves. And the mastication. The long, odious mastication: death of conversation, consumer of time. Jude's petty bites, Bjørn's efficient intakes, Jesse's wolfed mouthfuls. They needed no clock to cut them. Mortality spread like moonlight on the table.

All at once, in bustled Tomas, big-lipped and curly, in an army jacket. A faint smell of booze hung about him and he explained and excused it with a single word. The word was *medicine.* Jude smiled. A cover-all term if he'd heard one. Behind Tomas bustled a couple of bottles of Bordeaux and before the smile was off Jude's face he had a full glass before him. So, for that matter, did Tomas and Bjørn. Even Jesse beamed in the glow. 'I know a little vineyard,' began Tomas, recollecting picturesquely his journeys through France. 'We just came back from Morocco,' he finished. 'Decent but no must-see. Not much to talk about, honestly.' Tomas was a stickler for English, and had picked up all manner of eloquence. If Bjørn was all substance, Tomas was certainly style. This he explained by saying he had lived in North-London for a year, aged twelve, but this didn't really explain anything. He pointed at the table. 'I, that is my girlfriend and myself, shall probably return there next year. London being the Rome of the financial world, Reta may have to move there awhile. Actually, thinking about it, London is almost a Rome in matters medical, too.' He sighed and grimaced. 'But somehow I find it more unlikely that anyone will be sending me!'

Jude eyed him favourably. 'What exactly are you doing now?'

'Career-wise I'm struggling along with internships.' He smacked his lips. 'To be precise, I am in internal medicine. To be even more precise I am looking after what might be called in the trade, LOLs, or, for the benefit of non-medics here (which is of course all of you), little old ladies, with heart or lung problems, occasionally stumbling over a case of cancer.' A long slow smile lit up his face. It looked like you could store things on it. He lit a cigarette, leaned back in a chair and exuded an air of satisfaction. 'Well,' he said, changing subject with a wonderful delicacy. He frowned, still smiling. 'We have finally gotten our winter.' He gazed to moon and courtyard. 'That should dampen the talk of global-warming a while. Shouldn't it?' He opened this one to the table. Jude gazed too. If ever you were in the trenches, or at an awkward dinner-party, you would want Tomas beside you, trotting out such superb complacencies.

'Isn't it magnificent?' he replied, tightening his lips. 'Although I must admit, when it gets this cold, I could go without it.'

'Oh, it gets a LOTT colder than THIS in NORWAY!' put in Bjørn. Across the table, he and Tomas blinked at each other, as across a hundred miles of forest.

'Of course, Bergen is not so cold as the East of Norway, is it?' suggested Tomas, 'being warmed by the Gulf Stream.'

'Ohh, we gett pretty COLD winters over there from time to time.'

'Washington State gets rightly cold in winter,' said Jesse. 'It gets so cold and snowy you have to drive with chains on the wheels.'

'Oh, that's VERY COMMON in Norway.'

'I believe we have that tradition in Sweden too.' Jude eyed Tomas scurrilously. *I believe* was one of his favourite prefixes, often succeeded by *so*. Yet, Jude had never met such a reasonable man. Tomas might actually be the complete human; the apotheosis. Everything he did, everything he said, seemed to emanate from that liberal smile. Thousands of years of civilisation prompted his diplomacy. A classic eloquence in his every blush. He was a doctor, of course, but he might have been an ambassador. A real Renaissance man, and a better advertisement for the Enlightenment you could not find, with a touch of Modernism in his drainpiped angularity. Tomas wasn't right-wing, but he wasn't left-wing either. He didn't believe in God or State—but he didn't disbelieve either. All things to all men; yet he was no sycophant. No one forced his hand and he demurred with the best of them. In fact, the demur was his staple sound. Nor would he oscillate either. He just disagreed as agreeably as possible. No doubt there was distance in those small blue eyes; care to that aristocracy. But distance and care were essential qualities in a man. Those who had none were wretches or madmen—wretches, then. No, the funny thing about Tomas, to Jude's eyes, was that that liberal smile, that calm, that care, all made him more elect. What a paradox he would present in heaven. A curly gangly smile, strolling through the gates. A most complete man, at once undermining and restoring everyone's confidence. 'But, ah, Jesse,' he continued, 'you say Washington State. Where *exactly* in Washington State is it that you're from?'

'Well, it's a little island.' His tone rose at the end. 'Near Seattle.' It rose again. 'Samish, to be precise.' He appeared to be influenced by Tomas' exactitude.

'Seattle. Would that explain why you're wearing a *Seahawks* t-shirt?' said Tomas, combining acute observation with an alarming knowledge of American football, and using them to state the obvious.

‘That would.’

‘I see.’ Tomas tightened his lips against his teeth, smoked, rocked back in his chair. *I see* was another of his favourite expressions. He looked like a man for whom every subject is of finite, but equal, interest. In this he was similar, but different, to Bjørn, for whom every subject was of equal, infinite, interest. This obscure pass between finite and infinite was the Mason-Dixon line of the Scandinavian soul, all clogged with rocks and snow.

Jesse was beginning to giggle now, pitching curveballs from left-field. ‘The Seahawks were robbed!’ he was saying, exploring the table with a muscular hand. ‘*Sheesh*, the anger has taken till now to subside!’ He thumped the table. ‘I still hate Pittsburgh. But mostly I hate the men in black-white striped getup that made every call against the Hawks. Usually, when a team dominates total yardage, controls the clock, and wins the turnover battle—that team wins. The *X* factor is the officiating! And that enabled the *Steelers*, a team’—he struggled for words—‘*dominated*, in every facet of the game, to win.’ He looked round for approval. Jude winced a sideways smile; Tomas was reflecting; Bjørn was all ears, getting serious, pecking at the table with his hand. This was all the approval he needed. ‘All of the Northwest is brimming with hatred of the eastern establishment,’ he continued. 'The Southerners may cling to an archaic notion that the United States is divided North-South, but they are delusional.' His voice almost cracked entirely. 'The Southeast is simply the disenfranchised part of the East. The West is another country entirely. The referees,' he continued without pause, 'could not *imagine* a team from "South Alaska" winning over the "stalwart" *Steelers.*' It was reportage now. 'Polls taken beforehand showed an interesting thing: east of the Mississippi, the only state in which a majority were pulling for the *Seahawks* was the commonwealth of Massachusetts. And, I'm bound to say, that was probably an anomaly. No Westerners (except for soft southern Californians, an altogether despicable people) were pulling for the *Steelers.* The South is just more tribal than the west. The US is divided by the Rockies. The Mason-Dixon line is obsolete! All it refers to now is the weather.' Jesse threw his cap on the table, done with the unfairness of it all.

'I've, I've got to say, I'm a bit of a Southerner myself, so to say.' Bjørn chuckled modestly. 'I've always been a BIG, er, FAN of the MIAMI DOLPHINS!' he cried. 'Oh, well, fan is probably too strong of course, I've been a FOLLOWER, er, from a distance you'd have to say, of the Miami DOLPHINS, ah, all MY life, ever since I can remember, going way back now to nineteen eighty-three, four'—Bjørn winced himself, remembering—'ah, the first season of the GREAT, ah, AMAZING, DAN! MARINO!'

'Whooee! That would have been his rookie year. I'm too young to remember it, but I know for a fact that season they were upset in the divisional playoff by none other team than a certain *Seattle Seahawks!* Puttin' those south-easterners in their place.'

Here was much to cheer about, and, sure enough, a cheerful discussion followed, on another of mankind's favourite topics: America; its glories and pitfalls, punctuated by many a giggle and grimace. They heard the story of Harper, lost, benighted, three hours in the pouring rain, setting up tent on the verge of Highway 61, finally picked up—by a nurse, who took him home, fed and housed him, let him stay for days. His only responsibility: to walk the dog, through the summer floods. 'That's northern hospitality!' squeaked Jesse. A bottle was gone and Tomas was refilling in that quiet way of his when a glass was half-full. Bjørn drank up, finished the anecdote. Jude drank up too, looking down at his shoes. Once again, his head was heavy; stomach making moan. And as it moaned its most, in flapped Pilar Santana Artale and crew, carrying eggs, onions and potatoes, gesturing and laughing and drawing attention to themselves. There was no end to the gestures they employed. Olivia Ruiz twiddled at her navel,

Garcia Garcia shook a tiny hand and Maria Magdela Jesus Jose de Carmen passed a finger under her nose, reminiscent of the Lie. Laura Barbosa merely touched an eyelash. They looked like the birds of Bosch; they scarcely needed words at all. It was left to Pilar to apply the *coup de grace* and this she did by stroking the back of her fingers along her chin and flipping it away, as if removing unwonted shaving-cream. This was a gesture Jude could understand. He was always removing unwonted shaving-cream. Shaving-cream had a way of growing beneath the gaze, out of control, leaving you sorely compromised. You always had to flick it away.

There was an analogy here, but he couldn't spot it. Instead he spotted Pilar's rear, which she that moment obtruded to the room, in order to smoke at the window. A fine rear, sir. A wriggle on that rear. A curse be on her if she stay. '*¡Holaaa!*' they chorused when they realised no one was paying attention. 'Hey there,' said Jude. 'Uh, hullo,' said Bjørn, deep in a cup. 'Whatcha been eating?' said Santana Artale, looking over her shoulder. It was a bare shoulder from a black vest. A short skirt cupped stripy leggings. It was a look, undeniably a look. At a hundred and thirty-five degrees. You couldn't underestimate a look like that, though it could underestimate you at a second's glance.

'*Broccoli*,' said Jude. There was a measure of

defiance in his voice.

She shrugged. 'Whatever.' Up trembled the corners of her mouth. Jude struggled to focus. His head was pounding; even his feet were pounding. Anyone would have thought he had walked a lot today. Anyone would have thought he hadn't been sleeping well.

Barbosa reached for a frying-pan, Garcia for a chopping-board, Fernandez for a knife. 'How are you?' said Barbosa, looking round under lids. They began slicing things, working in concert. Garcia was heating oil in the pan. In no time at all they had a *tortilla* up and running. 'Ah, okay,' said Bjørn at length. 'What about you?' He stretched a curled hand toward Barbosa, taking in the others on the way.

'Even I have not much new to tell. I have these days, when I can't stop speaking. And I can't stop amazing myself, how the world is going,' said Barbosa. Nobody said anything. 'What...you did today?' she continued, glumly.

'Ah, MANY interesting things!' retorted Bjørn suddenly. 'Ah, of course, I myself probably stayed around here too long this morning. Although that also can be a fantastic way to spend time. Me, I don't believe in just BUSTLING about from one attraction to the other, ah, just to say you've been there. I can gett just as good a time in my room. But of course, on the other hand, it's important to, to gett outt there and see LIFE. Just learning about LIFE. Even at eleven years old!' he said, pointing at Jude and chuckling. 'Ah, but this evening, WE had a fanTAStic CHESS session, over at the CAFE MUSEUM, oh that's a great place, smoky old men in there.' Bjørn drew out a monotone further than anyone thought possible. '—All changing in and out of position with waiters and CARD-SHARPERS and bohemian types just reading, er, as Jude likes to do, or sitting watching people, best of all, with the mutter of voices and everything just merging into ONE.'

'Sounds an ideal location,' said Tomas. Rico shuffled suddenly into the room and everyone turned to watch him. He was scratching himself, blear-eyed and hopeless-looking.

'*¡Que Ricoo!*' said the girls and fell about laughing.

Rico grinned. He looked like a bear in the circus.

Tomas felt obliged to include him. 'Rico. You're from Azerbaijan, are you not?'

Rico nodded.

'Whereabouts, may I ask?'

Rico didn't understand.

'*Welche Stadt?*'

Rico shrugged. 'Baku.'

Bjørn's grin could not have been wider. 'Garry KASPAROV!' he half-cheered, with half-fisted fingers half-raised to the air.

'No,' said Rico.

'Ha!' said Jude.

Tomas had his turned face on his shoulder. 'Why not? Ah, perhaps it's because he's Jewish, is he not? That would probably be the reason.'

'No,' said Rico, understanding more than they'd credited.

'Not that?' Tomas said quickly. 'What then?'

Rico shrugged again, smiled slyly. 'Armenian *bloood*,' he drawled. Then he shuffled from the room.

There was a silence in his wake. 'Ah, but that wasn't ALL!' resumed Bjørn. His guns rotated back to Barbosa. 'THEN, going off to see the MIDNIGHT SHOWING of The THIRD MAN OH what a treasure that was, all there, ALMOST the only people there, just, ah ONE or TWO others I think, in, ah, the back row there, with that great film before us, which you just got to SEE if you're gonna be living in this city.'

'You should have told us,' said Pilar. 'Maybe we'd have joined you.'

'Yes, we didn't think about it,' said Jude. He wasn't sure it came out as he intended.

'I've not seen it,' said Tomas. 'It's thought to be one of the great British movies of all time, is it not?'

'Apparently so.'

'You weren't impressed, Jude?'

‘I *was* impressed. I was.’ He reached for words but they wouldn’t come. He realised someone had put the light on. Now it was him who was the Holly Martins, reeling on a chair, with Tomas as his Callaghan, putting to him very reasonable questions, and Jesse as the jolly Sergeant. All of which made Bjørn a wholly unlikely Orson Welles, split by the light. ‘I was impressed,’ he said again. ‘Especially so, considering it was a film, and that all films are, by their nature, rubbish.’

‘Oh no, THAT I can’t AGREE with.’

‘Hah-hah, mmm, *all films are rubbish*. Can you elaborate on this theory of yours?’

‘No, that’s just the point. Something too much of *elaboration*. To discuss, to notice film at all, is *necessarily* intellectualising the banal, to justify a lifetime of idlesse.’ Jude’s head was near his chest.

‘*Something too much of elaboration*,’ mused Tomas. ‘*A lifetime of idlesse*, I like it.’ He drew breath sharply. ‘But why films in particular? Why not theatre, or music?’

‘It’s a question of *appetite*,’ mumbled Jude.

‘You want a piece of tortilla?’ said Barbosa.

‘No.’ Jude’s stomach was playing tricks with him. The wine wasn’t helping either, and what was that if not a full glass before him? He took a cigarette from Tomas and looked at it, tapped it, realised the light had gone off again. The moonlight too had left the tabletop, as if a conjuror had swept it away. Bjørn had commenced on music now and there was no stopping him. 'Ah, we were just STROLLING round town, bought some FANTASTIC records—records YOU there,' and he pointed at Jesse now, 'have just GOTT to be HEARING! Ah, some, er, good old Mississippi SHEIKS, er, Lead-BELLY, of course! Ah, some BLIND! WILLIE! JOHNSON!' Tomas returned with four bottles of Bordeaux, though no one had noticed him leave. 'But he—he,' continued Bjørn, intent on doing his friend a favour. The finger swung back to Jude, as to its usual object. 'HE came out with the BARGAIN of the day! HE did the best of all us HUSTLERS here! HE came out of there, with the best discovery of them ALL: the SMITTSONIAN! FOLKWAYS! COLLECTION!' Bjørn was like some blind Ringmaster, drumming up enthusiasm in an empty marquee. He carried on pointing though, grimacing round. Some effect it had, because, leaving a piece of tortilla hanging in the air, Pilar inclined her head. 'Oh yeah,' she said. 'That's a find. On vinyl?'

'Unfortunately not.' Jude was weighing her up, wondering what a Spanish hipster would be doing, knowing about the Smithsonian Folkways Collection. But then Santana Artale had many a trick down those armholes of hers, and one or two up those leggings. Like Orson Welles refusing to leave his hotel room, Jude wanted to see some of those tricks. Pilar smirked lopsidedly, saying 'I'd like to listen to that.' He regarded the table. What was he supposed to say: 'come to my room and listen'? The more he thought about it, the more it enraged him. This was how women exercised their power: offering everything and nothing. And they had the gall to call it wit. They didn't actually have to *do* anything, make a single edifying contribution, compromise themselves in the slightest. All they had to do was serve the bullet. To answer was foolish; not to answer, equally so. It was a delicate balance. Jude, not as great a pretender as he would have liked, felt the scorn rising in him, and it rose the faster for this awareness. 'I'll lend it to you,' he said, thoroughly annoyed.

'Er, nott before me, I hope,' put in Bjørn, bemused by Jude's reaction to a clear come-on and thinking to smooth things over, floundering in mid-table. 'Er, ah, THAT'S another thing we've got to learn from the SOUTH!' he continued, turning back to Jesse. 'All that GREAT music which just er, was BORN in the CRADLE of the MISSISSIPPI and WHOREHOUSES of NEW ORLEANS!'

'A little more wine,' said Tomas, refilling glasses all over. Jude hardly noticed. Spanish ladies swam before his eyes, but that was nothing to relish. After all, Bjørn swam there too, and Tomas, and Jesse, forming together the Mount Rushmore of his mental geography, declaring all kinds of independence. Jesse had taken advantage of this apparition and was saying that he had 'come to this conclusion, regarding the South.' He twisted a hand. 'The less one has, the more vigorously one defends it. That explains many things: the Civil War, Rebel Pride, Soul Food.' His voice caught in his throat, as if all the Rockies, its peaks and gorges, were included within.

'Oh oh no no. Ah, I'VE GOTT to SAY!' Bjørn was tapping the table, smiling defiantly. 'Ah, a LOTT of the best things come up from the South there.'

'Crumbs. Must be the broccoli,' said Jude, finding form again. Tomas exhaled indulgently. Pilar was collecting plates.

'Sure,' croaked Jesse. 'Alligators, snakes, tarantulas, hurricanes. What more? Ticks, for example—and a miserable climate.'

'Good old SOUTHERN hospitality, for instance.'

'Let me tell you somethin' about Southern hospitality. I worked as a security guard in Tennessee. I used to hitch-hike, to and from these malls where I worked. An' the only people who ever picked me up were the truckers.'

'I see. I've never hitch-hiked myself. It's not worth it in Sweden. Too many lonely forests.'

'What's hutch-hick?' said Barbosa. She looked miserable.

'Jude. How would you explain hitch-hiking?'

'Sounds like a racial slur.'

'*Slur.*' Tomas mused. He didn't understand that one. 'Hitch-hiking is putting your thumb out and asking people for a ride.' He put his thumb out. 'A practice sometimes fraught with danger, at least *uncertainty*. Perhaps that's what you mean by *slur*.'

'Pilar did it, no?' said Barbosa, as if the world were ending in an hour.

'Yeah, I hitch-hiked a while round New Hampshire and Massachusetts,' said Pilar. 'Just a few weeks. Never had a problem.'

'*New Hampshire and Massachusetts*. You were in America for a long time, I take it?'

'I did a year of high school there.' She piled the plates by the sink.

'*A year of high school*. That would explain your really *excellent* command of English.' There was a Nordic shade in the *t* of *excellent*.

'Nah, I'm losing it.'

'I think not.' Tomas turned up the corners of his mouth, frowning. 'I saw you the other day with a copy of—I believe it was a copy of Thomas Stearns Eliot's *The Waste Land*, would that be right, Jude?'

Pilar shrugged it off. Jude said nothing. The kitchen was dark as a harbour, lit by lights in the eye. He was watching her at the sink, washing up, like a buoy in tides of steam. It was the most erotic thing Jude had ever watched. And he had watched a lot. A variety of positions were taken up and abandoned. The pony-tail was out of control. The rear was a boxing match. One time a foot splayed out, next minute it tucked back in and the body shook like a divining rod. Jude was like a divining rod too, with a very particular divination. He hardly noticed, for instance, that Jesse's audience, in the discussion of Little Big Horn, had dwindled to little Maria. Or that Kara had slipped back in to talk Swedish folk-music with Bjørn. What he divined absolutely was that Tomas was a man in his element, and it was *templado*.

'A work I have not myself read,' continued Tomas, helping Jude to some more of his element. 'To my shame and disgrace.' He looked neither shamed nor disgraced. He looked like a man of men, whose collective psyche had so well absorbed *The Waste Land* that reading it was unnecessary; the man all books aspire to. A more elegant education you could not hope to find. 'Though I mean one day to change that.'

'I'll lend it to you,' said Pilar. Jude heard it all from underwater. So she would lend it to him, would she? Go to his room, perhaps, take turns with the lines, joke over mispronunciations, ask why Jude wasn't there to correct them. *So elegant, so intelligent. We shall play a game of chess. Hurry up please it's April.* Hee hee, ho ho. Just like Kara, back sallied the moon. She had never really been away, just hid by cloud. Again she spread her sheet on the table, preparing for the feast. He could see her now: toes dipped and testing the shallows, white as the virgins of Vienna. All ten of them. '*Perhaps*,' said Tomas; as artful a *perhaps* as you'll hear. 'But I'm in the middle of something at the moment.' He turned to Jude, inclusive. 'A humble tip from an ignorant. If you should ever get lost in the National Library's interiors—falling asleep perhaps, among the shelves of old books, printed in, and untouched since, the eighteenth century—'

'Which makes them younger than my house.'

'Is that so? And if from that sound sleep you wake, realising that your head has been resting on a copy of *Eugene Onegin*, by one Aleksandr Pusjkin, I recommend you to read it.'

'That's a great one.' Pilar appeared on a pulled stool, on the other side of Tomas. She was feeling in the pockets of a bright wool cardigan, emerging with a large, armoured lighter. 'Have you read Rilke?'

'I've not read a lot of poetry. Like most medics who affect an interest in the arts, I plough endlessly through novels. No doubt we identify with the prosaic. Or perhaps it's a lack of concentration.' Tomas touched ash on tray. 'But I'm impressed. Your German must be, really, *ex-cellent*.'

'My grandma lives here.'

'I see.'

‘It’s a complicated story.’ She pinched at tobacco. ‘My grandfather was Viennese-Jewish. He left Vienna in the thirties—with his brother. Went to live with cousins in Bilbao. Pretty funny, he walked straight into Civil War. His cousins actually fought for the Republic. Actually my grandmother was in Guernica the day it was bombed. Yeah. She was sitting in a cafe, says she felt something coming. Or maybe she just had an appointment. Got out hours before it started.’

‘Is that so?’

‘Yeah, really. So that was pretty hard. Anyway, synagogues were closed, Jews were persecuted, and my grandfather converted when he met my grandmother.’

‘Where was that?’

Pilar wasn’t quite ready for the interruption. ‘Er, I don’t know actually. Maybe San Sebastian?’

‘Hmm, it’s unusual, isn’t it, in those circumstances?’ Tomas elaborated. ‘Escaping persecution in Vienna, then converting when he gets to Spain. Exiles often hold tightly to to their beliefs.’

Pilar had a rasping sort of snigger. ‘You don’t know my grandmother.’

‘True, true. I’m sure she was—and *is*—quite something.’

Jude took his time, but took note nonetheless. Tomas was sure Pilar’s grandmother was—and *is*—

quite something. Plus, he had further half-sureties on the subject of exile. What was the basis of all this surety? Anatomy? Money? A liberal tallness? No doubt all of these things lent a certain surety where Pilar and her grandmother were concerned, but what did they have to do with exile? Jude was willing to bet Tomas couldn't be exiled if he tried. He stared at the table, feeling somewhat aggressively protective of Pilar's grandfather. Meanwhile, his voice clambered up from somewhere craggy and unconvinced—The Crags, perhaps:

'Perhaps he just couldn't be bothered with it either way. Perhaps he found the whole persecution, followed by dogmatic reaction to persecution business all very tedious.'

Everyone looked briefly at Jude. Curiously, this version of events seemed to agree with Pilar, because she continued as if where Jude had left off. 'So they married, and he took her name: that's the Santana. After the war—the World War—his brother moved back to Vienna, but my grandparents stayed, had my Dad. After my Dad married my Mom, my grandfather decides he wants to go back to Vienna. This is late sixties. Says he never felt comfortable, always wanted to go home. So they move back to Vienna in nineteen sixty-eight, actually just after the—what?—four hundred and fifty year law was—how do you say that?—

cancelled? Which exiled the Jews from Spain. Imagine.'

'I didn't know that. We're going back to Philip, no—that would be Ferdinand and Isabella, would it not?'

'Fourteen ninety-two.' She began rolling a joint, slowly, like one concerned with particulars. 'You know they were actually given an ultimatum. Hundreds of thousands of 'em. They had to leave—when?—by the end of July. That's what they ordered. The end of fuckin' July. Jewish people actually gave their cemeteries to the public, to stop them being desecrated. Made them municipal parks. That happened. A lot of 'em were desecrated anyway. They spent days in the cemeteries, last days of July, just mourning and crying—like, remembering Zion.'

'I'm intrigued. Your surname isn't Basque.'

'My grandma's from Pamplona.' She stuck her tongue between teeth.

'But your mother—'

'From Sicily. *Tomas*,' she said, and punched him on the arm.

'The plot grows thicker.'

'Plot is about right.' Smile-lines went on and off, like lights at her eyes.

'Can you elaborate?'

'*Too much of elaboration.*' Both smiled, looking to Jude. He reached for his glass, ignored them.

‘But would this explain the American connection?’

‘No.’ She licked the paper, put it in her lips and lit it. She did it all slowly. ‘They sent me to high-school there. To learn English. I lived with host-families.’

‘What, if I may ask, does he do for a living?’

‘Yeah, he owns a sardine factory.’

‘I see.’

Jude could not help but find this funny. From the top of his glass he spluttered a *ha!* with more venom than he intended.

‘What’s so funny?’ said Pilar, blowing smoke. It got in his lashes, up his nose. He was thinking of trawlers, storms and enormous nets. He thought of the coasts of home; the greensward at the cliffs and the spread sand. He thought of Kynance Cove, Cornwall, every summer. Heavy yeasty waves. He saw the sleek yellow flag, and the divers assembling. The heavy waves were his stomach, yellow flag, his brain.

‘Sardines. Sardines are hilarious.’

She sprawled a moment over the table, angling at Jude. ‘What’s your father do?’

‘My father,’ began Jude, rehearsing old lines, ‘is a *Time-Lord.*’

‘I see,’ said Tomas, doubtfully. ‘Are you able to elaborate on that?’

Jude stared round the room. He wasn’t sure that

he was. The moon had gone for good this time and he was thinking to do the same. Come to think of it, everyone had gone, except them. What time was it? There was no clock in the kitchen. There were six bottles though, and Bjørn's *Divine Comedy*. What did it matter? Whatever he said, the magnificent Tomas (and he *was* magnificent) was going to imply elaboration, and no doubt Pilar would supply it. They could elaborate together (to) their hearts' contents.

'He's in charge of Greenwich Mean Time. And British Summer Time, for that matter. He probably has a hand in the *Prime Meridian*. Or should I say, finger.'

'I see. How does he do all that from the Glum Valley?'

'He commutes.'

'What about your mom?'

'She's the whole round globe.'

They laughed but Jude didn't see the funny side. He didn't see any particular side. He got up from his chair, huffed as though the world must know it, and traipsed from the room, without so much as *goodnight.* It had reached a weary end and there was nowhere to go. He thought if he just lay down it would blow like the unloosed windsock of Bjørn's bag. Dreams would lift him like a crowd of birds. But he had to lie down first. He had to make it to his door and shut it, and Bjørn could go to

Hell. He did make it to his door, did shut it, did lie down in the dark. This he could do. He did manage to cast last eyes round the room (not much to cast your eyes on), make out in the corner the cold, narrow radiator, anoint it the symbol of his chastity, fix them on its iron rungs, that long running pipe up the wall. He did drift off into tolerable dreams, of losing men in the cemeteries. Of appearances of other men, where you didn't expect them. Of Bjørn in all manner of ferris wheels, not that difficult to get rid of. Of his mother, milking applause in the *Burgtheater*, showered by Tomas with oriental tea. Of the labyrinthine backstage, the plunge through seven levels, and his father there, winding the scenery with *fin-de-siecle* articulations. Looking old now, looking weary. Bent over task and ignoring his son. It was a hard task. All fathers' tasks were hard. But as he came closer, the man turned his face and it wasn't his father, it was Rico. The shame of it. He heard the *tick-tock* of the cogs, very regular, revolving the stages above. The *tick-tock* became steps. It was Bjørn coming down to Hell, where he belonged. No, it was Bjørn coming down the corridor, to Jude's room, where he had no business. Funny though. It was unusual for Bjørn to knock—especially softly. Bjørn knocked to wake the dead, if he knocked at all. Just ask Kara Kundera. Quick smart raps were his stock in trade. And he didn't wait for answers, he leaned straight in just like a man about town. This knock was more like a mouse's, and it fell into patters like a spider on the wall.

'Come in.'

The door creaked. It took an age in opening. Pilar's head poked round, and her pony-tail followed. She didn't put the light on. She could see by the outlight. Jude was lying on the quilt in t-shirt and boxers, bathed in sweat. His body was straight, arms by his side. 'Sorry,' she said. 'Did I say something wrong back there?'

Only his head moved. 'Not at all.'

'You looked a bit pissed. Pissed-off I mean.' She added: 'maybe both.'

'Not at all. A little under the weather.'

'Well the window's open.'

Jude lifted his head. She was right, the curtains were parted and window wide open. That would explain why it was freezing cold. Mists were coming in, hit by the outlight. From the courtyard tree a bird broke singing. Dawn must be near.

'That won't help,' she continued, closing it, drawing the curtains. Jude noticed that she crossed the room silently. Bjørn had never done that. 'I don't know you very well. Perhaps you're normally like that.'

'No, I don't think so.'

'Well I thought I'd apologise. In case.' She quivered for a moment, mid room. She looked a little stoned.

'No I don't think so.'

'Alright, good night then.'

'No no, I appreciate. I appreciate you coming.' He was staring at the ceiling.

'Why?'

'I was a little *short*.'

'You were surrounded by Scandinavians.'

'Yes, that's enough to make anyone short.'

There was occasion for a laugh here, and it came in quiet snorts. Laughing *with* someone had its place after all.

'*Magnificent* as they are.'

'They're great. How long have you known Bjørn?'

'You don't really get to know Bjorn. Bjorn has always existed. It's merely a question of facing up to him.'

She sat down on the bed. Still Jude didn't stir. He could see wild strands of hair against the faint outlight. Her face was pale, just visible.

'When did you face up to him?'

'He was always there, at my shoulder, like Antonius Bloch. Like a man shaking a palm tree. I ignored him for a while, but then the whole charade grows tiresome. That was around three or four years ago. Where is he anyway?'

'I think he's gone with Kara.'

'He's easy pickings. Like taking rocks from a

troll.'

'He sleeps here.' She scuffed at the sleeping-bag.

'Yes. Don't know how it looks to other people.'

'How does it look to other people?'

'Ridiculous, I imagine. But then they're *looking*.'

'How long is he here?'

'Until he outstays his welcome so long that he's welcome again. Could be years.'

'So I should go.'

'No. No I don't think you *should*.' His stomach grumbled loudly. She put her hand on it.

'Must be the broccoli.'

He huffed like a steam-train, put his hand on it too. 'I don't think I'm at my best.'

'I'm smashed.'

'You should probably lie down.'

Fingers were gripped, hair ran in hair. There were scuffles, gurgles, all the drowning sounds.

3. The Fourth Man

Once again Jude found himself in a tunnel. He didn't even like tunnels. *Once again* sounded like an apology. And finding yourself was becoming tiresome. Especially when you knew exactly—in *meticulous* detail—how you had got there and what you were about to do next. Years of school-bus rides had imposed upon Jude the certainty of who he was and where he came from. Nothing was more premeditated than surprise.

Yet, for some reason, people wanted to put him in the ground. Rosa's words came ringing at him like so many clamorous alarum bells, in a mad expostulation to the fury of the fire. 'People are there to kill you.' This time though, his killer was not Magnus but Bjørn Morten Bjørnsen. Not so competent a guide; a wholly absent-minded one; but one with innate Norwegian knowledges. Tracking, fishing, stonemasonry, snowcrafts, these things to him were as engraven laws, their currency unquestioned. Above all Bjørn was lucky. Ridiculously lucky.

And it wasn't the Glum Valley this time. It was the outskirts of central Vienna, beyond the

Ringstrasse, near one of the many tributaries to the great *Danau Kanal*, at *6:14* on a December evening. A shade of snow lined every pole, post and yard. They had jumped a bent mesh-fence, tramped over a tip and entered the sewer system through an iron door. Now they stood with flaming torches, ready to penetrate the city.

Jude had been here before. 'Seen one, you've seen them all' he said darkly. '*Except*'—turning to Bjørn—'that the thing about seeing *one* and seeing *them all* is that both are dependent on *seeing*; a precarious dependence, in the light, as it were, of your fetishist insistence on fire.' Jude's back arched peremptorily. Under the torch he was sallow, rouge-edged. Behind him was the oil can. He put a flask of vodka in Bjørn's rucksack—for the inner and outer fires—left the can where it stood, moved into the abyss.

'Wh, you're talking about the torch?' said Bjørn. 'But, I mainTAIN, if we're going to do this, we've—we've got to be doing this au-TENTIC. We've got to be completely dependent on our FIRE. Build up a close relation. Er, we've got to be feeling that it's a matter of surVIVAL. Nn, keep your LAMP TRIMMED and BURNING! Besides,' he added, 'if we use a flashlight, we might have to be asking ourselves if we're insane'.

'Yes, much as I hate to agree with Saint, nothing is more *rational* than fire,' said Jude, unusually placatory. All the same he tapped a cold hand on the pen-torch in his pocket.

'Nn, you've got to be on the edge a little bit, feeling that sense of DANGER when you're inside a TUNNEL like this.' Bjørn hesitated, then perked: 'Nnn, like you ARE inside a tunnel!' he rejoined, '—and—and AT ANY MOMENT could fall—er— eighty-nine, ninety feet,'—there was no way out— 'over a BARBED WIRE CLIFF'.

Jude was discomfited. Where could you turn now? Both toyed a while with finality, before, like a tall mouse, Bjørn dove his arm into a gesture of continuation. 'Mmmm, this was the WAY,' he said, emphatically. In many ways, Bjørn's whole life was about the struggle *for*, climax *in* and recovery *from*, emphasis—a routine which practice had made perfect, and which he maintained in fast disregard for public approbation. 'Those guys at my CHESS CLUB—they—er—could show you around better than I could. Maybe we will not be able to see all the, ah, nooks and CRANNIES in the THIRD MAN because uh ah I know that one place you have to be turning down a certain OTHER tunnel, which I might not remember when we come to it.'

'They use your so-called *flashlights* in The Third Man'.

'Nnn, they would probably be better guides than me. I have no doubts about that, I, er, don't mind, er, to adMITT that is probably a FACTT.' Bjørn had an unerring instinct for turning admission into assertion; or, Jude might have said, a decidedly *erring*, not to say pathological, inability to avoid doing so. 'But, ah, we have to be PIONEERS!' Bjørn also spoke slowly, in clockwork cycles, through six-ish hesitations to twelve-like triumphs, each reacting to each. He leapt easily from overcompensation to conviction, as over a chasm's creaking bridge.

'Though, of course, all conviction is overcompensation,' meditated Jude. 'The decisions have been made and positions long since taken. Conviction is *necessarily* unconvinced.'

Either way, they continued to the city's heart. It was a cold heart, a freezing, kitsch, pre-Christmas heart, but, wearing only a thin rain-jacket, Bjørn was gesturing long-windedly at nooks, cruel-handedly at crannies, as if one could forget context entirely. Jude, an experienced slighter of the elements, conscious scotcher of the worldwide exaggeration of meteorological significance, was nevertheless annoyed by the imperviousness of the Norwegian—even to the dialectic of pervious and impervious. 'A pervious logic,' he muttered, huddled in his parka, eyeing the slides of droplets on the walls, the confluence of endless channels. 'And, like all perviosity, deeply sexless.' Down to the light's end went his eyes, and fled the picture.

But, 'uhh, we did not come for SEXUAL CONQUEST,' retorted Bjørn, sensing a general unwillingness. 'Mmmh, not everything has to be sexual. Sometimes we just gotta put the SEXUAL to the back of our MINDS. A HIBERNATION period, I guess, you could say.'

'Before its climactic rediscovery by psychoanalysis.' Jude's mouth was as dry as his voice.

'Nn, I'm up for a little bit of PSYCHOANALYSIS.'

'Look—*look*—around you. Consider *extremely consciously* the fact that *you, Bjorn Morten Bjornsen*, are *extremely consciously* exploring a sewer, at *six fifty-six* on a Friday night. See the *channel running*. Feel that cold *along your spine! Behold*, in your *earthquake-begotten Norwegian heart*, the *origin and end* of your psychoanalysis.'

'Mmmh...wha...' strained Bjørn. 'Of course, I'm always up for a little bit of SEX as well. But, er, we men, we don't need to be seeing the sexual in everything. We need to, we need to be seeing a clear—separation, sometimes, between the functional and the aes-TETIC.' He curled his fingers as if the water was fine. 'Ah, of course, sex can be functional too. As a biologist, I would HAVE to take that position! But sometimes, when we got a job to do, we got to stick to that quite—er, ah'—he staggered to stop Jude interrupting—

'UNSPARINGLY.'

'I bet you'd like to be seeing Kara Kundera's aestetic.'

'Oh—oh no—But that—that—'

'No, sir, I suspect your *clear separation*: an aesthetic fantasy, masking, like all aesthetics, a terrifying function.'

'Ohh, er—but—ha ha—but that is how we can be concentrating MORE on the sexual. I, I would not be saying that I'm too much of a sexist'—Jude tried to interrupt him but—'Mmwe're no different from NEANDERTHALS in some ways! But we men, we shouldn't be feeling bad when we come in the face of something not—DEFINED by sexuality, er, even if I myself am reading, maybe too much, sexual metaphors into certain BLUES lyrics. I MYSELF may do that too much! But, sometimes, real action, that can be the CLEAR BREAK that can set us up, ah, for sexual RENEWAL.'

Jude attempted to say something again, but—'EeerONCE again the magnificent game of CHESS shows so many, er, metaphors which you see in life. Because'—warming to his theme now—'because in CHESSS you can be seeing the game in TWO WAYS!'

They chuckled in sudden benignity, in the general direction of Studs Terkel.

They were momentarily waylaid.

'Mmm, there's TWO WAYS of seeing how we

can—approach the game of chess. Because they often say there are, in chess, TACTICS and STRATEGY! TACTICS, that's your functional play, when you look to, ya, to make combinations, or capture a quick piece, or make short-term gains. Often this is a more flashy, yee-aah—a showmanship type of game, with perhaps tech-nic-al wizardry and ATTACKING FIREWORKS. An example of this type of player would be—perhaps MAX **EUWE!**' So strong was the emphasis here, it seemed to contain the upper and lower vocal registers at the same time. 'MAX **EUWE** could see combinations probably in SECONDS that most other people would never be able to calculate. But they say perhaps his STRATEGIC play was not so strong, even though he, er, struggled for a long time to MASTER that side of the game. He couldn't do—ah of course, he could do it far better than ninety-nine PER CENT of ordinary mortals—but among the top levels of CHESS he was not so able to be seeing the more strategic AS-PECTSS of the game. That is where you need to be seeing more LONG-TERM patterns, where you might be making more quiet moves, or thinking about the controlling of certain KEY SQUARES....Ah, like the successor to Euwe, the great MIKHAIL **BOTVINNIKKK**!' Bjørn fed on the historic consonants, as on mountain air. 'Right there you can be seeing the contrast in styles. MIKHAIL **BOTVINNIKKK**, maah, they say was a great STRATEGIC thinker, with a fantastical level of ah OPENING PREPARATION.'

Unfailingly astonished, if not at all surprised, by Bjørn's epic persistence, Jude nevertheless made noises of interest. He was at too much mercy to spurn the combined might of Euwe and Botvinnik altogether, and had been, after only five minutes, so far stepped that to go back would be as weary as to go on. A single step, in fact, was enough to precipitate this contradiction, so that Macbeth's prognosis still looked optimistic, not to say delusional. 'Macbeth,' declared Jude, more Beckett than Shakespeare, 'is a drama queen. Real weariness walks belligerently from the stage.' But Jude, sociable misanthrope, theatrical in his own right, stepped neither back nor off, but plunged into the very depths and expanses of the stage, as if backstage were none.

They walked for half an hour. It was slow-going and you walked so close to the flame, privileging tactical fireworks over strategic progress. 'But CAPABLANCA, in nineteen TWENTY FOUR, against ah TartaKOWER, I think it is, is playing g**3**! in a similar position, which is certainly an EXCLAMATION POINT MOVE!' Bjørn was saying, 'sacrificing pawn material in the short term, for, er, a more CLASSICAL F**6** KING POSITION and the benefits of LONG TERM GAIN! Er, ALEKHINE is quite well known for saying about this game, ah, quite with poetical chess licence, that the black RIPE PAWNS are falling like APPLES.'

Drips and litter got in their way, and always at their left ran the water-course. In front, Bjørn pranced like an elf, on the balls of small feet. Around the feet, a pair of perfect-fit, brown trainers he had found in Budapest, utterly unconscious of his luck: 'Mmmh, my sneakers?' he sniffed, looking down with a drop at his nostrils, 'No, I bought them—er, in Budapest. Quite good old sneakers—.' But the subject failed to distract him and, although his eyes still stared at his shoes, his brain returned to its wonted ways. He was grizzled with flame on rain-jacketed shoulders, and his black hair shone red. Jude was hot on the face and his arm ached. But his back was cold. The darkness kept unfolding, and they passed a system of tunnels to their right. Arcs wept like angels over the thresholds. Now the stench began to rise. Rats pattered claws on the concrete. Jude bunched up. Bjørn flipped his raincoat collar. He felt like Tex Willer, with a dash of The Phantom thrown in.

'Nnn, if my chess colleague, Gerhard, was right, this pillar with this yellow stain means that we are not too far right now from one of the great old monuments of Vienna, the KARLSKIRCHE. And we are now coming close—I THINK—to one of the shots you are seeing in the THIRD MAN.'

They came to it, and, even by firelight, Jude's exacting eye saw clearly it was not the place.

'But, ah, I THINK it IS. Look! That curve! That'—Bjørn gestured with a straight arm, 'PERPENDICULAR!'

'*No*. I know the shot you mean. For a start that pillar is not there.'

'That—that what?' The echo was interfering.

'That *pillar*.'

'Willer?'

'*Pillar!*' said Jude, angrily.

'Nyah, okay, the angle of the shot does not include the pillar, but—'

'You *can't remember* a scene we watched only *last week*. For the *third time*.'

'Are you sure? It is true I DON'T remember the pillar.' The guide stood in thought. 'Oh, HOLD ON, a little bit further on—I could be confusing it,' he said, wandering vaguely forward. Jude trudged behind. Mishearings were the bane of his life; misremembrances, the death of him. He cast his mind back, to the last *Third Man*. It seemed only yesterday. He cast his mind a moon further, right into October. It wasn't long but it seemed like lifetimes. Arrival, obstruction, insistence, refusal, rage. *Landesamts*, *Wohnungsvermittlungs*, *Studentenheims*. Shenanigans at the Embassy.

Sleeping on Darko's illegal floor. Darko's general illegality; the etiquette it required. A room of *Jude's* (not *one's)* own. Bjørn's arrival, lingering, settling, laying his head in a bed on your floor, quoting and misquoting. More obstructions. The tragic bureaucratic cycles of denial, recognition, resignation. Baumgarten, Wellhausen, Putzfrau. The same tragic cycles. Intransigency, penury, sickness, despair, cynicism. Then rage again. Always rage. Familiar bedfellow, constant companion, at least before he stormed off, which was all the time. Bjørn's brief stint, almost *sojourn,* working at the porcelain factory. The added complication, not to say permutation, of A. The problem of the Modigliani exhibition. That moment, in *Mariahilfestrasse*, when he thought of packing it in. And then today, this afternoon, beside the *Riesenrad*, sunlight glancing off snow and the turning cubicles; hearing a pounding of fist on glass, seeing in the dazzle a familiar flash of teeth, a dash of black and white.

It was puzzling. In fact it was preposterous. No doubt the fact he had not eaten for two days had something to do with it, bar a nibble of soup at the Jewish Museum. And even then, only because Baumgarten smiled at him over *The Jewish Chronicle. Der Hungerkünstler* had actually got it right, albeit he was a feckless, adolescent wastrel, and non-vegan to boot; which meant that not only did he have no excuse, he had no shame either. No, there was no way round it, *Der Hungerkünstler* had got it *entirely* wrong. Not eating was not hard; you just had to not put things in your gullet. Naturally, this was made easier by the *Geldautomat* swallowing your card and discontinuing the flow of *Taschengeld* indefinitely. Vienna was a place where indefinition could go a long way. Everywhere you went they sold lingerie and flowers. Behind every Baroque façade was a socialist staircase; at every traffic-light a redundant button; through every closed door an Austrian, reluctant to confirm. Down every street, paved with the blood of Jews; by every plaque, gilt with the teeth of gypsies; into every personal space, built with the flesh of perverts, inverts, subverts of all kinds, gathered the breath of the indefinite, smelling of *Bratwurst*. All this Jude mulled over, slopping in his *all-stars* through the pools, returning, as if for the thousandth time, to the *Riesenrad*. There was the Wheel; there was Martins, rangy and darkened against the shifting sky; himself shifting too, restless, but manly, obstinate, self-affirming, bound to turn up anti-romantically in history; to infuriate but never to disappoint. And there—barely substance, little but signifier—the *anonym*. There it moved; was seen only in stages; appeared not to have moved at all from the last time we looked; paused, with emphasis, so that we would recognise it as such, perhaps even question it (what trick of bluff and counter-bluff?); then developed into the oncoming third man, breezily real. And this third man developing into the somewhat waddling and vicious Orson Welles, 'with his cheeks in a chunk and his cheese in the cash', suddenly upon us and through the open gate of the encounter; and still insignificant, despite all the stagy staginess of his imminence.

He couldn't wipe the scene from his mind. How could someone go from being an absence to a presence so unspectacularly? Perfect deferral to fat killer in twenty waddling steps. The world was a cheat. There was nothing to see down here. There was nothing to see up there. No need to dig deeper than a grave. The stench was lurid now, touching every tip of them. Foul sludge floated by, with an air of destiny. Vienna. The winter city, the erotic city, city of secrecy and cakes. This is what it was founded on. All that *Wurst* had to go somewhere. Down here, in fact, and up your nostrils till you gagged. 'No Wurst, there is none,' mulled Jude. 'The Wurst is not, while we can say *this is the Wurst*. Murder most foul, as in the Wurst it is.'

'Nn,' said Bjørn. 'It's not THATT bad.'

Either way, the air was warmer for it. For a while they stared, replete, as the main course cleared, dessert drifted by, sugars did their slow dissolve, and creams collected at the edges, seeming to sue for mercy. They listened, newly sceptical. Even Bjørn breathed the fog of disenchantment. A *flip-flap*, as of steps, decorated round; same steps that had haunted them earlier this evening, as they left Rosa's apartment, fresh from painting. A faint light and hum suggested vents or exits; the nearness of surface. They scattered on, imitating the rats, via cavern, under archway, past sudden pillars, affording them the merest of rueful glances, forgetting all but bent on exteriors. And with speed, in Jude's soft heart, came fear—of flight itself. But the dark drew again and the hum was dimmer. The *flip-flap* faded, or was surpassed, by a thin rush of water down stone. They held their torches low, watching their steps as they fell to a trot. The tunnel was bending, floor sloping, and abruptly they plunged, scissor-limbed, stifle-cried, into blank and flood, *and the sacred fires slept with their hallelujahs.*

'Oh, oh no,' said Bjørn, picking up his arms and legs. His jacket was wet the way down, and his trousers too. This was a matter of sensation. It was so dark you didn't remember you had eyes. He turned, expecting to hear a torrent of curses and recrimination.

'*Wahahaha-craheee! Aaaah! Aaaah!*' gibbered Jude, freezing and delighted, slipping and sliding on the rock and, head down in the stream, trying to pivot himself on the torch-stick, suddenly the only constant in his world. Everything else was chaos.

Bjørn couldn't see it, but he listened—conscious, like the cream, of small mercies. He slid a little on the incline, where four inches of water cascaded right to left, shelfing over his fallen torch. 'Four inches of water in a lonely ditch,' he said to himself. After a while, he perceived the gleam of the fall, like the light of one star. He picked up the torch, all real and useless now.

'Nn, darkness', he said. He stood like the Long Man of Wilmington, up for a little bit of sex and sadly disabused.

'*Waaah! Weee!*' screamed Jude, and laughed like a breaking machine-gun.

'Where is your torch?'

'My *hand!* In my *hahahahaha!*' The water streamed into his mouth and so what if he drank it?

'You should keep it DRY!'

'Dry. *Drahahahahahahahah*!' Jude slipped on his back and lay there, with the torch-stick triumphant, water assuming his hair. Bjørn felt his way and took the stick from Jude's hand. He tiptoed across the stream in the pure Norwegian tradition, instinct with the ice of millennia. Into his mind came the great Bergenian grannies toing and froing with shopping on the steep ice-slopes. Into his mind came Peer Gynt, Bjørn Daehlie, Harald Haarfaar and his seaborne sword; and in their famous toesteps he stepped, reaching the side with a sprinkle. Jude joined him, bumping into his shins. He was wet both sides, and shivering.

'You idiot, Bjornsen. Of course we are ruined.'

'Not RUINED. It is dry ground here. And there is the FAINTESTT light. We are not too far from the surface. Ah, in fact, I think, if I remember, we may be QUITE NEAR the OPERA HOUSE. Maybe we can be out, er, after half an hour, or LESS, if we could RE-LIGHTT the TORCH. Ah, we would need of course to find some old rags. And, don't forget, I still have my BOX of MATCHES!' Bjørn's enthusiasm was fading, but reason was emerging in its stead. He crawled about, a large full-circle, feeling for rags, papers, anything to burn.

Jude lifted his chin. 'Well count yourself kissed, Bjornsen, and the cock thrice crowing.' Like a great betrayer, he produced the small pen-torch from his pocket. He shook it once, blinked, and twisted the head. A cold beam broke from the bulb, slightly disappointing. If anything it made the dark seem more voluminous. All it brought into focus were Bjørn's elfin nostrils, trembling as he rose from his emptyhanded knees.

'Nn, WHAT! That's, er, that's INCREDIBLY SMART THINKING! Ah, nnnNI'M just gonna have to take back everything I SAID back there! Na, I had some FANCY IDEA about

PROMETHEAN FIRE, and all the WHILE, you were secretly carrying the fruits of mankind's labours in the vineyard of TECHNOLOGY!'

'My pocket.'

'It was, ah, of course, YOU, in the end, who was the STRATEGIST, and ME, after all, that was the TACTICAL PLAYER, wanting, ah, short-term effects over long-term VISION. Er, I suppose you could say, of course, that the strategic player is just thinking TOO MUCH about VISIONS and ABSTRACTIONS, in which case it might be THAT one which you associate with me. Nn, whereas YOU were actually the TACTICAL PLAYER!' Bjørn shook in the air a hook-like hand, thrilled with the irony of it all. He was determined that Jude would see his point. He had carried it so far now, he couldn't very well give up on it. 'Nn, just disMISSING in an instant all that JIVING AROUND, all that CHATTER, about autenTICITY, ah, although, of course, I feel there is something TO that, ah, that's not wholly out of the question, even now, but, ah, of course, there's always the possibility that we can take that TOO FAR and make MARTYRS and SACRIFICES of ourselves, in the ROMANTIC name of—'

As Bjørn reached a crescendo, the beam shortened and died, as if swallowed by the pen.

'N—'

'Fuck.'

‘Oh no.’

Jude rattled the pen, pressed the face, twisted its head this way and that, and unscrewed the tail. He turned the battery about, tried again. He turned it back about, flourished it conductor-like. But the band wouldn’t play.

‘Daa, what’s happening there?’

‘Do you have a battery by any chance? For a pen-torch.’

‘Er—nnNO,’ said Bjørn, beginning in hesitation but ending in emphasis.

Jude threw the torch to the void. There was a smash above the rush. ‘*Fuck!*’ he said again. He rummaged in the dark of his parka. ‘*Hmmm.*’ He patted. He rustled. Fingers felt swiftly over silver. ‘*Notwithstanding*,’ he demurred. There was a new slyness to him. He was not, after all, to be denied the glory of betrayal. ‘Notwith*standing*.’ And he drew something invisibly from his side. ‘There is always Pilar Santana Artale, and her stolen fire.’ There was a scrape, a *click,* and a big, expensive lighter leapt reliably into life. Better than hopeful, it was appropriate. ‘The opposite of light,’ confirmed Jude, flame triumphant at his thumb. Bjørn handled it, amazed at mystic womankind. ‘IGnem VENi!’ he marvelled. ‘MittERe in TERRam!’ They collected themselves, cheered by fortune; but as they turned to go, Bjørn stopped and angled his foot ninety degrees, smelling with an outraised finger.

'But—what is that?' he asked.
'What?'
'On my hand.' He dithered about, gesturing high and diminishing low. 'And, oh, look here on the floor. Blood!'
'Well, you've cut yourself.'
'No, LOTS of blood. Here, in a puddle.' He inched along the ground. 'And—here—in—front—dripping—here—leading—and HERE—wandering—to the WATER'S EDGE!'
Jude joined him, scrutinising his hand. Bjørn was right. It was a lot of blood. They examined themselves in the flame; turned cut palms, rolled trouser legs, checked backs: scrapes and scratches, but nothing so viscous.
'Uhhh, this is INTERESTING! PerHAPS our quest has not been all in VAIN!' said Bjørn. As if it were child's play, he recrossed the stream. The trail had vanished. Wherever it derived, the stream absorbed it. Crossing back, in the thrown illumings, Bjørn saw Jude standing stock still, with slight eyes, weighing the flood, and judging it too. To his right the cascade levelled off, rushing into blackness.
'The blood stops at the WATER' intoned the Norwegian. 'None beyond'.
Jude said nothing.
Bjørn looked excited. 'An, an ADVENTURE.' He wanted to share his sheepishness. 'Nn, this

could almost be like a FILM.'

'Isn't this cascade the one in *The Third Man?*' said Jude. 'Where *Orson Welles* realises the game is up.'

'Nn what? Gih, uh, ah the game is UP. Er, now, you're right—of course you are right. How could I forGET? I thought we had come to this by another WAY. Now I see it! The same slope, the water RUSHING. But, that means, we might only be five or ten minutes away. I seemm to have been MISS-LED. I think we just need to go down here, and here, to follow, in FACT, inciDENTally, though as if by DESIGN—THIS TRAIL OF BLOOD!'

They followed the trail of blood, now scarce, now abundant, as it staggered through the tunnel, with the lighter low and Bjørn bent, a philanthropic Long Man, administering charities. Occasionally, he lost sight of it, but looking round, found he had followed it nonetheless. Or perhaps it had followed him, it was hard to know. Either way, in five minutes the darkness coloured like a beaten eye and they emerged in a chamber with a ladder ascending under what might have been the lit edges of a manhole. The blood approached them over the floor, leading back whence they came. Bjørn was exultant now, able at last to justify his role:

'THIS! THIS—ah, could this be—where they filmed the great DEATH scene of the THIRD MAN! No, ah, perhaps not. When Orson WELLES is wanting to climb that ladder to the light. And he is shot DOWN!—ah, not by a hungry kid trying to make a name for himself, but by a hungry man in any case, who already has a small name for himself as a WRITER. HOLLY MARTINS, er, of course, is his name. But a man who is still HUNGRY, in a way, trying to discover the TRUTH behind the MYSTERY of the THIRD MAN!'

'Do we exit here?' Jude was shivering uncontrollably.

'And now, right here, we have our own MYSTERY, our own trail of BLOOD, our own THIRD MAN to be following, hungry every bit as Holly MARTINS HIMSELF.'

'Do we *exit* here?'

'Not here. That does not open. We tried it before. But—better STILL—we exitt somewhere else QUITE CLOSE now, which you just gotta SEE.'

'I have because I'm actually hyperthermic now.'

Bjørn could see whole carven lists of possibilities. 'But just before we get there, there is a fanTASTIC, ah, NOOKK, which you just gotta be seeing, back—'

'*No*. No. I'm not going to be seeing neither nook, nor cranny, no not prominence, protuberance, alcove, slit or ingle, and I care not who KNOWS IT,' said Jude loudly. 'You must understand that, unlike Monsieur Valdemar, I am DYING.'

Bjørn, who, for all his huge immunity, did

understand that final Harlovian tone, began to concede. 'Ahh, I suppose, you must be cold. I acCEPT that' he grimaced, sheepish again. 'And, probably TIRED. NN, ah, THAT cannot be discounted! But tiredness cannot be allowed to rule our consciousness here. There will be time for sleep, eventually. And, ah, as we know, SLEEP ravels up the RAVELLED SLEEVE OF DAY! Surely we just have to follow this trail, at least while it goes in our direction. NnnNNNNweCANNOT allow ourselves to LOSE this OPPORTUNITY, even at the expense of our health. We have to be thinking what is more IMPORTANT.' He turned and tried a new tack. 'Er, just come this way. I think anyway it may lead to our own EXIT OF CHOICE.'

Bjørn was pleased with these last well-chosen words in a language not his own, well-chosen because they involved the suggestion of choice, so dear to well-choosing and those who sail in her. Bjørn knew Jude sailed in her. Well-chosen words were Jude's fort and bastion, and it was cunning flattery to make him think the exit he necessarily sought was in fact his exit of choice. Becalmed for the present, he pressed on behind the lit black wick Bjørn's back figured in the dark. But the blood bothered him, and, in the back of his mind and therefore his body, what bothered him more was the motiveless absence behind him, ready at any moment to motivelessly and absently go mad. And the back of his mind was itself that absence, inseparable from the front of it! Maybe it was him. Maybe *he* was the one.

Two minutes and they came to another, smaller chamber, darker than the last, but with a similar iron-runged ladder scaling the wall to one side. Bjørn peered at the rungs, pointing the lighter.

'*It is AS I THOUGHT*!' he loudly whispered. His whisper was always escaping into emphasis. It wasn't even clear why he was whispering in the first place. '*The blood climbs the LADDER. Or, er rather, DESCENDS the LADDER!*' He ran a straight, pointing arm from top to bottom. '*And this is our exit!*' This last for solidarity. '*So we can kill TWO FLIES with ONE SMACKK!*'

Pleased at this coincidence of motives, Bjørn began robustly and long-leggedly to climb the ladder, lighter in hand, murmuring '*what you just gotta SEE.*' Jude watched him from below, avoiding the flakes snowing from his sneakers. He looked a comet, shooting to the void to the ringing of iron. Just when it was a small ball of red in the immensity, it broke abruptly into general light, reflecting on close interior walls. Bjørn must have reached a narrow room. Jude began to climb. There was something conspicuously like dried blood on the rungs. He didn't like it, sir. He thought of his own hands, cut on the rocks. He began to think about the probability of infection. He liked it even less. Everywhere he put his hand he encountered crags and volcanoes of blood, replete with diseases. *All-stars* flashing, he leapt terrified and harmless into a painted kiosk, about five feet wide on all sides, with head-height blackwashed windows where the roof domed over and the street-light was dimmed. Bjørn stood there, sweaty and sharp, an origami-man. He held aloft the lighter and, in the green and reddish glow, the kiosk seemed just then the last homely house, warmer and safer; a between-worlds Jude had no love to leave.

*

'Where—*WHERE*—do you think we two are standing right now?' said Bjørn, poised. Jude exhaled through the anticipant quiet. He guessed where he was, or at least where Bjørn thought he was, but acknowledging it was another matter. Always sceptical of ends, here, at last, was his clapboard limbo; makeshift, temporary, apt to blow away with the first whipping *Marchfeld* wind. It was strangely comfortable. But there was a grasping strain to his softness, as if, here, in a silly green hut, at the tail end of the Viennese evening, he could let it all slip, a lifetime of carniverous restraint, and vegan rage, do the unthinkable and curl in a cosy corner. Bjørn made a nudging noise.

The flame crackled. Even the blood on the floor was comforting.

'In the *kiosk*, I presume, via which Orson Welles escapes the unwanted attentions of Holly Martins,' he puffed.

'That, er, THAT would be MY ESTIMATION,' said Bjørn. He tapped the walls, as if confirming the theory. 'We just gotta be following this trail outside now.'

Jude nodded. The door had a bathroom-style slide lock, but it wasn't pulled across. Bjørn nudged at the door and they stood in a square, blinking. Lamps ranged round the corners; cobbles gleamed; the road was sane and reasonable. It wasn't the square in which Orson Welles disappeared. It wasn't the kiosk either. It was an entirely different looking contraption, covered with posters advertising Jules Arles.

Somewhere a bell tolled nine. 'Nnn, could THIS be, ah, oh no, no,' said Bjørn, still as a statue, pointing with half an arm. The want of coincidence was overbearing. Also overbearing was a sudden wind which whipped round the corner. 'There you go,' said Jude, tensing. 'Your *Marchfeld*, *Wienerwalder*, *Vindabonan* wind. Wont to whip round a corner at the slightest of provocations. Anything to invade a personal space.'

As if balking that wind, the blood led back round the corner, then staggered away down sidestreets.

They staggered after it, from point to point, until it hit an arched green door opposite the *Ruprechtskirche.* With resignation bordering on disgust, Jude voiced what they both were thinking. 'Yes yes, the trail—the *bloodline*, if you will—leads directly, *compulsively*, to Rosa Wellhausen's. An Origin and End if ever there was one. *Causa Bellum* and *Grand Desideratum*, rolled *voluptuously* into one.'

They beat toward the door. It opened to a small courtyard, crowded with flowers. There were bikes, barrels, and a bench too, which, combined with the flowers, lent the whole a sort of orderly dishevelment. Halfway along the left-hand wall was an open arch; within, a spiral stair. The stairwell looked as always: pale, impassive, never more than six steps from disappearance. It wound and tapered like something from Pirandelli—a comparison, no doubt, which would have pleased the occupants. Loathe to play the foil, either to Pirandelli or the stairwell, Jude chased the blood two flights up and hammered on another green door, ringing the bell for good measure. At length, it was opened and Rosa leaned in the door, wine-glass in hand, looking from one to the other.

'What is it?' She seemed in no hurry to admit them.

'There's blood on your stair.' Jude pointed to the stair. It was the kind of pale that blood bounces from.

'So there is.'

'It's all over Vienna.'

'What's new?'

'It leads to your door, by the look of it.'

'Yes, or from it—potentially.'

'Ha! *Potentially.*'

'You don't seem particularly concerned.'

'Neither do you.'

'You're not the one who may have been hurt.'

'Is that an excuse?'

'Not for you.'

Jude cleared his throat. 'Anyone who contrives a situation in which an incriminating—incriminatingly *repetitive*—bloodstain links a sewer to their door, or *vice-versa*, does not require sympathy. Excuses *perhaps*.'

'Even if they were mortally wounded.'

'Especially so.'

'Then you'd better come in while I come up with them.'

They shuffled feet on the doormat, removed their shoes, and went into a yellow panelled hall, with a packed hat-stand and a large framed photograph of postwar Vienna, 'bombed about a bit'. Strangely, from down the hall came the smell of fresh baked bread. Rosa was already in the living room, facing the street. 'It's late for dinner,' she said. 'What will you drink? And don't sit down. I'll see if I can find some blankets. Otherwise you'll have to take your clothes off.'

She disappeared for blankets, came back, threw them on the furniture, went away again. They eyed each other, eyeing the room, eyed in their turn by an astonishing grey Siamese, draped along the windowsill, name of Raoul. In the hall were old newspapers, cans, paintbrushes, but, except for some careless daubs over the door, the new coat had not spread this far. Here, all was neat and faded. There was little furniture; just a fine, redwine settle where Bjørn sat down, carefully, on his blanket, and a couple of elegant grey armchairs, one of which Jude more carelessly reclined in. They were arranged round a coffee-table and fireplace, unused. In a corner was a large wood cabinet, and the rest was shelves, stuffed with magazines, newspapers, journals, photography, vinyl and books, piled up and spilling over: books on everything from origami to autism, Catherine the Great to the Great Barrier Reef, Harlequins and head-dresses, sandstone, limestone and brownstone walk-ups, Cycladean burials and Yukon cairns. There was Ibsen, Beckett and Brecht. Cervantes, Chekhov, Montesquieu and Paine. Dumas, Defoe, Dostoevsky. It was all too much. You needed a crowbar to tell them apart. There were Voltaire's letters, Blake's illuminations, the Complete Casanova, and, over here, on the gnarled old table,

Nashe's *Lenten Stuff*. Jude pulled at this last and thumbed through it, remarking Rosa's indiscrimination. But, as if remarking the contrary, the book bent to a particular page, where several lines were thickly marked. Jude regarded the fireplace. If Rosa *would* leave the room, *busying* herself in the most languorous possible manner, what could a man do but take advantage? If a woman was going to let her guard down, it practically *behoved* a man to take an unabashed gander. Jude took an unabashed gander now.

'Noble Caesarian Charlemagne herring,' said the *Lenten Stuff*.

> *Pliny and Gesner were to blame they slubbered thee over so negligently. I do not see why any man should envy thee, since thou art none of those lurcones or epulones, gluttons or fleshpots of Egypt (as one that writes of the Christians' captivity under the Turk enstyleth us English men), nor livest thou by the unliving or eviscerating of others, as most fishes do, or by any extraordinary filth whatsoever, but, as the chameleon liveth by the air and the salamander by the fire, so only by the water art thou nourished and nought else, and must swim as well dead as live.*

Jude frowned, once more remarking Rosa's

indiscrimination. But Bjørn decided enough was enough. He slapped his knees. 'Na ya, a—a glass of, er, RED WINE,' he called. Rosa came to the doorway. 'Er, for me. Ah, of course, that is if you have any RED WINE.'

Rosa raised her eyebrows. Jude raised his higher. The astonishing cat pricked its ears, wore an irked look in those amber eyes.

'Red wine?' said Jude, apologetically.

Rosa brought a bottle and worked the cork till it crumbled. Bjørn lapsed his eyes. *Gusto* and *sabor*, said the bottle. *Carne*. It stood on the table like a crusted scar: together they spoke of shipwreck. Rosa disappeared, returning again with a knife, a breadboard and a loaf of bread. It was *Schwarzbrot,* heavy as theology, and she cut them both a slab.

Jude examined his. 'You know what I like about you, *Rosa*,' he said, abusing slab and eyelashes both. 'Not only are you a *junkyard angel*, but, more importantly, you *always give me bread*.' This was an exceptionally long emphasis, and he put a lot into it. But however much he put into it, Rosa took more away. It was a moot point whether nose or eyebrow was raised the higher. 'But then nose and eyebrow, and their *conjunction*, are points inherently *moot*,' observed Jude later, 'indeed, could be said to be the very embodiment of the *moot*, without which it is but theory.'

Either way, she sat beside Bjørn, tucking up her

legs on one side. She was wearing grey stockings, a short dress, navy blue, and a black baggy jumper. Nothing she did—nothing she wore—was any surprise to Jude. That was what she hadn't banked on. It rendered irrelevant all her moves and feints. Just like the Lizard Lie. He was even prepared to tolerate that baggy jumper, the mood he was in. At least her rear was tidy. She was like a mermaid in that respect—a mess on top, but damn fine from the waist down.

She filled beakers and they clinked them.

'Now what are you doing here?'

'And everything was going so hospitably.'

Bjørn was still chuckling. 'Err, mmgh, trying to KILL somebody or DIE TRYING.'

The astonishing cat stretched its fine, brilliant length, one side then the other, arced from the windowsill and was down the hall with a patter. An open copy of *The Cenci* was left in its wake, silvered with hairs.

Rosa lit a cigarette, offering one to Jude. 'They smoke my cigarettes, they drink my wine,' she said.

'They, er, DIG my EARTH.' Bjørn looked knowingly at his lap. He seemed amused by his wine. His hand was clamped on the glass.

'With your bare hands, from the look of you. Why don't you wash them before you touch things?'

'Yes.' Jude's smile was pacific. 'Like a weary

westerly moon, we've seen enough earth for one night.' He leaned forward. 'But the blood which *cries* from it—is another *issue.*' He raised a single eyebrow.

'You're very concerned about that.'

'I think, er, maybe you need a bit of CONTEXT here. We have just—er—I don't mind saying—we have just been exploring CENTRAL VIENNA, via the SEWER SYSTEM.'

'Ah, you've been doing the sewer thing.'

Jude started up. 'Yes, that's right. The re*cycled*, re*gurg*itated sewer-thing. The veritable *cliché* of blood.' He tapped the window, indicating the street. 'The *tiresome* trail, to the *boring* door.'

Rosa blew a jet. 'Benjamin Kepperly-Lie,' she said.

'Ha! What about him?'

She touched the ash. 'It's him.'

'Benjamin *McCormack* Kepperly-Lie?'

'The same.'

Jude took it in. '*What?*' he said. It was the shock that scorned itself. 'Why?'

'You'll have to ask him yourself, if you can find him.'

Rosa relit the cigarette, serious-seeming. Jude was clenching and unclenching his jaw, furious with the world. 'No, you're all *losing your grip*,' he said at length. 'You, Harper, The Spectre—even Kepperly-Lie (though hardest to credit). *Losing your minds.*' He tapped his head this time. '*Get* that grip. *Don't go insane.*'

'Why would I lie?'

Bjørn feinted for a instant. Jude didn't let him in.

'You mistake me. I accuse your *sincerity.*'

'You really think it all revolves around you?'

'No, *you* think so. I know it *doesn't.*'

'He was in a fight, of all absurdities, with a friend of mine. Right there.' She indicated the stairwell. 'Just a bloody nose. Why he went into the sewer is anyone's guess.'

'And the cause—the *cause?*'

'Me.' Rosa emitted a chuckle.

'Any special reason why he happens to be in Vienna?'

'Me.'

'Oh I see.'

'You're quick.'

'Well you pick things up. Don't you.'

'Occasionally.'

Jude looked icy. Rosa was an idiot. The Lie was an idiot. The whole thing was completely credible, not so much because it was so hard to credit, as because it asserted as much. What was worse—and most credible of all—it did so silently, knowingly, daring you to interrogate it. And if there was one thing Jude refused to do, it was *interrogate*—a moral compromise, if ever there was one. Not fortunately, but inevitably, Jude had had plenty of practice at this sort of thing with Magnus. There was nothing for it but total acceptance, followed by swift dismissal, of the premise.

'I see,' he said. 'And you're not going to go after him then.'

'He's really old enough to look after himself.' Rosa could see the turn this was taking. It was her room but she didn't want to be the last to leave. 'I won't stop you, though' she said, unfolding her legs. 'Go back to the God-damn sewer. Or the *Wohnungsvermittlung*. He's been looking for a room, I gather. Or try the *Casanova*—he's a regular there. Fallen in with some preposterous old man.' She said it as if they didn't all know exactly who she was talking about.

'And tell me,' said Jude, exhaling. He was looking to the side, through half-closed eyes, as if that were where the joke was hiding. 'This old man—who is fond, no doubt, of nick-nack and paddy-wack too—is he on the rotund side?' They knew he was. With precise hands, Jude designated rotundity, as if it had specific dimensions. The jokes were down to him again. Who else here was even remotely funny? 'Wearing a white suit,' he persisted, 'a Homburg hat, large tinted glasses—before a pair of *plaguey* eyes?' His stretched eyes expressed plagueyness, and threw in rheum and dropsy for good measure. 'With a rotten frog's mouth and teeth like a church window?'

'You know him well,' said Rosa. But she cocked a knee, impressed with the charade.

'Oh he's a total nonentity. Nevertheless, an obvious nonentity, whom it will be almost as easy to trace as to *describe*.'

'Then try the *Casanova.* Or you can finish the bottle.' Rosa reached the door, pointed back at them, swung into the hall. 'Either way, I'm taking a bath.'

Bjørn thought they should go, but Jude was in no hurry. He was willing to finish the bottle—and the *Lenten Stuff* while he was at it. This could take all night. Rosa would find them in the morning—Bjørn curled woodenly on the settle and he, Jude, red-eyed over his *Lenten Stuff.*

'Ah, ahem, don't you think we should LOOK for him?'

Jude didn't. Rosa was right. The Lie could look after himself. And even if he couldn't, no skin off Jude's chin. If he couldn't stand the heat, he shouldn't come in the kitchen. He shouldn't come to Vienna either.

'Nn, but it's BOUND TO BE RAINING OUTSIDE!' said Bjørn, removing *The Poems of John Taylor the Water Poet* from a side-table, to get at *Ulysses* underneath. He began to purr with pleasure. All of a sudden, Jude tired of Thomas Nashe. He folded his *Lenten Stuff*, and the book too, and looked around the room. It was an undecided place after all.

'Let's go.'

'Ah, okay.'

They pulled the door *zu,* tripped down the stairs and scattered into the street, all two of them. It was a cold, empty night. They returned along the trail, loitered by the kiosk, stared absently at doorways. Rosa. Kepperly-Lie. The sewers. They were sobering thoughts for anyone. What else was there to do? A siren wailed nearby. They trudged through the Christmas stalls, to the *Wohnungsvermittlung*, where the lights still blazed. Finding out where everyone boarded was a full-time job, for a great many people. Knocking thrice, they were admitted, and easily described their man. The *Vermittlung* denied all knowledge, but at the third time of asking revealed everything. '*War Gestern hier*,' it seemed. '*Ging sofort zum Palmenhaus, fragte nach dem Weg.*'

'*Das Palmenhaus*,' said Bjørn, between question and affirmation.

They liked Bjørn's way of going about things. Leastwise they preferred it to Jude's. It was a good-cop, bad-cop scenario. *'Wo bleibt dann der Dapperly-Lay?*' enquired the *Vermittlung,* but they were asking the wrong people. Jude and Bjørn made their way through the *Burggarten* towards Ohmann's bright-lit *Palmenhaus*, stopping for a *Glühwein* along the way. The *Burggarten* grew in the wake of Napoleon: a lateral reaction, Bjørn's type of reaction. Call it a quiet move, strategic.

Bjørn's feet scuffed on the gravel path. He had stopped to admire a bush. It was a short, stout thing, starting narrow, but shaping outward. At the top it drew in again, like an urn. Jude stared at it, confronted with self-comparisons. Brown, branchy; a thick twisted interior the eyes could get lost in. His were doing just this when they fastened on a glimmer. He looked closer. A white throat. A bird. In the bush, no less. Here was a thing. But on the other hand nothing could be done about it. He was removing his gaze when—another show of throat. Two birds. There were no stones around, only gravel, but, even if there had been, Jude was not in a killing mood, and Bjørn, he felt sure, was equally pacific, certainly while very precise conditions remained unmet, concerning the proximity of flies to smacks, upon the meeting of which he could become shockingly violent. Again Jude flicked his gaze, like so much shaving-cream, when at the furthest extremity of the bush, another throat unfolded, like a perfect expression. It was positively voluptuous. It might have been a bud, a fruit, a protuberance; but it was a bird. Typical. You wait for ages, then three come along.

He stood back, framing the bush in his gaze. Luminous throats gyred all over. Every conceivable nook was replete with bird-life, in all imaginable attitudes: all silent, all awake, fidgeting in the gloom. Finches, to be precise, with thick bills and brown plumage. Fat, too, and suspicious, with that dash of lace at the neck, like odd Dr. Johnsons, mixed mass and grace. The bush held them like a heaven. It was a balancing act. What little weight they had went to confirm its strength. Jude, on the other hand, lent it no strength, uplifted nothing. They were right to be suspicious. His part was two-dimensional, but the bush and its birds were a thrilling three. The whole round world, as Leadbelly might have said, and Bjørn actually did.

'The whole round WORLD.'

'A cosmos, sir.'

They stared at this phenomenon for a full five minutes. Passers-by passed by, equally suspicious. But the starers paid no heed. The *Glühwein* strengthened the stare, located it, as if it had stained the edges. Perhaps Bjørn was right. They could stay like this for hours, weighing *pros* and *cons*, pleased with themselves like Don Quixote. But the birds burst asunder, all together, all at once, swerving into evening over the *Hofburg*.

They cut through the *Palmenhaus*, through butterflies and teacups, pretending they wanted tea. *Hat ein Dapperly-Lay hier gegessen?*, they wanted to know. *Klein. Weiss. Mit Zähne?* '*Nein*,' said a waiter, '*aber so jemand hat gefragt, wann die Oper anfängt. Was möchten Sie?*'

'*Na, ja, er, ein kleines Kaffe,*' said Bjørn, wary of prices. The waiter went and they slipped from the door. At the *Operhaus* an usher had met a Dapperly-Lay, had had an in-depth discussion with him only last night, on the nature of acoustics. She could give them his email, suggested they try the *Kunsthistorisches* museum. He was into art. They trudged down the *Opernring*. The *Kunsthistorisches* was shut. They stared, disconsolate, at the *Heldenplatz*, 'lonesome for its heroes', relieved, in turn, of their enraptured fans. The city seemed a wake of funny customers asking for a bald albino. A man called Dapperly-Lay. They stumbled, unawares, upon the *Rathaus Weihnachtsmarkt,* brilliant with tinsel. It was a heavy crowd, and they stopped for another *Glühwein*, wondering what the mayor did in the *Rathaus*. Bjørn thought it was like Kafka in there, that there were a thousand different rooms, each one dedicated to some incomprehensible detail. At a fat desk, in some darkened office, the mayor was paddling a secretary's palm, deferring forever your vital petition. Jude disagreed. He thought the mayor spent his entire time roller-blading through cavernous ballrooms, in a state of exhilaration.

If you gave back your mug you got back a mark, but there was no incentive for that. They kept their mugs, slinking in the dark backs of the stalls. It was difficult to cross the streets, so getting home took longer than it should. They huddled from the wind under a road sign, where no shelter was afforded. Two poles was what it was, and a space for the wind to shoot through. Jude moved to one side where the traffic-light stood. He wiggled his finger under the crotch of the button box, where the suggestive button depended.

'This kind of thing,' he advanced, 'is the unwritten constitution of a nation. I mean, what could be more infrastructural than a nation's traffic lights? And that one has to wiggle—till it opens, shuts, bites and cuts—with a surreptitious finger, right here, under the belly and hindmost, is that not entirely indicative of national character? Not for nothing was this the birthplace of that singularly ignorant movement, National Socialism, which curled up its fists like a baby, and wiggled on its hands and knees. Not for nothing does an unscrupulous silence still roadblock the streets and stay in, stroking the thigh of Inquiry with a large feather. Not for nought does the Spectre of Fascism still drink tea on its apologetic arse, troubling you for the sugar. Everywhere you peer, silk and linen, the hint of perversion. No cataclysm will smash this Sodom. Just an ongoing network of disassociation among the monuments. What God works in seconds, we wait millenia for the industrious ants to do—unstack these bricks and mortar, tease the screws from the brass, split under the soles the slavish pavings. See how they slap them, the brave civilians! See how I stand all alone at this traffic light, wiggling my finger, waiting for the signal at the deserted road. See, on all sides, the *vast hectares* of unpeopled space. Now see that man in the distance, see his oncoming; observe the way he *rolls* from side to side, as if he were Orson Welles acting the part of Orson Welles acting the part of a man who has *imperiously faked his own death*; watch if he doesn't even check slightly in order to correct the angle of his attack and make a very *beeline* to the speaker of these words; study if you will the way he approacheth right up to me and stands directly beside me—*even here beside me!*— AND BREATHES A-DOWN MY NECK!'

This last tirade was indeed directed at a man in an overcoat, who had done exactly that, moving within a foot of Jude to await crossing the road. The man, taken aback by an outburst so specific, retreated to the distance of a metre. Bjørn stood apart beside the sign. He looked like the *Burghers of Calais*. Then they crossed the road.

*

The *Studentenheim* looked unusually spotless, but they shimmered up the staircase anyway, ate a weary-hearted bowl of oats. Back in Darko's room, where he was sleeping for reasons he could not remember, Jude had hot dreams. His dreams tended either to the monolithic, far outstripping the ravings of De Quincey (he had once dreamed, for several minutes, of nothing more than a quivering sea of beans) or the *extremely* elaborate—intricate, fully-formed narratives, packed with dialogue. This was one of the latter. He and Bjørn were visiting the *Casanova*, looking for the Lie. The Infidel had the night off. So did the big blonde, who made all the effort. A squat blonde had effortlessly replaced her, heels clacking, hips gyrating, hair shooting up like an oil strike. The moves were similar but the music was pumped from a sound-system and all the fire was gone. Jude Arles was nowhere to be seen. Neither was Columbo. You'd hardly have thought it was the same place.

The Panther was still there though. Jude resisted the temptation to have her disrobe him, opting instead for some serious flirtation on the subject of that very resistance, at the end of which she gave him a piece of paper and two of advice.

'Just take a right after the cinema. There's no sign, it's just a building. But I wouldn't bother if I were you. It's a weird place. I worked there for a night. Just—wwrrr!' She covered her face. Starting in the hips, an orchestrated shiver ran through her as if she were shaking herself from packaging. 'Weird.'

'We'll see.' Jude held up the paper, brushed

through avenues of coats, drapes, bouncers in no particular order.

Bjørn followed him onto the street, saying: 'Can't beLIEVE she's married to that singer. Nn, ah of course, he was an aMAZing musician—I've got to say, I've never HEARD anything like that—ah of course, I don't say it was the best thing I've ever heard, but then we don't need words like BEST and WORST, and all of that constant evaluATION of what is an experience in itself, unique and—as Soren KIERKeGAARD would say, incomMENSurable, although admittedly I have only read him in the English translation, which is ridiculous when you think about it. I really should read him in DANISH! Ah, we're getting on well with the DANES, we NorWEGians. We, we, see some kind of shared history of opPRESSION with them.' He tailed off, but not for long. 'It just goes to SHOW, though,' he said, anticipating Jude's interception with an interception of his own. 'What's he doing in a place like that? A sweetheart LIKE him, so to speak. I mean, here you have a fanTASTic musician performing—just inCREDible songs, and not only is he not a worldwide star, but he's doing the lowlife, East European CABARET circuit.'

'I can't think of a better place for it.'

'No, of COURSE! Not to say that being a worldwide STAR is somehow better than being a local performer, perhaps doing a small circuit, with a small degree of fame in your immediate environment. That in fact is probably better for achieving your musical goals, than getting caught up in the GLAMOUR and CIRCUS of the music industry. That in fact is probably exactly what he CHOSE! He most probably had that chance to take it to the next level, in terms of money and fame. He most probably DIDN'T miss that chance—rather he SCORNED—ah, BUKED and SCORNED—all the TRAPPings of it all, all the old conditions and CHAINS, which come along with it, like putting—er, what do you call that big, muscular creature like a bull, which would, er, PULL machinery in the field?'

'An ox.'

'Er, of course, an ox—in the YOKE of the PLOUGH!'

'I'm sure it's all part of his masterplan.'

'Not that there's anything inTRINSically wrong with fame, of course. Great Artists, they're using their fame, er—in all kinds of fascinating ways.' Bjørn capered through this clause like a ferret in the grass. 'Er, Shakespeare, he's inCREDibly AWARE of all these things in his writing, somehow concealing himself. Lord BYRON, I would say, is using fame as his STARTING-POINT, somehow accepting it as a birthright, or a curse, and everything he does is just a COMMENTARY on that completely PUBLIC self. An artist like Picasso, or REMBRANDT! Robert JOHNSON!—or a filmmaker like Hitchcock even, although, er, I myself am not such a fan of Hitchcock—these people are appealing to posTERity much more than to the audience of their day.' They pounded up *Löwelstrasse*, catching a glimpse of the *Minoritenkirche*. 'The audience of their DAY, they were probably not understanding what was going on—they didn't see the GREATNESS of it all. Ah, to them, it was probably all random gestures, some kind of HITT and MISS strategy. Most probably they didn't get the subVERsiveness of it all—because they themselves are obsessed with fame, with recogNITion, with some body of public oPINion, JUSTifying them to themselves. Otherwise they don't feel like a complete person. Whereas, these artists, even though they knew that public opinion is important, that there's some kind of MORAL force exerted by the public marketplace, but also that it's not just a matter of being tapped on the back and told how good you are.' With middle and forefinger extended, Bjørn mimicked the action for the sake of his audience.

'No, the *public marketplace* should be very careful who it taps on the back, telling them how good they are. If it doesn't want a nosebleed.' They boarded the southbound tram, rattling gently into night beyond the flood of shopwindows.

'Ah, what characterises all these people is their PLAYfulness in the face of fame. They're not taking it too seriously. They don't believe in basking in the sunshine on ParNASSus—er, or should that be ParnaSSUS?—they're much more like Dante's vision of limbo, where some of those great old Greeks are asking questions of each. They believe in the "SAD DUST GLORIES", that's what they believe in.' *Ringstrasse*, *Karlsplatz*, *Hauptstrasse*, the tram took it all in its stride. Bjørn was rubbing his hands, chuckling about how they were 'rolling a LONG WAY out of our WAY, ah, like some kind of ALTO CLUMULUS, just taking it all in, here, all the old southern part of Vienna, as if we had ALL the TIME in the WORLD.' They changed at the *Gürtel*, rolling back north and west, out to the undecided red-light districts between *Gumpendorfer* and *Mariahilferstrasse*, where brothels rubbed shoulders with chess-parlours, and sometimes of them too. Here a grocery, there a gambling den. Here hummus, there a *grosse würtzel*. Over there, behind that boarded-up window beside the open door, who knew what dubious trades? They stepped from the tram, and Bjørn gazed about him, wondering about the level of rent. 'Ah, but SPEAKing of the PLOUGH,' he said, poking the nightsky, 'there it is right there! Just casCADing down the heavens! There you've got Cassiopeia. And there the DOLPHIN, diving down! InCREDibly clear skies, considering we're in a great, lamplit city!'

Bjørn continued gazing for a full ten minutes. Jude left him to it. That was the thing about Bjørn. He had that rare thing: unassuming humility. Not a trace of the grasp in his face, unless he were playing chess, or football—or any kind of competitive sport. But who more abstract in the face of contingencies? Who thought less about them? Not that he scorned contingencies—there was no craft to it. He actually *didn't think* about them. Jude wondered if this lack of thought—which one could not call ignorance—was superior to scorn. Something in him resisted this conclusion. Was it even a virtue? He puffed. It wasn't courage, nor restraint. Could you even call it humility? It was nothing earthly. Nothing catalogued in the skills or virtues. Yet it looked like virtue all the same. Were you to place Bjørn and a virtuous man side by side—and with Bjørn it was difficult to place him any other way—and observe only their movements, they would very likely be identical, but for a little less stiffness in the virtuous man, unless he too were from Norway. But then, that being the case, Bjørn must be a virtuous man, for what was *motivation* but idle freaks and flaps? At the very least, Bjørn's effects were related to virtues. Suppose, for example, his abstraction were merely thoughtlessness, after all. Such mere thoughtlessness was a life's work to many. The world was not his home. A Norseman perhaps, but a Christian one, Bjørn could not have been a viking. Hewn from rock, he was all milk and honey. The halls of Valhalla were debarred him forever. Certainly he was devoid of vice: ambition, avarice, lust he had none, except for being honestly up for a bit of sex. And in Christendom, what constituted a virtue but to lack vice? Bjørn was a knight, born like Quixote, after his time. Nothing trite about him. Content to be alone, content with others. He would never turn round and say he *needed some space*. His space was in his head when he walked around. He could share a bunk with you, six months in a shrimp boat, never once have bad dreams. Oppression wouldn't have occurred to him. He was what the world needed if it was to survive the population explosion. Bjørn was likeable—and the more time you spent with him, the more likeable he was. And that he had not the slightest inkling of it was the best of all. For in Jude's book, the only thing better than to be virtuous was to be *likeable.*

Jude was watching a man leaving a bouquet of roses on a doorstep. He could smell falafal. Soon he was tasting it too. Bjørn got a kebab and they sauntered down *Sechshauserstrasse.*

'Mm, which *gasse* is it?' said Bjørn, from amidst greasy paper.

Jude couldn't remember. A swing-door bar-cum-saloon took their notice. A large chess knight hung over the facade. Inside two rows of old men faced each other over chessboards, lit by art-deco desklamps. In the corner, a stripper hugged a listless pole. A couple of men were taking time out from the chess to chat with her. It all looked very distracting. They turned right, and Jude studied the Spectre's card, looking up at one of the boarded up buildings. It had an open gateway, and three steps to a nondescript door.

'This must be the place,' he said, depositing the falafal remains in a cardboard-box. Two kittens sat either side of the doors, figureheads, straight from ancient Egypt. They looked at Jude like reservoirs. He trailed string and the kittens chased them, in and out of their legs, unravelling all the symbolism. Yet the ancient strangeness remained. It was good to live in cities, good to pass among passers, to stop to savour passage. Could the Glum ever satisfy again? It would require renewed investment. It could not be sandwiched between times. It would have to be routine, generative. You would have to gaze on minutiae, the way they paused to gaze now. But who would deliberately gaze on *minutiae?* Jude would rather gaze on *motley*. On crowds, statues, doorsteps, streets, bats on the faces of cathedrals. Gazing on minutiae smacked of stubborn ambition.

The kittens left off the string and began batting

each other. They were clean kittens—not a trace of mange. Vienna may not have been Istanbul, nor even Athens, but it was a good cat city all the same. It was that edge-of-the-Ottoman-Empire thing. The closer you got to patriarchy and coffee, the closer to the essence of cat. Clean cats too. Noble, privileged. Given the run of the city.

'No,' said Jude, approvingly. 'Animals are there to be fetishised.' He watched them circling a dustbin. 'Of course, they're also there to be sacrificed—*eaten* even.' He mused. Bjørn was still biting the kebab. 'I have no problem with the jugular-slitting, blood-letting, flesh-devouring consumption of animals—*per se*.' He slit the latin jugular. 'I *do* have a problem with the vast industrial slaughter of animals—the process, the *packaging*. I *do* have a problem with that.'

'It's, ah, imMORAL?' said Bjørn, through meat.

'Well, no. Immoral would be too weak a term, for the genocide we practise on animals. It *augurs ill for the human race*. The human race will pay—*dearly*—for its fish fingers and its chicken wings. It will wake up, of a morning—and a terrible one too—stare down, horrified—in a manner inconceivable to Kafka, though all too conceivable to Dante—at its *fish fingers* and its *chicken wings*, and realise forever that *you are what you eat*.'

Bjørn fidgeted. 'No,' continued Jude. 'It's not about morality; it's about punishment, or reward.

These things have their *manifestations.* What is morality but doing what's best for you? The human race does what is worst for it. It punishes itself. This is its immorality: a total absence of self-pity.'

'Mm, you speak in ABSOLUTE terms.'

'Everything's absolute. Show me something—no, really, point to something—now!—right here, in this very *gasse*—that is not absolute. That is somehow only partial'—he sneered—'somehow inchoate, embryonic, evolving.' He knocked on a wall, slapped a traffic light.

'Nn, ANIMALS,' retorted Bjørn, pointing triumphantly at the kittens, who had run out in front of a car, fled up a wall, and were now dangling ridiculously from a wrought-iron gate. 'ANIMALS are evolving.'

Jude considered, more hard than long. 'No,' he said, inevitably. '*Species* evolve—and a species is just a way of thinking. An animal is itself—*forever.* A glance at a cat could tell you that. And the glance *of* a cat could tell you more again. Shocking things. Tragic, inhuman things. Outside of all your morality. Cats, sir, belong to the dead—and their proper haunts, Xanadu, Atlantis, Acheron.'

'Nn, SPEAKING of CATS!' retorted Bjørn, as if he had only just realised they were. 'The great ALEXANDER ALEKHINE knew a little bitt about CATTS. Nah, ehah, ah this you've just got to hear this amazing fact er story about alekhine world championship holland sometime maybe nineteen thirty five.' Bjørn was mumbling, chin down, absently grinning, gathering his strength. 'Max EUWE was the opponent. This, ah, was of course the match Euwe went on eventually to WIN. And Alekhine, he ah would carry about with him his cats, couple of them, ah, they would be around him, just padding about on stage there, even SNIFFING THE PIECES before a match. Ahah.' He was laughing quietly, almost silently, uncertain if laughter was appropriate. 'Max Euwe, he's even talking about this, you can catch it in books and, yuh, various information and the LEGEND that's just GROWN UP around this event. Max Euwe, he's saying that one time the cats were just SNIFFING the PIECES. This kind of thing seemed to be increasing as the match went on, he's saying, and he couldn't understand it. Yuh, ah, cats here, cats there, getting up during moves to talk to his cats. Ah, until one time Euwe was just there to start the game, and Alexander ALEKHINE has a CAT, ah, DRAPED along his shoulder!' 'And they walk up to the table, and Alekhine, ah, OFFERS HIS CAT, for, ah, EUWE to stroke.' Bjørn was bobbing with comic profundity. The grin had stuck at its extremes. 'All a little bit, ah, SPOOKY.'

'*Ha!*'

'Ah, Max Euwe, he's wondering if this was designed to SPOOK him. But he's just shrugging it off, and continuing CONCENTRATING on the match, not really letting these SIDE issues get in his way. But then, one time, it's getting to be quite a close game, quite a crucial stage of the match, and Alekhine, he really needed a win at this point to keep his hopes alive, and there are hundreds of people all cramming into the hall there, up the stairs and hanging off the rails, where was it, ah, I CAN'T remember, probably in Amsterdam perhaps, and the tension is mounting, and then they see the players walking into the hall, and as he looked up over the chess board, he saw a CAT, KNITTED into Alekhine's JUMPER. Ahih.' Bjørn glanced from under his eyebrows. 'And an, ah, INVOLUNTARY shudder goes through the audience.' He mimed an involuntary shudder. 'It might not SURPRISE you,' he said, wincing suddenly, 'that Alekhine won the match. But really, ah, CREEPY,' he concluded.

Jude stared at him. It was. They mounted the stairs, pushed through the door and shuffled to the interior. It was dark in there. Only a fire-exit sign gave light, and a glass pane over the door. They hit a staircase and groped their way up, holding their collective breath. A white door with brass handles opened noiselessly, warmth wafted out, and a large L-shaped room spread a cream carpet before them. It was lined with thin table-legs, like black canes. The tables were circular, glass-covered. There were some thirty or so, ranged orderly along the walls, from which a black-leather bench protruded, running also the room's length. At each table, opposite the bench, was a single chair, in the same vein—thin, round legs, round seat, hollow back, clean as whistles. The general impression was cream, black-framed; like slick spectacles, liqueur chocolates, all dressed up and nowhere to go. A twelve foot Christmas tree bent its tip on the ceiling the fruit of both fertile imagination and overweaning ambition—and are not the two the same, observed Jude, with his crafty eye. It was floated with baubles in blacks and silvers. The whole operation was obviously colour-coded, blending art-deco with a contemporary Scandinavian minimalism. Jude looked haughtily at Bjørn, black against the wallpaper, flaunting his Scandinavian minimalism for all to see. The wallpaper was the cream of the carpet, ornately woven with fantastical candelabra, which, prinked at intervals with birds and leaves, revealed themselves to be such—not branches—only when you traced their whimsical tendrils to the fixed flames at their ends. These were picked out in a beige velveteen, raised from the paper whose wide strips' seams were apparent in places. Evidently the paper was older than the carpet, which looked freshly laid. Freshly laid, too, looked the cheeks of the gentlemen, littering the room in expensive penguin suits, all decked out retro-Victorian. Some wore bow-ties, some waistcoats of pearl or vermillion. Here, one with monocle, another with wings for tails. This was one with a cigarillo-holder, whose smoke was gay regalia. Top-hats and bowlers were *de rigeur*, but one feature only they all shared—a white carnation in the breast pocket. There were as many as fifteen of them, seated alone at various tables, but multiplied and thrown into interiors by ornamental mirrors, which grandly furnished each wall, deepening the cream.

Not that Jude and Bjørn were counting. Like Benedick, they saw them but noted them not. There were only two they noted: a nude at the grand-piano and the Spectre in white flannel. The piano was a display of dark largesse, here in the near corner, right-hand side. Candles burned on its tossed hood; a book of melodies on the stand. The nude displayed everything but largesse. She was a slim, shiny brunette, six-foot, with hair greased sideways. Her shoulders were tight, but hands delicate, velvet gloved, playing what may or may not have been a jazz-standard. *Take a book from off the shelf*, she sang, dreamily, with a Dietrich ease:

Make a present to yourself
Santa Claus is a jolly old elf
But he ain't got nothin' on me

Sing the baby's lullaby
Don't you make that baby cry
Peter Pan didn't want to die
But he ain't got nothin' on me

The notes started alto and descended, browsing first where the chandeliers made whorls in the ceiling, using their shards for staircases, dropping upon gins and tonic, whiskeys and soda, rums and coca-cola, stirring them like sticks. They ran pitter-patter over the tables, down the walking-canes, to tread like greyhounds on the carpet, rise as disorganised geese, steer at last to sleep—to be trod in their turn by the Spectre's foot, tapping under the table, treading softly because he trod upon your dreams. He was from Chicago, he liked the blues. He liked jazz more though. He sat at the far end, sucking a cigar, like an elegant worm, battened on human flesh. Now he noticed our newcomers, staring without welcome or recognition, as if daring their entry.

Pour yourself a slug of booze
Toast the other fella who's
Comin' out in quite a bruise
Though he ain't got nothin' on me

Light a burner on the stove
Don't you let that eyeball rove

If you're on the tail of love
You know you won't get nothin' on me

Jude looked about, delaying the inevitable. He and Bjørn appeared to be the only people standing. Even the mini-bar was empty. It was obvious that the Lie was not here.

Turn that television on
Ain't that Edward Robinson?
They don't make 'em like they done
When they didn't got nothin' on me

Apparently to confirm this suspicion, Jude pressed on, with Bjørn toeing his kibe. Passing through it, the room became rather grey than cream as if a lid had been placed on it. Thirty fish-eyes ignored them as they walked, but the Spectre's sick dog's were on them, screened by familiar tints.

Just a bad old Christmastime
Looking round for Harry Lime
He's the archetype of crime
But he ain't got nothin' on me.

I swear that I was home alone
Alibi was Al Capone
Po-lice even tapped my phone
But they couldn't get nothin' on me

The Spectre nodded contentedly at this observation. His foot tapped a mite firmer, gaining in emphasis what it lost in rhythm so that he was at a loss for some moments to get it back. The nude ceased singing and got to flourishing the ivories.

'Ah,' said the Spectre, as the notes cascaded round, 'my Anglican congregation.' It hardly occurred to Bjørn to insist on his nationality. He was in no mood for repartee. He wanted to get to the bottom of the mystery and then out of it. 'My gentle Norse,' said the Spectre, when Bjørn did not bite. 'Good collaborators. Cowards, but collaborators still.' He turned to Jude. 'Good strong necks to stand on. We use 'em, then we wipe 'em, like so much dogshit from our shoes.'

Jude was cool too. 'I thought you were going to say from your mouth. Or do the nurses do that?'

The Spectre chuckled. 'They always act shocked at first. It assuages the conscience.'

'The nurses?'

'After that—huh huh—well, you pull them in in droves.' He fumbled for the cigar box. '*Ecco*,' he continued, opening his palm toward them. His accent was crude.

'Well, it's your only means of conversation.'

The Spectre paused. A lip looked contempt. 'I've been expecting you one of these nights. God knows I've seen your friend enough. That bald albino.

Dapperly-Lay? Mmm.' He paddled his tongue as if it tasted good. 'I've been wanting to make him a proposition consistent with his name.' He chuckled shortly. Then, 'I say "God knows",' he launched, lazily, 'meaning a hypothetical god of course. A god who doesn't rape virgins, slaughter sons. An inhuman god. Not a god exhumed from the tomb of Elijah, stood on two legs and commanded to dance. A just god.' He turned back to Bjørn. 'Do you believe in a just God, my gentle Norse?' He offered him a cigar.

'I'm just keeping my opinions to myself.'

'You're just doing nothing at all. You know what I liked about Quisling? Took a neat bullet. Kept his house in order. Probably his opinions too.'

'Yes, yes,' said an impatient Jude. The situation was real. Even the Spectre was real enough. Irrelevant certainly, but remnant nonetheless. No doubt he had some power in his pond. You could still end up on the wrong side of his irrelevance. 'You've got the old combinations going. A threat here, a titillation there. A discomforting truth, a ridiculous lie. A little bit of divide and rule.' Jude relaxed his foreleg. 'Come on, throw a little *Sturm und Drang* in there for good measure. After all, you are an earnest outworn curio of that earnest outworn curio, *German Romanticism*, which like all archaeologies delights in discovering itself. But then ambition fattens on itself—as you, if I may, amply demonstrate.'

'I can call in a little *Sturm und Drang* now,' said the Spectre calmly, 'and there'll be nothing outworn about it.' He snapped his fingers. 'But I prefer to offer you a drink on the house.' Over to the table came one of the penguins, whom Bjørn, on closer inspection, found to be a woman. They were all women. They three were the only men in the place.

The Spectre fondled her buttock. 'What are you drinking? Scotch? On ice? On ice,' he ordered, revealing as much Chicago as suited his purpose. 'You know, I hope you've brought some fruit with you—artificial or otherwise, they're not fussy, though I find the prosthetic lasts longer. Organic is so mushy, huh-huh. You know what Adam shouldda done with the apple?'

'You're keen to tell.'

'Hmh.' The Spectre ploughed into an elaborate blasphemy, involving Adam, Eve, the Archangel Gabriel and the Tree of the Knowledge of Good and Evil. He proceeded to give precise instructions as to where they should sit, what they should say to the waitress, when exactly they should produce the fruit in question, etc.

'Yes,' said Jude looking round. 'You've been through this already. No, I came about a Lie—or a Lay if you will—if you *can*.'

'You've come to the right place.'

'No, I can see that I haven't.' The Spectre made no reply. 'But let's imagine—hypothetically speaking—that I wanted to take part in this desperate spectacle, tell me, where would I get my hands on this fabled fruit?'

The Spectre waited for the Scotch to arrive. 'Go root it out,' he said at length. 'Meantime, pull up a fuckin' chair.'

'No come on, where do you get yours?'

It was the Spectre's turn to look away, drumming his fingers.

'See I can't help be curious about your dealer.'

'You know what they say about curiosity my young friend.' He mopped his brow. It was stiflingly warm.

'Yes! I know what they say. They're nothing if not repetitive.' Jude was looking away again, drumming his own fingers, pushing from the table. 'They're a garrulous lot to hide behind the third-person plural.' He ran an eye along piping and encountered the nude. Nudity needed constant reinforcement from the armoury of plumbing. A nude with gooseflesh was unlikely to do justice to Gershwin or Harold Arlen. This one was doing justice enough. Too much justice in fact. For a second, not without gooseflesh of his own, he thought it was A., hair all lopped and constrained. She paid him no attention however, staring at the piano, resuming:

Drop a needle in the groove
Show 'em how to make a move
You're gonna find it hard to prove
That you ain't got nothin' on me

Whose house this is I think I know
I swear that he was made of snow
Come the spring he'll have to go
'Cause he can't got nothin' on me.

She was still holding the last note when they slipped through the brass-handled doors. The last they saw of the Spectre, he was producing a coin from the Penguin's ear. Bjørn was in the dark of the hallway, muttering about how every man's conscience is VILE and dePRAVED—how you CANnot dePEND on IT TO be your GUIDE!' Nevertheless, they found their way out of the hallway by virtue of the wainscot. From there it was all about slithering downstairs, clutching the balustrade, and making for that frosted doorpane.

'Not only can you not depend on it to be your guide—you shouldn't trust it with the smallest responsibility—if only because it's so keen to be trusted.'

They hit the street.

'Those were all WOMEN up there.'

'Yes.'

'Did you see the wallpaper?'

'Yes. Clearly, if you're into erotic ritual, disguised as megalomania, disguised as racial genocide, you don't sit for any length of time in a room without a colour scheme.'

They traipsed home to a spotless *Studentenheim*, climbed weary stairs, ate oats from shimmering bowls, couldn't remember at which point or where they hit the sack. But in Darko's room, into Jude's dream, came a rumbling sound: an aeroplane flying toward the open window. Disaster, surely! No. Disaster was averted. Only a propeller span into the room and lay there turning half-heartedly—*flippety-flappety, flippety-flappety*.

Jude awoke. Something gibbered outside the door. He leapt up, wrenched at the handle, fist cocked and drenched in sweat. A ghost was flapping in the dark corridor. Far down the passage he heard a giggle: a woman of uncertain age rumbled off with a shopping-trolley. Jude threw himself on the ghost and it sprawled on the floor. From what appeared a protuberant nose, blood began staining its sheet.

'Arright?' came a muffled voice.

Jude lifted its skirts. There, covered equally in blood, ectoplasm and shame, was Benjamin Kepperly-Lie.

'Got a room for the night?' he said.

It was two in the morning. Bjørn awoke, confused, moving his forearms back and forward like scissors. For some reason he was on Darko's floor. 'Urrr,' he said, and 'Whh—'. To no avail. But as he subsided back to sleep, snow falling in the courtyards, and spoons tinkering at soya-yoghurt and tea, he heard—or dreamt—the following:

'So it's like that. *In flagrante*. It makes the mind boggle.'

'The sewer?'

'In "The Third Man" wasn't it? Seemed a good place to lie low.'

'How'd you get in here?'

'Would have been the *Putzfrau*. One second she was talking about State Funerals; next thing I knew—'

But Jude raised an eyebrow and looked at the falling snow. Bjørn was asleep. Darko wasn't there. Benjamin wanted to explain, and he could have, but Jude didn't care for explanations. Some things were best unspoken. The Lie settled into his sleeping-bag and slept the sleep of the dead.

4. The Ravelled Sleeve

In Vienna, sleep definitely knit up the ravelled sleeve of day—and night too betimes. In fact the thread got so tangled, and cloths of heaven so bundled together, the two became confused and no one knew which day it was and who was sleeping with who. Or whom.

The situation was only exacerbated by the appearance of Benjamin Lie. This was entirely to be expected. But that did not mean it should not be *sus*pected too. In fact, Jude was convinced that it should be. The Lie kept stressing the 'temporary nature' of his stay. He had only been here a short while and already he was nowhere to be found. He would think nothing of turning up late and sneaking off 'early doors,' as he put it. 'Ohohono.' You would wake up a-night, drop off a-morn, stare through the day to find him disappeared. Early doors indeed. It was disconcerting. One wondered why he came at all.

Then there was Bjørn. Finally he had a room-share, with a little blonde boy in the civilian army. Occasionally, as now, you would wake into dimness and lean over the bed. On the floor: an empty sleeping bag. You would get up, shave, pull on your clothes, if not already in them. You would go out to the corridor, trundle down it, barefoot. Through kitchen, by toilets, by hallway, to Bjørn's door. An early door. Without knocking, you would enter and he'd be there, lank-haired, chopping forearms on the pillow, pretending not to have been asleep. The boy-scout would be annoyed with you, tutting and tapping at his computer. You stared, daring him to tut. But occasionally you would go in there and the boy-scout would not be there, and his bed would be unslept in. He would be with his parents. And in Bjørn's bed would be Bjørn and Kara Kundera, smiling private smiles. Some insisting would take place; some denial; some stutter and emphasis. You were in no mood for delicacy. You barged straight in. You didn't care whom you found. You informed Bjørn in no uncertain terms. Kara's breasts you unanimously approved. 'Bjorn,' you asserted, through haughty lashes. 'I like your girlfriend's breasts.'

Bjørn would give the rueful grin of a man who has won the lottery. Much blushing and chuckling went on. Not on your part though. You did like Kara's breasts, but they reminded you of what you missed, tumbling like monkeys in a tree. Where was Pilar Santana Artale when you needed her? Smoking pot, wrapped in a *PACE* flag, ultimate product of those new Europeans, Economic Union and Court of Human Rights, not to mention those twin Commons: Monetary Fund and Agricultural Policy. Ay, madam, but what could you expect? Was it not the same all over? Sexual and monetary currencies, increasingly tied. If he wasn't careful, a man could end up on the wrong end of the sea-exchange: his island pound, turn dry and continental. You were sceptical, but more, you were *wary*. After all, what was the alternative? Stay in your counting-house, counting out your pounds? Damn their insidious trade agreements, tacit tax reliefs. A little taxation went a long way. We all knew where we stood.

Jude knew where he stood. He stood in Bjørn's doorway, nine-o-clock in the morning, staring at Kara's breasts, far away, with the sexual compromises he would be bound to. There was Ava, the brunette from the library; the jetty Sara Baumgarten from the Jewish Museum; and the altogether swarthy Infidel from the *Casanova*. Ben and Bjørn had got there before, but if he could put up with that, so could they. It took a thief to catch a thief, or indeed to steal from one. And, at the same time, what could be easier than thieving loyalty from the loyal? It wasn't as if loyalty hadn't been thieved before. Apostasy had grown so fashionable; ambivalence, more fashionable still. To make matters worse, Barbosa was hanging from his coat-tails, appropriating his taste in music. She was doing a Bjørn (and it wouldn't have surprised him), trying to get her own room, and meanwhile spilling over Jude's with her clothes and creams. He didn't know how it looked to other people, but she could do her spilling on the brown-ribbed floor. That left Pilar, roaming outside his *Ringstrasse*, never so contented. And this, if not quite a passion, was a pain.

On Kara's breasts, falling snow glimmered. Hair fell there too, more light than heat. Here were the alpine peaks she came from, transposed from grandmother, mother to daughter. Here: take this for heirloom. Do this, *Liebling*, in remembrance of me. Jude glanced at Bjørn, beneficiary of this collective wisdom. Bjørn wanted to do this in remembrance of something, he wasn't fussy. He was keen to practice his Telemark landing, as if he had not exhausted that particular trick. Jude let him, pulled the door shut and wandered through the kitchen. There he encountered a roll, doing it justice by a knob of alpine butter. Next he found tofu yoghurt. It was a no-contest. Finally he stole one of Bjørn's bananas. If he was just going to leave them around. Bjørn had taken his eye off the ball, rolled it on the ice like one of those curling pucks he was so transfixed by. Jude would teach him to watch winter sports.

A glass of water washed it down. Superiority flooded his veins. Proper *Übermenschlichkeit*. He strutted off to pack a satchel and in a matter of minutes on *Auerspergstrasse* was out walking. Walking in this instance, in three inches of snow, meant a high-step stomp, with plenty of knee-lift, something that came naturally to Jude. Snow was his natural sphere, sorting wheat from chaff in the most effortless manner. His hair was raffishly swept. He was scarfed and overcoated, belted at the waist, pointy shoed below. A fearful plutocrat, come unto his own, wielding his Pound at the expense of your euro. People will pay what they have to pay for a needful commodity. Jude had a needful commodity. *Commodity* was his speciality. He sometimes wondered if he was anything more.

Breath streamed out easy. Pigeons flew to the statues and fountains. They had made tracks outside the *Kunsthistorisches*, across the *Heldenplatz*, over to the *Neue Berg*, angling at culture. But evidently they had got cold feet, had made for the air, to shit on the crannies of the mighty, their helms and epaulettes. Jude stopped to roll a cigarette, leaning on a pedestal. It was cold. Snow clashed lightly with his eyes. He licked the water, staring at the *Neue Berg*. It was a useless place, made for looking at through the vagaries of weather. People had misconstrued it. They thought there was something to be gained from its innards. It wasn't an unseamed chicken. Or perhaps it was; perhaps that was exactly what it was. Because, after all, nothing could be gained from unseamed chickens. Chickens were about eggs: free-range, organic ones. Here was a miracle even a vegan could admit to. But you had to stand back, let it lay in proper time. Jude stood back from the library, turned away. It would lay when it was good and ready. So would he. In the meantime, he would amuse himself in the Jewish Museum.

Sara was in there. 'Sara Baumgarten getting in there,' said Jude warily. She watched him, unsmiling, as he entered. She was drying a bowl. It was warm in the Jewish Museum. A good place to while away a morning. He stamped his shoes on the ribbed blue carpet. A pool formed beneath him.

'Jude Harlow.'

He picked tobacco from a tooth. 'How are you?'

'Good.'

He was taller than her, which was an unusual thing. He made use of it, in his overcoat, looking fatherly. 'Ah, it's the old washing-up game.'

'It never goes away.'

'No. Almost religious isn't it?'

'It's a routine. I don't think about it.'

'Exactly.'

'I don't mind it if no one is watching.'

'But *I'm* watching,' said Jude, leaning in.

'I'm not enjoying it anymore.' She put down the bowl and went behind the counter. Jude was thinking about the erotica of washing-up, but he wasn't about to say so. That was Harper's little peccadillo.

'What can I get you,' she continued.

'Um. An *orange juice*.'

'Anything else?' She looked pragmatic: a bad sign.

'No, I've eaten.' He swept to his table by the window, undraped, and leafed through the papers on the sill. The usual fare: *The Jewish Chronicle*; *Frankfurter Allgemeine*; Heralds *Tribune* and *Morning*. *Time* magazine was loitering beneath. Jude felt a little needled, needed a pick-up. He went straight for the *Herald Tribune*, read *Riots in London, England*. People were standing on statues, holding bollards. They might have been celebrating a sporting victory. It was all of a piece, their praise and blame, aimed at cementing the status quo. *Uprisings imminent* thought the paper. Anger would become violence. A cycle of vengeance was forming; political strife turning personal. Sara brought the orange-juice. Jude folded it away. It was sheer unreality, hysteria, a hoax to justify rising in the morning. The onanism of the secular organ; mock death-throes of the cult of the individual. As if death could be solved by *mimesis*: death, thou might'st die. Snakes and skins, the constant crying of *wolf*, *wolf* no more than a word. No use opposing with a real, live wolf. The real one wouldn't be believed, would go shrinking to his den, disillusioned. The whole *wolf* idea had to be dismantled. There was no wolf; there was no den. They were long since extinct. That was why they had Highland repatriation schemes. That was they imported panthers, set them loose on the fictional moors.

With small irony, this was how it would happen. The death they pretended: creeping by degrees from the high horizons. Loping effortless, negotiating slopes, easy on the needles. Left a bit, right a bit, on the slats and levels. Jude recalled Tomas, himself recalling. Tomas had spent time in Arabia, watching from roofs when the sun went down, the wild dogs breaching from the desert. No better balm to tired eyes. Sun like a scimitar under the pylons. A plane drawing in the runway sand. It was an amazing range: a hundred and eighty degrees of view, to outcrops, pylons, old city walls. There went the sun: a dropped coin under the horizon. Here came the dogs, on parchment rocks, silent as pencils. Below, birds circled in the palms. Both their descriptions, the hyphenated trot and incessant wheeling, disrupted the frames: the rows of palms, roads, grains in the rock. Like erasers now, they re-blanked the parchments, unseamed them, threw them on the earth. The view became vast and three-dimensional. Tomas himself was implicated, on his terrace, with his cigarette. And all because of animals.

And deaths would be like this. Catastrophe was a posture, a pout. Deaths would steal like those dogs into town, down to the rubbish dumps, feeding on waste. Silent as pencil-lines, white as erasers. They would ride the vehicle, replace the *wolf* with the literal wolves, make off with all the chickens. And the bookworms too. And the lines would melt away: the hard-drawn, ploughed in lines, like ripples in water. It would be all-inclusive. The whole country would get its come-uppance. It would rise like an island, into three dimensions.

And the papers would be powerless. Jude folded *The Herald Tribune*, taking up *The Jewish Chronicle*. Here was an article on Lenny Bruce. Jude settled in to the usual spiel. Trial and retrial; *klutz* and *cocksucker*; Moses, Jesus and the whole nine yards. Bruce had been a good boy at school, he just ran off at the mouth. Jude looked at his picture. He was a good boy as an adult too: anyone could see. Beautiful rings round fastidious eyes. The kind of smile the stars don't have any more. Ragged and gapped and tobacco-stained. He looked like he was consumed from within. But it was hard to identify with. Why take seriously what was so absurd? So you do a little time inside: it's the making of you, you come out on a roll. Friends in high places want to shake your hand. What was so unsettling? Bruce was no Keats, killed by *The Quarterly*, no Josef K, reduced to bureaucracy, condemned to endlessness.

He saw through the court-cases. They were transparent to him; he made transparencies of them. He turned them into his show. He read them out, line by ridiculous line. He dismantled them. In their mechanical waltz, he saw all the mass of biography, reportage, interpretation. He saw someone reading of his trials, sipping orange-juice in a minimalist chair. He saw the teleology; the glorious act of hindsight; someone seeing someone seeing. And all this he could handle, all this was hip to. But he also saw an underworld, of significant acts, where you stood or fell in the mouth, where the entry onstage was seminal, salutary, hour for which he he'd waited. To speak not to oneself in a cell, but in the sunlight, on the public square: this was his and everyone's aim. Outside that cell, he saw judges and lawyers, scribes and Pharisees, rolling on the human heart a stone. And they were neither man nor woman, they were neither brute nor human, they were Ghouls. He felt it like a spear in the side. Not a man of little deaths, incremental deaths. A man of stabbed-in-the-back. The death of a man, not the death of a country, culture, ideology. Bruce could teach Britain a thing or two. When had it come up with a man like that? A loud-mouthed incantatory man. Britain was mealy-mouthed, drooling at the lip. What it wanted to say it had long since swallowed. It could not muster a vital blow, even at itself. Decay was its inheritance.

'So what have you been up to?' asked Sara. Jude folded *The Jewish Chronicle*.

'Much.' He paused. 'Tons. Masses.'

'Such as?' She drew a chair and sat in it. In her hand was a glass of green tea.

'Oh the usual carousel. Wake, wonder who is on my floor this morning, or whose floor I am in fact on. Arise, arise, cry so loud, shower, shave, bat eyes at the washerwoman, seek friends, money, confirmation of my existence, be thrice denied *on all three counts*, sit in the library, meditate a deadline, ogle some illustrious legs, get hungry, scrape together some money to spend in one of various refectory establishments, confront the sudden evening, give up on study, go home, satisfy various appetites, and wind up a-nights in the Café Museum, reading Robert Musel and watching Bjorn play chess through various stages of intoxication. The usual grind. What about yourself?'

'Studying, painting. I split with my boyfriend.'

'Oh really?' Jude raised his eyebrows, contemplated sympathy, opted for sincerity. 'Congratulations.'

She smiled. It was that charming smile, a lot of teeth crowding round. 'Yeah, well.'

Jude fingered his glass. 'Of course, I don't know him from *Adam*. But that in no way disqualifies me from calling him an *idiot*.'

'You're quite perceptive.'

'Not particularly. All boyfriends are *idiots*. It's *congenital*. It's genital too of course. The minute they're defined by their *partnerships*, they become social cripples, incapable of ease.' Jude flicked the table. He wouldn't give it up. 'Really, basic functions such as talking, walking, *distinguishing*, become difficult for them. Other men become deadweights—obelisks!—Succubi!' He raised a finger in the air. 'Clamped upon their chests, preventing breath! The boyfriend tries, he really tries, but it's too late. He struggles, shudders, gasps, pressed into *homosex*.'

'As an alternative to what?'

'Well exactly.' Jude clutched at his t-shirt, revealing a stone-white stomach. 'Birth, death, dissolution. So long as those are repressed, anything goes. It's the basic principle of a liberal-democratic, capitalist society. Capitalism,' Jude pronounced, 'is *gay*.'

'So all the gays are repressed, is it?'

'No, only the heterosexual ones.'

'Hmmm. And I suppose it's the same for women.'

'Both wither in partnership. But women like withering. It's safe enough.' He stroked the side of *Time*. His t-shirt was white and long-sleeved, one of them ravelled. His face was pale and shaded. Behind him the street was white. The window was shiny. He looked like he had slept in the snow, with that weird, wide stomach empty as night.

'You don't like women.'

'No, I love them. I—' Jude paused for thought. 'I don't admire many of them. But I love them. And it's better to be loved than admired.'

'I never understood that.'

'Women may be starry, but they are not *actually stars*. Not *actually eternal*. Of course, neither are men—apart from Bjorn.'

'Are they starry though?'

'No. Men are dusty asteroids, dumb meteors, pummelling lonely moons.'

'What do you love about women?'

'I don't know.' He flexed his jaw, pondered Cleopatra. Fran Peters came to mind. The way she approached him, meandered to his lap. A deep summer day, turning evening. They were seated for a photograph, smiles all round. 'A certain grace,' he said. 'A lilt, if you will.' He saw her firm perfect rump descending. Was it there yet? It was there already. A tall willowy girl, among the grass and flagstones, seated on his thigh, weighing nothing. She might have been a dove's wafted feather. 'The being while seeming not to.' Baumgarten would like this.

'I don't get it.' She had her head cocked, eyes inquiring. For a sceptic she was fatally curious.

'There's no mystery in it.' She would like that

even more.

‘But you do admire some?’

‘One or two.’

‘Alright, what do you admire?’

‘The same things you’d admire in men. Courage, acumen, sporting excellence. Which, though it *sounds* like a recipe for fascism, omits the crucial ingredients: sentiment, stupidity, *sports science*.’

‘Kindness?’

‘Yes, another crucial ingredient.’

‘What about charity?’ It was hard to tell if this was sarcastic.

‘What about it?’

‘You don’t admire it?’

‘Not unless it involves the *above*.’ And he tossed his head at the above.

She sipped politely. ‘Give some names: women you admire.’

‘Nina Simone, Derartu Tulu, Benazir Bhutto. Though I can’t honestly say I’m not in love with all three.’

‘Some think they love, when they only admire.’

‘They’re probably in *partnerships*.’ The word might have been a fishbone.

‘So love must be unrequited.’

‘It must be interrupted. Not necessarily *dramatically*. Preferably with as little fuss as possible. A laugh, a cough, a crying child—anything can do it.’

'You sound like you're speaking from experience.'

'Why?'

'You're full of opinions.'

'Opinion is bourgeois. I reject opinion. Besides, opinions change every two minutes, as they should. There's nothing worse than someone whose opinion is *unwavering*. Love never wavers. It just dies a death.'

'You sound like Wilde.'

'No. Wilde was a prick.'

'Mm.' She didn't feel like bantering. She cupped the tea. He was three feet away, but her head inclined towards him, as though magnetised, so that the thick spiral of the crown pointed to his chin. She was watching the glass of the table-top, which the snow ran along in chains.

'Actually I think I might have that bagel,' said Jude.

'Avocado?'

'*Nno*. Tofu and cucumber.'

She slipped away. He slipped his neck, noose-like, in the scarf. 'Oh the moose, the moose is up!' he chuckled to himself. 'There'll be no moose!' He shouldered the overcoat and loped after her. '*Hchm*, can you put it in a bag? I have to get to the library.'

'What are you doing tonight?'

'Well, we're going to the *Hawelka*. At least that's the plan. You should come.'

‘What time?’

‘Around nine.’ He stared up at her, lucent; nose like a sundial, pointing to earth. The look of someone who lies for the good of all. A difficult look to resist.

‘Okay. I’ll see.’

‘I say *we*. It’s supposed to be Bjorn and the Lie and me. But it’s proving hard to get hold of them.’

‘How are they? I haven’t seen Benjamin for three weeks.’

‘Well, as I say, I’ve no idea. Exaltant in all probability.’

‘Do you have a mobile yet?’ She gave him the bagel.

‘None of us do.’

‘You’re so obsolete.’ There was that smile again, right at the death. He went out like a hunchback.

After that everything went like clockwork, from the scuffing about, through the hanging around, via the insertion of and extraction *from*, incorporating also the turning on and the logging in, all the way to Harper’s email:

Sir,

It’s all been happening. What you might call Developments. In the crumbling, decrepit, urgently-in-need-of-redevelopment (but not, sir, NOT regeneration) sense of the word.

Nevertheless, some WEIRD SHIT if you will (and even if you won't) is going down. Evidently there is a mole in the wall, a leak in the kettle, four and twenty blackbirds twixt cup and lip? For either my life, and your life, are INEXTRICABLY LINKED, or someone with access to both is very consciously, therefore eminently EXTRICABLY, linking them.

The smart money, of course, is on the Lie. But then is he not himself only a pawn in a larger, deadlier Game (chess, obviously)? Or is he, all the while, unbeknownst to the players, preparing to Queen himself, being, in the last resort, in TOTAL CONTROL of said game, and placing the Smart Money on himself?

The mind BOGGLES.

It all started at the Seaman's Church—Olaf Adolf's Kyrka, to be precise, that asymmetrical Victorian pile, throwing up nooks and crannies, spires and turrets, crosses and weather-vanes with reckless abandon. Once again I found myself in a sauna, surrounded by A's yearning masses, among whom yearning and mass were about equally proportioned. I, in trunk and hose, sir, they, in flagrante, occasionally draped with luxury towelling. The sauna brandished its usual accoutrements. Above the door, a feebly-lit lozenge, dirt-yellow. More vivid, the somnolent coal-stove, all lambent power. The smell of eucalyptus. Revolution in the air, positively manifesting, large and slow and curling into corners. The activists lounged on pinewood, pining, supining. They felt pine! the pinewood creaky with suppleness. It was a wood-from-trees scenario: limbs like ladders on the Freely-Lowe farm. Forearm, calf, conch-like stomach, emergent from folds. A thick sight, sir: cut black crescents, creamy marble, draped with rose. Hands rode steam like Marcel Marceau's. The stove was a purse of monies, fortune's dregs, reef where all ships founder. We looked to it, as to a cairn on the mountain. The barometer, our compass, troubled in the red; the thermometer climbed through ninety. Someone was saying something about escaping the loop of history, the farce of repetition, but he kept forgetting what he was saying and having to start again. Sometimes someone would remind him where he was, then forget what it was they were reminding. G., on the lower level, would reach for the ladle, urging, as he went, the relevant word, with a groan overloud. Then he would sink back to his bench, like a carpet unrolling, disappearing altogether in a press of steam. And so it went on. I didn't count their number. It may have been as many as twelve. One or two had passed in and out, in an arc of cold: desecrators of those marble limbs; spadecutters in the vegetable plot. At each rupture, the activists died little deaths, murmured like the dead, resenting the living. The light was a salted wound. Then the cold was grown upon, limbs to sleep subsided. The violators were forgiven; pity reigned supreme. No one likes to call another's bluff.

We had been promised the portentous X., but it became plain he wasn't coming, which A. (now) insisted was entirely as he had expected. Apparently, X was a sensitive one, especially if he smelt a rat. W., nearest the stove, kept rousing and quiescing—in his face, a residue of offence, blent with guilt (as it invariably is). G. was propped against a petite oriental woman, hand flung along his brow. K. was bolt upright at the back, with a fixed smile melting from his face. Strangely, the Fat Woman from the Cafe was there, I know not why (unless she had been eavesdropping on our conversation—on reflection, highly likely). A. had made a big show of getting out when the others came in, preferring to gorge on waffles in the solitude of the adjacent sauna. Occasionally we saw his eye at a tiny hole in a wood-knot. We heard a Scots curse echo in the hall. Flapping feet went by. The lozenge buzzed a little, then was silent. The sweat was like strings on our limbs. They responded to its feints and pressures; leaning, widening, adjusting. We might have been A.'s puppet show; a kind of Roman comedy.

My plan was simple. Wait for their guards to lower, then pose a few innocuous salients, sir, concerning the hypothetical existence of some chap called Jade, Judd, something like that, in some central-to-east European former seat of luxury and empire, a tale of espionage and/or exploitation of innocent youth, the possible pertinency and/or impertinency of artificial fruit, etc. But it was hard to find the right moment. If this was revolution, it was in the implosion phase, already shutting up shop. In fact, I was about to do the same, when who should enter but the High Priestess herself. She stood on the threshold like a Degas, stained with fire. Reddest of red hair, spiralling to shoulders; breasts like camphor and sulphur; and the auburn burn beneath, intricate with shade. A sight, sir, to warm sore eyes, turn blind cockles, cut the kettled lip. Them reds did it—I know they did, them hardcore ones. And hardcore was the word. Here a nook, there a cranny, sometimes swapping places. Concaves bottomed out, swelled to convexes, tapered to parapets topped with watchmen. The grounds were unstable. Today's hills could be tomorrow's valleys, and drought turn merciful flood. I had to stare at the stove.

She moved to the lower seat, followed by the cold. 'Well well,' she said. 'It looks like the Garden of Eden in here.' 'Minus,' said G., spitefully, 'a bloodthirsty, arbitrary dictator to send us into exile. Unless, my dear,' he added, with what he thought was effortless charm, 'you are less angelic than you look.' 'Oh, I wouldn't say dictator,' said the P, softly. 'I AM sorry to hurt your feelings,' says G. 'What would you call Him, pray?' The P. considers it, shuffling deeper on the bench. 'More of a Landlord,' she says. 'Oh, I assure you,' titters G. '—and I have some authority in the matter, you will allow—a landlord is nothing if not a dictator, profiting from the arbitrary divisions of private property.' His tongue lingered on his upper lip. 'Just like your God.' 'I was using a metaphor,' she explains, tolerant as you like. 'In which,' says G., 'the garden is the vehicle (we will leave the landlord out of this). What, pray, is the tenor?' 'We're the fuckin' vehicles,' says W., misreading the situation. 'An' the tenors too.'

He is quite motivated. 'Gonna come down like locusts, waste the private fuckin' garden.' 'Dear boy,' yawns the prostrate G. 'I think you're mixing your metaphors. Or should I say, "cross-pollinating", ahah? Besides,' he added, for the benefit of the P, 'surely, we'd do better to cultivate what GOD has so KINDLY provided?' The door is jerked open. 'Ah think ye'll find the Sister there was talkin' 'boot the garden of the soul,' rasps the naked, potbellied A., unable to refrain. 'An' yours could do with a little fertiliser.' He stands there, hands outstretched, splay-feet on the mat. 'W. points to the ground, as if imitating A. 'Do you have to be so fuckin' facetious?' he asks. 'Couldn't be more fuckin' serious,' rejoins A. 'That's what I'm afraid of,' jabbers W. A. is not interested though, tanked up on wine and waffles. He continues in his vein, flapping his tail and thrusting ample hips. 'I'll fuckin' teach you a thing or two about pollination!' he roars. W. is disgusted but G. titters unexpectedly. '"Pollination!". That's very good, Artie.' 'How can YOU—fuckin'—say that's good?' glares W., sweat berolling his brow. 'My dear Richard,' says G., a-flutter at the coming aphorism, very like a moth shut out from heaven. 'If you will BOMBARD us with your symbolic artillery, we can but resort to misreading. Artie here is merely digging the trenches. Depend upon it,' (with a single raised finger) 'in the overflowered fields of Rhetoric, innuENDO (sigh) is a sad survivor.' 'Well, he ain't sad enough for my liking,' frowns W. 'He only wants,' say I, ' to put a simile on people's faces.' A. threw a simile at me: a big bushy one, with a thumbs-up attached. 'Good on ya, lad!' he chuckled, 'fuckin' similes.' The P. looked sad herself, crouching over, as if warming at the stove.' 'Yeah?' says W., as if himself the stove (or ambitious to be so), 'if you don't like my fuckin' similes, I've got some literal artillery for you.' I sense my moment. 'Good' (I says) because we judge but by the FRUITS,' (this as portentous as possible). 'Yeh, and what fruits you got in mind' says W., who won't let it lie. His hands are gripping the bench-front. 'Oh, a real fruit salad,' says I. 'It's a global market, after all.' 'They grow on fuckin' trees!' says A., grinning at me, showing a surprising swathe of goof. He looks back at W. W. has stood up, folding his arms. He is a short man, and sturdy. Hair besprinkles his chest. 'I've got a feelin',' he says, insulted, 'there's a—fuckin'—subtext here. Some private fuckin' joke. I've got a be honest—if there's one thing I hate more than private property, it's a private fuckin' joke.' He tosses at A. 'What ya doin' here anyway? We're promised spooky fuckin' Mr X, and we get a bunch a flatulent folk singers. Instead of serious fuckin' insurrection'ry discussion, we get an array of insults an' thrown-off fuckin' hints doubtin' our integrity. Sorry, Artie, the only one spyin' round 'ere is you through the fuckin' keyhole, mate. I mean, what's the difference between spyin' and fuckin' voyeurism, when it's said and done?' This was the first thing W. had said to the point. Nevertheless, rather than pursue it, his tongue lolled at his lip as if substantiation enough. 'That's it, isn't it mon?' he said after that lolling pause. 'Is that all this is about? Fuckin' voyeurism? How do we know you're not the fuckin' spy? Or you?' He confronts my eye. 'Snoopin' about, coverin' your loins, gath'rin' intelligence like.' 'That would be a FRUITLESS job,' says I. 'Ah think,' says A., catching on, 'the intelligence around here is somewhat imPEARed.' He jabs at the ground. 'Oh yeah,' retorts W., as if those who cannot be beaten should be joined, 'well yer not exactly the APPLE of our eye.' 'I think you PLUMbed the depths with that one,' says G. languidly. He bursts into giggles, falls into hisses, erupts into sighs. But W. is strutting the matting, ire fixed on A. Someone tries to intervene, but 'no, man, I'm tired of it all—all the hint droppin' and double talk. This ain't fuckin' Shakespeare any more,' he flourishes. 'Not that you were great shakes at that.' There is a tired titter, but W., it appears, went too far with that one. A. extends an arm and softly, deliberately, slaps the wraithly cheek, like a sign of things to come. Some moments they are locked in shoulder grips. There is a strange quiet, punctuated by squeakings from the mat, until the F. W. cries 'I got some MELONS for ya!' and peals with laughter. Then A. shoves W. away—onto the F. W., who shoves him back. W., whose wraithly nature is becoming increasingly compromised, accidentally knees a square-shaped, ruddy-faced man in the head and down they go with a man of no discernible feature. The F. W. grabs the tongs, crying 'bunch of fuckin' LEMONS!' Others get involved, trying to break us up, and if they take a little collateral, they dole out some of their own. We are gasping for air, faint for heat. Bodies are writhing over matting, under benches, somehow up benches as well. I gaze on them a moment from somewhere under the back bench, bepuddled, belly-floored, dodging blows. The mass, frantic as it is, seems motionless: a dense epicenter, shooting beam-like limbs. On its edge, A. is cackling wildly, throwing ceaseless water on the coals like a demon of Goya. Now he stokes the fire, now he runs out to refill and throw icy buckets on us. 'There is a tide!' he cries during these sallies, 'which taken at the fuckin' flood!' then bursts into violent coughing. Wide ribbons run down his face, wiping browns for ruds. Meanwhile, the P. has retreated, sadly, to the door. She has turned both back and head, one to leave, other to take last looks. One of Blake's angels, wrapped indiscriminately in allegory and towelling. Behind, and framing her, the bashed bronze of the porthole; her hair, sunset water, poured on the fire; her back, a marble tomb. Magnificent, exact, unrequiring. The more you stared, the more her nudeness threw you. Winds blew in, the masthead fell away. Nothing you could do. You were capsized on ocean, in love but rudderless, despairing of the port. You had seen all you needed to see.

As had I.

Jude puffed, exasperated. He was only halfway through. How was he supposed to follow Harper's elaborate narratives if he kept reducing the nondescript nobodies he hung around with to self-important initials? Indulging him this once, Jude swung to the very start of the stream, looking to put names to faces, and kick arse too if need be. The source of this particular stream, was entitled

That...that Burying Ground...that one, over THERE!, a title to which each subsequent mail was solemnly referred. Jude took a breath and read, realising, too late, the source was himself:

Dear Sir

Apologies for my tardiness, and retardedness, in writing. You may recall that just before the phone cut out, I mentioned an...an Encounter with Artale. You will not recall, because I did not tell you, that I woke, not knowing where I was. Airport, Studentenheim, Yew Tree Lawn, floated before my mind, apt for selection. I opted Studentenheim, and settled in, awaiting the (precious, houseproud) furnishings of memory. I opened my eyes to assist it. Pitch past pitch, sir! Veritable tar!—like...like a road!—a Dream of the Road!—across my eyes! The next pressing question: who was I? A host of sensations, almost identities (far from faces) jostled for attention: Bjorn (impossible!), Pilar (don't love her enough), the Lizard (unlikely), you (rang a bell). My mother drifted by, disappointed with me. Finally, sensation of myself came back, like...like someone with Stockholm Syndrome, the most deluded part of which (and reeking of contrived psychological irony—because, Mad Jen, real psychological irony is impossible) being that he lived in Vienna. Last of all, and most important: what had happened? I put out a hand. Nothing. I felt my body. Covered in sweat. I flexed my nostrils. Scent, sir! Drifting, like...like the wake...of a battle...over wide fields of bed! A woman's smell. A chemical, animal-tested smell, all musk and Arabia. And what had I had to do with, how implicated by, this seductive scent? I lay there, eyeballing (like a black) the invisible ceiling. In vain. I couldn't remember. Whatever scenes seen there, scents sent, I had passed out before the denouement. I felt the sheets. Even more disarrayed than usual. Some kind of struggle. A skirmish, perhaps. No doubt negotiations, and a pact or two. But treatise, colloquy, consummation? Heaven only knows, and is too discreet to say.

Meanwhile, I was ill. I knew it before I rose. And when I rose, I rose like a man who is falling. I stumbled to the sink and vomited. I stumbled to the toilet and all hell broke loose. I stumbled back to my room, closed the door and fell over in the dark. My last thought was 'what happened to the outlight?' And this was most mysterious of all.

Apparently I was found by Bjorn. Apparently.

He could be lying, of course, trying to cover his ribbed (not to say cragged) Norwegian back. He had come in to go to the library with me (so he says). He had some serious deleting of military injunctions to do (I suppose). Instead he had to get me to hospital where I was put on a drip and detained overnight (although we only have his word for it). Next day they released me, with all kinds of instructions which I proceeded to ignore. I returned home to the kind of hero's welcome reserved for sociopathic Vietnam Vets (and for American soldiers who have experienced war in the Far East)—i.e. a grinning Rico following me sluggishly upstairs, singing an Azerbaijanian lament, punctuated by bursts of hip-hop and shapes thrown on the walls—and spent the next five days a-bed, sir, nursed only by Bjorn, although I suspect the hand of Kara Kundera in the occasional vegetable pasty he places before me, if not the more frequent bowls of oats and jam. Jam! He is a ridiculous creature. But I don't know what I'd have done without him. Felt funny in my Mind for sure, if not flat out fixed to die, Fixed To Die, FIXED TO DIE!

When I finally took it upon myself to venture from the building, with the one fixed intention of entrenching myself in some familiar nook, with only The Financial Times and a glass of water for company, my plans were violently dashed by fascists the world over gathering in vast numbers to stroll vacantly, inconsolably, along great shopping boulevards, contemplating the atrocity of the latest Alpine fashions. This is called 'The Festival of the Immaculate Conception', and it is the cause of a dire dearth of seating at the Cafe Braunerhof. So, coming over all Marxist for a minute, I stormed on down to Freud and Friends, only to find the shop shut for an indefinite period—a strange development I could only put down to Rosa's secretly celebrating The Festival of the Immaculate Conception far more fervently, and self-interestedly, than anyone (except myself, who anticipated it long ago) might have supposed.

As it turns out, though, the bug begins to pass, and my illness with it. I'm still playing it key down, though, doing all kinds of dropping (both out and off) in all kinds of unexpected places. The vomitings, stomach-cramps, deathly pallors have subsided, morphing into mere influenzas, which I have encouraged to branch out among Bjorn and Jesse. For which purpose, I took them to the Wienerwald on Tuesday and spent a good few hours discussing English etymology in

Old Norse. And Old Norse in English etymology. Not to mention old etymology in English Norse—which, scrupulously, we didn't, aware of Bjorn's sensitivities on the matter. Etymology, that is, if not Norse.

Followed up yesterday with the Kandinsky exhibition, which was a lot of pink and white. Cornelius was there, as if he felt a kinship. Tried to escape but he WOULD keep me, foot-tapping, finger-drumming, until he had detailed every snapped twig and ticked second of his jaunt through the Wienerwald birches. And he would keep INSISTING that they were BIRCHES, sir, so much so that if I'd had a wand of said species, genus, and arboratory—and also irrationally motivated—class, I would have wielded it, sir, in the general direction of his corduroy britches, which would have been all too easy, though HIDEOUS, to hit. Contracting a severe case of Museum Foot, not to mention Art-Gallery Eye, I went to sit outside, thinking of buying myself a pair of pointed shoes. Bjorn needed a few hours more, to stubbornly defy both his influenza and the creeping feeling that Kandinksy may be vastly overrated. It was sunny outside for about half an hour. Then, the sun went in. Suddenly, in seconds, WHIPPING ROUND THE CORNER!

a Siberian wind, incredibly cold! Since which nothing but ice and stone. Bjorn is in his element, walking EXTREMELY funny, Lord, wearing a black ski-hat and lighting the dark places with his nose. He rubs his hands and flagrantly ignores it (the cold that is—his nose, tiny as it is, he is, once in a blue moon, aware of—in those rare moments of, you wouldn't call it doubt, but hesitation, when something niggles, not only at the front of his face, but at THE BACK OF HIS MIND: a drip, a nasal drip, that must, at some indefinite yet pressing—imminent?—moment, be stemmed), determined to show pure implacability. His whole life: a quest for the implacable. Hopefully his influenza will worsen and confine him to bed for an indefinite period.

Speaking of which, no concrete encounter yet with Artale, since THE encounter, obviously—the one in the crags (where, 'tis true, a man may only die once)—but, nevertheless, signs, traces, ephemera, all of which melt, thaw and resolve into Saint's lighter, its pleadingly significant inscription, which Artale not only understands, account of having more than a half-arse classical and religious education (and a pretty one too), but credits, account of being a sucker for pleading significance. AND which (as Bjorn would say), having stolen from me, she decided to deposit in my room—on my bedside table, of all places, while I was otherwise engaged, on the toilet in all probability. Mark you, sir. She decided it. Weighed it. Premeditated it. The theft itself. Its consequences. The exacerbation entailed in keeping the thieved object. The problem of restoration. She will have heard I was ill. She will have been worried for me. She will have wrestled with the idea of a personal, face-to-face visitation, deciding against it, opted for a careful, even delicate, placing ON THE BEDSIDE TABLE, not only on the grounds of awkwardness, but because she did not want to risk repulsion at seeing me in my incapacitated state. The incapacitated state which, even now, I have only suspended in order to write this email. That's right, this one

from

Jude.

P.S.—which, when you think about it, lacks only an A to make a holy trinity (Pater, Son and Apparition), whose (w)hole I would gladly supply. It's an absence-presence thing—Derrida would (under)stand. (Even if) no/one else 'would' [...]. Except Nemmins. ~~Conclusion~~: she's Post-Scriptum, sir: not th(o)rough it, nor resultant from it, neither set on trajectories of perspective; merely past (be-hind [certainly!] and be-fore [framing three]) the (said) (s)cript; placed aside, neither distinct from, nor one with it, but extant only in this variable tangentiality: a ~~shimmering~~ ghost, now here, now there; a see-through (perspex) Apparition, at no time through-seeing (per-spective). So pretty much the Trinity then—Christianity's slippery Post Script: Hypothetical Trifle and Final Word.

Conclusion: Derrida is a bit silly, but Martin Luther was a Dunce.

P.P.S. I include Magnus, whom I refuse to call by any abbreviation, and the Lie, whom I refuse to credit in any way whatever, among my addressees, without any real expectation that they will tear themselves away from their outlaw wanderings and fishing rods long enough to actually answer. Because that's the thing about fishing and outlaw wandering. They refuse both abbreviation and credibility—which are of course intimately related, though not as intimately as credibility would like. Because credibility, sir, is a CRETIN.

Notwithstanding, Lie, Lie! Did you see the MATCH?

>
>

Hello Jude. Hello Harper.

Yes, I did manage to watch the tail end of it, because I sneaked away from my rod for an hour to The King Richard. Apparently there's been a big falling-out between Manager and Board over a sixteen million pound Target Man. Just wait for the January Transfer Window. There'll be a lot of comings-and-goings.

Otherwise, I haven't followed it as much as I would have liked. To be honest, angling took a hold, and that is why you didn't hear from me. I found myself going almost every night for about 2 months, until the early hours of the morning. But I have stopped now—in fact just this last week. I have fully recognised the error of my ways, and won't be going back. Instead, I seem to have got involved in a dalliance with an older woman. Not married this time, fortunately. Don't think it will last long though.

She's a difficult one—never stays in one place for a minute.

What are you both up to at the moment? Jude, you must be settling in now. There must be a lot of opportunities in a city like Vienna. Isn't that where there's ten pretty women? Mind you, by that token he could have stayed in the Glum Valley. We've got about that many here, if you include Raquel Dullet.

Benjamin.

>
>

Dear Sirs,

Good to hear from you Benjamin. Any chance of you getting on the blower one of these days? It's not so difficult. Just pick it up and blow, as Jude said to Rowan Rush. Speaking of whom (Jude, that is), what's all this about a pair of pointy shoes. Whatever next? I think you ought to point him in the right direction.

As for the Old Lady, I don't need to warn you to watch out for her veteran tricks—the stepover, shimmy and the old Cruyff turn. You shouldn't have any problem, as you've had plenty of chance to defend against Jude's over the years. In any case, there are more fish in the sea, as you of all people should know. Lots of other women too. I note that even when you sneak away from the rod, you still end up with the tail. You might explain to us how you manage to pull that off.

Speaking of which, I was walking home after work, all three of your storm-laden metropolitan miles. It was half-past six. Outside the town hall, a crowd of waifs, possibly strays, demanding peace, in a variety of languages. Peace flags, too, along Cess Street. Half–way along the road we have to go (Gut Street, as it turns out), I stopped for a beer, being thirsty. I got a bit drunk, sir. Sozzled, as Neady (the Beak at the Pomp and Prestige) would say. I sidled out. I snuck into the laundry. I handed the Ethiop a magazine I had borrowed—on Marathon Running. We stared darkly, flirted obliquely. A black-magic woman, sassy, seditious. Fixed me with a look under the eyebrows, chin down, laughing horrid—low African cackle. Terrifying. Me, looking back, seated on bench, bound to the rumbling machine. Cloths, sheets and swag, dragging their endless round. It wasn't funny but I was laughing anyway—laughing at her laughing at me—menace under the eyebrows, green fringes to her gums. Rain began. Fingers touched, hand rested in hand, then withdrew. Goodbyes were indicated. I had hardly known what was happening. But I knew when I left, sir, staggering home, under horse-chestnuts: love, sir, and with the washerwoman! All nineteen years of her, no clue to her name.

Returning home, I went into my kitchen and what did I find over the radiator? A huge multicoloured flag. And across its colours, a four letter word: PACE. Now if Alan Hansen were to drape this across the Spion Kop, with perhaps another billowing over the Annie Road End, proclaiming POWER, it might be another matter. But he hasn't and it isn't, and the whole thing might have had a very violent conclusion, had not five girls, and Romanies by G-d, BURST into the kitchen, jabbering in the language of Rom! All vagrant hair, nomadic smiles, positively exiled legs. And such noses, sir, such noses! 'Hullo,' says I. 'Hullo,' says they. Well, what with one thing and another, sir, a bottle of wine went down and another opened up. Damned if they didn't giggle, sir, GIGGLE among themselves. There was a lizardly one (no relation) with thick black hair, black stockings under a tight green dress, and she was eyein' I, sir (in creation where one's nature neither honours nor forgives). And I was eyein' her (in a similar postlapsarian state, as the Caveman would say). And what with all this lack of honour, not to say forgiveness, things went tol'able well and it became quite clear what was required and the specific conditions necessary to make it happen. Thunder rumbled, rain hammered on the windows (that was two of them). They put on some music, fell to dancing after their kind. And such a dancing, sir! to turn a Christian man heathen. Stampings, burnings, and the snapping of fingers! The Lizard girl approached me, sir, dancing like a DERVISH! Flailing and pointing and writhing. Right up she came, trussing up her hair—and immediately letting it fall! Turning and turning, in the widening gyre. What was a man to do—start dancing? No sir. Anguish! Impotence! SADDAM SAID HE HAD A BOMB, BUSH SAID A BETTER BOMB! I sat there, sipping, looking up and down, as if in a dictionary. Finally, they spent themselves. She stopped dancing, sat down near me. She looks at I, I looks at 'ee, jiggered if we didn't see each other. But vileness! Obscenity! She couldna speak English—hardly a word, and I couldna speak Rom for life of me. It became a problem. I could twinkle and leer as much as I liked, refill glasses all over, but at some point I had to cross that bridge. THAT bridge—that one, over THERE, LOOMING, between verse and chorus. This was the po(i)nt when I was supposed to seduce her by whispering low that the world was not Doomed. When in reality, Doom is as good a basis for seduction as I can think of. The Corridor of Uncertainty seemed a long way away, down a Corridor of Greater Uncertainty Still. We began looking away from each other, taking too much interest in the others' conversation. Something turned sour. I issued like litter through the doorway, accidentally flinging the PACE flag to the floor. I blew down the hall, flapped through the door, scattered over the bed in a Corridor of Absolute Certainty. And bitterness, sir. Melancholia. Enough to turn a heathen man Christian.

Again.

Harper.

>
>

Sir,

It's Biblical—baleful, bilious, Babylonian, and the red-devil TOWER THEREOF!

You should have cut out her tongue! Dragged her by the hair! Entered her forcibly if necessary!

But you couldn't. None of us could. I was there! in the retelling of it, there in the corner, weeping for you, and for me. I could barely watch, remembering (if only) Kent, remembering Holland, remembering Cleopatra. Remembering, too, the fifth of November; what was attempted, what was foiled, why, and its repercussions. The tunnelling, the Betrayal, the vile Peter Heywood. Who's that knocking at the window? Who's that knocking at the door? Fal-a-dee, fal-a-day, fal-a-diddly-i-do-day. A penny or a ha'penny'll do you no harm.

But what could you have done? Learn every language under the sun? Even if one wanted to keep things to a minimum one would still NEED Ro-may, Spanish, Italian, Arabic, Rus, Turk, a smidgen of Icelandic (not too much), a million Indian dialects in ADDITION to Hindi, Czech and Hebraic.

And so it is with no small amount of reluctance,

frustration, occasionally ascending into outright RAGE at the tawdry, attritional career called LIFE, which, as we all know, and to Bjorn's great delight, not to say moral self-congratulation, is a Marathon, not a Sprint, that I have joined a German language class (I am, apparently, only 'slightly advanced'), populated almost exclusively by Kosovars, Chechens, Turk, and the occasional spitting image of Raquel Dullet—were Raquel Dullet entirely orange-coloured and dressed as only a cheap Romanian whore could dress.

Oh. Hang on....

But it's all good fun. My favourites thus far are, in order of preference Drazenko—aus Bosnia. Forty-something, married with two kids, currently stuck in a five-year-long lack of visa-induced unemployment limbo. Purveyor of chewing gum. Consumer of local Croatian specialities. Speak no English. Holds no currency. Then there's Williams—a Negro from Nigeria, somehow washed up on Aryan shores. Lastly, and least convincingly, there is Gianpaulo, a waxwork Italian who has ambitions to cram the study of the Law, and all its Tenets, into his miniscule brain, and who says very little but 'Wuuunderschon' while smiling gleamingly at every female in the room who does not look as if she has just stepped out of a brothel, which (as that is probably what he has just done) is not only contradictory, but severely reduces his scope. Together we talk about hobbies, book theatre tickets, buy groceries, and perform all manner of semi-improvised, barely sensible 'dialogues' with an abundance of artificial fruit and vegetables. Then there's a short break in order to allow everyone to file out into the lobby-cum-cafe area and smoke the place up a storm. Then it's back to the classroom for some more knockabout fun and the inevitable casual anti-Semitism, until, finally, I'm released into the freezing airs, setting myself a course for the Neue Burg, wherein I feel compelled to remain until fully 8 o' clock in the evening. Back home it's a blur of eating in total silence, possibly scanning the financial pages of the Guardian, ever on the look-out for corporate, socio-environmental misdeeds. Music follows, very often of the type sometimes referred to, glibly, horribly! as 'Americana' . A bit of reading—though nothing related to what is portentously, PERVERTEDLY! known as 'Academia'—and suddenly it's 3am.

Other than which, I have gar nichts to report,

except that last weekend my card was inexplicably seized by a cash machine—AGAIN—causing me to have to eke out the whole of Friday night to Monday morning on 10 of your doomed Austrian Marks. Marks, mark you. For what is your euro, but a prostituted economy, a suppurative currency, a million-pierced pussy, stamped and numbed with monumental nonentities? And what is Europe but a great flat mattress, stained by a million multinational corpuses? And what is a multinational corpus but—but, like the euro, you GET MY POINT.

A stick or a stake for King James' sake, will you please to give us a fagot? If you can't give us one, then we'll take two, etc.

Jude

>
>

Hello again.

It sounds as if you are both having an interesting time in your respective cities.

I hope you have not been having too much fun

to miss out on the latest transfer gossip. The manager looks safe now, but there'll be a January clear-out. Allegedly he's been keeping tabs on a Congolese Enforcer and an eye on a young Belgian Ace. Meanwhile, he's been running the rule over a tricky Ukranian Starlet who plays in the hole.

But that's enough of Mr. Harlow. It doesn't look as if much will come of my dalliance. I have learnt a valuable lesson over the last days: women will always lead you up the proverbial. Trouble is, that's the only thing they'll lead you up.

You're absolutely right about the fish, though. The problem is, we get hooked, don't we? I need to metaphorically recast, and hope that something takes the bait. Have you got any ideas? I'm looking for inside information.

As for Mr. Harlow, you could never accuse him of missing the point. Someone needs to tell him it's about time he had a word with himself.

Maybe we will meet for Christmas. You never know where I'm going to turn up next, like the proverbial bad penny.

Benjamin.

>

>

Dear Sirs,

If turning up is your Thing, you would be perfectly welcome on any number of floors in the Immigrants' Home—perhaps more welcome than you bargained for (though no doubt you would bargain hard). Myself I've been keeping my eye out for a good deal, but it's getting to the point when I'd accept a raw one. My haggling must leave something to be desired. I'm thinking of heading down to the Bargain Basement.

Yesterday I was nearly priced right out of the market. My last fair deal had obviously gone down (no great loss), but I was in serious danger of my last swarthy, not to say dark, deal going the same way, and not just because shadows were falling, and I had been there all day. In the Corridor of Uncertainty, that is, with the lamp burning, staring on a glimmer in the garden. For no apparent reason, I put on my shoes and went down to Starling Lane to look for jobs at the plant nursery, wondering if the Flower Man would provide me a reference.

There was a wetness on the pavement but for once it wasn't raining. On the contrary, it was misty, sirs. The laundry was a cat's eye, all yellow walled. The Ethiope was shovelling clothes. I heard a click, a clang, the rumble of deep machines. I walked on down the road, past magnificent Africans, incredible Indians, dazzling Pakistanis, the glory of the colonies heavy in the air, like...like MENE, MENE, TEKEL, UPHARSIN, dripping down the plaster. I wandered through the park, to the desirable residences. I passed Pablo's cafe-cum-bar, eyeing the waitresses. Lithe Lithuanians, working their lissomes for a bit of loose change (not loose enough for my liking). Savage Serbs with knives for eyes, they could cleanse my ethnicity any time they liked. Best of all, your sulky Bulgars, sweet buns bulging, with their silver platters reflected in the floor. I walked on, past oblivious Brazilians, wealthy divorcees, French women of uncertain age—but so fine—in the chemist, or photography shop. I stopped by at the organic store to talk Italian with the ragazza there, desirous of her organs. I studiously ignored the elderly—the ubiquitous, monocular elderly—hobbling with sticks, allowed to carry weapons. I went up the street, took a right and a left. There was the lighted nursery arch, leading down a tunnel between houses. It was all Swedish craftwork, Norwegian Christmas-trees—pillars of the Scandinavian economy. I thought of Bjorn, his glacial formation in the fjords of Bergen. I thought of you, sir, with your great trapped grin in the freezing night; hysterical, handsome—with a hat on. I saddened among the greenhouses, flushed round the outdoor stalls, stopping things falling off tables. In the flower-bunching shelter, more angular girls from the other edge of Europe, feeling instinctively the absence of Test Match Special. I got a phone number, unfortunately the owner's. There was nothing more to do. I went back down the tunnel, staring down the opposite road, descending to mist and levels.

I continued to the canalside, mist rolling through the mansions, past house-boats, flower-shops, washing-lines, the inhabitants of the Zoo, watching from behind their snouts/trunks/muzzles. I moped, mooned, meandered for ages—AGES, sir!—which started me thinking of Agnes Rikovic, the Latvian girl. That and the smell of the canal. I saw myself taking her arm; kissing her teeth under the road-loud bridge. Moving along the canal, I sang, soft and croaky. Cyclists came out of the blue, silhouetted. Dark night now, and lights along the water. Bends, bridges, boat-trip signs. Dogs sniffing the ground. Maybe they had seen Rikovic too. Trees went by, vast and unnoticed, fronting opulent houses. But things changed quickly. Pretty soon there were glass blocks, corporate walkways, regeneration schemes. I saw metallic paint, gliding steps, a pedestrian-bridge, all steel and aluminium. I turned around. Vast apartments, immense lobbies, financial oases. Designer walkways, grafted plants, secular water streaming over marble. All still, all godless, built on whose authority? Huge flyovers made a permanent rushing. You could see the odd person, still in the offices. On the right, warehouses stored bathtubs, pipework, anything related to heating and plumbing. I crossed the pedestrian-bridge with its architectural phantasmagoria and followed the canal again, sucking air, passing couples, slipping on cobbles. It was then that I climbed a gate, walked a little way and found myself trapped in a garden, apparently dedicated to Gauguin. Something shuffled in the bushes. 'How do I get out of here?' I thought. Either I had to retrace my steps or I had to climb a bramble-covered wall and leap into the fog, covered in thorns. Naturally I chose the latter. Picking the thorns from my skin, I saw a bedraggled Artie peeking over the brick. For a second he wore an expression of terror. Then he disappeared. But he must have dropped into the thorn bush, because immediately 'JESUS CHRIST!' burst upon the night, as if he had newly risen.

Harper.

P.S. Merry Christmas all.

>
>

Sir,

A strange thing has happened. A weird thing, sir. A seminal (though hardly surprising) one, in every conceivable sense, and, in short, not to put too fine a point on it, in so many words, a RIDICKILOUS.

Thing.

The Thing, to be precise.

The Lie. The Lizard Lie. Turned up in Vienna.

Like the bad pennies he insists on tossing.

And his explanation for this flagrant flouting of the laws of time and space? A friend of the female persuasion. In fact, the very same girl who works at the Jewish Museum. She as sketched I, as let I in, several hours afore opening time, as outrageously flirted with I, matter of fact. She. Sara Baumgarten, her ludicrous name. Whom he claims, of all Absurdities, to have met during a Language Exchange Programme. All of which, though it explains a great many Things, does not explain the fact that, having spent hours tramping the sewers of Vienna, on Christmas Eve, with fiery torches, chasing wild geese and almost losing both torch and way, Bjorn and I followed a trail of blood up a ladder, out of a kiosk, to Rosa's flat. Which same Rosa, apart from admitting that it was indeed the Blood of Benjamin, refused to yield any more information beyond the odd innuendo, highly, and unsurprisingly, incriminating of the Lie and his sexual mores, not to say proclivities (though I'm sure he would, and with silently—invisibly—inverted commas). Which ridiculous admission, however, I have in no way imparted to the Lie, reasoning that three can play at that game, and relying on the fact that, however much he is mothered, he is entirely incapable of keeping mum—if only because mum happens to be a paranoid, anarchic sympathiser, whose idea of sympathising consists of drinking herself to an early grave while 'keeping an eye' on reckless young men who once in a decade or so come dashing through Vienna. The irony being that the Lie is probably the most reckless young man to come dashing through Vienna—ears pressed back to his head—since Dora Ratjen. Notwithstanding, like Dora Ratjen he persists with the charade, explaining that the Whole Thing was "one of those remarkable coincidences", and attempting to divert me with tales of the fabled river of Epirus that put out any lighted torch. Incredibly, he succeeds.

Meanwhile, I proceed to turn the tables on him in other, more devious ways, by shamelessly appropriating his style and getting up to language exchange escapades of my own—not least (though not only) by exchanging languages with P.S. (A). Words were spoken, grins exchanged, and before anyone (except Bjorn) knew it, I had invited her to see The Maltese Falcon last night, which could only have been more appropriate if it had been entitled The Sicilian Dragon, and if Bjorn and Barbosa had not been either side of us, like two craggy sentinels, avalanching away. Notwithstanding, the curtains opened and I came over all tired. I yawned, I stretched, arm coming down around her shoulder. Brilliant. Yet sufficient. For I am, as she points out, a mere stylist. Nevertheless, she points it out to me in an email written at 2 am, which I had to get up and step over Barbosa to read (a Barbosa, lest you ask, who is currently staying in my room—on the floor, sir—because Maria has some friends over, and cooking for Bjorn and Jesse, the former of whom seizes on the opportunity to ingest as much salchichon as he can gnaw when he thinks I'm not looking). I replied in the affirmative, observing, however, that the last time I was called a stylist, I was arrested, tried, and sentenced to six months in exile. From there, it was all about striding (STRIDING, sir, with GIANT STRIDES) over Barbosa, LEAPING into bed, and falling noisily asleep. ALL about, sir—i.e. me, in my iron-clad bed, BB., lounging as longingly as she could on the hard ribbed carpet, and never the twain to meet. For my tail is not, like that floating signifier the Lizard would call the 'proverbial', to be pinned on every passing donkey. And this is PRECISELY according to plan, and EXACTLY as I have foreseen it. Because the boom-chasing, wagon-jumping, Johnny-come-

lately Sicilian will have no option but to consider the awesome power implicit in my room—not least in its slight effeminacy. Which, she fails to realise, being so slight yet so perfect, is in fact as total a demonstration of patriarchal hegemony as one cares to imagine.

Word will spread.

As for my malaises, the Viennese sewers did me the world of good, but (and) finally did for Bjornsen. He's now laid up in bed, being fed an eternal diet of porridge and pasties while the snow blows past the window, filling each intricate nook and cranny.

As the Lizard might say, what goes around comes around.

Jude.

P.S. Oh, a merry Christmas, sir. Merry as in Godawful.

>
>

Sir.

The Lie is a Law Unto Himself. I can only assume he heard you were in Vienna and decided to see What That Was All About (Then), without breathing a word in case you felt tempted to Trouble Yourself on His Account. No doubt assuaging his Aryan conscience at the Jewish Museum led (as assuaging an Aryan conscience always will) to all kinds of other Aryan assuagings the difficulty of justifying which naturally led him to that last of all resorts, the Language Exchange Programme. Clearly he hoped that revealing such a sordid hand would clear him of all suspicion. A White Lie, if you will. How far does he intend to run with it? For Lies, as Carlotta, the magnificent Columbian above me (if only) says, have short legs.

And speaking of short legs, though shapely, I returned home last night to find Garfield in the kitchen, talking to the magnificent Italian below me (hold your horses, sir), namely Carmela Farina, from the first floor: a short, taut beauty from the school of hard knocks and even harder knockers. Eventually Garfield sighed, pronounced some banal poetry at the refrigerator and waltzed through the doorway, trailing a hand. At which point I brilliantly broke the silence with: 'Cosa fai?' (What are you doing?). 'No, niente.' (No, nothing). 'Pero, per chi stai aspettando?' (But, for whom are you waiting?). 'Dai! per nessuno.' (Fie! for nobody). 'Va bene,', says I. 'Allora!' says she. 'Comunque—' says I. 'Dimmi!' says she. Now I love this 'dimmi!' sir (and note, sir, the exclamation mark, marking an exacting imperative, not to say imprecative). In that simple imperative lies a world of promiscuity (as is invariably the case). 'Tell me'—lit. 'say me'—lit. 'take me if you want me'. And, sir, how I wanted! And how could I not, what was so generously given? Not to would have been churlish, not to say delusional. 'Dimmi,' says she and I could but obey. I looked at 'ee, she looked at me (droopy, fulsome eyes) and a pact was made on the spot. All that remained was the protocol, the token premises to foregone conclusions, the workings in the margin. And such a wide margin too. What the Lie might call a Margin of Error. 'No,' says I, with a swirl of hand, 'se vuoi una bevanda?' I moved among wines. Pretty soon she moved among them too. The lighting was fluorescent. Conversation was tilted at, Italian sorely abused. At last we dispensed with the niceties, adjourned with a wealth of excuses to the Corridor of Uncertainty, in all its symbolic glory. It was dimly lit, sir. Only a desk-lamp to chase the shade. A little music, a little conversation, a photographic study of family history, and we were home and hosed. Crucifixes were noticed, approved, dangled in mouths. Mouths were put in mouths, to catch crucifixes. They all got mixed up: margins, music, crucifixes. It was like the Exorcist in there. We fell amidst boxes, books, sleeping-bags galore, hearing a goofy, fallen-eyed, half-spastic man (not myself), singing in between strokes, that he didn't like the government where he lived, and that curly pubis, velvet cock, highschool thigh, were ashes, all ashes again. And when it was done, and there was no more to be said, she passed the night with I, with her thigh across my loins, putting the sign on me. You know the one, the blood sign, sir. And it stayed there all night, printed on my side, and the angel passing over. And this was best of all, sir. Nothing better, sir, than the Elisabeth Regina, nestled all night on your thigh, an eight-hour kiss, still-wet gesture of ownership.

As Louis Pasteur would say: 'it's all about the terrain'.

Harper.

>

>

S...so...c...c...c...cold......Sir…so...c…

Had it not been, however, your story would have fair knocked my socks gleich off. Or, at the very least, I would feel compelled to remove them myself. But sir, you are lucky. Lucky bounce laser-guided pea-roller pot-boiler, page-turner 'arper, you have an Iti! Do 'er! Do 'er! Lucky lucky blighted blighter. Lucky Piers Harlow/Kepperly-Lie/Big Quentin hoofing blighter. Where do you meetm it, this...this....CREATURE. And I bet it is a creature, fine of fettle, of locks for- and fet-. Bah! Bah, fet-! Bobbafet! But the associations, sir, the associations. It must be a terrible trial; a terrible trial; a terrible trailing trial. But GLORY! I envy. I jealous. I dread to think what it must be doing to your mind, though I know all too well.

ALL TOO WELL.

'Cause she done me, sir. PSA. Bombed me. Like a Palestinian, happening under a Vickers Vernon, with its nose cut off for to spite his face.

And what a nose, sir. What a nose. Once again, I adjure you: remember Cleopatra. Remember (again!) the Fifth of November. Recall everything about it. The confederacy, the barrels, best of all sir, the burning.

THE BURNING!

Not the Burning that was, but the Burning that should have been. Place to one side, for a second, those historical humbugs (written, remember, by the victors), messrs Gunpowder, Treason and Plot. Focus on the Burning. This is the language of the victim. That flame—that leaper—is his tongue. That ember—that sleeper—his chary heart. I'll give 'ee charity, sir, make a saint of you yet. Remember the Burning. One autumn night in every year. Concentrate on the Burning, sir (an umbrella term if ever I saw one). Roll up. Read all a-sodding-bout it (and weep). It's a hot-off-the-press Biblioclasm.

Curses! Seven of 'em! On her if she stay. On me, if she go. Curses on Magnus and his relentlessly mnemonic poetry, as if it were something to master.

So there I was, just mulling—MULLING, sir!—like so much Gluhwein in Alpine earthenware, a croquet stick in hand and long, rat-like hair, mincing down my neck. In the kitchen, sir, where most of your mulling gets done. Your ornery, everyday mulling. Your tuppence-ha'penny, five for a pound, financial meltdown, everything-must-go kind of mull. Poking into cupboards. Peering round fridges, swatting perfunctorily at Bjorn's Metamorphoses. Yes, and also at his Latin Classic. ALRIGHT! and at his Ovidian fables.

Jesus, you drive a hard bargain.

Yes, yes, and you too. Listen, I was just doing all of that and more, when who should walk into the kitchen but, curse be upon her! Laura Barbosa, with a mind that multiplied the smallest matter. When questioned who had sent for her, she answered with her THUMB. For her tongue it could not speak but only gibber. Viz:

Barbosa: [glumly] Holaa

Me: [slyly] Laura Barbosa, getting in there.

BB: [hesitantly] How are you?

M: [affirmatively] Okay. How's it going?

BB: [with determination]

I feel much better
Although the things
Are not as I would like to

M: [with interest] Oh really?

BB: [getting a hold]

But I'm doing fine
And having much fun
In those last days

M: [getting bored] Good.

BB: [persistent]

Discussions and arguments
Went away
And I focus it positively

M: [piqued] I see. What kinds of arguments? And with whom?

BB: [shrugs]

So my life goes on
And I have many things to do
New people to meet
And I have to keep my friends
And not forget them

M: [spreading hand on table] Which friends, in particular, are we talking about?

BB: [adagio]

So I will keep on working
In this capitalist society
Although I don't think capitalism
Is the best solution

M: [appassionata] Yes, yes. But what are you talking about?

BB: [piano]

Hoping to do what I want
As long that the rest let me

M: [stately] Do I detect some kind of bust-up with Artale?

BB: [pianissimo] Yus.

And so it transpired, sir. She and P.S. (A), at loggerheads, bored to death with each other no doubt. One joint, one gesture, one proclamation of peace too many, and—suddenly!—hatred rips through them! At each others' throats, like so many stoats and weasels. And I should know. Or rather knew. I should knew. Because, it also transpired, by the sound of it (and the size, too, if I'm not much mistaken—which, given her diminuitiveness, is always a possibility), if one can make any sense of her rancid ramblings, I'm very much passed and decidedly tense. Done and dusted. Soundly whipped and taken to the cleaners (and, no sir, unfortunately, lamentably, NOT LIKE THAT). And for why, sir? For why?

For a sly, swart, greasy Hispanic slime-monster called Manolo (note the subtle and so so obvious concealment of the word Man in his name). Apparently P.S. has been brainwashed into believing this—this THING! (in no way related to the Lie, I might add)—is not only her boyfriend, but a bona fide (and that's probably the root of it, or vice-versa) Hominim, Pithecanthropus Erectus (and, again—and I stress—in no way related to the Lie) even, in his later evolutions, member of the subspecies,

Homo Sapien Sapien (at this point, Bjorn, God rot his incessant philosophy, would begin to say, 'Nnnnnn, to be sapien once might be considered unfortunate, but to be sapien twice,' whereupon I would be forced to decapitate him, for once bitten, twice shy, and in any case warned is forewarned; there is wise and there is wise after the occasion), distinguished by social intercourse, language acquisition, problem-solving capabilities, etc (cf. Boyd and Silk, 'How Humans Evolved'), of the species, Homo Sapien (there he goes again), of the genus, Homo (despicable), of the order, Primate (I might have known), and of the class Mammalia (I always said it). That's right, sir: Homo. From hemo, meaning earth, dirt, soil. Connote, sir, with humus. That's right: humus.

Already I smell him, sir: all spice and incense. I hear him, communicating (barely) in a preposterously quiet and mystical voice, with an oppressive, yet easy, sexually-competent command of English, featuring indiscriminate use of the word 'beautiful'. If I were to see him, sauntering down the corridor, with the long hair, the goatee, the relentless guitar-playing, I seriously think that, without a word exchanged, I might beat him to a pulp, leaving nothing but a greasy spot outside Cornelius's door as proof of his existence. An existence I would instruct Cornelius to DENY! And he would. He would lie when Stefan came calling. He would lie in court. He would lie on his deathbed, while all the time the clues…the clues…were all there in his last and possibly finest symphony.

Jude.

P.S. There is a Kroner abroad. Or rather, a Kroner is NOT abroad, it is still (stubbornly, ridiculously) at home, which is exactly why, according to the Lizard, it is after my arse, trying to get me to get in touch. I'm going to try to persuade him to get in touch for a change. It's time for a little reciprocity. Nevertheless, I shall copy him in on this email. I hope he's still alive. Can you remember his phone number?

>
>

Dear Sir,

Crumbs, some people ain't human, they got no heart or soil. But I hear you, sir, I catch your drift, and, simultaneously, understand where you are coming from. Dimly, to be precise; the Cooley Valley. I have lingered in that Valley, sir. Lain and limbered up in it—laughed I'll be bound. I have passed from that Valley to mine own, the Glum, and have barely known the difference. I have known their intervening hills. Their steps and stoops, slopes and slips. Muscular, inviting; obstinately steep, then preposterously shallow; thick as thieves and slight as gossamer; each overlapping the last. For both Glum and Cooley are about steps, extents, gradations. Unlike Redwoods, Himalaya, Giants of all kinds, staring is not enough; you have to have walked among them. I have, you have; Artale, the Iti, the Panther, the Pole, Wellhausen, Baumgarten and Rom: none of them have done this. None, I'll wager, will. For this reason, sir, they must be scrupulously exoticised, orientalised, Othered. No one will appreciate this so much as them (though we take this on trust). No offhand remark must break this restraint. No conspiratorial jest to leaven conversation. Not so much as a kiss, if it smudge the rouge. The alternative is incest.

And speaking of conspiratorial jests, Artie knocked on my door early this evening, half dead and frozen to the bone. He wanted to know, in the whiniest of voices, if I was coming to the Mendicant's Café to meet X and his anarchic political plotters. I could even bring some friends. I promised to see him there, and turned up at 8 with a feckless company comprising Kostas, Garfield and Garfield's curmudgeonly (because?) unfortunately-named acolyte, Richard Wraith.

So there we all are, crowding in out of the rain. The balustraded, brownyellow stairwell is filled with leaflets, pamphlets, posters, selling all kinds of New Age remedies: Feng-shui, T'ai Chi, the Wigan Beer Festival. A poster advertises Alfonso and his Muchachas. Under the headline is a picture of said Alfonso (and his guitar), surrounded by Muchachas and moustaches in equal measure. At the top is a red door. This opens on an L-shaped attic, what Neady (the Beak from the Pomp and Prestige) would call a 'space', privileging exposure, be it of pipes, floorboards, brickwork, women, etc. At the counter are trays of salads, soups, quiches etc. Beans aplenty, none of 'em baked, leastwise not how Tollett (the pipesmoking hummer and hah-er and friend of, though not, I suspect, in, Neady) likes 'em. How Artie likes 'em, however, because no sooner had we ordered bread and humus, he leapt up from a table and ordered lasagna, roasted vegetables, a vast bean salad and a couple of bottles of wine, all of which Garfield footed. The waitress, though neither handsome, nor wearing a powder blue cape, nor with long white shining legs, nonetheless weren't no woman, she was a man! An enormous man, at that, in a long dress and heels. He pointed out that they didn't serve alcohol but could open bottles for us, at which Artie looked apoplectic but Garfield twinkled, patting his expensive leathern bag, and saying 'savoir faire, dear boy.' He had brought along four vintage Burgundies, partly to salvage the evening, mainly to make sure everyone knew it, and to silently laud himself for having done so. I carried four glasses to a corner table. Artie had the corner seat; I was facing the wall, where a framed nude walked among awnings. 'You've only four glasses, dear boy,' said Garfield peremptorily. 'No no, the barman's bringing them,' said I, as the barman emerged from behind a screen saying 'that's barmaid to you, love,' with a weary tone while Garfield clapped hands and warbled for joy. Joy in the sense of despair of course. 'Do ye mind not drawin' attention,' says Artie, from within a mouthful of beans. 'Oh—ha-ha—I'm sorry, Artie, I—ha-ha—' says Garfield, watering at the eyes, 'that's very good, that, don't you think so, Richard —"barmaid to you"—ha-ha. Very apt.' 'Garfield, mate, don't start,' says Wraith, disconcerted. Artie stares, red-faced, as if he'd long since started. 'Very louche,' persists Garfield, aspiring to fuse the roles of patrician, homme d'affaires and Wildean wit. 'BAM!' he cries suddenly, slamming his hand, taking it far too far. 'A direct hit!' 'You're drawin' fuckin' attention to yourself,' says Artie, this time through grit teeth. 'Oh am I,' shrills Garfield, rolling back his eyes. 'Well then I do apologise, Citizen ARTie; only when the barmaid corrected young Harper here, on the subject of her identity, I held it had relevance for all.' 'An' what d'ye mean with that?' says the tramp, fork a-pointing. Garfield pauses, folding a napkin. 'Only,' he says, 'that our barmaid is not the only one here who suffers from a little duality.' 'Is that fuckin' right?' champs Artie. 'Keep insinuatin' and ye'll suffer from a little duality.' 'My dear man, I shall INSINUATE,' announces Garfield, 'all I LIKE' (placing the napkin squarely on the table). 'I was under the impression—or should I say, Harper, through no fault of his small experience and tender years, gave us to believe—that this'—and he casts his hand about the room—'was a hotbed of rrrevoLUTionarrry ferrrvor. His rrr's are out of control (cue comment from B. K. Lie). 'And we were to be entertained with a right royal republican CONTRETEMPS. But so far, it amounts preCISEly, if you'll pardon the opportunism, to a hill of beans.' The hand wafted in the direction of Artie's meal, already a lasagna and a plate of vegetables down. 'Funny ye should say that,' comes Artie back at him, making shift with the beans, 'because I was expectin' the same thing. But if they're—that's what ye might call ma "contacts"—if they're no gonnee show, which it's how it's lookin', it's because they've had wind of a li'l fuckin' duality of their own.' He looked pleased with himself, eyes cast down behind his glass. 'What ye might call a mole in the system.' He was still quaffing. 'A rat in the fuckin' henhouse.' He set down the glass with a smack. 'Ye wouldn't happen to know anything about that, would ye?' he says, looking each of us in the eye. 'Ah mean, that'd be a dangerous fuckin' scenario for everyone concerned, if it turned out we had apostates an' turncoats an' fuckin' backslashers in the system. Cause when these carles get together, they don't talk pussy. These are pretty fuckin' sensitive subjects up fer discussion, an' what they revile most is a spy, ye comprehend?' He looked at Garfield. 'They're neither too fond of gossipin' fuckin' women.' 'I see!' says Garfield, mock-offended. 'Who's INSINUATING now?' And with a fold of hands, upturn of eyes and much clucking of tongue, he ceases. Artie is enjoying himself so much he orders up a chocolate brownie 'on the tab'. To my left is Kostas, staring at the window. It is a big, warehouse window, beaten with slovenly rain. He looks mournful, as if a love-affair has ended. Behind him is a fat middle-aged woman, staring at a candle in the manner of someone who wishes to appear preoccupied. That left Wraith who really was offended. 'Still,' he begins, like someone who won't drop it. 'Since we're here now, an' deprived of the company of these bona fide—fuckin'—reformers, you can at least tell us a bit about the plan, naïve an' tender-yeared an' lackin' in fuckin' integri'y as we are.' 'Rrrrichard!' snaps Garfield. 'Do you mean to tell me you intend to discourse with this man?' 'What's the fuckin' alternative?' protests Wraith. 'Alternative!' shrieks Garfield into his glass. 'I was brought up to believe that before venturing upon an "other", or "alter", we must first avail ourselves of a "same"—a "native" if you will—but the only native you and your rrradical friends are displaying at present is, forgive me dear Richard, native CHARM.' 'Sorry Garfield,' chimes Wraith, 'but I think you're well out of order.' They would have continued like that, but Artie saw the waitress coming with his brownie. 'Hssst!' he says, tapping his ear. 'The walls have ears'. Kostas looks at the walls. All he sees is nudity. 'In that case, is it impertinent to ask what the FUCK' (sensuous, full-mouthed) 'we're doing here?' says Garfield, 'and how we may profitably discuss anything, while the walls are so aurally endowed? No no, never mind the Plan, the whole thing reeks of ill-planning, and you know full well, Richard, if there's one thing I can't abide it's ill-planning.' 'Joker can't keep his mouth shut,' says Artie, half mirth half menace. His mouth is half full of brownie. 'And how is one to discuss anything with a shut mouth?!' yells Garfield, inviting the participation of the whole Mendicancy. 'Though such be preferable in the consumption of BRRROWNIES!' Garfield is a man who takes pleasure in delicacy and boorishness alike, often at the same time. A man who attaches overmuch import to his all too obvious comments. 'Far as I'm concerned,' chirrups Wraith. 'There's only one topic we should be fuckin' discussin' today. An' that's how can a corrupt—fuckin'—power structure best be destroyed?' 'It's a good question,' muses Garfield, breaking dry wax from the bottle and replenishing the candle. 'I have to say, Richard—really—you could make a very fine speaker if you learned to control your tongue. Ha ha. But, really, very fine. Take note, dear boy' (tapping the table in front of me) 'for all your erudition, you haven't, bless you, an eloquent bone in your body—ha-ha-ha!' He closes his eyes, laughed lightly at his eloquence. 'The young,' he pronounces, twinkling long enough to ascertain his audience, 'are untaught in rhetoric, poor things. Be they ever so brilliant—and, by the way, I am of the opinion that this generation far exceeds mine in aptitude and intelligence' (composing a noble face) 'ever so embedded in books' (spitting this out, so as you could see he esteemed 'em), 'they have not the art of oratory. (Sigh). I flatter myself' (he plants five fingers to his chest) 'though I have not half their education, toiling the furrows of intellect just as my father chipped at the walls of Yorkshire's unforgiving mines, gifted little in the way of abstraction, I have yet—in my dotage—a greater grasp of oral fluency' (his eyes rolling back) 'nay, the FUND-a-ments of grammar, than any of this cherished generation.' He waves a hand, surrendering the case to our appraisal. Kostas smiles faintly. Wraith looks discomfited. His eyes hardens, tongue comes to the fore. 'I don't know, Garfield,' he juts, 'it's like Goethe says, in Faust innit man? It's what you say, not how you say it. That is,' he says, regarding Artie accusingly, 'so long as you ain't too drunk to enunciate.' 'I think, dear boy,' lisps Garfield, 'you might cite our own Bard rather than the Kraut's.' And, placing a hand on his chest, he summons a sententious tone. 'Videlicet: "The weight of this sad time we must obey. Speak what we feel, not what we ought to say." Now there's rhetoric for you.' '"Nothin'll come o' nothin', speak again,"' mutters Artie, tucking into his glass like a man whose territory has been invaded. There is an ascetic in Wraith which disagrees with him. 'The Auld Cause was none o' yer teetotal enterprises, that's sure. None o' yer bloodless coups. Blood everywhere—that was us. Menstrual, sacrificial, you name it. Plenty o' the red stuff too' (he says, raising his glass), 'milk o' human kindness. Only water we drank was to the King across it.' He is in his cups now. Nothing can tear him from soliloquy. Nothing, that is, except for louder soliloquy, aided by modern microphone technology, for a Poetry Event is starting. A tall, earnest American—in a roll-neck jumper no less—is whispering loudly (yet spiritually!) into the microphone, 'You know, huc-hum' (tap tap) 'huc-HUM, OUT ON THE PRAIRIE, YOU CAN JUST FEEL THE WEIGHT OF THE AMERICAN LAND, IN YOUR AMERICAN BLOOD, TRAVELLING ALONG YOUR AMERICAN VEINS.' 'Greeeece,' begins Kostas, apropos of what no

one is certain, 'was the crrradle...' There is a terrible pause in which the American expounds on Wallace Stevens. '...Of Demooocracy.' A foolish smile spreads over Kostas' face. Yet not an embarrassed one. At the end of its spreading, it fixes, confirmed. The eyes above it blink. It is a sad smile suddenly. Artie pats him on the back, understands Greece's pain. 'Scawtland was a free land once,' he explains, but the American begins declaiming: 'THE LONG BLUE HOWL OF WYOMING COYOTE.' 'An'll be agin, when we're done.' 'AROOO! COYOTE! PURE AMERICAN ASOPHAGUS!' 'Arthurrr is...an Eeengleesh name?' (smile). 'It's a funny thing, ye ken, 'cause ma grandfather,' 'MELTING INTO THE AMERICAN NIGHT,' 'my grandfather!' 'CALLING OCEAN TO OCEAN, COIL ON COIL,' 'MY FUCKIN' GRANDFATHER!!!' 'LIKE A CHAIN GANG GHOSTLY HOLLER ALL ALONG THE MASON-DIXON!' It is all too much. Artie goes over to the poetry table, simultaneously like a robin redbreast in a cage AND like a Heaven in a Rage, and begins to harangue the American: 'DON'T YE KNAW HOW RUDE IT IS INTERRUPTIN' A MAN'?' he bawls. 'I'M SORRY, WHO'S INTERRUPTING WHO?' says the Poet. 'HOW'D D'YE LIKE IT IF I INTERRUPT YE

IN ILK MANNER YE FUCKIN' YANKEE PRICK?' 'CAREFUL OF THE MICROPHONE.' 'YOU CAN SHOVE YER FUCKIN' MICROPHAWN UP YER AMERICAN ARSEHOLE!' (dashing microphone to floor). 'Hey!' cries the Fat Woman behind Kostas, 'there's fuckin' poetry happening here!' 'Oh, the poetry! Do let us know, dear woman, when the poetry starts!' 'AH'LL GI' YE POETRY,' shouts Artie, vehemently pointing. 'Poetry in fuckin' motion.' He starts prancing, circling fists like a gentleman fighter. He is hauled off by the barman and coaxed back to our table with a bottle of Burgundy, while the poets pick up the microphone. 'Fuckin' poetry,' mutters Artie. 'Ah couldn't agree more,' says Wraith. 'Sheer bloody self-aggrandizin'—.' They share a moment of sympathy. 'Grrreeece,' says Kostas again, 'was the crrradle...' 'Too right. Plato was fuckin' spot on,' says Wraith, keen to agree. 'Poets should be exiled. Put in the fuckin' stocks, more like.' Kostas is still moving his mouth when: 'Plastic FUCKIN' explosive!' belches Artie. 'Is that poetry enough for you?' 'That's more like it, dear man!' 'HERE'S A POEM ABOUT...ABOUT DEATH!' 'Bring down the fuckin' city from within.' 'That's what I adore about you, Artie, you're never one to fuss over details!' 'DRIP, DRIP, DRIP, LIKE ACID ON MY SKULL!' 'But how exactly?' 'We blow up City fuckin' Hall.' THE IRIDESCENT OCEAN PAIN SHUDDERING IN JESUS!' 'City Hall! Such ambition!' 'SEEPING DOWN THROUGH MY COSMIC MIRRORED MIND!' 'A real fuckin' Coup d'Etat.' 'Aaaathens is a city very laaaarge...' 'Ye should come to the Scandinavian Church. Fuckin' Kirk job, Paradise Street, ye ken. Bomber'll show ye, here.' '...With many forests very laaaarge.' 'This time ye'll meet 'em fer sure. X an' the rest of 'em.' 'Aaaathens has...suffered...many time.' 'I'll let 'em know you're alright.' '...Frrrom FIRE!' etc. And Artie storms off, and I (and Kostas) go storming after him, and the Fat Woman unfolding a poem of her own, and Wraith is offended and Garfield delighted, and the barman is waltzing from bottle to bottle, unscrewing 'em all and earning not a penny.

Harper.

P.S. No, sir, I have forgotten it.

Jude sighed. That seemed to answer the initial question (i.e. of the initials), but, like all answers, it was vaguely unsatisfactory. Harper was infatuated with narrative, but he wasn't in control of his materials. His self-deprecation, which he convinced himself was irony, was a defence mechanism designed, *specifically,* to ostracise himself and demonise The World. Jude was more interested in his own story, which he, by contrast, had *perfectly consciously* constructed. He pursued the correspondence upstream, which was to say downstream, if you spoke chronologically—but Jude had little time for that—right into the present.

Sir,

Woke up this morning in a cold sweat. Struggled to breathe. Opened my eyes. There, on the ceiling—three letters, one shimmering as if only partially extant (to the extent that I suspected my own tired eye):

P S (A)

Struggled to breathe, etc.

Speaking of which, yesterday Barbosa took her ridiculous collection of Girl's Things (for even Barbosa is a Girl), comprising all manner of creams, ointments, emoluments—necessary, as the Lie would say, on a Daily Basis, merely to keep them from disintegrating—and went back to her room, Maria's friends having upped and left, having long since overstayed their welcome, therefore Barbosa's into the bargain. When the time came—a dark, electrically-lit, nondescript hour—it was an almost Emotional goodbye. There she stood, by the door, her arms full of tubs, tubes, bottles of every description (not to mention pads, cottons, applications—NOT TO MENTION THEM!), gazing on me mournfully—and I tricked into gazing mournfully back.

BB: [lugubriously]

I'm almost sure
This relationship will end
In friendship

M: [relieved] Which one?

BB: [smilingly]

It's too complicated to depend on that
Unless it changes,
That I'm not sure at all about that.

M: [cautiously] I see.

BB: [With an air of sad martyrdom]

I will go home,
Read for a while
And rest.

And I will keep on making breaks
To this working live,
Travelling now and then, from time to time.

M: [momentarily stumped]

BB: [waxing lyrical]

When you'd like to come
To Barcelona or their surroundings
I will be pleased
To let you a place to stay.

M: [putting a hand to the door] Brilliant. In the meantime, by which I mean at least a month or two, I'll be just down the corridor.

L: [insistent]

I'm sure you will recover
all the little pieces of your heart
to have again a splendid whole

Which will take you to those
incredible situations

everyone want to be in
and never be ended.

M: [solemnly again] Yes, well. I'm sure you will too.

BB: [confidentially]

I know you love women
and they are your debility,
but it has to give you strength.
Use it.

But you have to be brave enough
to say no and forget.
Your harem is around the world.
Look for it you will find it.

M: [tolerantly] No, you're right.

BB: [daringly]

Although if you think about harems,
think about them,
they, as girls they are,
would like to have a harem too.

Big hig.

M: [affirmatively] Big hig.

She trembled with her load, caught in two minds. With an uncommon, calculated—and so much the more genuine therefore (that's right, sir, GENWYNE)—display of understanding, instinctively perceiving the requirements of the si'u-ashun, I raised an heroic hand, preventing the necessity of opening bosom and spilling various, nefarious, moist conglomerates over the carpet (ribbed, mark you) and merely moved toward her, the way a friendly ship comes under the lee to starboard, or two rappers of uncertain ethnicity bump bodies. Cheek to cheek, then, and (slapping) hand to back, breasts separated by a mountain of cosmetics, we shared not only a hig, but a moment. Then away she shuffled, looking back with riduckulous eyes.

Nevertheless, I noticed one or two things remained on my beside table—lip-salve and hand-cream to be precise—which cosmetic falsities add up, Harper, to a pharmaceutical truth, namely, that girls KEEP staying in my room. The place overflows with them. They are going to think it the NORM. They will consider it (the Lizard aside) the Next Big Thing and come in their hordes to my ambiguous room.

And, as with Schrodinger's Cat, no one will know what on earth is going on in there, until they open the door and find us fast asleep. Or as if so. For what is sleep, Mad Jenny, but imitation?

Speaking of which, tonight Bjorn and I are going to the vast, and quite probably empty, Gartenbaukino, to watch the vast and quite probably empty 2001: A Space Odyssey. Already I feel him getting quite uptight and excited at the words 'Space' and 'Odyssey', though I wouldn't be surprised if the number 2001 also sent a tremor or two up his icy spine.

Jude.

P.S. Some girl's stolen my seat. Intolerable.

>
>

A Happy New Year, Gentlemen,

Humus: the last stage, or state (lasting centuries, millennia), Thule Ultima if you will, of decomposition, differing from soil in that, while the latter will typically contain traces of vegetable matter, humus is amorphous, uniform, without discernible character. (True, some identify an 'active humus' with the potential for further decomposition; others, among whom we find the venerable Flower Man, protest that this CANNOT be humus, by definition.) It is beneficial to soil, however, in both its physical and chemical capacities. Dark and jelly-like, it keeps soil warm and moist, enabling plant-nutrition. Earthworm humus is particularly good: the Champagne of humi if you will.

I recommend the 1991 study, 'Food Resources and Diets of Soil Animals in a Small Area of Scots Pine Litter', by the intriguingly named J. H. Ponge, the psychology of whose interest in manure would furnish an article of its own. The article appears in volume 49 of the excellent soil journal, Geoderma. I borrowed said journal once from the town library, read it religiously and promptly lost it. Running up a tremendous fine, instead of trying to get it back, I had the idea to renew it perpetually. I remember I was in the process of renewal when I pressed the wrong button. Up flashed a box, in which was written the following dire warning:

'IF YOU END THIS SESSION, YOUR HISTORY WILL BE LOST.'

Incidentally, I saw lights in the school hall the other night, climbed on the roof and witnessed The Man Formerly (and Even Now) Known As The Man Who Would Be King with a group about forty strong, all standing in a circle. They were coming one by one to the centre, gesticulating, hanging their heads as if confessing something about themselves, then weeping and returning to the rim to be comforted. After, they began linking arms and pushing individuals into the arms of the others, raising each other up, and weeping again. Finally they stood around heaving their chests (as if sighing) and eating cakes. It went on for about an hour. When they'd gone, I tilted at the window (open), slid down the gym rope and scoured the place looking for clues. Nothing but a few remaining cakes and some pamphlets expounding upon dynamics, infrastructure, wellbeing, and the like. I left a note of my own, at the end of a tunnel under the stage. I think you might have liked it. It read: THE PLAY'S THE THING.

Continue to report status and location. At some point you may be called upon to return. Myself, I will remain until I deem it unfeasible or unnecessary—whichever comes first.

T.

>
>

Messrs,

Think about it. Moist. Jelly-like. No discernible character or form. But, as Lenny Bruce, Dustin Hoffman, Martin Scorsese might say, annoyingly beneficial to the soil.

WE HAVE SEEN THIS SOMEWHERE BEFORE.

That's right, I'm talking about a moist, formless delicacy, some kind of conglomerate of chickpea and tahina, mixed with a little Syrian/Palestinian olive oil, Babylonian garlic and Indian lemon, origin unknown (and, according to The Jewish Chronicle, much disputed), although legend puts the source (refrain!) in a 12th Century concoction of the Kurdish-Armenian-Mesopotamian Sultan of Egypt, Saladin (origin unknown), whom Bjorn is quick—in the slowest possible sense, obviously—to point out languishes forever in Dante's Limbo, and whose two sarcophagi (a wooden one: occupied; a marble one: empty!) grace a mausoleum in Damascus; a man who captured Jerusalem, defied the Coeur de Lion, and once said, on personally executing Raynald de Chatillon: 'It is not for Kings to kill Kings, only THAT MAN overstepped the mark' (completely brilliant, and well worth memorising for future reference); moreover, the psychology of whose interest in some kind of semi-solid, hors-d'oeuvre accompaniment to a tossed composition of certain esculent plants and herbs (including the Egyptian lettuce, sogennante for its milk-like liquids) would stand little, if any, scrutiny, for one who did not wish to decompose into his own vegetable matter, specimens of which I see all round me as I speak. Nevertheless (as is the case for said specimens) in the event that such is a consummation devoutly to be wished, you might do worse than turn to John Evelyn, friend of Samuel Pepys, witness of the Fire of London, and author of 'Sylva, or a Discourse of Forest Trees', a semi-vegetarian after Bjorn's own heart, equally patronised and esteemed by vegans, whose skull, not long ago—like Thomas Browne's, and Mata Hari's before it—was stolen from its sarcophagus in St. John's Church, Wooten, by someone who REALLY wanted it, and the fortune of whose family, I might add, was founded

on GUNPOWDER.

So you see, it all begins to add up.

The same man, mark you, who writes:

...We are by Sallets to understand a particular Composition of certain Crude and fresh Herbs, such as usually are or may safely be eaten with some Acetous Juice, Oyl, Salt & c. to give them a grateful Gust and Vehicle...And hence indeed the more frugal Italians and French, to this Day, gather Ogni Verdura, any thing almost that's Green and Tender, to the very Tops of Nettles; so as every Hedge affords a Sallet (not unagreeable) season'd with its proper Oxybaphon of Vinegar, Salt, Oyl & c. which doubtless gives it both the Relish and Name of Salad, Ensalada, as with us of Sallet: from the Sapidity, which renders not Plants and Herbs alone, but Men themselves and their Conversations, pleasant and agreeable: But of this enough, and perhaps too much; lest whilst I write of Salt and Sallet, I appear myself Insipid...

in his much-loved Classic, 'Acetaria: A

Discourse of Sallets', as recommended, indeed presented, to me, on the occasion of my birthday, by my mother.

Which returns us to the origin, lest we had forgotten

Jude.

>
>

Dear Sirs,

Following your carefully-laid clues (the Lizard aside), I not only discovered red stripes on the American flag, but the said Evelyn's teachings on the 'Four (vulgarly reputed) Elements: Fire, Air, Water, Earth'; the 'Stercoration, Repastination, Dressing and Stirring the Earth and Mould of a Garden'; and the aforementioned 'Sylva, or a Discourse of Forest Trees', wherein he includes the following advice:

...As to that of earth, we shall need at present to penetrate no deeper into her bosom, than after paring of the turfe, scarrifiying the upper mould, and digging convenient pits and

trenches, not far from the natural surface, without disturbing the several strata and remoter layers...

Therefore we should take notice, how many great wits and ingenious persons, who have leisure and faculty, are in pain for improvements of their heaths and barren Hills, cold and starving places, which causes them to be neglected and despaired of, whilst they flatter their hopes and vain expectations with fructifying liquors, chymical menstruums, and such vast conceptions.

...Chuse not your seed always from the most fruitful trees, which are commonly the most aged and decayed; but from such as are found most solid and fair. This observation we deduce from fruit-trees, which we seldom find to bear so kindly and plentifully from a sound stock, smooth rind, and firm wood, as from a rough, lax and untoward tree; which is rather prone to spend itself in fruit, (the ultimate effort, and final endeavour of its most delicate sap,) than in solid and close substance to encrease the timber. And this shall suffice, though some haply might here recommend to us a more accurate microscopical examen, to interpret their most secret schematismes, which were an

over-nicety for these great plantations.

In the mean time, for the simple imbibition of some seeds and kernels, when they prove extraordinary dry, as the season may fall out, it might not be amiss to macerate them in milk or water only, a little impregnated with cow-dung & c. during the space of twenty four hours, to give them a spirit to sprout and chet the sooner; especially if you have been retarded in your sowing.

As to the air and water, they are certainly of almost as great importance to the life and prosperity of trees and vegetables; and therefore it is to be wished for and sought, where they are defective, and which commonly follow, or indicate the nature of the soil, or the soil of them (taking soil here promiscuously for the mould;) that they be neither too keen or sharp, too cold or hot; not infected with fogs and poys'nous vapours, or expos'd to sulphurous exhalations, or frigiverous winds, reverberating from the hills, and other ill-situate eminencies, pressing down the incumbent particles so tainted, or convey'd through the inclosed valleys: But such as may gently enter and pervade the cenabs and vessels destin'd and appointed for their reception, intromission, respiration, and passage, in almost continual motion: In a word, such as is most agreeable to the life of man, the inverted head compared to the root, both vegetables and animals alike affected with those necessary principles, air and water, soon suffocated and perishable for the want of either, duly qualified with their proper mixts, be it nitre, or any other vegetable matter; though we neither see, nor distinctly taste it: So as all aquatics, how deeply soever submerg'd, could not subsist without this active element the air.

Harper.

P.S. One rule I must not omit, that you cast no seeds into the earth whilst it either actually rain, or that it be over-sobb'd, till moderately dry.

>
>

Sir,

I confess it. I have been retarded in my sowing. However, FLYING, like airborne pollen, in the FACE of the eminent Evelyn (causing no small amount of sneezing, I shouldn't wonder), I deduce that it is precisely a rough, lax and untoward tree that answers my needs. PRONE, sir, to spend itself in fruit. For what cares I for timber? I have all the timber I need. And yet, sir, I wager I'll find one solid and fair, as well as fruitful; howso it be, that if it prove aged and decayed in the soil, I shall not reap it long enough to know. I mean to become a factory forester. A planter of pine and eucalyptus. And the soil—I mean the SOIL—may go to waste for all I care. For What Is To Be Done? The SOIL is defective (taking the soil promiscuously for mould), typically containing traces of vegetable matter. By the rood, man, I mean my seeds to sprout and chet the sooner, dung or no dung. With great Gust and Vehicle I shall make great plantations to match my vast conceptions; notwithstanding I shall ALSO subject the entire process to over-nice microscopical examens. No amount of secret schemata shall avoid my piercing, penetrating, positively impregnating gaze.

As for the mould (taking the soil precisely for soil), by which I mean the tubes, canals and other emulgent passages, for the elaboration, concoction and digestion (meeting with no noxious vapours in the descent, though occasionally leading to the vomiting of pestiferous fervor), which, sir, we can most certainly, analogically and otherwise, characterise as the STOMACH, how I hate it, demanding Wretch! And the stomach, too. With that hunger, that UNCEASING hunger. A hunger which assails me every couple of hours, no matter where I go, what I do, or what measures I take to placate it financially.

Speaking of which (assailing, placating, etc), Bjorn has taken up running. Not just running either, sir. No, he has been running in the Wienerwald, in Austria (which we may loosely—yet with considerable justice—term Germania) in a RACE. He is a GERMAN RACIST. Suddenly it all seems so obvious. The abstraction, the eyes, the classical form.

Speaking of which, stayed up until 3am last night watching Afle'iks. It was INCREDIBLE, sir, INCREDIBLE. And yet at the same time, totally credible. Then, sometime in the middle of the night, it began to RAIN. Not a rubbish rain, mind, a FANTASTIC rain. Thunder and lightning, sir! Just myself, Bjorn and Rico, staring at each other with the whites of eyes, grinning, in the empty television room, where I go of an evening to take my mind off tortuous hunger pangs, whilst explaining to Bjorn how he's got it ALL WRONG on EVERY FRONT.

As for your Tonight (fine), we, the homo erecti of the Heim, are walking (erectly), in a troop, to an UNSPECIFIED LOCATION of DARKO'S CHOOSING, to execute your retaliations in first, your welcomes to the Premiership, your short balls and your lumping it longs, your effing and blinding and fancy-dan dives—all manner of Cruyff turns, Garrincha dribbles and Platini slide-rulers, while, all along, the terraces ripple with obscene anthems relating to various historical calamities, sexual perversions and the unwarranted (not to say suspicious!) consumption of pies.

Playing football, in the freezing Viennese night.

Until which certain term, I am doomed to walk the watches of the library, watching (constantly). Staring even. AND, as it turns out, being stared AT. For a FANTAHSTIC girl in here (the Neue Burg), a leggy brunette, sir, whom Cornelius has long had his beady, snaky, worm-like eye on, is currently seated at the computer opposite, giving me the

I

P.S. Suddenly, sir. Suddenly. That leggy German brunette I was speaking of—bit of a looker, object of Cornelius Barry's affections (and just about everyone else's in the library), name of Ava as it turns out—that's right, as in Gardner, and yes I would, on both counts—which innocuous name can be cynically reduced to a single letter, without any loss of hermeneutic suggestion, signification or semiology (the last especially, despite her immoderate attractiveness). Well, while the Crimson Visage is gone, the rodents emerge to gad about. She has just plum—that's right, Plum—asked me out—or in rather, because apparently there's some play on, and what with us sitting opposite each other and all, one thing led to another until she invited me along. I told her I probably wouldn't go. Then I will send her an email from some UNSPECIFIED location to say something along the lines of, 'I'm away. Back at some point—not exactly sure when. Did you still want to go for that drink?' Putty in me 'ands. Putt-EYE...in me 'ANDS!

'Cos I'm COURTIN' En oi!?!

An' oim a-WOOin'!!!

P.P.S.

That

Man

(you know the one. The one just There.)

That man

is

a

WRETCH!!!

>
>

Sir,

My aunt and uncle and their neighbour dropped by yesterday evening, on their way across the country. We sat in the kitchen eating and talking, my uncle spinning yarn on a sturdy Welsh loom. He was also leaning over me rather imposingly. The neighbour was a magnificent old man named Idris, as in 'Cader'. He is very small, very taciturn and very white, like something from the end of an Edgar Allen Poe novella. He can only go out at night because he has a skin condition, which means that it blisters and is ruined by the sun.

His favourite hobby? Gardening.

It's ridiculous. He has to get up before dawn to do his gardening, before going back into his house and shutting all the curtains till nightfall. His skin is luminously white, and blotched. His hair is preternaturally white. Taken all in all, he is a very white man, with all the social handicaps pertaining thereto. I sat there listening to him and my uncle and aunt speaking Welsh. Apparently, if he ever decided to visit it again in what little remains of his life, he would have the FREEDOM of a village in Normandy, because he was one of three men out of 180 who survived, when his company liberated it from the Germans. Think about it. A small Welshman in his eighties, with a permanent pallor and love of gardening. The Freedom. Of the Entire Village. Harem-scarem on the cobbled streets. Pledging in the choicest Bourgognes. Riotous debauchery with a host of Madames, and some few Mademoiselles. And of all it not only tolerated but indulged. I'm telling you, sir: not the war did for them, but the aftermath.

Speaking of which, the Iti is gone now, and with her the world's generosity (taking the mould promiscuously for mould). No, sir. Away with your fluffed 'spirit', your fudged 'symbol', your flatulent 'pneumatics'. Give me real presence, real remembrance, bounty in the mouth. As Neady would say, 'that's kind, that's kind'. As if to reinforce which, when night was established, and my uncle finally gone (Idris waving sadly from the back-seat), I wandered back to the Corridor and fell asleep under a picture of the Virgin into carnal Carmelan dreams, whereupon, on the very verge and lip of consummation, I was violently woken by the insane jangling of an all too adjacent alarum. A fire alarum no less. Joining a disaffected throng of Serbs, Kurds and Somalians, plus a couple of Ugandans and a Georgian—all of them torn from the lip of consummation—I traipsed downstairs, filed through the door and stood shivering, in t-shirt and shorts, watching the rain fall slowly through the streetlight. It was only when a hundred or so immigrants had assembled on the lawn, and a glazed-eyed Artie had emerged coughing from the computer room, that I noticed Kostas, about an inch behind my shoulder, in a large maroon dressing-gown, chest-hair sprouting over towelling, grinning the most heavy-lidded grin. He stood there, high-chinned, regarding me through dead, unflinching eyes, as if he had known I was there a lot longer than I had he. Not a word was spoke between us, despite the fact that, having followed the fire-alarm procedure to the letter, NO RISK WHATSOEVER was involved. After he had done that for about a minute, possibly two—time itself falling as slowly as the rain, so that I was beginning to think that what they are wont to term an unflinching regard was nothing other than vapid stupefaction—he raised his chin still further, cranium almost touching his spine, cranked open his jaw, levered up his tongue, and, with a sort of gutteral buzz, low in the larynx, uttered the following word:

'FIIIIIIIIIIIRE!'

At last, having tortured this single syllable as long as air could endure, the chin fell a fibril, jaw fractioned back, tongue tucked a tad, and left only the grin. And there he continued, silent, implacable, in an immensity of night and time, offering for contemplation the epic hypothesis of fire. A hypothesis not at all subverted but backed up by the streetlight, reflecting from impenetrable Athenian teeth.

Until Garfield came bustling out, also in robe and slippers, to assure us, in the most noble manner possible, and with a perfect plethora of words, that, there was indeed no risk whatsoever involved, as if we had not known that all along, and that the alarm, such as it was, being entirely false, we might disperse our several ways, to soothe our limbs and compose ourselves to sleep, perchance to dream, etc.

Which, naturally, gave not only pause but insomnia

To

Harper.

>
>

My dear Sir,

Speaking of gardens (not Baum gardens, although I shall gladly explore that subject later—particularly the garden aspect, although, it is true, I am more than salubriously interested in the Baum), I done 'er, dunni. Decked 'er, 'ad 'er, and, as Gianpaulo might, and does frequently (having first lit a solemnising cigarette, put a conspiratorial arm around my shoulder and addressed me by name), croon, somewhere between advice and confession, 'tomba la bomba' (and bear in mind that, bar, a 'yes' or two from my side, that is the ENTIRE EXTENT of our conversation). A. that is, not B., which obvious monosyllables will not only induct me through an alphabet of intrigue, but have that alpha-male, Bjorn, champing at all kinds of intriguing bits.

But I shall give you a taste of your own putrid medicine, and narrate the whole day, and chronologically at that. It began, as days do, with the Dawn, which meant attempting to step over Barbosa, who can be easily reduced to anything you like, provided it involves tears, but not quite attempting hard enough. Hard enough, however, that she woke up and cleared out with many a reproachful gaze, bordering on somnambulant stupor. It continued into Morning, which meant Bagels with B. in the Jewish Museum. Two Bs, actually, or not two Bs, because, since he has already reduced himself to a hard, lean penury, one doesn't like to reduce Bjorn any further. Fortunately the Bs were on the house (comparing truss, perhaps, with prop and lintel); but when I had persuaded them to come down (as far as was possible, in Bjorn's case), we breakfasted kostenlos. Because, here's the thing, sir. There comes a point, a very distinct point, when a man has to eat. And this is not something I can AFFORD, unless I seduce women into buying food for me, which Bjorn triumphantly informed me is a very Henry Miller-esque thing to do, at which point I wondered whether or not this was something I could AFFORD, and, planting my nose very precisely in the Jewish Chronicle, resumed reading about Brother Theodore—chess hustler, Dachau-survivor, Einstein-associate, stand-up tragedian and cameo actor in Orson

Welles' The Stranger, a cameo subsequently cut to an appearance, whittled to a credit, pared to a total null—all of which would have been a red rag to Bjorn's interlocutory bull, so I share none of it.

WHICH artful economy, sufficient for the Morning but spent by Noon, landed me in Freud and Friends, seeking employ. So far the only thing I have is an agreement that at 9.30am on Thursday 11th January I will turn up at Rosa's apartment to spend the day painting her bathroom. While I am performing the aforementioned task, she will probably recline in a chair and drink wine, and, adopting an air of extremely scrutable, excruciating, scrotum-tightening inscrutability on the subject of her recent disappearance, insist on expounding at great length my future career, which she seems to think can only be brilliant. Money has not yet been discussed. But it will be, sir. It will be.

Notwithstanding, the expectation of getting hands on some of Rosa's (considerable, I suspect) cash-money, gave me extra motivation to desist from returning home and, instead, go the library to put in a serious late shift till all of 7 in your Viennese Evening. Not but I found time amidst all the furious Reading of Books and the intensive Taking of Notes to write a message. A message saying something along the lines of, in fact exactly: 'Pssssssssst! The Library is Stuffy. Want to step out of the air?' This message I wrote on a blank piece of A4 paper, which I proceeded to fold up into the shape of an aeroplane and throw in the direction of A.. Fortunately she did not send it back saying 'Into my grave?' which would have been either intimidating or witless but (and) nothing in between. Instead she wrote, 'O.K.', and threw it so rubbishly that I had to pick it up from under the desk. Cue much foolish smiling and regrettable clowning, and in minutes I was lighting her cigarette in the Late Afternoon fog and agreeing, at the second time of asking, to go to a play.

After that, it was all about (that's right, ALL ABOUT) the Evening, which, like me, had a STORMER. There we were, both of us, the Evening and I, blazing in, giving it the old one-two, the shin-kick, rib-tickle and downright 50-50 there-to-be-won elbow in the face. It began, as so many things do, with A. and Drink. One became two, morphed into three, transmogrified into four, and just when you thought evolution had achieved all it was likely to, lo, it mutated into, of all ridiculous things, an Austrian version of Macbeth, apparently inspired by a Hungarian opera, itself apparently inspired by a play by a man with the all too apparent—yet inspired!—name of Toth, whose obvious monosyllable will defeat Bjorn utterly. This latest apparition was staged, completely uninspiringly, at the Volksteater, and set, quite apparently, almost blatantly, in Hungary, during the baronial feuds of Matthias Corvinus (a distant cousin, let us remember, of Vlad the Impaler, aka Count Dracula, aka Klaus Kinski, a man, incidentally, whose Viennese flat was filled with nothing but autumn leaves) and various Ladislaus's, including his brother, Ladislaus Hunyadi, and the improbably if not unluckily-styled, Ladislaus the Posthumous. After triumphing in which, the redheaded, straight-nosed Corvinus, in tandem with an unsexed, chessplaying (and tomes, sir, tomes and reams could we write of the correlation) Beatrice of Naples, financed his philanthropic ambitions and patronly longings (including the ludicrously named Bibliotheca Corviniana), by overtaxing the exhausted peasantry, before letting loose a Black Army to pillage their property and ravish their wives. Meanwhile, inspired by his successful juvenile portrayal of a Woman Covered In Ribbons, Corvinus added insult to injury by disguising himself as peasants, soldiers, wheelwrights—any satirical figure he could cut—and went around spying on everyone. Naturally, he became a National Hero, popularly styled The Just. Naturally, too, he headed for Vienna and, having been there, done that and scoffed the Sachertorte, again quite naturally he died without an heir, leaving Malcolm, aka Vladislaus Jagiellon, to walk off with all the posterity—at least until Banquo's family trees stumble his way. And that, of course, should be that, except that, as luck and legend would have it, Corvinus, like Finn MacCool and Sir Francis Drake (and, as it happens, Vlad the Impaler) is a so-called 'sleeping king', ready at any moment to arise from any given mountain, rescue Hungary, Transylvania, Slovenia and Vienna (but not, repeat NOT, sir, the Tirol) from their extremely pressing concerns (a three per cent drop in sleighbell production, skulduggery at the Eurovision Song Contest, etc) and put a myriad Infidel foes to the pale. Just like the Lie. And, apparently, just like Macbeth.

So there we were, A. and I, in Creation obviously, but more precisely in the Volksteater, eagerly anticipating a bloody tragic catastrophe, developed through a brilliant historical parallel subtly comparing the woes of poor oppressed Austria with those of Scotland, Ireland, Palestine, Sri Lanka and the Basque Country. And also to see Macbeth. Her call, remember. Hers. Which put her at an immediate disadvantage, of course, and one which I did not scruple to exploit. We sat down. Shuffling commenced, the spurious removing of coats, procuring of comfort, etc. Legs touched, backs came into contact with shoulders. I was cool, she, distinctly tipsy. This in itself set her at a distinct disadvantage. She reiterated that it was a play she particularly wanted to see. Good, said I, with the air of a man who, by virtue of an ornate, but partially-concealed, mirror, has just glimpsed his opponent's ENTIRE HAND. Then the play started. And guess what? It was risible. Utter toth, as they say in Hungary. I sat there positively, and quite negatively, LAFFING. What was that, sir, up there, blocking the light of the elaborate chandelier? Why, it was my UPPER HAND. What happened next was sheer routine. Her place by Night, with a little Chick Corea. 'I think I should warn you,' said I, choosing my words carefully, 'that I have other irons in the fire'. 'A daring gambit,' said she, shuffling up onto the kitchen surface and reaching for a bottle. 'Not at all,' I continues. 'I don't do gambits—that would be Bjorn. I just play fool's mate,' (she plying the corkscrew) 'suck my opponent in,' (she extracting the cork) 'and then—just when said opponent is about to execute the coup de grace—slope off, as a marvellous spout of water sweeps the pieces from the board.' Out popped the cork, the smell of wine drifting up in a way Cornelius might have described, after much intellectual deliberation, as 'effortless', and Bob (to my disgust) was proven to be my uncle.

'Was' being the operative word, sir—'proven' being an inflated and supplementary past-participle, and 'to be', why! 'to be' (as I pointed out to A.) being a theatrical ham of an infinitive, in need of considerable down-sizing, yet which, in its various significations, conjugations, negations even, a man cannot escape, it seems. Because I learned this morning, during a phone-call with my father, that my uncle, whom, subsequent to his sex-change, and (subsequent) removal to Argentina, it became increasingly difficult, though tempting, to classify as such, is dead, sir. Dead.

But not in the water.

No, sir. In a swarm of bees.

That's right. My uncle: killed by an enormous

swarm of bees, which attacked him whilst he staggered home drunk through Buenos Aires. At night! mark you. There he was, rolling along. Maybe singing a song. Down a cobbled street. The sky was inky, the moon was full. He did something...something he did...we don't know what...to enrage some BEES, which came from...where? All we do know is anyone sitting up that night would first have heard the rapid clip-clop of his hob-nailed boots as he ran, terrified, down the street, hotly pursued by a buzzing, seething, deafening mass. A cry! A scuffling. Then silence. And at dawn, there, lying on the ground, the spreadeagled body of a middle-aged ambiguous person, in a sea of bee-corpses.

I am Jude.

P.S. You should keep up that Hamlet thing we had going.

P.P.S. AND A BALL! Suddenly thrown at you! KEEP IT UP!

>
>

Sir,

I woke very suddenly, caught the bus and got to wiping, polishing, disinfecting, etc. Then I started work, etc. I scraped the last obscenity from the wall and decided to go for lunch, at The Pomp and Prestige, where I have become a regular, and whose other regulars now greet me with a nod, a point or a look of familiar scorn, depending in part on who they are, and in part on how bespattered with excrements, detergents, lineaments (of gratified desire)—all the ents—I happen to be that day. Thus bespattered, I sat in the corner with my ale and sandwiches, reading Von Eichendorf's Life of a Good-for-Nothing—of which no one could get enough of the symbolism. The blondes leant over the counter, showing meagre breasts, smirking and pointing at the title. 'Alright,' they were saying, 'look at the symbolism!' and 'I'nt it APPROPRIATE!' and chuckling to themselves. The red-faced man noticed it too, he of the horse-racing. 'Alright,' he choked, as if about to die (and he is, sir, mark my words, he is), 'un-fuckin' fortunate CORRELATION, in't there—heh, heh, heh, etc.' And he actually said 'etc'. Needless to say, they all shrieked with laughter, in the most understated way and carried on watching their nails and adjusting their paper crowns and wishing the world on fire (including the red-faced man, staring, as if unknowingly, at the electric heater).

Meanwhile, the caveman, name of Loth, came in and carried a pint to the opposite corner. Next came the Beak, Neady, folding his eyes, full of elegant apology. Lastly came the graven image, the granite-faced one called Tollet. When Tollet is on a roll (as he invariably is), you can't stop him, and he knows it—and you still can't stop him. He will trundle past, flashing and growling, cackling and yackety-yacking, pointing his finger at you to deflect the attention you dare to throw his way. 'How are you?' you say to him, he says it back to you. Behind the electric fire is a kitchen. From the kitchen came an old crone. 'Shall we lunchify?' said Tollet eagerly. The crone, whom one only ever sees at lunchtimes, and who only ever proceeds from that same kitchen door, was happy to oblige. She took her orders and disappeared. 'Yees, it's a good place to lunchify,' said Neady, as if he hadn't been here before. He had his palm on his cheek, looking round at the stained wallpaper, sports trophies, winsome illustrations on the walls. Loth also had his palm on his cheek. 'M, mm,' he nodded. 'An articulate place,' continued Neady. 'Y, yes,' said Loth, 'a, a sort of synergist quality. N, nodal.' He stared at the table-top. 'Not like Number Nine' says Neady (with some repulsion) '—which is just a space.' 'A sort of diabolical r, realm,' agreed Loth. 'A Gnostic chaos.' 'Hm-hmf,' chortled Neady. Pretty soon it was as you were. Potato waffles and baked-beans, salad sandwiches and wine, were wolfed and munched at, while the world span round. 'Marvellous, hmf-hmf,' chortled Neady, placing a paper crown on his head and watching Tollet eat. 'That looks delicious, Len.' 'MmmWONderful!' growled Tollet in return, unwilling to reflect on food till it was eaten. 'Beans are really important,' continued Neady. 'Really important. A lifeblood kind of thing.' He sipped the wine. 'I was in a village in Mexico, in the seventies,' said Loth, who must have had a peculiar past, 'w, where the clockmaker was accepting beans in payment for mending clocks.' He paused long enough for you to realise he was laughing. His laugh was almost silent; a breathy beginning which subsided into teeth—pure teeth. 'Not much money. People paying—huh huh—in sacks of beans.' His teeth gleamed. 'Different concept of wealth accumulation. Beans. The e, engine of time. Huh-huh.' His eyes could not have been more lidded and still been open. 'I, I have no money,' he continued, massive and flickering. 'Just give me a sack of beans.' From the floor beside him, he lifted an imaginary sack of beans to the table. 'Would, would you like some beans with your time?' There was a riotous silence. 'Oh, well, yes, Mexico,' chortled Neady. 'I'd like to visit Mexico. If only because it's not America. Almost—and unfortunately—definitively so.' There was general silence while he thought. At last he cleared his throat, as if about to pass sentence; yet his voice had an offhand tone, as if the silence had not been. 'American food is abysmal.' He seemed saddened. 'Largeness and success are their only discriminations so far as I can see, so their food is tasteless—and this in turn leads to, or proceeds from,' (he cleared his throat again—a slight clearance, two little clicks) 'a general inability to notice things in detail or to know how to find pleasure in things.' He stared at his interlocutors in turn; he looked almost surprised. Then came a faint, explanatory smile. 'After a time, this begins to infect the visitor. The least educated are the best and are infected the least by circumambient non-pleasure-taking.' Again he looked round, pleased with himself. 'Y, yes, not taking the comedic seriously,' offered Loth. Neady chortled, offended by America. 'Pleasure is a severe instructor.' 'A p, pre-Aristotelian consciousness.' There was another silence, then a wave of Neady's hand. 'They gather together for such non-pleasures as listening to Rachmaninov's second symphony whilst watching coloured fountains jump to the music. Enchanting for a moment or so but only for a moment. But they just listen and listen!' He was warming to his theme. 'Or stand about as though they are listening, like flipping Stepford wives! It's a vicarious life.' He looked aside, frowning. 'No one dies in America,' he said, sadly. 'No one dies in America.'

There was a pause while this washed over. It was impossible to know what he was going to come out with next. He might suddenly lament the demise of Welsh. On the other hand he could turn round and champion Elvis. 'No, Elvis was a good thing,' he might easily argue—and who could remonstrate? He drank again. 'I remember one Sunday lunch—at a small hotel in Blois—' (he cleared his throat again, mentioning detail) 'A thin man sat in a corner.' He proceeded to act it out, taking up his napkin, tucking it in his collar, miming a particular eating. 'Munching his way through shell-fish,' (he puffed himself up, shelling imaginary shrimps) 'then sole,' (he flicked the sleeves from his hands, took up knife and fork and parted imaginary layers), 'then vegetables,' (prodding at them), 'then various meats,' (he pattered with his mouth, toing and froing with the fork) 'with a different small bottle of wine to go with each,' (saying 'yes, yes', shaking an imaginary glass) 'and a look of rapt concentration (ho-ho-ho).'

A fold of eyes marked the close of the charade; he was serious again. 'Such fastidious stamina.' 'A Cal, Calvinist hedonism,' mused the Caveman, looming over his pint. 'The god, the god of appetite.' 'America saps all the appetites except for size and success.' A palm upturned in acknowledgement. 'Which are girded around with insecurity. Next year something else will be larger or more successful.' Neady bit into a cucumber sandwich, chewed and continued. 'The only antidote I found to this was raw oysters and clams from Chesapeake Bay which I ate in large quantities in a pub called The Trap—unspoiled by indifferent cooking, and delicious. I got healthier and healthier!' he breezed, 'though in order to reach the venerable Trap I had to survive nightly monsoons. Indifferent American Merlot too, called Jekyll, I believe.' His voice fell to a burr, pondering that aside. But again he rallied. 'Yees, I sound like exactly the sort of thing that the Reformation was supposed to stop!' This was almost a protest, palm to the sky. 'Boston,

Delaware, New York are full of Catholics but their Puritan origins are everywhere. You can't drink or smoke or do anything much but you can look at half-baked porno films on hotel TV or muzzle more less continuously like a cab-horse from one of those horrible, large cardboard cones full of popcorn or noodles or indescribable horribles which, avoiding the light in the eye, make straight for girth.' He chortled again, without opening his mouth, so that air rifled the lips. 'Notwithstanding, I had rather a good time. Hmf-hmf-hmf-hmf-hmf.'

'Y, you like travelling?' asked Loth, who must have asked the question a thousand times before. The spirit of Eiron hovered over the table. Neady gave it thought. 'I don't know what I think about travel. I always enjoy it when I do it but I don't do that much of it so it can't be that important to me I suppose. Unlike Rog,' he demurred, 'who travels all the time and seems to have to.' There was a pause in honour of Rog. 'I wanted quite strongly to live abroad—Italy ideally—when I was in my early twenties, but I was different then. And the world was different then.' It was sheer pathos, hard and devastating. Between them, Eiron dissolved in tears. Neady sipped some wine, swirling it with thought. 'I've lived most of my life in the

same small town, and don't get tired of it at all. I love walking across the medieval bridge and looking at the river tides, seeing how it changes. I like routine. I like routine.'

'Y, you've just been to France?' persisted Loth, a coat of foam on his lip. He wiped it with the back of his hand. 'I had a good time,' responded Neady quickly. 'Visited Vezelay for the first time,' (quieter now) 'though I've wanted to go since nineteen-fifty-six. I was bowled over by it. Everything seems to have gone downhill since about eleven-fifty. Voltaire saw the sculpture on the tympanum at Autun (about the same date as Vezelay) and thought the dynamic, twisted Romanesque figures,' (twisting his mouth accordingly) 'were ridiculous. So the cowardly Autunians promptly plastered it over in shame! Hmph! With the result that—come the nasty revolution which destroyed some of the best such—there it lay! hid behind its plaster only to be unveiled in perfect condition in about eighteen-forty.' One hand unveiled like a glove from the other. It was like a flower in sudden bloom. 'So good comes out of evil or in this case confident stupidity, which is a sort of evil I suppose.' He munched on the sandwich. 'I've just been reading about the nasty revolution in Hugo's

Quatre Vingt Treize. Over the top, but rather good.' The sandwich removed, he smoothed his hands. 'Actually it isn't eleven-fifty which is the downhill point but about sixteen-seventy when French buildings suddenly get that pomposity of style which they still have,' (the twirl of a finger), 'though all the Gothic and Romanesque ones are being restored at great expense everywhere—and emerge gleaming white. So perhaps the older aesthetic is stronger now than the one that killed it off.'

The finger metronomed from one to the other. 'Y, yes, I like, like France,' said Loth. 'It's very near, huh-huh. Of relatively easy, easy access.' He seemed to find this quite amusing. 'We've always found Spain harder to get, get to.' 'That's true, that's true,' said Neady. 'Indubitably.' He sank in small chins. 'I would very much like to go to the Prado,' he burred, 'and kind of corny places like Avila and Segovia. The Castile plain, or the idea of it, enchanted me when I first read Don Quixote. (The book enchanted me too, through I've never been able to recapture that). You get a sense of it in John of the Cross. Must be quite like Anatolia,' he observed, 'which I liked.' Evidently more could have been said on this, but Tollet, who had scraped up and washed down, brought out the cigars and handed them round. They slit the sheaths and lit up. There was silence for a while. I was just back in my book when Neady's raised voice said: 'What are you reading, if I may ask?' He had turned to me, casual, not patronising. I showed him. 'Yes,' said Neady, curling a finger at my book as if it were a rare species on the tip of his tongue. 'Vienna. I like Vienna.' He didn't look convinced. 'I should do,' he said, as if it were a genuine, though troublesome, obligation. He closed his eyes, repressing a burp, speaking as if to himself. 'I was taught by Wittgenstein's star pupil.' Like a conductor's, the finger beat the air and drew a line across him. 'So you can draw a direct line from Wittgenstein...to me! Hmf hmf hmf!' The eyes peeped. 'Although I am more unequivocally Catholic.' He was gathered in a while, arms folded, creased at the chin. He had a sprinkle of boyish stubble, comically, liberally permitted, as if, flourish though he would, time, or memory, were not quite subject to his baton. 'I like Vienna,' he repeated. It had become a mantra now; an odd, qualified, penitent sort of mantra, plainly confessing a doubt. It wasn't clear why coming in a direct, though wavering, line from Wittgenstein meant he must like Vienna. It wasn't even sure he'd been there. 'I like Vienna. Ha-ha, there's a 'but' coming isn't there? BUT—ha ha, there it is now—(the Caveman chuckled low)—and I'm repeating myself here, the best thing about is that it's not Germany! It gets better as you go south. Most of Germany is nasty kind of thing, but you get through the Black Forest to Bavaria, and things start brightening up, and Austria kind of continues the trend.' He lifted palms, as though the sun were rising. 'Then Vienna has the Hapsburgy Baroquey type of thing and that's worth something. That's worth something,' he repeated. He nodded sagely. He seemed to be conducting his own Grand Tour. One arm was folded on his stomach, and the other rested an elbow on it, clasping his chin with the hand. Two fingers rose like antennae on the cheek. He didn't seem to be addressing me any more. I went back to my book. Two minutes later, 'Venice!' he was exclaiming, as if it were painful to him. 'Don't flipping talk to me about Venice—humph! One can never have enough of Venice!'

'I went last, last summer,' said Loth. 'Lot, lot of human activity. High, high level of consciousness. Difficult to plot, plot co-ordinates as it were. Interruptions of frequency. A sort of universalised tourism.' 'Yes,' said Neady, looking blankly at Loth, as if he didn't

follow. 'Ah like tourists,' said Tollet, puffing. 'They're so INGENUOUS!' Neady was frowning, as if he found this alarming; not liking tourists, but having to consider them. 'Yes. There are a lot of tourists.' He dismissed the thought with a fold of his eyes. 'I found an extraordinary little church there last time, not far from the Grand Canal, but tucked away. Never seen it before, though I must have passed it three or four times. Fantastically ornate frescos!' He screwed up his face as if the sun were blinding. 'Pietas and Ascension type of things.' He spoke absently, puffed on the cigar. 'I stayed there an hour, just sitting. It was—well, it's pious kind of thing—but it was a religious experience. And you can do that! You can do that in Venice! It's current! It's current!' He looked round as if this was amusing. Y, yes,' said Loth, cupping his face. This currency evidently appealed to him. 'A a sort of stillness in motion, centri, centrifugal com, compulsion. The comm, command-centre of the cosmos.' He chuckled, showing a white wall of teeth. 'It doesn't look like it, does it,' said Neady, ignoring him completely, 'but I'm never happier than wandering round little churches.' The caveman looked bowed, as if he knew it very well and never dreamed that it didn't look like it, but that there was nothing he could do about it. 'I could do that all day,' concluded Neady.

'Ah love Venice,' said Tollet, billowed round with smoke.

I continued with my book. Their voices, running the gamut of pitches, so that they might have formed a whole chorus for themselves, receded into tentative forays, like the middle lull in a symphony. 'Re-reading Goethe's Travels in Italy,' Neady was saying, 'has got me into Lavater about whom I know almost nothing. Seems to exist only in very old editions.' His mouth dropped like a frog's. 'He doesn't sound that promising, and Blake admired him which is never much recommendation, but, after being all over him, Goethe turned violently against him, so he might be worth defending.' I fell into my book again, followed the violinist on his own travels. He was trapped in a garden, climbing trees to hide from hounds, not too far from 'Rome,' Neady was saying, as if it spoke for itself. He had reached the end of his pilgrimage. 'Rome. It's a pleasant city is Rome.' The air was heavy with confusion. Loth said something I couldn't hear, then 'I like Bernini,' continued Neady. 'Fantastically ornate!' He screwed up his mouth again. 'It's those Baroquey externals. Almost painfully distinct. And the tomb works, doesn't it? It couldn't have been some blocky, neoclassical affair. It wouldn't have suited the space. Had to offer something different. A lead, a thread. And so those marvellous sinewy columns, directing the eye.' Again I lost track of the conversation, well into my second pint, until the bar-maid brought a couple of chocolate bars and put them on their table, at which Neady looked positively overcome with gratitude, making all kinds of smiles and bows, without so much as speaking a word.

Suddenly, 'Ah abHORRED Norway!' boomed Tollet, in response to a question by the Caveman. In one fell, prehistoric swoop I was thrown northward. 'And you wouldn't THINK that, since me ancestors are from there!' He wheezed with laughter. 'Ohhh, AWWWFUL, wasn't it? I went fell-walking with a friend.' No one could imagine what kind of friend, and Tollet wasn't about to elaborate. No one could imagine what kind of fell either. 'Spent a week climbing some of the Western peaks. ExCRUCIATING, wasn't it? All that rock and snow, and the endless SCREEEEEEE HEE HEE HAH HAH HAH!' Gone in a word from bass to shrill, he broke into the most elaborate laugh I ever heard. He was almost crying with laughter, staring fiercely round. He looked as if he would fall apart at the seams, in his shabby brown jacket with the elbow patches. 'AHAHAHAHAHAH!' he continued, like a cockerel, well beyond the bounds of expectation, spittle flecking from his lips, bringing barmaids and regulars into the sphere of his gaze. A more serious laugh you cannot imagine, impugning the soul. A face like a land of dry rivers, hit with sudden floods. 'ISN'T ITTTTTAHAHAH?' he roared, for all the pub, and much of the surrounding wilderness, to hear, and, leaning full forward in his chair and rocking to one side, he folded hands on his knees, as if clutching a cap, and slowly, leisurely, like one foredooming, brought upon me the full gimlet blankness of his stare.

Then, all at once, he stopped, just like that. Buttoned lip and stopped outright. All that was left was a snorting from the nostrils, the pinched eyes and a fierce staring round.

Suddenly the day was a drained glass, a squeezed zestless lemon. I wasn't sure it was worth going on with at all. The bar-maid saw my predicament, cleared my plate away, and I was on the street

Again

Harper.

>
>

Astonishing, sir, astonishing.

In any case, I was compelled to return to the British Embassy, in order to renew my legitimacy. So back I went, and was ushered—like a wild, white-haired, madman in an Edgar Allan Poe short story—into a waiting room, with sofas, magazines and watercolours on the walls. A man only has so much time, and most of it he spends HANGING AROUND (waiting, I shouldn't wonder) being pelted with watercolours. In any case, I was finally ushered—ushered, mark you—into the office of a wild, white-haired madwoman calling herself the Naturalised Citizens' Secretary or somesuch barely credible thing. 'Well you see,' she said, very quickly and inestimably poshly, 'I'm not at all SURPRISED.....but I'm APPALLED!!! How much have you written?' 'Well now' (says I). 'I THINK I might have a chapter. 6,000 words, but I might edit it down a bit, though that would involve having to look at it again, which in turn would IMPLY, I presume, some measure....of.....what The Man Who Would Be King would call...(sigh) responsibility, Harp, responsibility.' She stared at me, sir, then ushered me—for the third time that day—into the presence of a younger woman (45?) from Hampstead whom I had seen last time, and who took me for a drink and told me about the work hard/play hard lifestyle.

So once again, there I was, in a bar, drinking, talking, flirting outrageously with a highly sympathetic older woman and discussing my plans for the future. She wanted to know if I was going to extend my studies. Hmmm, ah, mmm, I said. 'Well,' she wittered. 'I really think you should.' 'But why?' said I. 'You have the temperament for it.' This cut, sir, cut me deep inside, like...a wound...a cutting...wound. I began to work the point of a paperclip into the ball of my hand. 'Really,' she frothed all over the place, 'I mean, darling, you write SO WELL! Oh yes, Oh I KNOW it's PAINful for you. I can see it in your work. But you'd be PUH-ER!-FECK-T!!!'

I could feel the vomit beginning to rise. A cold cliched sweat broke out somewhere between back and brow. Hot, salty tears slipped the length of my hollow cheek, agglomerating at the chin. Blood poured from open wrist. My colon was in spasm. My head began to jerk back ferociously. Off in the distance the sound of children playing.

'And for now?' I said. For now, she said, I would have to reapply for funding, while in the meantime producing more research and working—FOR NOTHING—mind you—in the Embassy archives. 'But enough shoptalk,' says she, ladling sparkling wines into carafes, goblets, any receptacle she could lay her hands on, 'how is Vienna TREATING you?!' 'Oh,' says I. 'Apart from the penury, starvation, cancer, influenza, and the general air of eroticopathic idiocy, just fine.' 'That's simply WUNDERFUL,' she bubbles. 'And have you had, you know, any special ENCOUNTERS?' 'What,' says I, genuinely baffled, 'you mean, as in The Crags?' 'Terrific!' she sluices. 'I suppose they are,' say I. 'Any what you might call FRUITFUL experiences?' 'You mean apart from Bjorn's bananas?' 'Oh yes? Tell me more.' 'Well, it's like this,' says I, taking her as literally as possible (though not as literally as she would have liked), 'I was in the kitchen, casting around for something to eat. And not

having anything of my own, except for a few shrivelled onions, lounging around in what Benjamin McCormack Kepperly Lie might, entirely inappropriately, not to say rather rudely, term the 'old onion bag', I made a beeline for Bjorn's cupboard...' And so it went on, with her positively spewing with delight at my every word, until she could bear it no longer and gave voice to long pent up feelings regarding the Embassy Dinner and the (necessary) production of various imitation cunts, wombs and ovaries otherwise known as FRUIT. Whereupon I produced such a specimen (a pomegranate, I think it was) and, when she had recovered from her orgasmic swoon, she leaned in, showing me all of her copious cleft-hoofed, two-leaf-clover, inverted horseshoe breasts (unluckily for me) and whispered: 'And...and where did you GET this...this MARVELLOUS THING?' At which point I judged the whole thing had gone as far as I wanted it to and sloped out, tapping my nose, and leaving her to foot the bill, which no doubt she did, shoelessly, under the table, to her (and the bill's) heart's content.

Well I mean I did all the things she told me. And in the end, after many a form filled, many an application made, I calculated I could buy myself a bowl of soup to celebrate, which amounts to celebrating by ensuring my continued survival. All of which (survival) is made more palatable by Barbosa shuffling back to her room, after a sojourn in mine, so now it's just me and the Lie, who seemed to think it safe to return to my floor. God knows where he has been sleeping in the interim: all we know for sure is that he has been sleeping in an Interim, a Caesura even, probably of the Feminine Medial kind, sir, though tending toward, not to say indistinguishable from, the Terminal. But then, like I always say, render unto the Caesura. Immediately he did so, however, (return, not render—as a Chinese Elvis Presley impersonator would say—REPUGNANT THOUGHT!) I lost my watch. I was sure I'd had it the night before. The Lie had no idea either. So I left the Heim. Upon returning the Lie said 'I found your watch, look.' 'Really,' I replied, 'where was it?' He goofed and started laughing: 'It was right at the back of the refrigerator, behind a bag of spring-onions!' Now, I asked him, and he said that not only did he not have anything to do with it, but that he hadn't once either removed or replaced the said spring-onions, thus negating the possibility that he'd actually swept up a large and rather noticeable timepiece in the process. Equally, I have no memory of putting it there, nor dealing with aforesaid vegetable. Conclusion: I am mental. I must have been sleepwalking the night before, taking my watch from its usual resting place on the desk in my room, carrying it to the kitchen, opening the fridge door, and secreting it behind the SPRING ONIONS. Then, job done, I went back up to bed and wiped the whole incident from my conscious mind. All very precisely,

Jude.

P.S. P.S.(A.) has been reading Blake. I spied 'er in the kitchen. At least the psychotic hallucinating hippy can be relied upon. And Pilar Santana Artale too.

>
>

Sir.

Regarding bombing, and being bombed, of wanting and NEEDING bombs, etc, I was on my way to work yesterday when, what to my wondering ears should appear, but A BOOM, sir. Perhaps a BANG. Short-lived, like a balloon exploding. Some kind of Bomb?

Difficult to say, never having heard one. It came from the street, fifty yards away. I was in a side-alley, because Heywood Road, my usual route, was closed. The police were there with barricades and guns. Hordes of people were herding off buses onto other buses, streaming out of the buildings. A couple of scabrous whores came complaining out of doorways, picking fights with the police. Even the tramps were disturbed. They rolled up sleeping-bags, shuffled disgruntled from the church columns. One of the police had a megaphone and he was counseling everyone (a loud counseling) that there had been some power surges in the area, to make their ways to work, use other bus routes, go about their business etc. They didn't want anyone panicking. What's going on? said I, when he paused. 'Power Surges,' says he. He looks disconcerted, annoyed even. Where? says I. 'The road is closed!' he barks. That much is obvious. There are orange barriers all across it and a sizeable police presence. Okay, say I, how can I get over there? Where? says he. 'There,' says I, pointing. Over THAT barrier.' I advise you to take other routes! he says, and then goes on with the megaphone. I advise you to take other routes! he roars. This is the Police! There have been some power surges in the area! Do not panic! You are advised to use other routes and means of transportation to get to work! This is the Police! etc

Of course I immediately took the rest of the day off, and went to the Pomp and Prestige to see what the news had to say. What they had to say, in feeble dribs and drabs, was that it was actually bombs. What I had heard was a bus going off. Apparently they'd been going off around town for almost an hour. The Police knew this. Not only did they not tell us—they lied, and herded us onto buses to be dismembered, apparently because they didn't want us to panic. 30 people dead.

It has just started to POUR with rain. And I mean BUCKET, BREACH, BARNSTORM. I was in town as evening was falling. I saw it coming: the rack of cloud drawn westward, to the river, the melancholy massing in the east.

Anyway, what with one thing and another, I stayed there most of the day, pondering the violent foreclosure of my Services to the Community, and a covert, trespassing return to the valley. Artie came in and, looking up at the news, made some heavy hints that he had a hand in the day's events and invited me down to the Seaman's Church to meet his crew, this time for real. I said not today. He insisted. I humoured him, promised to go next week. Several drinks later (all on me), I went to get the bus home. They were on a special, especially slow, schedule, 'count of the morning. Anyway, finally the number 80 came, and there I was, riding it, as was the lunatic next to me, evidently to the lunatic's amusement. He nudged me and intimated as much. 'Eighty,' he said, 'hic-heh (chuckle). Stuh (turn, shuffle). Eighty. Stuh. Stuh! Hic-heh! (turn, wring hands, turn again), eh?' I looked him in the eye and said nothing. The lunatic was subdued, but not broken. 'The old pub,' he resumed, as we went past the Pomp and Prestige. 'Hic-heh, an't been there for years.' He wasn't looking at me now. He was talking to the bus in general, gripping the rail with his hands. It wasn't uncommon, of course. It would be uncommon for a lunatic not to be on the bus. Sometimes there's some competition who can be the most deranged. He kept looking behind him, as if expecting, imminently, the approach of Banquo from the spare seats at the back. Rain began to patter. We passed a bridge over rail sidings and the lunatic looked down. 'One,' he said. 'Two. Three. Four.' I thought I could see what was coming. 'Five. Six. Seven.' Surely he wasn't going to go through with it. 'Eight. Nine.

Ten,' he concluded. 'Ten, yeah, ten. Hic-heh (chuckle). Stuh. Good-o, ten, hic-heh.' I looked at the train engines. I couldn't see ten. Tracks perhaps? Wires? Carriages? Far more than ten of any. He shuffled off the bus. I stared back behind me and realised it was lamp-posts. As I did so, I saw Loth, in a blue fleece, two seats behind. 'Huh-huh-hullo,' he said, as if sensing a gap in the lunacy market. 'Hello,' says I. 'Looks like a storm.' 'Y, yep,' says he, 'cl, climactic pressure-zones.' The motor hummed under his voice. 'Signs, signs of apocalypse.' We chuckled. It was warm in the bus; the heater was blasting. 'Good time to be going home,' says I. 'Y, yes,' says he, 'I, I like to be home before nightfall.' He was leaning in, as if to hear me better, looming on blacks and silvers. 'Why? Is it dangerous where you live?' I asked. 'No,' said he. His hair was black and silver, as if affected by the windows. I could see eyes behind his black/silver glasses, but his mouth was dark. 'When night falls,' he continued, 'y, you get that feeling that the w, the world is not our home.'

He carried on looking at

Me.

P.S. Hum Bom?

Hum (us?)

humus.

>
>

Dear, dear, Sir,

Agreed, and accepted, and impressed, and not at all surprised but shock and awe nevertheless...

NevertheLESS. Armageddon did the job. And it did; it worked.

But I'm glad you're alive, sir. Never gladder. Never more pleased to receive one of your preposterous emails. A tear—rolling down my cheek—testifies to this.

I knew of it. I had heard. And from a source, too, though far from humus you should understand. For it was none other than Barbosa, whom I met in the darkened corridor, the kitchen light behind her, so that she looked like a messenger of ill. Which is exactly what she was.

BB: [eery, portentous]

How are you doing
After the terrorist attacks
In England?

M: [half-asleep] What?

BB: [steamrolling on]

You were lucky
Not to be in the wrong place
At the wrong time.

M: [digesting] Was I?

BB: [pityingly]

It's incredible that there are people
Who still belive
That blood and death will change things.

M: [remembering] Oh, by the way, you left your lip-salve and hand-cream on my bedside table.

BB: [knowingly] Those aren't mine.

M: [confusedly] Whose are they?

BB: [places a finger aside her nose—taps it, grinning]

Seriously, it might be time for you to get out of there now. Forget exile, screw community service, get on your hind legs if need be and make your way home. I may be doing the same thing myself, if Rosa Wellhausen has her way. I was painting her bathroom the other day and she wanted to know what my Plan was. Plan? says I, there's no Plan. 'It's pathetic,' says she, pouring wine (ten-o-clock in the morning). 'You're exiled from home, duped into espionage for Queen and country, and so penniless, you're reduced to painting an old woman's bathroom.' For the second time in a week, I merely dug something into the palm of my hand, this time the paint-stripper, and asked how much she was paying me.

But she had a point. Cause I'm nigh done with it. Dusted it. Hung it on the wall. A., B., PSA, the whole Viennese whorl. At least for a week or so. It all went wrong with A. principally because she invited me to ANOTHER PLAY. A PLAY WITHIN A PLAY. I wrote her an email saying that I had no intention of subjecting myself to another such debacle. Misinterpreting this as a break-up letter, she wrote back saying that perhaps we could talk about it more openly when we saw each other again and I said, Okay, until then. But what I meant was: it'll be OKAY...until...THEN. THEN I stormed off to play Talisman with Bjorn at the Games Cafe (the Prophetess, sir. YES, she is a floosy, YES, it IS unfair that she ALWAYS HAS AT LEAST ONE SPELL. YES, there is nothing better than seeing her trampled underfoot by Messrs Troll or Ghoul. And yet. And YET. She EXISTS. And life IS unfair. As Magnus would say: DEAL with it. Needless to say, she—which is to say I—mercilessly crushed Bjorn's ridiculous Dwarf, Unaffected by the Maze though he was—and remains, strangely enough.)

The Lie came home late this morning and confessed himself at a loss—said he'd spent the night wandering by the river, found himself reduced to eating kebabs and going to fruit-machine shops. Tell me about it, I said. No, tell me about it. Finally I convinced him that I wanted him to tell me about it, and he complied. I told him things relating to myself, and finally we lit out on a sunny day, and headed to the Cafe Museum to talk about modernism. I introduced the idea of radical uncertainty and he said 'Alright' and 'Look' and looked at me in a very identificatory kind of a way, though each all too aware of Utter Ridiculousness (as it is known). It was almost warm. Sunlight shafted in but the Lie declined to comment. After that we went our separate ways.

And NOW I have to go and get a haircut.

Jude.

>
>

Sir?

No word from you. As with all silences, I assume that this is a meticulously constructed, self-aggrandizing mystification. But I trust you are well, not scattered over a wide area, limbs and loins akimbo, reeking of mortality.

'Cause that's what I've been, sir, all too often of late, so much so that my bedsheets are covered in blood, caused by a great graze across my right knee, caused by being shoved repeatedly into a metal fence by Bjorn, somewhere in the vicinity of a football, on a freezing Viennese night, in the name of a

'contact sport' a 'man's game' and 'playing to win', and which opens up more times than Jesse's de-fence. To which rational instruction in the Social Contract, I even more rationally, not to say cold-bloodedly, retaliated by returning home, having a shower (my first in three days) and dining upon oats, an apple, and a banana. Cutting right to the chase I drank a glass of water. Then, just to be sure, another glass of water. You see my point—which is more than I can say for the Social Contract, or Bjorn, its unlikely enforcer.

You might also, if you came to Vienna, see my paint, for it continues to lather Rosa's flat, for a few spare Marks and as much alcohol as she can muster, and I manage, at ten in the morning—amounts, I might add, vastly disproportionate (and not in my favour), as Rosa knows only too well. After a whole lot of none-so-subtle enquiries into my various courtships, comprising silent approbations (P.S.A.), general indifference (A.) and vehement sarcasms (B.), followed by a cold, exhausted courtship of our own, she will then get down to the serious business of my future, the future of the world, etc, as if the two were remotely connected. Really, sir, a man could grow tired of The Future, constantly looming, imminating,

IMPENDING even (FOUL thought), or being made so to seem by those who have none—to the extent that he might, of an evening, book in hand, rain pattering at his window, listening perchance to Bach or Stravinsky, a single lamp burning at his desk, and a rare skin condition pock-marking his torso, mutter quietly to himself: 'Oh, go away, The Future.'

This time she (Rosa, not the Future, although given its looming, immin—and imMAN—ating—like certain fundamentalist Christians—and notice the concealed MAN within the word—IMPENDING nature, chances are, like Fate, Luck, Moon, and all those other caprices, it's a female, and either a notorious hag or a damn fine 'un, possibly both at the same time, which come to think of it is an exact description of Rosa) was practising on my love of the Glum, not to mention the Cooley (as also of my home and its environs), speaking, with horrific rationale, of my ties, my roots, my bonds, sir (and also my familiar and geosocial connections and obligations) and the Odyssey every man must make, etc. All tosh of course. Far stronger impression was made by her appeal to my pocket, or lack thereof, sending one into a spirals of speculation about the absence of absence, its not equating to presence, etc, although, on leaving, she did make me a gift of an expensive, immaculately bound, Blake's illustrated Plate, Print, Illumination, Etching, Manuscript, Palimpsest, Facsimile, Stencil, Papier-mache, Plasticine, Tie-dye, Tracing paper, Bark-rubbing, Daguerreotype relief type-things (relief!), which was nice, if odd, not to say pedantic (what, sir, is she suggesting about the Marriage of Heaven and Hell, the Collusion of Innocence and Experience—Messrs Pebble and Clod included—the Grudging Agreement between Bowlahoola & Allamanda, Scotland and Wales, Los and the Spectre—both of whom, particularly in their cursing, raging and stamping capacities, I understand only too well?) and perversely dismissive of the fact that, as she well knows, I would have much preferred the equivalent in cash.

Conclusion: she wants me to remain poor. She wants us all to remain poor, a. so that we will have no choice but to effect revolution and b. (naturally, the primary motive, not to say URGE) so that we will be forced into dependency on her, construe a maternal-filial bond, mistake/accurately-interpret it as sexual attraction and wind up making love in a bathtub, covered in paint.

In any case, all that talk of Glum and Cooley got me thinking, thinking got me sleeping, sleeping got me dreaming the following:

I went for a walk in the Glum, fell in the river up to my ankles and stung my hands. Even that didn't feel good. I straggled home, smelling of sewage, picking little sticky bobbles off me. I spent HOURS walking in that selfsame valley, sir. Ostensible reason: None. This is what no one understands. It goes well beyond what anyone could reasonably expect—if for no other reason than it is so reasonable.

Woke up and started thinking Rosa might actually be, if not right (if, in fact, entirely wrong—about EVERYTHING), at least (accidentally) spot-on. Started thinking of going home, if I can avoid getting arrested. Oh Sir, I plan to get so muddy. So very, very muddy. Like...Muddy Waters, a Mud-Skipper fish, like....like soil mixed with so much water....from....a container. I wonder what Magnus would advise. Not that I would take said advice. But I would mull it over, sir, and that's as much as anyone can ask.

Now I have to write an e-mail to the friend of a

friend, who has invited me for dinner. I have already accepted twice over, but am about to decline—conjuring some imaginary prior engagement. Which there is, in fact: with me. An imaginary one, mind. In my room. At night. With a book. And Washington Phillips.

At any rate,

Jude.

P.S. From whom no word, since I promised her that if we ever meet up in the Glum or Cooley Valleys I'll let her ride my BMX—guaranteed to bowl over any right-thinking woman. 'Bowl over' in the sense that I'll probably crash into her and snap her fibula.

P.P.S. To make matters worse, Jesse left last night, on some kind of travels. That wasn't what any of us needed.

P.P.P.S. Hang on a minute. Loth and the Spectre? Someone's having us on. Someone with a pronounced lisp (isn't it always the case?)

>
>

Sir,

No, no, I'm fine. Only I discovered the other week that Artie had been spying on my emails. There he was, outside the computer room, doing his usual coughing, banging, whimpering act, threatening to die of cold/hunger/plague/despair if he did not get a chance to check his emails and peek a wee bit at 'the GURRRRLS', and there I was, all tolerance and eye-strain, making off for bed and leaving him to it, when I realise, halfway up the stairs we have to go, that I've forgotten my hat. Back to the ambitiously named computer room I go, only to find Artie, splayed disgustingly before the computer, except that where I expect to see cracks and crevices of various descriptions, I see our very own email correspondence (the cracks and crevices being minimised at the bottom of the screen). And when I challenge him on it, all he can say is 'Och, ye left it on the screen. I could ne help but make use of ma eyes. An' a little natural curiosity.' This couldn't be, says I, because I signed out. 'God's trewth,' says he, hand on heart. Impossible, says I. 'How'm ah readin' 'em then?' says he. A question to which I had no answer, apart from to pluck his bituminous beard and swear that if he did it again, I would have him banned from Garfield's, the Seaman's Church and the Mendicant's Cafe into the bargain, at which he veered between rage and destitution, and backed out of the computer room, pointing a crippled finger in my face, and accusing me of exposing an old man to the incoherent, irreverent narratives of youth.

Since then, being quite busy, and having no idea how he had got access to my account, I have neglected using it. Till now, that is, when, signing in, I realised that the computer, whether of its own or another's accord, was 'remembering' my username and password.

So that, as I say, I am fine. Fine, that is, apart from a collapsed eye, gotten, sir, would you believe, in a DREAM.

It was like this. I was on a road, a quiet long lane. The Ghost of King Hamlet, whom, I gradually realised, was X in disguise (only, gradually mark you, to realise he was actually The Ghost of King Hamlet), appeared in the distance, disappeared, appeared again, on the other side of the road, like...like a shimmering ghost? a little closer than before. He was singing in a meandering falsetto. Again he disappeared, again appeared, closer again, still far away. Annoying manner of approach! Smug, complacent, easy as lions in their power. The disappearances like winks—it could have been my eyes, how was I to know? The Ghost of King Hamlet knew this, riding the intervals as a plank rides waves, sewing ambivalence in those eyes. I turned away. Instead of looking up the lane, I was looking down it. Was The Ghost of King Hamlet moving behind me? That old chestnut. Cue all kinds of falling forests. I couldn't stand it—the silent crashing. I turned to face him. At that point, of course, he reappeared to the right, halfway down the lane. I think I knew I was dreaming. Terrified, I decided to meet him. It would go hard but I would embrace him, Proteus-like. He was wearing a white shawl, a white wool-hat, some kind of habit under. Sackcloth I thought. His hands were bunched at the neck, holding the shawl just like Magnus of old.

I stepped forward. He skipped to the left, faster now, in for the kill. Suddenly he was before me, central as hell. He was singing in my face, high and eerie, like a siren. It was horrid, but I embraced him, keeping my face away. This wasn't enough. I had to relax, assume him in my veins. I let go my neck and leaned.

At which point G. pottered in and woke me up, asking questions, adjusting curtains, busybodying about with a 'tut' and a 'cluck' and a 'dear boy,' for good measure. I invited him to the Seaman's Church, feigning an interest in his life and politics. He drummed and he shrilled and he fiddled it three, and then told me almost everything there was to tell, keeping back only so much as to beg another telling (which much he advertised with many a high glance and choked silence), so that it was questionable which was more titillating—the grand confession or this little reserve. He would stump up hundreds of thousands, not to say millions, of your English pounds—from his personal fortune, mind—for a cause he believed in. 'Grassroots!' he scoffed. 'Show me a million—in cold, hard, CASH!' (luxuriously enunciated)—'and I'll show you grassroots! It works like manure I've found. Just spread it around, you'll be amazed what will grow.' The man desires nothing more than to throw away his money on an only hope. He patters a hand on my radiator, stares forlornly from the window. Rain answers him with a patter of its own. W. was valiant but naïve, apparently. They met one early evening at The All and Sundry Theatre, become embroiled in argument, and swiftly realised that between W.'s radical socialism and G.'s voluptuous fascism was much common ground. A bare, sodden ground, sir, sated with confession, tinged with late-afternoon humanism. Where jollity and despair share a hug and cry. A hugh and cry, as your Barbosa might say.

He rises from the armchair. 'But money is nothing in the end,' he sighs. Wisdom is nothing. It's all about beauty.' He smiles wanly. 'You'll go far, dear boy.'

'In the meantime,' says I, 'can I get dressed?' 'Go ahead!' he yells, 'I'm not stopping you!' He looks thoroughly offended, puffs up his feathers and off he waltzes to the door, when he checks, turns, lolls again. 'One question, Harper, if I may: this Artie chap, and his low-grade political plotters (whomever they may be!), are you in with them for the ''experience''' (with much saliva)? A bourgeois vicarious thrrrill?' (rolling vituperative r's). 'Or do you mean what you say?' 'What makes you think I've said anything?' said I. 'Ah-ha, very good, dear boy,' said he, acceptant. 'You'll rue the day that clogs me with this answer, hah-hah!'

He winked and vanished (through the door). I got dressed, went to the mirror, looked at it, saw that my eye had collapsed. Just like that—overnight. The right one. Twice as small as the left. Some kind of stress reaction? A wasp sting perhaps. No, the wasps all died in autumn. I blinked, insofar as I could. It was still there. It is still there.

I can see through it well. But it is twice as small—all round. The doctors are baffled. A hard thing to deal with. Not in the book of modern medicine. No one knows. All they can tell, peering close, is that, like Louis Pasteur (or is that Edward Jenner?) I have something

in my

EYE.

>
>

Sir, sir, a remarkable email. I would like to prostitute and send it to a girl, any girl, which one being immaterial, as if to say, 'look what remarkable friends and their dreams I have.' And I would mean 'Look what remarkable friends and their dreams I, sir, EYE have.' And then they would either not be interested, or, worse, would, and would start in with the QUESTIONS. 'What do you mean, you have their dreams? Do you mean you SHARE their dreams?'

Speaking of which, Rosa's latest wheeze to compensate me for painting her flat without ACTUALLY COMPENSATING ME AT ALL—more, sir, more, by actually demoralising me to the point where I drop brush, paint, and all, and devote myself to the writing of socially-conscious, ostensibly satirical, but beneath their peeling, scabbed, thin-skinned surface, horribly heartfelt, novels about writers suffering writer's block, from which they emerge only by virtue of having, by which I mean LUSTING TO HAVE, their sexual activities described in such tawdry, pedantic detail that they develop, necessarily, into a REALLY MEANINGFUL RELATIONSHIP, ultimately contributing to an inspiring journey of self-discovery happily divided between Hampstead, Bethnal Green and war-torn Iran—was to take me to see the laughably-titled Konig Lear at her favourite underground theatre, where, for reasons known only to rich, posh bookselling socialists, she procures free entrance, although it turns out that Konig Lear is only a front, a ruse, an excuse, to once again sing the woes and prostitute the wounds of the poor old Vaterland, who, having laboured seven years under the yoke of the filthy Nazi—only PRETENDING to welcome him with wild enthusiasm, brilliantly FEIGNING to send two hundred thousand people to the Heldenplatz to cheer his return to the Heimat—is then subject to the abuse of his ostensible liberators, the crass Russ, macho Yank, and dithering Brit, as represented, in reverse order, by a coward Cornwall in cricket whites, an oh-so-aptly named Regan, in gaudy Stars n' Stripes (so a Stars n' Stripes then) and a butch Goneril, constantly appending a hammer and sickle to an overdeveloped proletarian bicep—only, chances are, said hammer has not beaten wooden stakes all summerlong into fields full of young chrysanthemums, NOR has said sickle been purloined from Farmer Chile, NOR his scantily-clad wife, NOR borne aloft over the surface of Bullish Lake while she, Goneril, sank beneath the water and trudged the ENTIRE BREADTH of its swampy bottom, giving one to wonder what she, or Russia, can possibly know about Communism. Because it turns out it's 1945, somewhere between Yalta and Potsdam—although with nylon license we take in the entire postwar period, from Allied occupation, through the Cold War, McCarthyism and the Sino-Soviet split, up to and including the creation of the EU, with even a little comic nod to the impending euro in a pathetic attempt at contemporary relevance, the irony being that it is PRECISELY the setting in postwar Austria which makes relevance of any kind impossible to achieve—and the superannuated Austria, aka Konig Lear, is pretending to devolve his kingdom, while in reality having it devolved for him, into three parts, otherwise known as Powers, except of course that it ends up in the hands of only two, albeit one of those two is actually two Powers, in the form of the eternally bilaterally agreeable UK and USA, and albeit that collaborationist France, by courtship of Cordelia (the only person in the play who has no obvious metaphoric referent, which presumably is why Austria disinherited her) keeps attempting to come to the party and form a Four Powers occupation. In which foolish antics, Austria is aided by a faithful, nigh-on ideal, European Advisory Commission, aka EAC, aka Kent, and abetted—when the EAC is put out to graze, not only by an ungrateful Austria, who, madly, thinks it has any say in the matter, but by a more general mystification among the Powers as to its precise purpose—by the EAC's successor, namely the Allied Control

Council, aka ACC, aka Gloucester, who strongarms Lear to take 'due turns', by 'monthly course', between Regan and Goneril (herself temporarily allied to the newly-created Communist state-cum-protectorate of Albania) in the delicately poised International Zone (aka zone-swap), until he gets his eyeballs gouged by a newly Eurosceptical Cornwall, himself egged on by Regan, who is busy stabbing the First Servant in the back (UNESCO); while, incredibly, presciently, like a ghost from Christmas Future, Kent reappears to guide Lear again, this time in the guise of Caius (the European Economic Community). These are called parallels, I believe, and straighter, brittler, more fluorescent ones you will not find outside of Bjorn's cross-country skis, notwithstanding that cunningly placed between them was an age-old fiction of fraternal rivalry, embodied in the unlikely (yet tiresomely likely) bodies of Orson Welles, aka Edmund—himself caught up in a nasty internecine spat between Goneril and Regan, in their respective capacities of Stalinism and the House Committee of Un-American Activities, broadly morphing into McCarthyism as the play goes on and the 40s unfold the 50s—and Joseph Cotton, aka Edgar, who, before killing Goneril's puppet, Oswald (aka Karl Renner), escapes

Edmund's machinations by adopting the persona of Poor Tom (Holly Martins) and wandering naked on an inhospitable heath (the Prater). This welter of nods, winks and tickles is apparently called postmodernism, and is the cause of great backslapping, pelvis-rubbing glee among the players, the audience, Austria, Europe and the World. Only the Universe glimmers darkly over the whole twee proceeding, ready to pelt the World with rotten comets for this stupid abuse of its patience.

Of course, it was absolute toth. The only good actor was The Fool (a dead ringer for Wittgenstein), although, of course, that comes as no surprise. Let's face it, anyone can play The Fool. You just have to look wise and foolish at the same time. It's almost impossible not to. Nevertheless, I am getting an education in Shakespearean tragedy, and at the same time in female courtship, leading one to wonder whether there is an enormously obvious parallel between the two, so obvious and enormous that you actually can't see it at all, until it swings round and decapitates you. Which, promptly, almost happened when we went back to Rosa's flat and I declined to comment on the merits or demerits of democracy, on the grounds that it was flogging a dead horse, when I was far more interested in stroking a live cat—which, brilliantly, flirtatiously, I proceeded to do. At which point, Rosa shouts I'm wasting my time, should light out, go home, write my life story. As if proving her point, she throws Hemingway, Orwell, Lorca my way. She is half-drunk, but repetition lends her credence.

I excused myself, citing an important appointment with Bjorn, Rico and International Athletics, in the Television Room. So I go home, strangely elated, and immediately get this email from P.S. (A?) She'd heard from Bjorn we were going to watch a film the next night (The Birds, sir, appropriately enough), and could she follow us there? Also, how was I? What am I doing these days (these 2 days after we last saw each other). And if I was Around? Yes, I replied. But I shan't come Around because I'm with the Lie (which I was), who needs to be taken upstairs and fed, but I'll see you Around, later perhaps. And I did, sir, because she came Around, not only to my Way of Thinking, but to my Kitchen too (though they are often synonymous, as Robert Johnson would agree). And she came, and I REALLY amused her, sir, with my brilliant jokes. She brought back a couple of things she'd somehow managed to half-inch either from my kitchen (possibly from my refrigerator) or else from my bedroom, sir—a book, a compact disc, and half a garlic. Fine, I said, mock seriously, well if we're going to start giving and taking stuff back do you want to take your lip-salve and other beauty products from my bedside table?

'No,' she replied.

Now, Harper. A woman would only need those things there if she were intending on waking up in my room some time reasonably soon. I dare not speckalate (as the LIE would pronounce it), but there it is. As Barbosa would say: nothing remotely coherent, but a mere grinning and tapping of the nose. The same Barbosa, incidentally, who—having lost her last jabbering excuse, now that Jesse has gone, leaving a spare bed behind him—persists these last two nights, in sleeping on my floor; but I stress—the floor, sir. The floor. The thin, threadbare one. A man's bed is his CASTLE. Woke up yesterday with a terrible headache thanks to her, like the roses in her best-friend-and-worst-enemy's GODAWFUL poetry, sucking all my—MY—oxygen the whole night through. And now I have a cold, which not only gives Rosa the perfect opportunity to blather contentedly about Mary Wortley Montagu and the infectious Phlegm of Vienna, but which, if you are not careful, will soon be

Yours,

Jude.

P.S. Received a postcard from Slovenia, where Jesse has gone a-roaming, with a rucksack and baseball cap, in the bitter winter snow.

P.P.S. Rosa's cat gave me fleas. Pah! Like I never had fleas before.

>
>

Gentlemen,

Things are coming to a head. To the very Font in fact. I read in this month's EID (Emerging Infectious Diseases: a peer-reviewed journal tracking and analyzing disease trends) that Avian Flu is set to sweep Europe. Meanwhile, we have Foot and Mouth devouring the herds, and, to cap it all, countrywide floods—so that the reservoir begins to fill again. But Bullish expansions continue apace. And we are still persona non grata. Moreso, indeed, because some canny operator has just burned down Fourpoints Farm. You will guess who bears the blame.

Notwithstanding, know that I will expect both of you here by the 31st of March, exiled or not, and regardless of threatened punishments. Yes, I know: a day before your injunctions lift, but we have some serious scoping to do, and Dovecombe, I think, will bear the brunt of it. It has rather too many beasts abroad for my taste. Besides, our old friend The Man Who Would Be King is putting on a charity play on that night—Hamlet, you'll be interested to hear—in aid of St Swithen's collapsing graveyard, and if that doesn't serve as what a certain Liar might call a red herring, I don't know what will. Worm, I know your family's not around, and mine neither, so you'll just have to hunker down for the remaining time with whomever has stayed loyal. I'm sure there must be one or two. Your sacrifices will not go unappreciated. For, as my old biology mentor, Mr. Le Boeuf, used to say, 'you can only get METAL with FIRE!' Perhaps that was why he was so satisfied with the genocide I practiced on pumpkins and melons.

Continue to state location.

T.

Jude was nodding when he realised he had been reading without taking anything in. In fact, he had been drifting, right there in front of the computer, nodding not in agreement but sleep. There was a symbolic pool of drool between the letters *H* and *J*, not touching *U* but very close to the *N*. 'Well, what if it is?' thought Jude. 'About time, some would say.' Ava had gone. In front of him now was Cornelius Barry, no doubt looking up novelty watches on the net. He was back where he started, with Harper's implausible ravings, about tramps and saunas. He finished it off, less for interest than the sake of form.

I left the sauna, got dressed and went up to the cloakroom to get my shoes. There I was, kicking about among the boots and cagoules, when up rumbles A., sweating profusely, and pulling on a trench coat. 'Och,' he says, always on his guard. 'What are ye skirlin' round here for, like the scavenger ye're?' 'I was just looking for my shoes,' says I. 'Well grab a pair of fuckin' pumps, any'll do,' he puffs. 'No time to fuckin' lose.' I scuffed a suede glove on the floorboards and noticed a headline on a sheet of newspaper. It was the Evening Chronicle. RESIDENTS

REFUSE TO GIVE WAY TO BULLISH EXPANSION said a headline, and underneath was a photograph of a barricaded Fourpoints Farm. Alongside that, another caught my eye: WWII EXPLOSIVES FOUND IN TUNNEL. There was a picture of a hole with the caption: 'philanthropy'. 'Look at this shithole!' A. breaks in, skirling, himself, among the coats. 'All this crap litterin' the floor.' He pocketed a couple of wallets and a comb, and threw a pair of tennis shoes at me. Strangely, they fitted. 'Anyone would think a bomb had hit it,' he growled. I looked at him. He was buttoning on someone's trousers. 'Heh!' he slurped. 'Trouble was, a bomb DIDNAE hit it. Hit everything round it, 'cept this 'un. Shoddy fuckin' Jerry. Old Bomber'd got it.' He pulled on a pair of random boots, shoved a knife and a hip-flask down his trousers. 'I'll show ye demolition! I'll show ye,' he was muttering. He ogled me, tongue in the side of his mouth. 'Heeh, I'll show ye.' He grabbed me by the upper-arm and forced me through the door. 'Show 'em fuckin' Lutheran apostates, an' all, an' their hearty hymn-singin'.' His voice in the outdoors is reduced, precise. He seems sobered by it. 'Methodist, Millenarian, Wesleyan. Pres-by-fuckin'-tarian.' He looked up at the church. Slow rain fell through the lights. 'I'll give 'em a fuckin' sauna. Gonna get hot around here, sooner than ye know.' He shuffled quickly down the pavement, jabbing at the ground. 'Ye think I'm full o' shit, don't ye? Don't ye, eh?' 'I thought we were going to meet X again?' I said. 'How'd ye know ye haven't?' he grunted. 'You do him pretty well.' I said. 'X is that accomplished,' he said, 'he could act me acting hem, just well enough to de ye fuckin' head in.' He clicked his fingers. 'X can disappear, just like fuckin' that. If anyone asks—it was fuckin' Artie, fuckin' horsin' aroond. Na, mate, X is real enough. An' I should know. I went to actin' school with hem. I'll nae fergit it,' he chuntered, as if he could forget it easily. 'I was playin' the Dane, ma first big role. Guess who X was? Fuck me, if I weren't upstaged by a Ghost.' He stopped a moment, putting a paw on my shoulder, so that he shoved me into a brick wall. 'Ye know that's the part Shakespeare played?' he said profoundly, squinting in my eye. Then he started on ahead. 'What chance had fuckin' Hamlet?' he muttered. 'Play was over after Act fuckin' One. How d'ye follow that?' A car goes by. He thrusts me along, past empty lots, fences, weeds, with the smell of the river, rain in the night. 'Where am I following you?' says I. 'Trust me,' says he, and he winks. 'Like Louis fuckin' Pasteur—ah ken the terrain.' He points down the road. I can't see anything. 'See that!' he barks, but the bark doesn't last. 'What?' says I. The sky is a blank—nothing obstructs it. 'Look again!' he says, striving to sound angry. 'I can't see anything,' says I. 'Heh!' he cries. ''Cause there ain't nothin' here! Not a thing standin' since Forty-One.' He sweeps his hand a full one-eighty. 'Firebombin' mostly,' he champs. 'Jus' down there was the SS Willoughby. Knaw what happened to her? Heh, awnly a barrage balloon! – Ye ken wha' a barrage balloon is?' I didn't. 'Look like zeppelins. They had what was known as a Balloon Command back then, if ye can credit it. Used to float 'em low in the sky, ye ken, te entangle divers. Any case, either with the firebombin', or—they'd carry small explosives, these balloons—somehow the balloon caught fire, drifted t'ward the ship. BANG!' he snapped, clapping his hands. He was trying to scare me but his voice seemed smaller than ever. 'A thousand tons of fuckin' bombs, blew her sky high, an' a mile fuckin' wide.' He surveyed the scene. 'Balloon Command!' he tutted. 'I'll gi' ye fuckin' balloons.' He sounded wistful. 'I thought you said they'd done a shoddy job?' says I. 'Och an' they did,' says he. 'Bombin' wise. They awnly killed four thousand. Ye should have seen fuckin'

Hamburg. Over fuckin' forty. Heh! That's proper bombin'! Still,' he says, quiescing again. ''T's a lot more than bombs wipes a slate.' He points to a car park, although wasteland might be the better term. 'There was a church here, St. John's, a hundred years back. They closed it down, New Year's fuckin' Eve, nineteen-o-five. Knaw who was married there—an' buried there too?' His eye glinted. The river had got in it. 'Awnly Joshua Wilson.' 'Oh,' says I, 'the man who built the tunnels.' Artie checks, looked away. Evidently I wasn't supposed to know this. 'Tunnels,' he mutters, searching for cause of displeasure. He spits on a thistle. 'Tunnels. Labyrinths more like! Catacombs! Fuckin' mausoleum is what we're talkin' 'boot! Tunnels,' he disdains, and the wind disdains also. 'Another fuckin' philanthropist, weren't he,' he continues. 'Used to get people movin' bricks from one side o' the tunnel to another, an' back again, jus' to keep 'em employed. They called him The King o' Cutters Hill. Knaw when he died? Awnly May the first. Heh, In'ernational Worker's Day. That's a good 'un. 'Fore they called it that, o' course. Cause o' death: water on the lungs, heh. Hegh! Looks like I'll follow his footsteps.' He proceeds to hack theatrically. You can smell the wine on him. 'Anyway, St. John's closed an' they moved most a the graves. Not the fuckin' King's. He's under that car-park now, acre o' hard tar for his windin' sheet. Won't be pushin' up daisies, now will he?' He jams hands in his coat pockets. 'Safe as houses,' I say. It is a conciliatory remark, but, like all conciliatory remarks, it is destined to infuriate. 'Safe as houses!' he snorts. 'What's so safe aboot a house, that's what I want to know? What's so safe aboot a FUCKIN' house!' This was clearly a sore point. 'Show me a house, I'll show ye a fuckin' mantrap. Heh! Everywhere he dug them tunnels, the houses are fuckin' collapsin'. Everything he touched turned to wormholes.' He turned and the wind took his voice. We trudged up the road, did a long, bleak dogleg, and dropped in for a pint at The Water Hole, a tiny old establishment which A. assures me has slaked the thirsts of Herman Melville, Charles Dickens and Adolf 'fuckin'' Hitler down the years. Apparently it lies under imminent threat of luxury 'redevelopment', but A. and his chums are 'gonnee do somethin' boot that'. He slaps a finger on his nose, leaves me to pay and continues his potted mythological tour, stopping for a breather at the Strongarm Rooms, a sojourn at the All and Sundry, and ending up, where all things end, at the Pomp and Prestige, where he sings the International, follows a risible Anthony with a phenomenal Coriolanus, and passes out with his head face down in a plate. By the time the Goose evicts us, it's pissing down as much as up, and I assume A. has lost his thread forever. Far from it. 'Speakin' of the Führer,' he begins again, pointing down Spinney Street, suddenly sober. 'He stayed oover there, before World War fuckin' One.' 'Near the reservoir?' I ask. He looks askew. 'Not far fray the Synagogue,' he says quietly, and he leans in. 'Now. What was he doin' here, apart from spongin'?' 'I don't know,' I say. 'A Language Exchange Programme?' He grips my shoulder. 'Dodgin' military service!' he roars. 'Caaa-caachachachach!' A. dies laughing and resurrects in contempt. 'Like a feckless fuckin' wastrel!' he says, staring hard. 'Six months in this shithole an' he went runnin' back to war. Six months,' he reflects. 'In a shithole like this.' He pisses on a lamp-post. The rain pours. 'I'd shew it ye, but I cannee.' He throws wide his arms, as if he'd caught a whopper. 'Luftwaffe fuckin' flattened it! I guess ol' Adolf didna like the accommodation! Cachachachachaaaaaaach! Och, that's what I call bearin' a fuckin' grudge! Safe as fuckin' houses indeed! I'll shew ye. I'll shew ye. Be yer fuckin' Fuehrer an' all.'

We continued up the road, down another and slipped across a grass waste. Stopping at a crumbled wall, A. removed some rubble and a trapdoor appeared, blocked up with bricks. He got in, up to the waist and passed me the bricks, one by one. Lastly, he passed up a heavy plastic sheeting, stuck with rocks and nettles. A cold air drifted up. 'Ah'll show ye a fuckin' mantrap,' he repeated. 'A sight fer eyes.' He clambered out and motioned me in. 'Doont fret,' he says, looking furtively round. 'Ah'm the only one knows the place.'

I sat in the hole. 'Jump,' he said. About six feet under me appeared to be a huge pile of rubble. 'Ah said, fuckin' jump!' he rasps. I jumped down, downrolling that pile like an ancient barrow mound. A. pulled the plastic over the hole and jumped in after. He lit two candles, handed one to me, and we carried them before us. All they revealed was more rubble, capped with a darkness. We were in a long, tall tunnel, feeling our way, stumbling on stones, clambering over vast mounds, so high we had to crouch under the ceilings. Brickwork encircled us, rising to high, pointed arches where other tunnels, with crescent mouths, dropped toothy rubble. 'Ye wanna spectacle, acle, acle,' grunted A., coughing away. His voice bounded and rebounded from the walls, till what little sense it had was lost. 'Gi ye a spectacle, an' fer our eyes awnly, awnly, awnly.' And he turns to me, as if tearing his face from a painting.

At that moment a light hit the mound in front of us and another man comes into the chamber. 'What's going on here ere ere?' he says. 'What the fuck is going on HERE ERE ERE?' retorts A. 'I'm with GOWT, OWT, OWT' said the man. 'Heh heh heh!' says A. 'An' I'm with fuckin' PLAGUE AGUE AGUE!' 'Guardians of Wilson's Tunnels, unnels, unnels,' says the man. 'Are you supposed to be here?' 'S'posed! posed! posed!' says A. 'Do ye know who I am am am? Heh heh heh! Then ye'd best ask the gen'leman here ere ere.' 'That's right ight ight,' says I, twitching uncontrollably. 'He's Bomber Harris' son, son, son—or is it grandson, grandson, grandson?' etc, etc, etc. These genealogies, as they are wont to do, continue for a despairingly long time, before we go our respective ways, each giving permission to each. And just as we have slipped into a side-tunnel, scaled a huge mound and slid perilously down the other side, what do we see but another torch, shining full in our faces. A shrill voice cries, 'Alright, fuck's sake, Carl, we'll get lost in 'ere, 'ere, 'ere. AAAGH! Who the fuck are you, you, you?' 'Little Miss Muffet, uffet, uffet,' wheezes A. 'and this is Tom Fuckin' Thumb, umb, umb,' he demurs. 'Now get into the air an' oot ma fuckin' grave! rave! rave!' he foamed, and off scarper two urchins, not without first launching fireworks in our general direction and spraying some kind of poison in the air, so that we danced around the tunnel, dodging rockets, blinded by Catherine wheels and trying not to breathe. Finally, after a solid ten minutes' walk, we came upon what seemed to be a large chamber with divers recesses, one of which, by dint of slithering up and down mounds, we gained. Pushing back an awning stuck with bricks and plastic, A. revealed a narrow chute, three feet high. 'Now,' he rasped. 'We slip threugh here, creep along the chute, an' close now, real fuckin' close, in the very next chamber, lies my awld man's secret.' The candle almost singed his eyelashes. 'Just a little wooden crate,' he smiles, 'ye wouldn't blink te look at. But, my God, Bomber, it's what's inside that counts. Heh! Ain't that what they say?' What is inside?' says I. He looks as if he is attempting to snuff the candle in his eyesocket. 'Fruit,' says he, smiling. 'Heh! That's right. Lemons, melons, apples, oranges, bananas, pineapples, plums—you fuckin' name it. Even fuckin' avocados! Aye, son, a colourful collection. Glowin' like gold in that innocuous box.' A. stirred his hand in the air, like seamen in (whale) sperm. He had a rapt look. 'Aye, lad,' he breathes. 'Best bunch of explosive fuckin' fruit since the Fall.' He pulls a lemon from his pocket, slaps it in my hand, and squeezes them together. From the tip a thick paste oozes, dropping on the stones. I jerk back my hand, repulsed. 'Get a grip, son!' he remonstrates. 'Anyone'd think ah'm squeezin' yer fuckin' lemon! An' ah'm sure you don't need me to do that fer ya!' He shakes the candle at me. 'Lucky I didn't drop my fuckin' candle, or we'd be at groun' level again, an' faster than we'd wish! Na, nothin' wrong with that stuff,' he says tightly, putting back the lemon in my palm. 'That's Nobel 808. Plastic fuckin' explosive to yeu' (coughing again). All the wee from Vienna,' he repeated. 'Court'sey of Dad. Anyone asked, he was a travellin' fuckin' children's entertainer. No one asked what a children's entertainer needed with a whole crate o' prosthetic fuckin' fruit.' He laughs grittily, then sobers up, staring me wildly in the eyes. 'Listen up, son. X wanted me to give it ye, in case anything happens te us, ye ken. Said it would explain a lot. Said it was evidence.' He slots the lemon in my pocket, buttons it up and pats the bulge. 'Heh! He gargles. 'Pretty fuckin' convincing evidence. Heh! Evidence like that they can't just destroy. Might just fuckin' destroy 'em first!' He stifles a laugh-cum-death rattle, creeps up the chute, and by the time I've begun creeping after him, he's already emerging in the chamber. I see lights, hear a hollow cacophony of portentous terms, laughable jargons, syntactic fragments, doing the police in many echoey voices, viz: 'stop' 'trespass' 'bomb' 'diffusion' 'squad' 'material' 'sensitive' 'nature' 'hurry' 'up' 'please' 'it's' 'time', and so on. Then a pause, a mutter, a roar. A scuffle, a blow, and a single shot. Naturally, I inch round, creep INCREDIBLY FAST and scarper, candle in hand, all the way we had come, till with religious delight, I see a streetlamp straining on a square of plastic. Then it's scrabble up mound, shin through trapdoor, roll by brambly wall, and I'm in the waste land again, gazing on the lemon.

There it was, sir, in my hand, glowing softly in the dark. A piece of yellow plastic. There was the almond smell. A nice smell—warmer than the river. I held it, dreaming, with the cool air on me.

Still

H.

P.S. I think we should talk. On the blower. How does tonight grab you? Say 10 o' clock, GMT (as stipulated by your Father)?

Jude was sweating, prickling down his front. He was tired of the computer, tired of the library. Cornelius Barry was pretending not to have seen Jude, waiting, apoplectic, for Jude to acknowledge him. He looked like a man whose life was a continual struggle not to break wind. He could fuck right off. Clicking *Reply All*, Jude dashed off the following:

Sir,

Risible, sir. Deplorable. And Tawdry.

And that's just three of 'em.

Sounds like they all need a good pounding; the High Priestess especially. And you're the man to do it, sir! If it's revolution she want, stick it to 'er. Stow the gauche manifestos, kitsch electioneering, high-camp coups d'etat. Get straight to Red Terror. It's what she wants, what they all want, after all.

Except, it seems, the Sicilian Dragoon, whom, judging by her egomaniacal silence (and I shall, sir, IN THIS VERY ROOM, where I have SENTENCED MINE to polite conversation), I can only assume has been drafted into the King's Fusiliers. In any case, she's leaving next month—and with one of Rosa's cat's fleas in her ear, if I have anything to do with it—preferably the one she (Rosa, not the Sicilian, alas) bawled me out with this afternoon, for displaying pig ignorance of the specific details of the despoliation of Vienna during the Napoleonic invasion. Which, sir, is as far as her greed will try my charity, given that she (Rosa, not the Sicilian, alas) so clearly wants to be invaded and despoiled.

Speaking of charity, I've been on the receiving end of too much lately, in the form of copious tobacco and alcohol, though Tomas is perfectly, magnanimously, egalitarian about it, and in return I let him eat my rhubarb and apple crumble—so good it almost caused a major furore. Stole all the ingredients, naturally. Whereupon, indulging Mary Montagu's romantic notion that Vienna is inhabited by all nations, only so as to completely debunk her self-serving hypothesis that a conversation among esteemed friends is life's greatest happiness, everyone (sans P., sans S., sans Everything!) was sitting round ploughing through it last night in total silence (but for the rolling of reinstated Eyes, the gnashing of relocated Teeth, plus the obligatory scraping of spoons, coughing and snuffling between mouthfuls, etc) when Barbosa, who, for reasons known only to herself, had spent the previous week on my floor, causing me to kick her out that morning with an army of Rosa's cat's fleas in her scalp, extremely premeditatedly, piped up (a mournful, reedy pipe, mark you), as follows:

BB: [premeditatedly]

How is
Would be
That every one would like
To try living letting
The others live as well

The gathered hosts were momentarily dumbstruck by her moments of confused, which is also to say ill-informed genius. Before they had a chance to react, she pursued her broken tirade.

BB: [pursuant]

There is also another thing
That retains me those days.
I think you already know
That Maria is in Paris.

It's going to be her birthday
There are festivities from Girona.
We'll be drunk most of time, for sure.
We will remember of you
acting sharks or snakes.

Maybe we'll meet soon
In Barcelona,
Or maybe somewhere else.

Well, it is too complicated
To explain so briefly, but
Maybe we can talk about it

In a quiet evening drinking tea,
London.

Jude.

P.S. Looking quite unreasonably forward to Jesse's return (today). Have gone so far as to leave a note under his door, inviting him to the

Hawelka tonight.

P.P.S. Well look, I'll try to call you this evening. But if I don't, because I'm waylaid by the Hawelka, try to call me at the Studentenheim (Play Room) tomorrow evening (i.e. 1st of Feb), for definite between 8-10. I'll have gone running by then, and will probably be feverishly pressing and sitting up, while Bjorn beats the Lie at table-tennis by boring him to death.

P.P.P.S. Speaking of Magnanimity, I assume you intend to comply with his insane demands, and return to the valley for the tail end of March? Good then. I've a mind to meet on a hill, all overarched with trees, I walking up and you, you walking down. With your eyes in your pocket, my nose on the ground. But remember, before you come, first, please, TELEPHONE.

Jude signed out, pulled from the desk, as from water, and slopped to the exit, exhibiting both pencil and Bible. He stepped to the lighted square, faced the sudden cold. His skin was cool awake but his head swarmed. He slipped through the arches to the Michaelerplatz, eyed with suspicion the Roman walls, spotted with snow. 'Vindobona,' he thought. 'No more.' Sometimes the past is improved upon. Sometimes you hit a golden age and you know it;

everyone goes around safe in the knowledge. While people are convinced, they are content. The very thought is enough to inspire! But then something changes. The door is left open. People look carefully at one another, no one wants to be the last to leave. It's gone before it's left the building.

He fell to the left, curved round the Holocaust Memorial, dipped right out of consciousness angling several lefts and ended up chuckling in Orson Welles' doorway, pressed against the wall. Now he fell backwards, walked backwards on the cobbles, sent his shadow backwards by a streetlight. The sky held out on him. It was thick purple, pulling into night. He glimpsed the *Universität*, whirled near the *Burgteater* and, taking a nook, having a cranny, stumbled on a square. A huge, bearish, geometric puzzle swung into the evening, as if the square had grown round it. It was the *Minoritenkirche*. He laughed abruptly. When his breath finished fanning, he leaned on a wall. There it was again: the *Minoritenkirche*, three styles in one, its ragged cloisters, cracked skull, lopsided belltower, twice toppled when Suleiman peeped through the keyhole of Europe. The belltower looked like clapboard, jammed amidst Gothic. It reared skyward, dragging the building with it. A dead tree, climbed by its amber windows. More theatre than church. Ravaged by fashion, fire, armies. Divorced beheaded, died, divorced beheaded, survived. Every despot's favourite. Hitler's, Napoleon's, Jude's kind of *Kirche*. He rolled over the frozen flagstones. Up to the side-wall he went, under the cloistered walk. A lamp rolled a stained ball on the stones; a single, suspended lamp, like a sunset through dark glass. Arches were hoods overhead. In and out he stumbled, till the square swept under him, with all its eaten flags. They were clipped with tramped-down snow, as if a thousand men had marched there: thousand soldiers, sheltering, touched with candles. They had crossed the threshold, lain among the pews, close for warmth and quietened. Who owned it now? At what point did attack become defence? These questions sewed their dreams. There was an odd middle, when you were in, yet new, dwarfed yet sleeping, among columns, statues, tombs. Ducking the tympanum, its motley of Saints and Marys, through one of double doors, its concave rim on rim, and Jude also was in yet new. White walls wound, but a gloom presided, with irregular flames. A mass was taking place, it was that time of day. '*Noi ti lodiamo, ti benediciamo, ti adoriamo*,' the Priest was saying. He was far and fluid, 'wrapped in his own formless horror' in the pulpit of a left-hand column. His voice carried well into interiors, doing without the microphone. '*Ti glorifichiamo, ti rendiamo grazie per la tua gloria immensa, Signore Dio, re del cielo, Dio Padre onnipotente.*' Jude took a turn under the gallery. These were protected spaces, calm and wakeful. No one seemed to notice him. Emboldened, he moved through the left-hand aisle, only to be accosted by that grand imitation, The Last Supper (and also Raffaelli's representation of it). Here was Judas with his hand in the cookie-jar; there was Peter with his hand disconnected (just like Marty McFly's); and there was young John, dressed as Mary Magdalene, swooning to a *V*. Grails and wombs and significant gestures. The kind of tired old contrivance Magnus would have favoured; whetting appetites, outstaring eyes, passing dish after portentous dish, positively pregnant with the (suspension of the) suspension of disbelief. Verily, The Last Supper deserved its conspiracy theorists, clutching at signs, as if they signified *anything*. 'One of you shall betray me'—and they looked so surprised. A hammy reaction at the best of times—how much moreso to a prescribed narrative? No, no, it wasn't vegan. As far as prescribed narratives went, preferable by far was the Long Breakfast (with the Sunday Papers), the Late-Night Rummage in the Larder—even the despicable Afternoon Tea was redeemable, via Toast and Peanut Butter.

Jude's stomach growled. He frowned, put a hand across it, like Thaddeus, looked away. There was an Ur-text for you. 'Ugh,' he chuckled, spurning The

Last Supper, as he once had Pilar Santana Artale, and continuing down the aisle (*ditto*). The place was a treasure-chest, hulked round with shipwreck. Jude moved in the murk of the sea-bottom, accustoming. Gold and bronze, leather, silver, nuzzled the eye, rose like anemones from pools of gloom, sinking when the gaze departed. Only the Priest's robes remained. They slunk and billowed, like a ghost that refuses to go. '*Signore, figlio unigenito, Gesu Cristo*,' said the Priest, '*Signore Dio, Agnello di Dio, figlio del Padre, tue che togli i peccati del mondo*'. Jude approached the pulpit, side-on, as if extremities were dangerous, a row-boat under a gunship. *Tap* went his shoes on the floor. He was seeking lee of the column, to be once again invisible, stealing up a glance before he made it in. The Priest was human over the ghost of robe; thick glasses and a face like a cabbage. But the voice was clear, as if it came from the mind. And he cried then ghostly ever this one cry: '*Abbi pieta di noi; tu che togli i peccati del mondo, accogli la nostra supplica*'.

With the column upon him, Jude dropped a shoulder, rounded a font and came face-to-face with John the Baptist. This was a bit like bamboozling the goalkeeper (Piers), side-stepping a stray puddle and preparing to tap into an empty net, only to find Benjamin Kepperly-Lie in your way—a reed shaken with laughter: impossible, disarming, radiating Radical Uncertainty—so that you swiped, missed, overbalanced in the puddle. '*Tu che siedi alla destra del Padre, abbi pieta di noi*,' continued the Priest. John the Baptist was holding a crook-like cross, a sheep at his shoeless feet. He was slim, slope-shouldered, half-extending an arm. There was a swagger to him. He looked like a faun on a jaunt. But there was a stump at his foot which he appeared to have narrowly avoided. Jude identified with John. Not Christ, not Elias; a voice in the wilderness. Prophecy was seeing what was before you, headed straight your way. A rational man in exceptional times. A man who must decrease. A man who liked water, up to his belly, sun on the surfaces. Who baptised with water, not with fire, who baptised in Aenon, for that's where the water was. An easy equation, as the Lie would say. *'Perche tu solo il santo, tu solo il signore, tu solo l'altissimo, Gesu Cristo, con lo Spirito Santo: nella gloria di Dio Padre*,' said the Priest. *'Amen.' Amen* said the congregation.

Jude turned away, as if implicated. In a darkened corner—none other than King Ottokar of Bohemia, foremost of his race. Jude looked from John to Ottokar, John to Ottokar. The more he looked, the more similar they were. The curly hair, uncertain beard—just like Harper in fact. Ottokar even had his forearms extended, wrists cocked as if holding a rifle. Not such an easy swagger, but a swagger still, loins in the van, and the mirror foot forward. It had narrowly avoided tripping on a crown. They stood either side of a chapel, as if guarding its entrance. Ottokar, John: the Man of Action and the Knight of Faith, one mirroring the other. But that was the thing about your Knight of Faith: the *mirar* only went one way. 'How are you?' you said to him, he said it back to you. There was no point in admiring him. To do so would be a disservice. This is what Harper didn't get, constantly admiring, arranging his plays as if the world were not a stage—hence his tired hunt for *experience* (how Jude spurned the word). He should get together with Rosa. They could sing experience till senility set in, striding back and forth with pretend-rifles, tripping over crowns, implying dramatic ironies. It was all about *business* (Jude strangled the word) as *The Man Who Would Be King* would say. They were all actors. Democrats at heart, leaning on the people. Would-be Kings, stumbling on the *would*. If Harper weren't careful, he would end up in a concrete drain, a bullet through his (shrunken) eye. Not one with a name on; an ugly bullet, sprayed through an alley. And he would love it. *Bear Hamlet like a soldier to the stage*, only stage he really believed in.

Such a sight as this
Becomes the field, but here shows much amiss.

Jude stared at John the Baptist. Here was a man who didn't want to be King, who was not fit, *etcetera*, whose head dizzied at Salome's hips, no greater of woman born. Here was a closed circle. What had Jude to do with John? Prophecy was immanence after all, deed in word.

Jude frowned at John the Baptist, withdrew his unconditional sympathy. By contrast, Ottokar would shake your hand heartily, clap his own, seat you on cushions in some murmurous room, solace with wine a good day's hunting. Jude went to stand near Ottokar, a man who *was* a King, who fought his own father and married a woman thirty years senior (*ergo*, a mother). He had laid the foundation stone, here at the *Minoritenkirche*, twelve-seventy-six, when Vienna was besieged by Rudolph of Hapsburg. He had lost Austria, tried to retrieve it, died in battle, lain here himself, thirty weeks in state. Now he stood represented, in mid-swagger, somewhere between the word and deed. It must have felt good to arrive in pomp, to go through motions, to place a stone, with ritual slowness, a year after fire, two before death. In the fruit of that stone loin, Jude stood himself. The *Minoritenkirche*: a good place to stand, between word and deed. So he stood there, arms folded, right-leg protruding, as if controlling a bobbling ball.

Standing like that, he became aware the pass was

on, through the entrance to the chapel. He made that metaphorical pass, following up with a box-to-box sprint. Inside it was high and gloomy. Candles were banked round the altar, like tiny theatre seats. From there rose columns of polychrome marble. Between them stood San Antonio in lilies. He was holding the Christ-child on his arm, appearing to interest it in a picked lily. It was his chapel, patron of protection, lord of lost things, whose Austrian lilies bloomed the year of sixteen-eighty. Strangely enough, he died about the time that Ottokar was born. Above him soared three files of seventeenth-century stained-glass amidst white-panel walls. Two more windows closed round. You couldn't help but look up. On the rear wall, behind Jude's back, wood panelled galleries enabled glimpses from above, like boxes in the theatre. What kind of person hid in a chapel's private gallery, spying on those beneath? It took a romantic imagination, take it as pejoratively as you liked. Jude took it very pejoratively, and liked it too. Nearer at hand were two statues. To left of him, Antonio again, with the Christ-child and lily, atop a base of brick. He was brown and lilac. Fuchsias stood before him, all pressed in the dark. To his right was a large, handled urn, showing a shrub to the flame. Around him, climbing the walls, were plaques commemorating wealthy or important patrons, in German and Italian. *Dank und Bitte* read one;

Grazie read another. Initials were carved below the words. Some had full names, longer imploring, encomiums, epitaphs. Beyond twelve feet or so they were hard to read. Jude span on a heel, reading as he went. To his right hand, also on a brick-base, was a robed, veiled woman. *S. RITA DA CASCIA* read the base. She was holding a crown of thorns. It looked delicate, the way she handled it, cross dangling from her arm. Her face was pained but strong, almost scornful. The world was not her home. Plaques rose around her, recalling the dead. *Dank*, they read, and *DANK* again. Jude shivered, now he came to think of it. *DANK U. BITTE* read a third: *LEOPOLD RITTER, EUGEN HOPPE, W. I. M. EGON*. His eyes scanned the stones like ants unseaming them. It was systemic work. He was tracing that wall, left to right, right to left, higher and higher, busy and mindless. The roof was a blue gloom. It must have been forty, fifty feet high. Shadow fell like a chandelier. He almost overtoppled, knees crooking with a vertigo sensation. He crouched to ground for balance, and his attention was caught by a plaque near at hand, inscribed to *MATHILDA KRÖNER*. *KRÖNER*, thought Jude, slow on the uptake. That was Magnus' name. Magnus: a Kraut, a Hun, a Barbar at the gates of Rome, dismantling its hinges. Who knew from what cold wilds he hailed? What Rhineland or Danubian haunts took suck in ancestry? Could this same Mathilda be his *alma mater*, to whom he'd return in the marble harvest? Rolling the *KRÖNER* down the barren male line, being such troublesome bedfellow. All his exploratory life: a bid to get back to those wolfish wolds, boary firs, eagling mountain crags, where no doubt he must not roll. Magnus would have loved the idea; refuted it; loved it all the same. Jude suspected the secret of Magnus' strength lay in crediting, establishing even, a cheap psychological framework which he could strongly dismantle. There was nothing like a straw man. Jude stood again, fixed on the word which kept the ports of slumber open wide, many a watchful night. This, from thee, will I to mine leave, as was left to me.

He left the chapel and was surprised by pallor. Three huge windows gleamed on the eastern wall, over organ pipes and the capacious gallery. Even their dimness impressed: there was nothing like it to show refulgence by. A framed figure leaned from the balcony. Jude hunched, looking shiftily left. The Priest was breaking a large black loaf, getting crumbs all over the altar. A small queue formed before him, kneeling and receiving, kneeling and receiving, waves on stone shores. Jude sidled in the aisle, turning the dark to his advantage. He meant to slip out quietly, without word, certainly without importunity. If it was a question of bread, he would take Rosa's—black as Abaddon, with a dash of soya spread. And of course there would be wine, the redder the better. Rosa's was an altar, and a *mater* too, every bit as bountiful, and without all the trappings. '*Hoc est corpus,*' said the Priest. It seemed warmer in the nave than the chapel: all those breathing bodies. Jude rounded the font, left The Last Supper all ends up and was doing a column for pace when, utilising all of his peripheral vision, he spied in the pew a familiar shimmy, as rump and pony-tail jostled for position. It was her—right here—at the *Minoritenkirche*—Pilar Santana Artale—attending evening Mass! Crowding in among the bread and wine, came Rosa's advice. 'The *Minoritenkirche*,' she said. 'Worth a visit,' she said. 'It's a man's life,' she said. '*Bella gerant alii, tu, felix Judas, nube!*' There she went again, confusing Latin injunctions with maternal urges. She knew where she could stick her Latin. Right up the old vernacular. '*Et tu, Rosa?*' said Jude, wine running over the floor. He'd been done, sold a dummy, lost his man. It was a set-up, a blasted teed-up near-post volley, worked-out on the training ground. Nothing left to do but pick the ball from the onion bag. She was deep in the pew, praying. She wore a red roll-neck under a tight suede jacket. Candles made a sheen of her crown. From here he could see her long, fine nose, her lips, her cheek. That worn-marble stain under the eye. The smallish eye was a door pulled to; hardly closed; with living fire behind. He read love in those lids, that brow, beating on the spaces above. It was the most erotic thing he'd ever seen—and he was losing count of them. He stood there, hand on the pew, till, as if an extension of closure, she opened her eyes.

'*Theee*,' he rasped. '*And THIINE!*'

'How did you know?' whispered Pilar, spinning round, pony-tail horizontal.

He was still pointing at her, exacting reaction, a crabbed leer on his face. But he was wondering at her prescience.

'I might ask the same of you.'

'I didn't.' She shrugged.

'I said I *might*.'

'I just came for Mass.'

'Ah, the herd mentality.' He patted the pew, chuckling. People were walking out, as if unamused.

'Well, and to accompany *Abuela*.' She pointed to an aged woman, going through motions, crossing herself, touching her lips, applying inflexible fingers to the pew in front. She was hunched like a miser over gold. If Pilar's prayers were centred in the upper air, hers were in her midriff, as if she didn't want them to escape her. They were her child's toys, portentous, possessable, and she was jealous in their care.

The woman looked up, turned, as if catching her

name. She bent again.

'The herd mentality.' Jude raised his chin, determined to see this through. *Abeula* continued with her rhythms.

'Did you see the size of that loaf? *'Do this in memory of me.'* I was like, 'How could I forget?' She bobbed like salmon. Jude looked pleased. An adversary worthy of him.

'Yes, almost like something Rosa Wellhausen would make.'

She nodded to the altarpiece where a Maria portrait was held aloft by seraphs. 'That's *Maria della neve*. The Lady of Snow. There's another over there, by Rossellino. In Carrara marble. From Liguria?' Jude looked as if he knew. 'This is an Italian church you know.'

Jude merely gazed at the altar. His face mixed knowing and admiring.

'I'll show you around.' Unexpectedly she took his forearm, lead him like a mule from the pew. That was okay by him. Just at that moment she could have led him by the nose: his or hers, he wasn't fussy. 'Of course, that's the Last Supper there, in mosaic.'

'Yes, yes.'

They passed by.

'And here you've got St. Francis. This one's anonymous I think.'

'Right.'

'And there's John the Baptist.'

'Yes, I know all about him. He seems to have narrowly avoided tripping on a stump.'

'You've been round already, right?'

'Well, warned is forewarned.'

'What are you doing here?'

'No, it just seemed like a good place to come, in the circumstances.' He chuckled to himself, hands in pockets. The church had almost emptied.

Her head cocked. 'Are you religious?' It was asked archly.

Jude shifted from one foot to the other. Rosa, Pilar, women generally, were *obsessed* with this question, though of course only sentimentally so. On the other hand, when was obsession anything more? It was hard enough that it was *entirely the wrong question*; but the fact that one had seen it coming from several years away was incapacitating. 'Everyone's religious,' he grudged. 'Everyone believes. Everyone is explained by myth. What religion could tear itself from myth?' He dawdled with the font. 'Everyone lives in the world. The world (and this is my fundamental theorem), the world *exists*. Everyone's religious. Don't ask me that again.' And he slouched off to stand beside King Ottokar of Bohemia.

'That's the chapel of San Antonio.'

'You're a veritable tour-guide.'

'The saint of *lost stuff*.' She crept up and waved

like a ghost. Then she burst into giggles. He could see the ripple of her gums. 'Are you lost, Jude?' She bumped her hip on his. Her voice had that Spanish husk, all mocking. Jude didn't say anything. She was walking a fine line, becoming idiotic. But he was too, annoyed and transfixed by her, led by the nose. And it was her line he was walking, not his accustomed one. His was a controlled, precarious line, wherein length had some say. The kind you'd play a straight bat to, get an edge if you weren't watchful. Hers was more like a boundary-rope. You could fall half-asleep, sign a few autographs, still have time to patrol it. Jude wasn't used to subordination, much less speechlessness. Magnus sometimes induced it, by placing Jude where he was not quite comfortable. But Magnus had to realise, he was only able to do this because Jude himself *acquiesced.* Jude's self-subordination was, if not wearily superior, at least discerning. Because Jude was willing—yes *willing*—to go the extra mile, something Magnus himself would not have dreamed of doing. Pilar was different. That had been the thing about her. She got it, she understood the Specific Conditions. Now she was threatening to turn love into sentiment, as if it were not war. It was the same with Rosa, even with Sara Baumgarten. They could cut and thrust only so long, as if dialogue were an expediency. Somewhere along the line, they assumed too much. They leapt lightly into sentiment, as to the manner born, were lost to a man. Baumgarten was particularly adept at this. Assuming too much was her starting point. She knew no other way than Assumption. As-*sump*-tion. *Sump*. Jude sneered. *Schon*. Already sumped. You could say that again. Everyone was self-protective, desperately seeking disappointment. Magnus too was self-protective, ludicrously so, in his mollycoddled world He too assumed, but not too much. He assumed disillusion from the off, in that sense left it behind. You could take him or leave him, in the midst of his gothic hyperbole. No skin off him. But the others all awaited it. Pilar had started with the gothic hyperbole, but hers risked the Ridiculous. She was desirous for an intercedent, disappointed at his failure, desiring disappointment. She exposed herself. Not to a verbal male thrust—typical of woman, she evaded encounter, unwilling to close with him—but to verbless male silence, verging on boredom. How easy it would be to lose interest altogether. To vaguely remember something you'd forgotten. To mutter, to mope, maunder off in disconsolate state—just like King Ottokar. And it would be no success at all, and apparently no one's fault. But that was only apparently; underneath—underneath, sir—it would be *her* blasted fault, for her cowardly evasions, unwillingness to put herself on the Line, *his* line, that is.

And so he said nothing, stood, disappointed. But not seeking disappointment—having it thrust in his face. He hadn't made this appointment, Rosa had. But then he, Jude, had acquiesced in it. He too had set himself up for this appointment-disappointment exchange. He too was driving love from its native antagonism. He was as suspect as the others. He wasn't even thinking straight. There was nothing to be gained from these thoughts. Worst of all he had now left such a pause as she would think significant, as if her arrows had hit their mark. There was nothing else for it but to turn that slight pause into a lethargic silence.

Que lo olvidado se recordara
Que lo perdido se encontrara
Y que lo alejado se acercara

she said. She leant in on his shoulder, hanging with a hand from the chapel gate. Her mouth was mocking, lips sloping like the wings of swallows. Jude continued looking at Ottokar of Bohemia, although it was clear by now Ottokar of Bohemia was nothing more than a premise. He knew it, she knew it. Ottokar knew it better than anyone. 'That's Rita de Cascia,' she said, jerking back her thumb. 'Patron Saint—of the Impossible!' She chuckled again, throaty, like a lady of the night. Jude had underestimated her. She didn't seem at all to be courting disappointment. She seemed genuinely to pity him, pity, scorn and love, in equal measure. If anything she was mad, quite at home with the Ridiculous, Patron Saint of it even. No no, that was the Lie.

'I don't believe it.'

'Really—hah hah!'

'No, I don't believe it.'

She looked at him, gurning on a thought. Then she wobbled, dropped a shoulder, and she was gone in the chapel before he could react. He knew better than to follow. He stood his ground, next to old Ottokar, looking him up and down as if interested in appropriating his style. The crown he didn't run to; no way to warm a frozen ear. Perhaps that was why Ottokar had doffed it. He didn't go for the leggings either, although he knew a *Mistress Vampire* as would. The boots were a fine if effeminate mould, but he thought he could get away with them. Jude tapped his shoe on the floor, looking from Pilar to Ottokar to Pilar. She was adding to the banks of candles. The tunic was wide-waisted, would have suited him well. Jude had an unusually distended pelvis. She crossed herself in the flourish of fire, making obeisance to the gloomy San Rita. Finally was the cloak: a great steel-shield. Perfect for the Reaper's next appearance.

'Come and meet *Abeula*,' said Pilar. They slipped

up to the altar, took a right, between the pews. The place was almost empty. The Priest was busy behind the scenes. That figure had gone from the gallery. Last stragglers milled near the door, and there was the *Abuela*, three-quarters back, head fallen forward on the pew in front. The parting in her hair was a crack in stone. Long weakened curls moved, dust-like, from the centre. Those almost-masculine fingers, sepulchral pillars, were serried either side. It was hard to tell if she were praying or sleeping. They kept their distance, watching her shoulders rise and fall. They were mantled by a black wool-shawl, large holes between the strands. Under was an expensive fur. 'She's ninety-two,' said Pilar. 'Have I told you about her?'

'Is she the Jewish-Spanish-Viennese-Basque?'

'That was my grandfather. She's Spanish.'

'What's she doing in an Italian church?'

'So, my parents and me used to visit her in the holidays. My Mom's Sicilian, liked to go to mass in Italian. Grandma came too and got into a groove. She's been coming here thirty years or so. German, Italian, she doesn't care. That's the good thing about mass—it doesn't change much from place to place. She understands some Italian anyway.' They seated themselves in the pew across the way. *Abuela* remained still, but for the breathing. They looked at her, to avoid each other. It was marvellous that she persisted. Hands were blotched and mapped. A bloodless wrist extended from the fur. Back was a broken institution. Yet the will to live was fierce. The brow was all concentration. The fingers murmured on wood, they way a batsman tests a handle, or Ottokar might have gripped a sword. In couched shadow, against the farther flames, they saw trembles in lips and eye. She was like John. The longer she lived, the more of her life slipped out of understanding. Who knew the *Abuela?* Whom did she expect to? Only the dead ones. They were her standard and reference. She was half with them, yet not the less alive. Sometimes the busy world must have seemed an ignoramus. It must have baffled her like Pilar baffled Jude.

Elevating slowly, she removed her hands from the pew-back. They could see her eye was open, but staring straight down, as if moving her neck were painful. Then it flickered to the right, aware of being watched. The small of her back touched the back-rest; the upper part never would. The *Abeula* was with them, turning to look, working her mouth as if swallowing opinions.

'*Abuela, te presento a Jude, un amigo de la residencia de estudientes*.'

She rose with great difficulty, frowning, as if caught off her guard. Only when on her feet did she work a smile—the smile of a girl of twenty, just stepped off the cruise-ship. It was a brilliant smile, perfectly false, met in two front teeth a little rounder than the others. Her eyes were small and sunken. Round them were layered lilac rings, suggesting the natural development of Pilar's weary stains. Eyebrows climbed her brow like a difficult overhang. '*¡Holaa!*' she said, as if the world were lambs and verdure.

'*Hola.*'

She gestured with a hand. Jude stepped up to shake it, leaning in for the obligatory kisses. Just as he was retreating, however, she noticed his ravelled sleeve, poking out over the hand she was holding.

'*Y…y ¿qué es eso?*' she asked, pinching hold of the sleeve.

'Mmm?'

'*¿Qué es eso?*' she repeated. She smiled as if she saw the absurdity but that that was no reason to desist.

'She's asking about your sleeve,' said Pilar.

'Ah, my sleeve. A long story.'

'*Una larga historia.*'

Abuela turned slowly to Pilar. '*No…no me importa lo larga que sea la historia. ¿Qué es eso?*' And she turned slowly to Jude.

Jude was warming to *Abuela*. She must have been quite a thing in her prime. 'I got that,' he retorted, '*going over a stile.*' *Abuela* smiled disdainfully. 'Can you translate?' he continued.

'Forget about it.'

'No no, translate.'

Pilar shook her head. '*No es nada, Abuela. Los chicos son así.*'

'*No...no puedes ir a la iglesia vestido así,*' said *Abuela*, still smiling. Her smile was the soul of determination. Years of convent-school had inscribed it on her face. No matter the circumstances, so long as they were new she wheeled it out and pinned it to the chin.

'She says you can't come to church dressed like that.'

'Ha! Well, it's too late now.' Jude was getting some cheer back. So long as she was no relation, a really old woman was a good thing, especially if on the brink of the grave. She could say anything. *You* could say anything. Together you sewed chaos in conversation. Everyone was left floundering—you and she just went right ahead, pert, unembarrassable, beggaring belief. Poison in kisses, knives in the smiles. You could cannon her foredeck and she would chuckle back, torpedo your hull. The soul of anarchy, for no one had less to lose.

'*Dice, «es tarde».*'

'*Nunca...nunca es tarde para el Señor.*'

'She says it's never late for God.'

'Ha! I suppose she's right. And my sleeve?'

'*Dice «tiene razon».*'

'*Cl...Claro que sí. Claro que sí.*'

'She says "of course".'

Abuela still wasn't letting go. She beckoned with the left hand and Jude bent in again.

'Dá...dámelo...' she said, pronouncing carefully. *'Dámelo.'* For a moment she released his sleeve and made a sewing motion with her hands. Then she took the sleeve again, tugging it into line like a naughty boy. *'Dámelo.'*

'She wants you to give it to her.'

'What now?'

'¿Ahora?'

Abuela looked slowly but sharply at Pilar. She clenched her jaw before speaking. '*Claro...claro que no,*' she said, as if Pilar were in danger of being committed. She clenched her jaw again. '*Cogerá un re...un resfriado.*' She frowned, turning back to Jude. *'Fatal,'* she commented. She shook her head minutely. *'Fatal.'* Again she puckered up her lips. '*Más...más tarde,*' she croaked, taking the utmost care with her enunciation. '*Más...tarde.*' She patted his hand.

'Later.'

Jude nodded. He was just retreating again when he found his lean-back blocked. It was those same masculine fingers at his shoulder. He turned back to find *Abuela* in his face, staring down her nose at his mouth.

'¿Cómo...cómo tiene los dientes?' she said at last.

'¡Abuela, no puedes decir ese!'

'Enseñame tus dientes.' She smiled wide, as if for the birdie. She did it again, pointing at her mouth.

'¡Abuela, es increible!'

'Es...es muy importante. Hemos...hemos...tenido siempre buenes dientes.' With the same hand she squeezed his cheeks so that his lips pouted. His breath was visible, pouring from his throat.

'¡Abuela, estas no son maneras! Y de todas formas, no es mi novio.'

Abuela tactfully ignored this last statement. She merely stared at Pilar as if she came from another planet. Then she tilted back her head and resumed her scrutiny. A few seconds seemed to satisfy her on this point. She dropped his lips and nodded in Pilar's direction.

'Muy, muy bien,' she croaked, singing the second *muy*. *'De verdad.'*

'She likes your teeth,' said Pilar, grinning.

'Tell her I like hers too.'

'Dice que a el también le gustan los tuyos.'

'Claro, claro,' said *Abuela*, staring to the altar. It was the kind of unconscious response a mirror brings out. She pressed, re-pressed her lips. Her eyes were far away.

'¿Qué tienes, Abuela? ¿Quieres que nos vayamos?'

'¡Oh, tengo...tengo frío!' whined *Abuela*, still glazed, but mentally present. It was a real whine,

almost a cry. *'¡Pilar-har-har, ayúdame!'* She bunched the fur at her neck, on the point of tears. Pilar seated her again in the pew and rubbed her back with a hand.

'No pasa nada,' she said. *'Abuela, no pasa nada.'*

'¡Un frío, eh, de verdad!' haffed *Abeula*, looking pleased with the rubbing. Jude looked at them in the pew, clocked in shadow. Who knew what time it was now? This whole charade could go on all evening: wandering in pillars and aisles; kissing, shaking hands, rising and leaving; coming back again, watching halflit figures disappear here, appear again there; coming face to face with giants of history; lighting candles, rearranging beads, round and round the nave; weeping, smiling and weeping again, touching brow, lips, breast, back to lips, *ad infinitum*.

'Mira, mira,' said *Abeula*, pawing Jude's arm. She tapped the pew coquettishly. *'Todas las cosas bonitas—y caras, claro—que hay aqui.'*

'She says, look at all the beautiful things.'

'I'm looking.' Jude arched an eyebrow. Grins flew in blurs.

'Los cuadernos, las esculturas, las copas…todas…todas.'

'The paintings, the sculptures.' Pilar swept a desultory hand.

'La Virgin de…de…'

'¿Eso? ¿De Rossellino, Abuela?'

Abuela looked amused at the interruption. She turned her head, raised her own slow eyebrows, turned back with the faintest sarcastic smile.

'*El San Francisco...*'

'*Ya lo he explicado, Abuela.*'

'*La escultura de Juan...Juan...*' *Abuela* snaked a finger in that general direction. '*Un montón, eh?*' she said, patting Jude's arm. She really had tiny eyes.

'A lot of stuff.'

'Your family should run the tourist information.'

'My Mom used to go on about it. We kind of absorbed it.'

'*Todo tesoros, eh. Todo tesoros.*'

'*¿Qué tal estás, ahora?*'

'*Tesoros...tesoros...*'

'*¿Qué tal estás, Abuela?!*' said Pilar, raising her voice. It bounced round the aisles, much as Pilar herself might have done.

Abuela ignored her, tucking in a blouse-sleeve which crept from the fur. '*Tienen...tienen que tener cuidado.*' She was facing the floor, arranging her coat.

'*Ah sí, Abuela, por qué?*'

'*Nada está seguro, con los tiempos que corren.*' The lapel of the coat was pressed against the chest.

'*Mm-hmm.*' Pilar made a face at Jude, searched the church as if for exits. She was still rubbing *Abuela's* back.

'El crimen aumenta cada año...cada año mas.'

'Sí, sí. ¿Por qué?' said Pilar, innocently.

'¡Y yo qué se!' snapped *Abuela*. *'¡Vete a la calle y pregunta!'*

'Bueno, no sé, Abuela. Nada es como era. Incluso Vienna es moderna.'

'Moderna es una palabra sospechosa.' Abuela looked to Jude for confirmation. She found it.

'Vale, vale.' Pilar wiped *Abuela*'s nose with a tissue. *'¿Vamos juntos a preguntar?'*

'No quiero.'

'Tenemos que irnos, Abuela. La misa ha terminado.'

'¡Tengo...tengo frío!'

'¿Dónde está tu sombrero? ¿Está en el suelo? Is her hat on the floor there?' Jude ferreted in the darkness under the pew. *'¡Mira qué largos son tus pelos!'* Pilar ran a finger along *Abuela*'s curls. *'Me han preguntado por tí en la peliquería. «¿Donde está Mercedes?» me han dicho. «¿Donde está?»'*

'Claro que sí. ¿Por qué no?'

The hat was found and affixed. It was round and furred, with muffs.

'¡Ya está! Estás muy calentita ahora. Mmm, muy calentita. ¿Vamos a casa para cenar?'

Abuela folded her hands deliberately. That accomplished, she began shifting, in stages, until she was half-facing Pilar. Her eyes turned the remainder. *'Entonces, mi niña, ¿tienes algo que decir?*' She blinked, but continued staring at her grand-daughter, whose mouth alternated between smiles and surprise.

'*No, Abuela, nada. Ya te lo he dicho.*'

No-one moved. The boles about *Abuela*'s eyes, in the relief of flame, had the depth of church spaces. Again the cold hand felt for Jude's arm. *Abuela* attempted the long shift back. *'Tenía rizos tan bonitos,*' she said when she was almost there. *'Largos...abundantes.*'

'She had nice curls.'

'Y los dientes como tú...como Pilar. Todo perfecto. Todo...en orden.'

'And teeth like us. Sorry about that. Did I tell you, Abeula was Miss Pamplona, nineteen-thirty-three, I think it was?'

Jude nodded. It all made sense. Abuela took his hand in hers and patted it slowly, as if only remembering patting. *'Como su padre,*' she said, indicating Pilar with a curled forefinger. *'Su madre, no, pero su padre, sí.*' Pilar couldn't translate. *Abuela* was facing away from her, toward Jude's left ear. *'Tengo presente...*' continued *Abuela*, taking Pilar's hand now, so that both of them rested on her lap. *'Tengo presente el dia en que tu padre vino al mundo. No tengo presente las otras—Maria ni Alfonso—no. Pero tu padre, sí.*' She patted both hands, as if calming them down. *'Tengo presente...tengo presente.*'

‘She remembers giving birth to my dad.’

‘Era igual que tú, cuando…cuando era pequeño. Pero…pero con mis rizos.’

‘Same as me, with curls.’

‘Tenía rizos bonitos…cuando era pequeño.’

‘He had nice curls as a boy.’

‘*Tengo presente mi boda. Cuando…Cuando me los recogí, así.’* She drew a halo on the hat, already crusted with firelight. Her small eye was a black circle in the no-man’s-land between floor and air. *‘Pero cuando bailamos, los solté. Todos hablaban de lo guapa que estaba.’*

‘Claro.’

‘Tengo presente…tengo presente….¡Qué acontecimiento era! Todos…todos los jovenes bailando y sonriendo, todos contentos, todos contentos, bailando un walz.’

*

The well-known *Hawelka* was next the *Casanova*. It still is, although it’s not what it used to be and the *Casanova* has gone. Not that it was not not what it used to be before—not closed no soon as opened, on the outbreak of war. Not that it was not unscathed by war, when all around it fell. Not that it did not reopen to become a convenient Bohemian haunt in the postwar years, growing in notoriety with each plate of homemade cake. Not at all. Only that it may have known a waning, perhaps with the wane of its inimitable *Frau*. And not so much for self-consciousness' sake, straining like light in net-curtains. It was always self-conscious. Consciousness can be contained, ego tended; mulled until warm and flavoursome. But then you must lower the heat again, simmer down, stir routinely. You must construe routine, amidst your slovenly items; dive down in the décor and winter out. It's a question of waiting. If not, time, and the moment, will tell—the lid will blow and all the steam escape. A discharge, if you will. The *Hawelka* still burbles, but the door has blown open and the steam's escaping. This book will play its part, perhaps, unscrewing the door itself from its jamb—and doorpost too. But time, more than light, did what war could not. The span of the *Hawelka* was one with its owners. Soon it will be taken off the stove, or become a burnt pan with a crusted bottom. Let's hope there's not a fire.

'Mm, this is where Henry Miller came, in his good old Vienna days, just, er, MULLING aBOUT, defying the whole American emphasis on PRODUCTIVITY!'

'Not milling about then?'

'Ah, no.'

'Determined to escape his name. Ha! What he didn't realise was that a vowel wouldn't do it. He would end up, via the ethnic cleansing of *connotation,* in *exactly the same* pickle he was in before: milling unproductively in cafes, implicitly, but constantly (but *implicitly*) critiquing American productivity, while churning out American classics, nineteen-to-the-dozen—as classically American as you can get. And of course, that's the thing about your *classic*: it's a money-spinner. It's just a question of waiting. Which can be done in cafes as well as anywhere.'

'I see. "Just a question of waiting". Fff, indeed. So, Jude, are you saying we can never escape name or nation? We are always damned by association, so to speak—all the more when we defy them?'

'Nnn, some kind of VICIOUS CIRCLE?'

'No, I'm not convinced by your so-called vicious circle. I'm not sure it didn't shuffle its vice long ago, replacing it with that imitation: idlesse. Now it hangs around in cafes, stretched at its ease, to the extent that, *like an old woman's silver curl*, it has ceased to be a circle altogether, has become a *line*, albeit of the slackest kind.'

'Exactly like The SPECTRE, then.'

'*No*. The Spectre is a turd.'

Everyone laughed. Everyone was drinking mulled wine, in the corner-booth of the Hawelka, piled about with smoke and coats, cloth and lamps, bags and hatstands. The walls were dim gold and burgundy; the seats, striped, beige and crimson. Darkness locked the corners, where walls hit the ceiling, and out across close-placed tables was a limber mass of humanity—breathing and glowing, breathing and glowing. There were half-hid foreheads, hooks, chair-backs, climbed on by clothes and headwear. There were fillinged teeth, grooves in faces, pregnant veins in hands. Nostrils like caves and caverns. There were all kinds of things in the way: smiles, thighs, teaspoons. If you weren't squeezing past, you were ducking down, pushing aside, stepping nimbly over. If shawls didn't get you, bag-straps would. A tangle, a scuffle, the sound of shin on willow. There was a lot of self-excusing to be done. It was *Entschuldigung* this and *Danke sehr* that; an unwarranted *Gruß Gott!* over there. Eventually you made it to your place, wherever that was. It might be a booth, it might be the middle-tables, it might be the small ones, up against the wall. Under a painting, close by a globe, some leaflets troubling your neck. Through no fault of your own you could wind up touching toes, pressed against hips, making the best of the situation. This had happened to Jude. He had spent whole evenings, paralysed, tight in the bladder, waiting for the storm to pass. Other times you found yourself at the bar, under wood-panelling, inhaling fresh-baked *Buchteln*. You found yourself in posters, far as eye could see, running the gauntlet between art and dance. No soon as turned round, you turned up in the toilet, propped against the forward wall, pissing in the bowl. Without so much as an explanation, your trousers were buttoned, hands were washed, were drying on paper towels. Then it was the rigmarole all over: brushing curtain, slapping wall, lanced by an eye when you were almost back. One thing led to another and you were glad in your cups again and responding to Tomas on matters of so-called *reverse-psychology*, as if psychology were anything other than putting the cart before the horse.

'I see. But, to return to the earlier point, for a group of dye-in-the-wool Europhiles—'

'Crumbs. That's called killing them softly.'

'Ahem, is that incorrect? In any case, for a group of Europhiles (Jesse included—when convenient to himself, which I hope will be soon), I note we seem to talk rather a lot about our friends across the pond. Doesn't it say something about us, that we sit around troubled by America?'

'Europe is *continually* troubled by America, in the most culinarily-superior manner, obviously. But don't think America isn't sitting—sitting, mark you—over there—over *there*, mark you!' (pointing to the toilets in the west)—'on its obese arse—troubling about Europe—*even as we speak*, constantly haunted by Spectres: Marxism, Fascism, Ernst Stavro Blofeld: and all of them raging "Remember!"'

At this point Jesse fell into the booth, having

tripped on a bag-strap. He was wearing jeans, a trim, army-style jacket and had on his head a Russian-style fur hat with ear-flaps, lightly dusted with snow. His face was a beaming red.

Jude slapped a palm on the table. 'Where have you been?' he said slyly. 'My *blue eyed son*?' The palm pressed and repressed, as if it might melt through the surface. 'Where have you been, my *darling young one?*' A forefinger twitched at the top.

A quiet chuckle. 'He's stumbled on the side of TWELVE MISTY MOUNTAINS!'

Jesse slumped beside Bjørn, quietly effusive. 'That's more or less true. I've been in Croatia, Slovakia, but Slovenia mostly.'

'Ha!'

'Slovenia…I see. Another of those places I've meant to visit, but have been too lazy in the end. *Ja, Herr Ober! Noch vier Glühwein, wenn Sie können*. But I've heard good things, not all of them from Marcel.'

'That's right. *Rico*, for one, has a high opinion of Slovenia, largely on account of the dearth of Armenian blood, although, of course, were that blood to be flowing down the Alpine streets, it would be higher still, inversely proportional to the dearth, if not the Alps.'

'A member and signatory, Marcel proudly tells me, of the Council of Europe—brainchild, I believe, of your own Winston Churchill, and founded in nineteen-forty-nine—and the Organisation for Security and Co-operation in Europe—whose Secretariat, I discovered, is right here in Vienna. Not yet of the European Union, however, "neither of the Schengen Agreement.'

'It's going up in my estimation. No, *literally*.'

'Ff, "up in my estimation". But whereabouts in Slovenia?'

'I kind of went hiking—'

'He walked and he crawled on SIX CROOKED HIGHWAYS.'

'Down in the forests there.'

'He stepped in the MIDDLE of SEVEN SAD FORESTS!'

'I figured a Washington backwoodsman could deal with anything Europe could throw at him. So I just hitched up my sack and set out.'

Four mugs of *Glühwein* came to the table. Eight hands cupped them round, two of them blue.

'I believe the appropriate Viennese expression is "Prost". Jesse, it's good to have you back.' They clunked mugs.

'It's good to *be* back. At one time I thought I wouldn't be. I was thinking, "I wish Jude and Tomas and Bjorn were here now." I'd have given anything then to be sitting here with you guys and a mulled wine in my hand.'

'Hmm, sounds CRYPTICC.'

'That's probably a good word for it.'

'How about *uncanny*?' They leaned in. Their shoulders pulled the shadows.

'How about bloodcurdling?' said Jesse, exactly as Benjamin McCormack Kepperly-Lie appeared at the table. He was wearing black gloves and a green wool-hat. Over copious layers was a black-and-white football shirt, stretched to its extent. On his pale face, an old black eye.

'Ha! Speak of the *devil!*'

'Haff-haff. Haff-haff.'

'Hee-hee-hee,' cried Jesse.

'Benjamin Kepperly-Lie. We haven't seen you in a while.'

'No, I've been absent. "Without leave," you might say,' he said, looking significantly at Jude. His arms buoyed at his side.

'Ha!'

'Ha-ha-ha.'

'We thought for a minute you might have gone back home.'

'I was just a little tied-up. Ohohono.'

'Ahah.'

'Hee-hee-hee!' Jesse was already doubled over the table, anticipating hilarity to come.

'Ja, Herr Ober, wir möchten noch ein Glühwein, bitte! Und, haben Sie Buchteln? I think you can squeeze in here. *Ja.* So are you planning to do a Bjørn and stay?'

'Thanks Tomas, I'll just shuffle in here, shall I? Oh no. No,' said the Lie, responsibly, 'the nature of my stay is only "temporary".' He nodded solemnly at Jude.

'Ha!'

Jesse was wiping tears from his eyes. They looked bluely through the steam.

'But Benjamin—we've heard many things—many doubts, or qualms, have surfaced. This would appear to be the right place to put those qualms to rest, by answering a rather simple question, namely, what are you doing here actually?'

'Well, that's actually quite a hard question to answer. Haff-haff.'

'Ha-ha'

'Haff-haff-haff, oh no.'

'Ha-ha-ha-ha-ha.'

'It is isn't it! It's quite a hard question to answer!'

'It is! It is!'

'Haff-haff!'

'Ha-ha-ha-ha!'

It was impossible to get any sense out of them. Tomas gave up for a minute. Only for a minute though. He grinned along, tapping a foot in the air, looking beadily at the Lie until the laughter rolled away like Bjørn's *alto clumulus*.

'So!' he resumed.

'No, well it's still a difficult question to answer, ahaff-haff.' The Lizard planted a finger athwart his upper-lip. He wasn't budging though. On the contrary, he was entrenching himself.

Tomas approached it from another angle. Approaching from angles was a speciality of his.

'Let's put it this way: why did you come to Vienna? We all came for different reasons I suppose. Myself to study. Jude because it was…incumbent—is that the expression? Bjørn because…Bjørn, why did you come here?'

'Oh I just kinda BLEW into town.'

'Just so. What was *your* motive in coming?'

'I can't say I came here "of my own volition", can I?'

'No! Ha! You can't!'

'Let's face it, it wouldn't be very credible would it?'

'It wouldn't!'

'It's a shame, really, 'cause that's what I'd like to say.'

'No, I'm with Tomas all the way.' Jude was leaning back in his seat, smoking Tomas' cigarette, looking at the Lie with a sidelong look. 'You'll have to find something better than that.'

'I'm searchin', look.'

'We're waiting,' said Jude.

The Lie pressed his lips, put out both hands as if brokering a deal. 'There was a woman, look.' He was quite serious. Then very suddenly: 'there always is, isn't there, haff-a-haff!'

'Ha-ha-ha.' The Lie was like a cat which waits until the last moment, then scoots in front of a car with its ears pinned back.

'Ah,' said Tomas. 'Now you're talking about the mysterious Sara Baumgarten, esteemed barmaid of the Jewish Museum café, are you not?'

'I suppose I am really.'

'Funny,' said Jude, 'because I heard *different*. She told me the whole Language Exchange Programme was a tall story.'

'Now, strictly-speaking, that's true.'

'And what is it leniently-speaking?'

'Well, it's still true actually. Haff-haff!'

'Ha-ha-ha.'

'Hee-hee-hee.'

'But, you know, it does feel as if I've known her for ages. I suppose she's sort of wormed her way into my thoughts.'

'I thought that's what you did.'

'Well you know I've always been good with worms, oh no…no. But to use a footballing metaphor, in a short time, she's almost become part of the spine of the side. A thorn in the side, more like it!' he said, dashing over the road again. 'I told you I had a spine-chiller, naaoo.'

'Ha!'

'No,' he resumed, coaxingly. A winsome smile stretched his mouth, showed those famous teeth. 'I suppose I'd rather have my talent on the field than "warming the bench" so to speak. Grr, mind you, she can "warm my bench" any time she likes. Ohohono. Nao, I'm not really into "squad rotation", hahaha-ahaff. Not like Amos Jones, haff-a-haff.'

'She says she hasn't seen you in three weeks.'

'Well, that's true to some extent. There have been other…distractions. Ohohono, not those kind of distractions. Well, not entirely those. No, we had a falling-out you see.'

'Like LOVERS often WILL.'

'And that boyfriend of hers has been hanging around, look. He was none too happy I tell you, when he burst in—to his own flat, mind—and found us "*in flagrante*". Ah dear, his face was like a ragin' furnace! I was quite lucky to get out on that occasion. The fire escape came to my rescue, I'm afraid. Which is what you want, isn't it, when confronted with a ragin' furnace! Haff-a-haff! Poor "Fräulein" Baumgarten had to pour cold water on the situation. To be honest, I'm not sure she managed. It's a difficult thing to talk your way out of, isn't it? "*In flagrante*"'s "*in flagrante*" after all's said and done.'

'And before, by the sound of it.'

'Grrr, I stoked her fire good an' proper! Haff-a-haff-a, oh no.'

Another mug was slung upon the table and a plate of cakes. '*Danke schön*,' said the Lie, pressing lips as if the seal of his word. The cakes were hot from the oven. They were cut into squares, brown-crusted and blonde. In the midst was plum jam. They grabbed them up in handfuls.

'Yes, I heard about that. *Danke schön*. So, cheers again. Here's to Benjamin. Long may his stay be temporary.' Through mouthfuls of cake, they raised mugs and supped. Warm wine shot to their toes. 'But, speaking of women, Jude, what happened, by the way, with you and Ava? I heard that didn't work out.'

'No. She would insist on inviting me to the theatre. A sure way to court apathy.'

'I'm sorry to hear thatt.'

'She was drop-dead *gorgeous*, of course, as they invariably are.' He minced at the word *gorgeous* like a pan of oil. 'But that's the thing about the drop-dead gorgeous: there's only so much you can do with them—as she herself knows better than anyone.'

'The theatre. I see.'

'The final straw was the day I spent with her in the MuseumsQuartier, resolving never again to confuse sexual encounter with cultural aspiration. If it wasn't the *oohing* and *ahhing*, at titillatingly-subversive bourgeois artworks, it was the getting sore feet from a two-mile walk. What she has to understand is that it's *cumulative*. Like...like clouds, *massing* on the horizon. And *not*, sir, alto cumuli.' This with a surly look at Bjørn. 'Very much of the *cumulonimbus* variety, towering now and then into *cyclones*.'

'Hm,' said Tomas, but his poise couldn't hold. 'Ff-ff-ff, "sexual encounter with cultural aspiration".' He reddened, as if laughter were undiplomatic. 'Didn't you say Rosa might be coming tonight?'

'No. I suggested it, but she poured scorn on the idea, with what she perceived to be a witticism about painting the town red, and it becoming a habit. At which point I *retorted* that painting has that effect, constantly spilling over from business into pleasure. Which of course was both brilliantly flirtatious and horribly ambivalent. So, of course, she felt obliged to remark that there was nothing very pleasing about my painting, and I said the same was true of her wages. "Perhaps you need to find a new employer," says she. "Perhaps I do" says I. "Try the man at the Casanova," says she, meaning, of course, in her conspiracy-infested head, The *Spectre*. "He pays good money, I hear, for all kinds of things" says she, making a puny attempt at an ambivalence of her own. "That's true," I follow up. "Soup. *Brötchen. Schwarzwaldkuchen.*' She rejects the suggestion. "Until pleasure spills into business," she says. "Then he shoves you under a car". "Yes," I says. "That would be his fecklessly unoriginal solution," inferring The *Third Man*, of course, among other things. But she didn't get it. "He's not concerned by originality," she *snorts*. And she really *believes* this. "On the contrary," say I. "He's *obsessed* by it. It is the *raison d'être*, *cause célèbre,* and at the same time *bête noire* he has created for himself, to amuse his old age—and that of his civilisation." And there the dialogue comes to a paint-slapping, *Schwarzbrod*-kneading, drinking-and-smoking-yourself-into-an-early-grave conclusion.'

'A pity.'

'Not really. I'm seriously contemplating allowing her French-American ex-lover, ex-riverboat captain, current plyer of hybrid EuroAmerican music-hall blues to catch us *in flagrante*, so I can use that as a brilliant excuse to grab the hundreds of marks she owes me (and few hundred more), jump out of the window and never see her again.'

'Haff-haff. In my case, it was my fault you see,' continued the Lie, keen to explain. He made a gesture like the turning of a small pump-wheel. 'Honestly speaking, I just can't seem to stop my eye a-roving. Let's face it, variety is the spice of life.'

'No,' said Jude, suddenly assuming the highground. 'Nothing palls like *variety*. At some point a man has to put a cap (*Common Agricultural Policy*) on it. Crumbs.'—And a swarthy girl, swanning for all she was worth, escorted Jude's eye across the café. '—I'd put my Common

Agricultural Policy on her any day. Thus are problems involved with their solutions.'

'I wouldn't mind being involved with her solution,' said the Lie, spying a Turkish girl along the wall. Back went the ears. 'Haff-a-haff, ohno.'

'Alrightt,' said Tomas, folding his lips and sucking air through his teeth. It was the sound of chisel on the turned marble. 'But you mentioned there were other distractions. Do you care to comment on those?'

'Not really, no! Haff-ahaff!'

'Alrightt. Ffff.' Tomas was smiling round the teeth.

'I suppose I'd better though, hadn't I?'

'Well,' said Jude, with largesse; 'it's about that time of the evening.'

'I've kept you in the dark too long.'

'It looks that way.'

'A case of the blind leading the blind, so to speak.'

Tomas was puzzled. 'Why so?'

The Lie paused, catching his breath. 'I'm not quite sure! Haff-a-haff! That's probably why, isn't it?'

'Yes!' cried Jude, redly laughing.

'No, see, I'm not quite sure of events myself,' resumed the Lie, seriously.

'In the land of the BLIND!' reacted Bjørn, 'the one-eyed man is KING!'

'Where is he then?' sniggered the Lie, looking swiftly over his shoulders. He wagged in the direction of Jude. 'It's not The Man Who Would Be King, is it? Anyone can see that. 'Cause he "would be" King. That's not the same as "is", is it?'

'No, ha-ha, it's not!'

'Let's face it, he's an idiot, isn't he?'

'Yes, yes he is. A perfect idiot!'

'Goin' round with his charity group, talkin' about "business". "A little bit of business, yup, a little bit of business?" He should mind his *own* business, shouldn't he?'

'Would you prefer we did the same? Because, unless I'm mistaken, you were about to tell us what you've been up to.'

'He won't let me off the hook will he? Ohohno, sounds painful, doesn't it?'

'Ha-ha.'

'I'm talkin' nonsense, aren't I?'

'Are you?'

'Haff, haff, haff.' The laughter drained away. The Lie became doubly sober, sliding his finger over his lip. 'You've found me out, haven't you? Well, I might as well admit it. It's like this, you see. I've—I've been spying on Jude.'

There was a silence. Muffled mirth.

'No, no, not like that! It's for a good cause you see!'

Jude burst out laughing.

'No, no, see, I was asked to—for your own sake. You were in trouble, look.' And he worked open his fist in explanation. 'I was back in the valley, mindin' my own business, you might say.' His hand was an upsidedown crab. 'I was runnin' errands, look—for Magnus. The police were watching Magnus' house, see. And the Water Board too. So myself and Joe, you know, the "Flower Man", were helpin' him out a little, on the quiet. I took him "provisions", as it were. We had a system. A "rotation-system" if you like. I would leave them at a different place every week. We had four different places, and I'd come on a different day of the week each time, going forward through the week. It would change each month, with a different meeting place starting the month from the one before. It was very complicated! Ahaff-haff-ahaff! I had it all drawn up, look, in my room—or I never would have remembered it. I wouldn't!' He shook his head. 'Anyway, one evening, I'm in Latterly, at the The Cart and Horse, watching football actually—after a hard-day's fishin', ahaffohono, and this woman walks in, orders a pint and comes over to my table. Now, she was quite "advanced in years" as you might say, but "handsome" if you understand my meaning. Ohhh no! Not like that! She was definitely a woman. All woman, but, arrf no, I'll come to that. Naagh, no, perhaps I won't. But she still had, you know, a good bearing, and this hair to her shoulders. One of those who "would have been something in their day", as they say. Now,' and he clasped his pale hands on the table, 'I wouldn't lie. I believe you know the lady in question.'

There was a stunned silence. Everyone leapt to conclusions. No one knew how seriously to take them.

The Lie placed one hand athwart the table, solemnly but fast, as if staking his life. 'That's right,' he said. 'Heike.'

'Who might this be?' said Tomas, intrigued.

The Lie looked round. The hand staked his life again. 'No come on, you're having me on.'

Tomas looked around. 'Jude? Bjørn?'

'She seems to know you well. Haff-a. No.'

'Ha-ha!' roared Jude. 'He's mad! Mad! Nobody knows what he's talking about!'

'Now, now, come on!' encouraged the Lie, wagging his jaw. 'Heike.'

Blank looks.

'You're havin' a laugh,' he continued. 'Haff-a-haff.'

'I believe you're the only one laughing,' said Tomas, smoothly. 'But please continue, and perhaps we can piece this together.'

'It's impossible,' said the Lie, flabbergasted. His mouth opened and closed. 'She's been meeting up with you here. She knows everything about you.'

'And we appear to know nothing about her.'

'No, it's all very clear, *all very clear*,' Jude said haughtily, *'Clearly,* Heike is Rosa, in disguise if you will. *Clearly* she is completely mad. And *clearly* you are an idiot for being taken in by her.'

'Nevertheless, let us interrogate, and let you reiterate if you would, the point; namely, that she really came all the way to Latterly, Glum Valley, to demonstrate what Jude would call her lunacy?'

'That's right.'

'She's raving. Ha! Raving! And you, sir, are ridiculous! Ridiculous!'

'Well, hold on, let me explain. We're in The Cart and Horse, as I detailed "hitherto".' The Lie proceeded carefully, like a crab going sideways, aware of a sea of scepticism. 'She sits down opposite me and without so much as an introduction, she pronounces my name—an' let's face it, that's not as easy as it sounds, is it, in the first place? Most of Vienna seems to have got that wrong—although I might have encouraged them in that error, haff-a-haff. Grrr, as in a great many other errors too! Haff-a-haff, haff-a-haff! Argh, no. But, errors aside, she asks me how the fishin's goin'? She's got a slight German accent. Or it could've been East European. It's hard to tell. "Not really the season for it," I say. I was a bit "bemused" as you can imagine. An' I swear to God, she replies, "the season's about to change". "Portentous" you might call it. Or was that "pretentious"? Haff-a-haff, I never can tell! Now, she crosses her legs and I can't help but notice, you see, that she has this—how can I put it—above-knee-length skirt on, and she's wearin' these stockings, on what seems to be a nice pair of pins, as they say in football, ahahahah, arff, ohohono. "Small returns for a day's fishin'," I say, showin' her my box. Naaaooorgh, not that kind of box. Not yet! Haff-a-haff haff! It's got one fish in it, hasn't it! One measly fish!' He placed his finger under his nose, hesitating, almost wagging, about whether to make the expected joke. But the joke here was that he refrained.

'Ha!'

'Not a very substantial return, is it?' The Lie chuckled under his finger. 'But she says, "One may be enough", and she says it all ominously, as if there was a "multiplicity" of meanings in that single fish. Could have fooled me, ahaffahaff! It was a smelly old roach, weren't it!? Not worth the bones it was grown on. Anyway, I wasn't sure how "metaphorically" to take this, so I decide to play a straight bat, so to speak—to mix my sportin' metaphors. "It's gettin' to the middle of winter, look", I say. "A warm and wet one," she says—arrrrgh, I swear, I swear! Well, just then, someone scored on the television. But only on the television, unfortunately. Nooohoho, but you can imagine my confusion, can't you? I didn't know where to look, haff-a-haff! I was like Jude one place behind Sarah Kent in the lunch-queue. "Sorry—what's that?—offside?—where?" Haff-a-haff! I wish! Haff! Haff-a-haff haff! Ah dear.'

'Huh-huh-huh,' chuckled Bjørn.

'But I composed myself, look,' said the Lizard, composing himself. 'I was just trying to ride it out, so to speak, so I said: "It's the wettest one in years, apparently." Oh no, that probably wasn't the best thing to say was it? Probably wasn't the best thing to compose myself! I had to think of something to follow that with. So I tried to stick to the fishing. Some hope, ahaff-haff! "It's true though," I "reflected"; "in normal circumstances, the weather would be good for fishing. I should have been able to manage more than that." And I held up my fish again. "Why isn't it?" she "enquires". "I'm not wholly sure," I say, and it's true. I wasn't! "It's rained a lot, hasn't it?" she says. "That's right," I said, "ground can't hold any more". "Something will have to give," she "rejoins"; "the centre cannot hold". Haff, I didn't know what she was goin' on about! She looked a bit annoyed though. But she ploughed on, as it were, remarkin' that the lake was very low, considerin' the rain—you can actually see it, look, from The Cart and Horse—and I had to admit that it was, although not as low as it had been. It was even worse in August, September. It was down to the bare bones. Like my fish! You could see Ossly Bridge entire, and half of Folly Hall. In fact, the whole hamlet was sticking out o' the water, just like the ribcage of a decaying corpse. Well, hahaha, a little bit like that anyway, haff-a-haff! There was Birch Lodge and James Farm and Saddle Farm, where they say Hole's family used to live, look.'

'I didn't know Hole's family came from there.' Jude looked serious.

'Nor did I. My uncle told me a couple of months ago.'

'Is this he of *The Turnips* fame?'

'That would be the one, haff-a-haff.'

'So it's a total lie then.'

'Only on his father's side—haffahaffahaff! Oh no.'

'Ahah.' Tomas looked appreciative.

'Where do they live now?' said Jude, accepting another cigarette.

'Up at Woorish, look.' The Lie leaned in, conspiratorial. 'That's a strange place, innit? You can see both sides up there—down to the Glum on one side, and right over to town on the other.'

'That's right. It's hardly the Glum at all.'

'It's an interesting "etymology", I suppose you'd call it,' said the Lie, who was interested in etymology. If he hadn't had business leanings, he might have made it a study. 'It was originally

“Worn Ridge”, they think, on account of the sort-of wild, irregular lie of the land up there. Although some have speculated “Wooer’s Edge” on account of a story of “star-crossed lovers” who would meet up where the hill falls steeply toward town—there’s a kind of cut-away cliff—and they would have their secret “tristes” there. Until one night, after the woman was found to be pregnant, the man, her lover, pushed her down that little cliff and sent woman and child to the churchyard. The story goes, he hanged for it. On “Noose Hill” in fact. Near Upper Dovecombe, look.’

‘I suppose this is the subject of a *Turnips* ballad, belted out on wedding nights the length and breadth of the county.’

‘It was my uncle who told me that. It’s a strange place, though, the churchyard at Woorish. With that view over town, with all the lights sparkling, and so dark among the stones.’

‘I think the word is *bleak*.’

‘You know what I mean?’

‘I know exactly what you mean. I have crept through said churchyard, in the dead of night, following a *Harper* and a *Magnus*, on our way to a manhole, in a brick shed belonging to the Water Board, anticipating all-night travails, through cold and dark and damp, in despondent hatred of my companions, wondering why I was not in my bedroom, in The Yew-Lawn, Dimly, Cooley

Valley. Until I realised that that would have meant all-night travails, through cold and dark and damp, in despondent hatred of my companions.'

'I'm sure the sixteenth-century stone walls and oak doors of the famous Yew Lawn contain rooms and inhabitants which are the epitome of hospitable warmth and cheer,' said Tomas, pleasantly. 'So much so that I therefore must tell you: be not *surprised* should you find a tall skinny man with a funny accent at yours or Harper's doorstep. Or indeed yours, Benjamin. Maybe sooner than you think.'

Jude made a gracious gesture. 'The valleys, both Cooley and Glum, are yours to command, their singed carpets, their plastered walls, their masses of quilts and pillows always hunkerable down on.'

'I thank you, sir.' Tomas made an equally gracious gesture. '*Entschuldigung. Zwei Flaschen Rotwein, bitte. Und noch mehr Buchteln, wenn's geht.* Sorry Benjamin. Pray continue.'

'Well, to cut a long story short, she sits there smokin', and proceeds to grill me on the recent—"queer" I s'pose you'd call 'em, a-haff—events in the valley. An' it was quite "uncanny", as you might say.' He nodded in Tomas' direction. 'She seems to know all about Magnus, all about Harper, all about all of you. Imagine! I didn't know what to think! Well, next thing you know, there was one of those fake coal-fires, and the football droning on in the background, and she kind of "inveigled" herself into my confidence. She bought me a pint, look, and I ended up telling her the whole story, ohohono.' No one was laughing. 'I didn't tell her where Magnus was,' he added 'That was between me and him, of course. But I told her what I was doing for him. But it was you she seemed most interested in, to tell the truth' (nodding at Jude). 'She knew you were here, and stated, in no uncertain terms, that you were in danger. She said there were shady organisations, kind of cult-organisations, trying to rope you in. She said others in your position had come to—let's just say a sticky end. Ohohono! Not that kind of end, I assure you! otherwise I'd have been tempted to join a shady organisation. Haff a haff! As if I weren't shady enough! Haffa-dear. Hchm. She was asking a lot about the reservoir and the Pump House fire, and so on. She thought it was the work of anarchists, look. I wouldn't be surprised if she thought I was one. Seriously. She can't have been very "perspicacious" can she? Haff, she must have thought I was a bloody good actor, mustn't she? Hidin' my light under a bushel, so to speak. Nnngh, chance would be a fine thing—naaaooo, no, haffa! She even, I suppose, "surmised" is the right word, you'd been sent here as bait. To smoke out their suppliers. Ah dear, "smoke out" their suppliers. What was she smoking, haff-a-haff? Nao, I didn't get the last bit, but it had something to do with Harper. You're not convinced are you? I can't say I was either. She said you didn't believe her and wouldn't trust her anyway, but she wanted me to keep an eye on you over here, and would pay my boat-fare.' The finger went once to the nose and wagged outward. 'I have a bit of aerophobia, see,' he explained. 'Otherwise known as—haff-haff, wait for it—you'll have to wait for it, haff-a-haff!—could be waitin' an awfully long time, couldn't you, at this rate? Haff haff—no, otherwise known as "ptero-merhano-phobia".' There was a pause. 'Phew! Haff-haff, I think I got that right. You're not convinced, are you? "Fear of flyin'" to you and me—though that hardly does it justice, does it? "Complete bloody terror of flyin'" would be would be more to the point! Haff-a-haff! So I thought about it. I wasn't really doing that much at home, just fishing and helping Magnus, account of I was the only one who wasn't being watched, look. Apart from Alistair Hobbes, obviously. Let's face it, he's in no danger of attractin' suspicion, is he? He's about as suspicious as a bull in a china shop, isn't he? Haff-a. Ah, dear, I'm a bit like a china shop, aren't I? Full of bull—haffa, haff-a-haffa! No, at the end of the day, you see, I couldn't find work. The job market is very much on its knees, so to speak. Actually, to be fair, I'd given up looking. Taken a bit of a "year out"—nnnnarrrgh no! You're not convinced, are you? That's twice now! Three strikes an' you're out, haff-a-haff! "Year out" he says! When I was I ever "in", to be fair? Well, apart from—arrrgh, no! I won't go there! Well, if you insist, haff-a-haff! Ah dear, Jude's often "in", isn't he? Trouble is—haff-a-haff!—he's "out" again, half a second later! Haff-a-haff! Only takes a dolly-dropper, an' some undecided atmospheric conditions! Grrrr! He's had a few "dolly droppers" in his time, hasn't he! Haffa, in some decidedly "atmospheric" conditions! Haff-a-haff! Haff-a-haff! Arrrrgh, no!' The Lie wagged with stomach-patting laughter. Jude wept tears of joy. Everyone else was nonplussed. 'Or so I've heard, ahaff! Then there was Heike herself. What did you say her name is? Rosa? Nao. I've got a horrible feelin' you're not jokin'. One of us's been had, haven't we, an' I've got a funny feelin' it's me.' The Lie pointed at his chest. 'I've been stitched up, haven't I? Well and truly had. Chance'd be a fine thing, naooo.' He paused, frowned, bunched his lips. 'I'm goin' to have to think that one over,' he said. 'In the meantime, there was Rosa, as I'd better call her now, "whom", I admit, was an intriguing proposition from a psychological perspective.'

'Ha! From a *psychological perspective!*'

'But that about sealed it, as you can imagine. You'd probably rather not, wouldn't you, arrgh no! No, but in the end, I told Magnus about it—the trip to Vienna, a-haff. And he said it was an excellent idea, said he could do without me very well. He reckoned he could get supplies from the Flower Man. So there wasn't really much to think about in the end. It was a no-brainer, as you might say.'

'So it wasn't rocket science, presumably?'

'Hahahaha, ohohono.' The finger hovered commandingly over the table. 'No it wasn't to be fair. Latterly to Poole—'

'Oh yes, that direct train, Latterly to Poole!'

'Well, a-haff, maybe one day. Latterly will have to get onto the map first, won't it? Haff-a, ah dear. "Latterly". You can say that again, haff-a-haff. "Latterly"! Haff-a-haff-haff-haff!'

'Ha-ha-ha-ha-ha.'

'Ah dear. I've put it on the map, haven't I, one way or another. Probably "another" to be fair, haff-a. No, I've got an uncle in Poole, look.'

'Another one!'

'Nao, I've got uncles everywhere, haven't I? It's almost a "euphemism" isn't it?'

'Ha! Is it?'

'No, not really.' The Lie looked defeated. 'But I have got quite a few uncles. Five to be exact.'

'All of them experts in local history and local ale. Though not in that order.'

'They do "alevate" the truth a little, as John Taylor would say, a-haff. No, they do tell some tall tales. "Shaggy dog stories", you might call them.

Some of them shaggier than others, arrrrgh no. But we won't go into that. This one's sort of estranged from the rest of us. He's in the fishing trade, actually. That's not the "strange" part, a-haff. You're not surprised by that, are you? "Operates" out of Poole. "Holes Bay" to be exact. I'm not messin' around. It's called "Holes Bay".'

The Lie impressed the table with a look. The finger hovered again.

'So, as I say. Latterly-Poole; Poole-Jersey.' The finger pecked twice and stopped. 'I thought I'd do the scenic route, see. Since I was going that far.'

'Oh he *thought he'd do the scenic route!*'

'Haff-a-haff.'

'*Since he was going that far!*'

'I'm always going too far, aren't I? Usually via the scenic route, haff-a-haff! It makes sense, though, doesn't it? Why would you go that far otherwise? Haffa. I mean, what a waste of bloody time!'

'Ha ha ha ha.'

'No, but it's cheaper, an' convenient, look, because my uncle took me as far as Jersey. He fishes that route, you see. From there it's "plain sailin'" as it were. Jersey-Granville. That's in the "*Manche department*" of France, isn't it?' Another impressive look. 'I speak a bit of French, look.'

'Ha! Oh you do? You speak a bit of French?'

'Un *petit-peu*, ahaff. Puh!' he said, pretending to

spit. It must have been that Language Exchange with Sara Baumgarten. I learned double quick then, I can assure you, haff-a, role-playin' with the old "artificial fruit". I improved my French too! Haff-a-haff! Arrgh, no, I must seem a suspicious personage, mustn't I? Speakin' the "lingo", boastin' of my *savoir faire*. Next I'll be sayin' that I've got a little *je ne sais quois*—haff-a-haff! I'll find myself flyin' over the "*Manche*" in a minute, won't I, "aerophobia" or no!'

He leaned back as if to triumph, but was forward again before they could stop him.

'So it was easy, look. Jersey-Granville; Granville-Paris; Paris-Vienna.' The finger pecked three times. 'Night train, look.' The Lie looked crafty. 'We won't talk about the night train, will we? Not just yet anyhow, grrhaff. Choo-choo! Haff-a-haff! Arrrgh, no. But it was a lovely trip. I can recommend it.'

'And Rosa paid for all this?' said Tomas sublimely.

'Well, actually, she hasn't yet.' The Lie performed a barely-perceptible double-take. 'At least, not in Austrian Marks. A-haffa, you could of fooled me! That's an Austrian Mark right there, isn't it? Haff-a-haff! Right on the beady eye!' He pointed at his eye.

Jude slid two conciliatory elbows over the table. 'So you've been spying on me?'

‘Well, more like keeping an eye out. Ah, dear, I’ve been lucky to keep it in of late.’ He pointed again at the eye. ‘Ahaff-haff. It has a tendency to roam, doesn’t it? Haff, arrgh no. So there it is, you see. I accept that I’ve been “remiss”, you might say. “Miss” Kent, “Miss” Goodhead, “Miss” Chiles, haff-a-haff! Ohhh no. But I’ve been a bit slow coming forward haven’t I?—There’s always a first time for everything, haff-ahaff!’ At this point, the Lie rose in stages to his feet, pointing in the general direction of the toilet. ‘Toilet’s over there, is it?’ he said. ‘Yep. Yep.’ And then, registering the question, he hovered by the hat stand. ‘It looks like I’m trying to get out of it, doesn’t it?’ he suggested. ‘It looks like I’m trying to “extricate” myself from a difficult situation. Let’s face it, I’ve had enough practice.’ He didn’t know whether he was coming or going. His jokes had gone half-cold, one step removed from the table. ‘Seriously, I do need the toilet, actually. It’s “convenient”, though, isn’t it? Talk about playing your “get out of jail” card. Haff. I never seem to pass “GO”, though, do I? I suppose that’s why I’m still here talkin’, haff-a-haff!’ He was still pointing toward the toilet as he moved away.

A new darkness announced the waiter, who squeezed between Jesse and the hatstand, uncorked two bottles of wine and and set them down amidst five glasses. After some confusion over the ordering of cakes, a request to remove a stray bag-strap, and hesitation in Jesse as to the dispensing of wine, the waiter took that liberty, and there was quiet for a while. Jude stared forbiddingly through the window, Bjørn gazed at a painting, Jesse ran a nail repeatedly up a polished runnel. Only Tomas, arms folded, tilted of chin, seemed to have kept the thread, for, when the waiter was finished: 'Benjamin Kepperly Lie,' he began. 'I think that's what's called talking your way out of a corner. Speaking of which, Jesse, you are more or less in a corner there, certainly an edge, and you were just beginning what sounded like a macabre story.'

'Hee-hee-hee-wheee.'

'When we were momentarily distracted by Benjamin Lie.'

Jesse took some moments to collect himself. 'I'm sure his story is more interesting than mine. If, hee hee hee, he ever gets round to telling it.'

'That, it seems, is something we can't count on.'

'No no, we *can*. Because one thing you have to understand about the Lie: he *can't keep a secret for the life of him*.'

'But can he escape his name?'

'His ridiculous *name* is precisely his greatest *confession*.'

'Hmm. "Precisely his greatest confession".'

'Well, we have all night, don't we? I'll bet by the time we've finished those bottles we'll have winkled it out of him.'

'In the meantime,' sighed Tomas, swinging a leg into some newfound room, 'let us winkle out your eery tale.' A haffing sound signalled the return of the Lie. 'Set in Slovenia, I believe. But whereabouts?'

'Hee, oh, first I went to Ljubljana, then down to the south-west there, really close to Italy, to see the sinkholes. They've got miles of these limestone caves, on the Karst plateau, caused by disappearing rivers. The Skocjan caves, boy, they're really something. They've got this river that goes underground there, the Reka—'

'Maybe it's better underground then.' The Lizard's jaw wagged. 'Ohohohno,' he said.

'Ha-ha-ha.'

'Hee-hee, but you couldn't find a purer source. You can go see it, pouring into the earth, straight through the snow. Right to the Adriatic.'

'He's been out in front of a DOZEN DEAD OCEANS.'

'Not me, but the Reka does. It goes thirty some miles underground and actually comes out Italian.'

'Crumbs. Just like Harper.'

'With a new name, "Timavo".'

'That's what I call a BAPTISM.'

'Can you baptise yourself?' asked Tomas.

Jude meditated. '*Possibly,*' he said, with an air of authority. 'What do you think, Lie? Can you escape your name?'

'Haff haff, I think I'm going to go back to the toilet at this rate! Haff haff, and stay there! I'll need to, won't I, if we're to get through those bottles? That is, if I can make it that far.'

'Let's make a start then, shall we?' Tomas raised a glass. 'A baptism of sorts. To Churchill's Council of Europe, friend to the United States.' He nodded at Jesse.

Jude demurred. 'No, I propose an alternative toast,' he said. His eyelids were half-lifted silver, whetting the appetite, repelling the gaze. 'Or rather, I propose no toast at all—only a steady, solemn swallowing, completely devoid of encomia or enthusiasms of any kind—to a cheerfully treacherous, infuriatingly fractured, brilliantly disunited Europe, whose cultural and, more importantly, physiognomical repulsions are the basis of stranger cultural and physiognomical attractions, not to say *desires*; whose refusal to conform to the lingua franca of the day is the basis of a begrudging *understanding*; and whose own mutual suspicion is the basis of a collective incredulity towards America, an incredulity which occasionally, and necessarily, spills over into *outright ridicule*.'

'I see. You're not a fan of Churchill then?'

'There is a *case*,' established Jude, 'for dismissing Churchill entirely, as an alcoholic ham, in twofold thrall, to American amplitude and Churchillian rhetoric.'

'Ah, there's nothing wrong with a little bit of AMPLITUDE.'

'Well yes, we all know your feelings towards amplitude, Bjornsen. And we can make an educated guess about Churchill's.'

'Haff haff.'

'So you think Europe is in thrall to America?'

'Well yes, of course. But not as much as America is in thrall to Europe. Because that's the thing about your *thrall.* It thrives best in a vacuous expanse.'

'There's some truth in that,' squeaked Jesse. 'I think America *is* intimidated by Europe to a degree, France especially.' He moved the cake-plate. 'When we know where Europe is, of course, which down South is far from certain.'

'No,' countered Jude, 'especially when they don't know where Europe is. Especially when they've never heard of it. For, if America is in the *Mind*, Europe *in* America is even more in the Mind.' He looked significantly round. '*Even more*,' he leered, 'in the *Mind!*' And he tapped his mind, causing short-lived mirth in the circle.

'Myself, I can understand a small degree of Francophobia,' said Tomas smoothly. 'Particularly on the topic of foreign policy, I want you to know that, in difference to Kara, I offer my full support to you and your Queen in your Eastern interventions. I hope the future, perhaps even the near-future, will vindicate present policy with victory and peace, to reflect glory on the transatlantic union and shame on the European continent, France in particular. There is something inexorably supercilious about the French.'

Jude rejoined. 'Yes, what we do merely as a matter of course, they insist on making an ideology out of, completely failing to appreciate its self-evidence.' His eyes looked slyly to the window. 'No, sirs, while we may shake hands with *Liberté*'—he caught sight of the Lie's reflection—'and ogle her surreptitiously when her stare is turned, for *Egalité* and *Fraternité* we have *no time*.'

Bjørn couldn't let it alone. 'Ahhh,' he said, cornering the conversation while he meditated what he was going to say, 'on the other hand, I'VE gott to say,' he said, raising a forefinger from the table, 'that ah I myself ADMIRE the position of the French. Er, sometimes you just have to stand still, stay SILENT, just silently ACKNOWLEDGE your superiority—ah, unaSHAMEDly—ah, if that's what it is. And, make no mistake—ah, I of course LOVE America' (extending a palm to Jesse) 'no one needs to tell me what a fanTASticc country that is, I KNOW—but make no mistake, France IS superior to America in many ways.' He sniffed. 'Ah, we've just gott to acCEPT that, America just has to acCEPT that, and, maybe hardest of all,

FRANCE just has to accept that.'

Tomas wasn't sure. 'France has no trouble accepting that.'

'Well, good. Goodd. Ah, that's what I've got to say I admire about Harper's friend, er, VINCENT, his name is. He's French, of course, and er, he's just perfectly att EASE in his cultural heritage and assumptions. It's not even superiority, even. He would never call it that. It's just a kind of PLEASURE in wealth. Ah wealth of heritage, not capital. He just sits there, silently—ah Magnus is a bit like that too—and just lets you talk. And you know—you KNOW—that your thoughts are just running away with you, and you're just talking yourself into a HOLE, but you just keep talking, just inTIMidated.' Bjørn drew strength from the table-top. He looked anything but intimidated by the French.

But Jude was not convinced. 'No, it's easy to remain silent. People are continually confusing those precise positions—the washing of hands, the taking of *back seats*—with moral stances. They're not the ones with dirty hands. They're not the ones standing in the grave, crying crocodile tears—which are tears after all.'

'Hmm, "which are tears after all,"' repeated Tomas, sublimely amused. 'Nevertheless, Jude, you of all people should be perhaps less than satisfied by the behaviour of your own country.' He dabbed a butt in the well. 'By which you yourself have been most notoriously abused I should say, packed like—cattle across the sea.' Tomas frowned on his comparison.

'If I do not complain at being treated like *cattle,*' said Jude, with a sort of wounded nobility, surprisingly supportive of the comparison, 'it is because—honestly—I never expected anything else. This is how it will end, mangle-limbed in machinery. This negates nothing, least of all redemption.'

This statement might have induced incredulity, had not a source of more incredulity intervened, in the shape of an old woman with a plate of cakes. She was small and box-like, white hair clipped back from the face. She must have been most of ninety.

'*Buchteln für die jungen Männer,*' she said. '*Noch mehr. Direkt aus dem Ofen. Ja, ja, sie mögen meine Buchteln.*' And she cocked her head. '*Oder, Herr Lie?*'

'*Ich glaube so,*' he said, and haffed briefly round.

'*Oder, Jude?*' She looked at Jude in the corner. He was opposite Bjørn, with a wry look on his face, a look which the wine was flushing. '*Drei Gäste, die Sitzplätze benötigen,*' she said, putting down the cakes and ushering Pilar, Barbosa and Olivia Ruiz from behind her back. The problem was, there wasn't much room to be ushered into—a problem compounded by Jesse, who stood up, intending to retreat to the bathroom.

Tomas reacted like one simultaneously surprised and not at all surprised. 'Pilar, Laura, Olivia,' he counted. 'Splendid. *Ah, Frau Hawelka. Entschuldigung. Noch eine Flasche bitte.*' There were smiles and welcomes. 'You know Benjamin I believe. Yes of course.'

'How's it going?'

'Thanks.'

It was a complicated scenario. Jesse blushed and dithered. Frau Hawelka effected a slow turn, Pilar squeezed past, wearing a black quilt coat and a clownish expression, and the Lie, becoming at once very chivalrous, took her coat and hung it on the hatstand, without a word, except 'right' and 'yep'. This left him in a quandary, however, because there were too many coats to help with and he didn't think he ought, especially after Barbosa had knocked some things off the hatstand. In the end he gestured and blinked and did nothing in particular. Then, anticipating that seating would become an issue, Tomas got up to procure a chair, which gave Pilar the opportunity to slip in next to Jude. The Lie said 'okay then,' and 'right'. It was nice to feel the brushing-by of a woman like Pilar. Jude was a lucky man. Meanwhile, Barbosa parked herself next to Bjørn, who was not unhappy, but, realistically, this left only two more places in the booth: on that edge and this. The Lie wasn't convinced by either of them. That one had been innocently colonised by Jesse's jacket. This one was the Lie's original seat, but should probably be ceded to Olivia. The thing was, seeing the delicacy of the situation, the moreso because she couldn't understand a word, Olivia had retreated to the shadows, looking, as if for succour, to Tomas, who had got into conversation with a nearby table. With some reluctant puffing the Lie resumed his seat, then attempted to redeem himself by creating space where there was very little. 'No trouble,' he said, blending chameleon-like into the booth. 'Plenty of space, look.' Olivia perched herself beside him, chattering Spanish at Barbosa like a magpie, none of which would have been a bad thing if the Lie had been able to speak a word of Spanish, apart from 'el partido' obviously. You never knew, though, even that might be of some use on this most providential of nights. There was a period of jostling, settling, ascertaining. Jude looked to Barbosa who was looking for elbow room between Bjørn and the hat-stand. 'No chance,' he chuckled to himself. Olivia was over there, examining the wine-bottle. That was the Lie—unmistakably, if forever mistaken. Pilar, right next to him, was tying back her hair. Finally, Jesse returned, closely pursued by Tomas, the one red-faced from his excursion and oblivious to the entire situation, the other with his procured chair, which, with a discerning glance, he swung under his own weight at the head of the booth.

'Hey,' said Pilar.

'Hey,' said Jude.

'Been here long?'

'I have no idea.' He touched the stem of his glass.

'Like that is it?'

'Possibly. Ha-ha.'

'Seems like ages, doesn't it? Haff haff. Time to go now!'

Pilar grinned, first at Jude and then away, tossing her pony-tail accidentally in his face. It was still nice to feel the brushing-by of a woman like Pilar. Doubly so. 'We were just discussing redemption,' Tomas explained. 'Jude was contending that to die an ignominious death was no obstacle to redemption.' He bared his teeth. 'If I haven't simplified that too much?'

Jude looked haughty and shifty at the same time. 'No no. *Self-evidently.*'

'Then here's to redemption.' There followed quiet sipping and smoking, until Tomas refocused the lens. 'Jesse has just been telling us about the terrifying forests of Slovenia,' he preambled. 'If I may, these caves sound marvellous, but not macabre, I shouldn't have said.'

'Well I was getting to that part. I got a little tired of the tourist sites, so I decided to go hiking in the mountains.' He gripped the mug like the memory. 'Up in the Julian Alps, near a place called Kranjska Gora.'

'Ah, well, hold ON now. Isn't that near there—ah—they hold those famous, er, SKI-JUMPING tournaments?'

'Now that you mention it, I met a party of people who were up for the ski-jumping. That's in Planica, I think.'

'PLAN-ica!' said Bjørn, as if shot. 'Planica.' He nodded his head.

'There—'

'Ah, THAT'S! where we would always watch the ski-jumping from, over in Norway, er we would HUDDLE up there by the fire (or by the radiator, of course) and watch those good old SKI-jumping events from Planica, we…didn't know too much about it or where it WAS necessarily, but that name, PLANICA, that was quite a name in Norway.'

'I didn't see any of the jumping, but I was in a hostel not far from there. I would set off through the snow in the morning, in the lower mountains, and trek most of the day through the forests.' Jesse leaned both elbows on the table, with his back to the café. He seemed honoured to be in the midst of things, sandwiched between Norway and Sweden. 'I did three days like that, taking big baguettes, a couple of apples and a bottle of water. There's something so perfect about that, when you're out there, just you and the mountains, with the cold on your face and warming up to it. You know, setting out, with the sky still full of stars, and this big ball of a moon dropping low.'

'A bit like The Duchess of Malfi.'

'Ha!'

'Sarah Kent was a lusty widow, wasn't she?'

'Ha-ha-ha-ha-ha, yes she was.'

'I don't know about tennis balls, but she was a player, wasn't she?'

There was general, mechanical laughter, not because false—because familiar. The waiter came with three glasses and an open bottle, and was gone before his frown could be felt. Tomas poured the wine and a lull fell on the conversation. There were murmurs among selves but no one spoke aloud. Then Bjørn did, right across Barbosa.

'Nnyah, that just sounds FANTASTIC. The, the sense of SIMPLICITY, ah, when you're in a situation like that. Everything just seems so SIMPLE. Just REDUCED to the, er, simplest possible EQUATION.'

'Right—'

'YOU just FEEL the ancient oldness of it all, and the newness too. Right at the same time, those two sensations, of oldness and newness. But it's not a weary, tired oldness. It's a steady, CONTENT oldness. That's not really history at all, stRICTTly speaking. That's way beyond history. That's not about the, the chain or CHRONOLOGY of happenings and moments. That's about present and past, simply. Simply juxtaposed. That's got nothing to do with nostalgia, or attempting to reconSTRUCT a sense of history.'

'Sure, but—'

'Nn, that's what I was saying about AMERICA. We've just got to be looking past the recent, ah, WHITE history of America.' Bjørn acknowledged Jude. 'Or LACK of it. We've got to be seeing America as a great continent, with thousands, millions of years of time written upon it. We haven't got to be thinking about, oh, the STATE, or RACE, or IDEOLOGY. We've, er, got to be thinking about a, a LAND-MASS. The Mississippi, the Missouri, the JAMES RIVER. AH!' he interjected, not finished with his list, anticipating retorts. 'The ROCKIES, er of course, the SIERRA MADRE (although, er, obviously that is also in Mexico—AH! Because these lines aren't as CLEAR as the STATES, especially the UNITED STATES, would like you to think), the APPALACHIA. And, er, of course, some fantastic hills. LIKE!' he retaliated, 'the HILLS, er, the BLACK HILLS of DAKOTA,' seeming on more native land himself, smiling a little at Jude, 'the WEST VIRGINIA hills; the…' He cast around for some more hills to complete his trio.

‘Blueberry hills?’ said Jude. The Lie wagged his jaw. Tomas blew smoke through a smile.

‘Ah I’VE got to feel that America is actually completely ALIVE with history, in THAT sense. Whereas the FRENCH—er, the Europeans, GENERALLY—they, er, too easily fall into NOSTALGIA. That’s not a disease the Americans tend to, er, SUFFER from so much, they DON’T LOOK BACK. Although of course, LAWRENCE—ah, who you, of course, Jude, are not so fond of yourself—but, er, he’s seeing in that a FAULT, being too much interested in IDEAS. He maintains, ah, that America is not a BLOOD LAND—ah, that’s what he calls it—whereas ENGLAND—ah, the England he associates with, ah, Thomas HARDY, I think it was—although I must say, I’m not so fond of Hardy mySELF, I’ve got to be seeing that as a little bit INSULAR British fiction, that kind of easy PESSIMISM which just sometimes seems to characterise English fiction, although, of course, Norway is not IMMUNE in that respect—but, ah, LAWRENCE!’—rescuing his point just as his entire audience were on the point of mutiny—‘suggests the England of Thomas Hardy is a BLOOD LAND. He, er, seems to be associating that with some kind of, ya, involvement in, er CELEBRATION of history and, er, perhaps LINEAGE. Er, I don’t know whether I completely go along with that MYSELF. But Lawrence, he seems CONVINCED of that.' Bjørn nodded proudly, on the back of Lawrentian conviction.

'All the same, isn't it good to celebrate history?' said Tomas, briskly. 'Better than eradicating it, anyway.'

'You can't celebrate *or* eradicate history,' quibbled Jude. His quibbling was done at the lips. 'You can only be more or less aware of it. To be more aware of it is to be mixed up in it, for better or worse, glumly, generously, above all *maddeningly*.' He put some ice into this one. 'A curse and a benediction,' he said, dripping honey. 'Helplessly blessed! Hugely importuned!' He raised a finger. 'Which means, of course, to be *alive*.'

It was another extraordinary statement.

Feeling this, 'that doesn't mean impotent, incapacitated, *physically crippled*,' continued Jude, somewhere between sarcasm and patriotism. 'It may mean *moderated*.' Again, this last bore a great verbal scrutiny. 'It must mean death. That's good. Nobody dies in America,' he said, recalling something. 'Both nostalgia and America are less aware; *ergo*, America is nostalgic.' Everyone looked surprised at Jude's newfound investment in life, death and blessing. It wasn't newfound though. It was oldfound—Oldfoundland. Older than Rosa and her comrades could possibly conceive. His old magic against their new magic. He moved a leonine paw, lifted the wine, sipped leoninely.

Barbosa turned to Bjørn. 'What has Jude say?'

'I'm not sure I QUITE understood.'

Tomas' voice rode calmly through the colloquy, like a tea-clipper through the choppy Atlantic. 'Sounded good though.' Jude was still bleary with emotion. Pilar fell sentimentally for him all over again. She toyed with her glass, thought to grace his bed that night, given favouring winds. Jude saw her wizened smile, suddenly remembered he had forgotten his mother's birthday. She would be furious, distraught, and, at great cost, he would send her flowers. That was women for you. Motive was irrelevant; it was all about reception.

'In any case, whether or not people die in America,' said Tomas, grinning through smoke, 'they certainly die in Slovenia, or so I'm given to believe. Which brings us, I hope, to the sinister part to your tale.'

The light seemed to flutter and fall. It came from globe-lamps, hung from the ceiling—touched their shoulders like a large palm frond.

'So I was out in the woods,' said Jesse, 'and day was drawing on.' He took a bite from the last cake, inspecting the bead of jam. 'I'd gone on a kind of circle-walk, expecting to come home via a trail I'd been on the previous day. I reached this crossroads where there's this stone trough by the roadside. I knew it was the same as the day before because it had this white cross on it.' His finger squeaked on the plate. A cross appeared in the icing-sugar. 'Anyway, I wanted to get up this small peak in front of me, but it was quarter to three and I was still quite far from the hostel. I liked to be back by dark, about four.' He looked back at the lamp as if it were about to go out on him. 'So I set back along the path, the way I had come, following a creek, or stream, on my left. I was walking an hour, expecting any moment to come out into this junction, where the trail snakes out of the woods. You come onto this wide plateau, all snow-laden now, with the high mountains in front of you, and the road goes right up to the hostel.' His hand soared up to the right, near the net-curtain. All was dark on *Dorotheergasse*. Through the netting they saw themselves reflected: assertions of shape, negated by streetlights, by the corners of doorways. Sometimes the reflection had sway, sometimes the street. It was one long shadowbox, silent, irrelevant—just the chase of hand for wind.

'It was coming on evening now, the sun had fallen in the firs. I was beginning to get confused about the junction when—to my *horror*—I realised, looking into the trees to left of me, I had lost the creek. It should have been in a gulley, twenty, thirty yards to my left, but I couldn't see anything. There was a gulley, but not the gleam of water in the trees. I stopped dead still. So you could hear a bird hop. But not that familiar murmur of water. It occurred to me, maybe the creek had frozen over here—was oozing over ice. I crashed through ferns into the gulley and marched up and down the bottom. I was actually turning over snow, looking for the water. In vain. I must have mislaid the creek some way back. I tried to remember when I'd last been aware of it, but that was half-an-hour back or more. I'd been heavily involved with thinking about Vienna, about the *Studentenheim* and its array of characters, and I'd clean lost track of the outside world.' Jesse looked embarrassed. Many faces faced him, and twice the ears waited on his word. But he seemed to embrace the burden. 'Like I said, dark was coming on. I was cold. You couldn't see too far through the firs, and I didn't want to walk half-an hour back and start again. But, no problem, I thought, I must have taken a little right turn without realising, and put this new gulley between myself and the creek.' He began to arrange the *objets trouvé* of the table. The plate of cakes became the snowy plateau. Someone's green wool-hat became the forest. A pencil Bjørn had that minute dug up from the seat beneath him, served for the forest-trail, and a shoe-lace from Jesse's pocket became the disappearing stream. 'If I just head straight through the forest to the left, I'll surely hit it. So I clambered up the bank and started through the trees. Gee, that was one of the stupidest things I've ever done. I figured I'd come out on the road in five or ten minutes at most. The trail couldn't have diverged that much—that was my thinking—or I would have noticed when I took the wrong way. It must have headed in much the same way as the original one. After twenty-five minutes, I was still ploughing through the firs. It was getting difficult to see my way. I had the flashlight, but that just lit the immediate ground, and made everything else look darker. Beyond the circle, there was just that heavy blue glowing the snow makes. I began to get a bit panicked. I was thinking about the hostel, eating supper, taking my book to the parlour-fire there. I gave it five minutes more and was still in the midst of the trees. So I decided to retrace my footsteps, back to the trail and walk back on it, slowly, till I found the fork. I just wanted to do things correctly, not take any more chances.' He drained the mug of wine. 'Some hope I had. I went back another half-hour through the trees but I didn't come out at any trail. I had walked noticeably more quickly than before, so I should have hit it by now. Now I was really panicking. I went on another five minutes, ten, twenty—still no trail. I couldn't believe it. I had tears standing in my eyes! I was convinced I was heading in the right direction. It was really just a case of walking straight ahead, turning around, walking straight back. It's hard to credit how difficult that simple manoeuvre can be when you're surrounded by miles of forest. After about an hour of this I really got angry. It was quarter-past five. I ate the last of the baguette and decided to walk in what I thought was the right direction—to my left now—the direction I thought I'd been walking in originally. So I hit out, at quite a pace now, trying to stay in the wider avenues, while keeping my direction. I didn't even look at my watch. I just kept the flashlight trained on the snow and tramped on, keeping my rhythm. I had to come out on a trail—I was just telling myself—it was impossible that I could miss a trail if I walked in the same direction. There were many trails in the area. It's a popular place for hiking.'

'Ja, Herr Ober!' said Tomas, snaking up a hand. He swung his long crossed legs. *'Buchteln, wenn's geht, und noch zwei Flaschen Wein.'* He frowned on his interruption. *'Ja, das war's. Danke sehr.* Sorry, Jesse, pray continue.'

'Okay, so I walked like that for what seemed ages. Eventually I came to a slope. I followed it halfway down into a small valley or shallow gorge. It was properly night by now. The trees were thick there too. But, as I was going up the other side, I thought I saw a light through them, off to my left. I shut off the flashlight. Just a faint, dim light, like candlelight. I put the torch back on and made my way towards it, more scared than relieved, and about halfway between myself and the light, I came upon a clearing. And what do you think was in that clearing?' Jesse paused. He was beginning to enjoy himself. 'An old stone well.' He edged the ash-tray a little closer. 'Kind of a stone circle with the gabled wood roof. No pail, no handle, just this metal grid across the top, I don't know, to stop people falling in. That was a little spooky in itself. From there I could see the light more clearly. It *was* candlelight—in the window of some kind of dwelling. A hut or lodge of some sort.' He moved his own brown hat—with the ear-flaps—to the edge of the table, just in front of Tomas. 'I turned off the flashlight and stood beside the well,' he said, tapping the ash-tray, 'just wondering what the heck it was doing here, what the heck I was doing here. I honestly didn't know whether to go back or go on.'

'Well, well, well.'

'Haff-haff.'

Bear in mind, though,' began Jesse again, croaking in his throat. 'I was cold and hungry. There was a candle, there had to be someone there. They could show me the best way out, I thought. Maybe it's a hostel and I can stay there. I'm not sure I want to stay there though. It's kinda lonely. So here I am, I'm freezing cold and lost in the Slovenian forests, but I'm getting picky. I figure, you only need to be one step up from starvation and you start distinguishing between turnips and potatoes.'

'I don't know. It's all the same to Harper!'

'Ha-ha-ha-ha.'

'I would have preferred to just find my quiet way back to the hostel. I was thinking about my room, the super-pressed bedsheets, that old hostess's quite excellent cooking. But I was getting ahead of myself. It was hopeless thinking like that, as if I could just skip this inconvenient interim. As if that's all it was! Here I was, standing by a well, in a clearing,' (circling the ash-tray) 'in the middle of a forest,' (palming the green wool-hat), 'at six thirty on a January night' (pulling his strawlike forelocks). 'Shoot, was I compromised! So I kind of shifted toward this lodge—with the candle burning in what looked like some kind of dirty plastic window—and, you know, the light just splurging up the pane. Like a nicotine stain or something. And you know what the weird thing was? I'm edging closer—from tree to tree almost, like the wolf in the cartoons—trying not to step on any twigs or rabbit-traps—'cause I know from experience, you can never be too sure about rabbit-traps—'

'Haff-haff,' said the Lizard sympathetically.

'—watching this spread of light on the pane, and listening out, with all my ears straining, for sounds of any kind, except the shuffle of my own feet in the snow—and I see myself a second, my black gloves, blacker than the forest round me, and my boots on the white below—and my breath coming in hot shafts—and it's me I start to get scared of! It's *me* I'm going goosey over. Maybe *I'm* the one! The killer in the woods, and when whoever it is in there sees me—watching from behind the candle flame—they're going to scream blue murder. I don't know. You can't account for people's actions in those situations. One thing can lead to another. I could imagine someone going nuts in a situation like that. Two people meeting, in the middle of a forest, in the dark of night, dying of fright—or quailing a second and flying at each other—not a word said—just for fear's sake.'

Jude was with him there. He frowned at the distinct possibility. Bjørn looked up from under his brows, diagonally to his right. One hand was round his mug. His head was inclined to the table, listening intently. He wet a meditative lip, turned his eyes back to the table.

'So I'm pretty terrified by now. I don't want to creep up there. I want to make as much noise as possible, crack every twig in the book. Funny how there's never any twigs when you want 'em though. I start making a big song and dance about approaching that house. I turn on the flashlight, I'm tramping the snow, pushing back branches. I even cough a couple times. I even say "hello!", coming close to the house now, but somehow my voice seems small—really localised—as if outside and inside were two different things. Now, I'm about twenty yards away, still screened by trees. I'm kind of diagonally-on to the window at his point,' (cutting a palm toward the flapped, brown hat). I turn the flashlight on the house and I see wood piled up outside. There's a collection of things. An old wood-seat, some rusted machinery—some kind of strimmer, I think, there's a rake there, and a lawn-mower. Would you believe that? A lawn-mower. I don't know, maybe there's a lawn round front. At what seems the back of the house, you've got some kind of outdoor pump. There's this covered part to the back, under the gable, with work surfaces. You can't see quite into that—it's a dark space. The flashlight doesn't show enough. There's more wood laying around, and, then, what do you know—to my *horror*—the flashlight comes to rest on an axe, plum in the middle of a chopping-stump. That's right,' said Jesse, deep in his cups, well in the swing of things, 'middle of the forests, lonely house, don't speak the language, hold very little currency—hee hee—and an axe, blade half-buried in a tree. Alright, there's nothing more normal than that, in the midst of a forest, in wintertime, with firewood laying around, but darn! if I don't shudder to a halt, almost wincing. I actually feel my heart thump, like a ball in a sock. I don't know. I don't consider myself easily scared, but I'm worried I'll die of a heart-attack before I make it to the house. Automatically I shut off the flashlight. That in itself scares me though. The constant oscillating—on, off, on, off. Anyone watching would have to think it suspicious. It *was* suspicious! Try explaining that to a jury.'

'Haff.'

'I want to go round to the front door, but I just can't walk that way—not past the dark space. So I come out of the trees, round about the corner of the house and I'm exposed! It's too late to turn back now, even if I would. Even the flashlight's pointless now—the candlelight's bright enough to walk by. I'm kind of squinting into it, trying to look friendly, as if I can half-see someone behind it, which of course I can't. But then I start imagining I can. I start seeing—or imposing—on the oily screen some old woman's face, staring out at me: a kind of knobbled face, gnarly cheeks and eyes. I start to see the tips of fingers on the pane. I try to shake it off, but I'm shaking. I'm sure it's my imagination, but that doesn't mean it's not scary. I was going to go round to the front, but the way I see it, I have to pass in front of the window, I may as well get it over with. The last thing I want is someone seeing me pass and moving on, giving them time to get scared of me. So I bite the bullet. I go—too quickly—straight for the window, quickly knock it, to give them time to adjust—but not really enough time, because I'm impatient to wait—press my gloves to the window and peer inside.' He cupped his hands around his temples, peered into the audience, who sat around, mouths open, in a halo of gloom and wine.

'A room. All perfectly, pristinely, furnished. Not a speck outta place. Kinda like lookin' at a—what's his name—a Vermeer painting? Have I pronounced that right? You know what I mean? I remember there's this cold, dead fireplace. Paintings on the wall, I can't tell what of, but old, gold frames. Tables and chairs, old fashioned furniture. Ornate. Some of it quite massy and solid. Some delicate-looking. I'm—huhh—I'm gettin' an impression of material, of heavy, stuffy material. There's carpet, I'm quite sure there's thick carpet, ornately patterned, though I couldn't swear to that. There's just this candle glowin' on the window sill, the one I'd seen from the woods. And it's blurring my sight, don't forget. It's hard to see into a room, when you're staring past a candle which is the only light source. So I'm cuppin' my hands, pressing my nose against this window, and I'm half wanting to take to my heels, half wanting to show my hand, shout my name, pound upon the window. And I'm getting this impression of heaviness, breathiness, kinda suffocation. And my eyes are adjustin' to the gloom. 'Cept it's not gloom. There's a kinda whiteness, wellin' up to 'em. And as the wellin' floods over, as it were, I realise.' He paused. 'Everything.' He paused again. 'Every piece of furniture in the room. Dining table, coffee table, couch—kinda more of a divan—armchairs, dining chairs, lamp-tables, lampstands, I forgot the piano—upright piano—record player, speakers, mantlepiece, you name it. Even the sill the candle stands on. Is covered.' Jesse swung wet eyes about the table. There was a breathiness there too.

'In lace,' he sighed.

'Oh my *God!*'

'This really immaculate milk-white lace.'

'Haff.'

'Seriously.'

'MmhUH!'

'Like a snowfall in the interior. Fact, for a moment, I don't remember if I'm inside or out.' He took in the circle. 'You could forget what century you were in.'

'You could, couldn't you. Haff-a-haff! What millenium, in fact.'

'Nn, perhaps it was a MUSEUM.'

'It did cross my mind. A kind of lodge for tourists, showing scenes from bygone days.'

'A museum. Hm. Or a craft centre.' Tomas blew smoke, smiling. 'Slightly odd, perhaps. Not altogether unremarkable.' He drew in his lips. 'But, if I may, not completely remarkable either.' He looked like troubled water. It was hard to tell which direction his lips went in.

'Except that, as I peered, I heard somethin' too.

Low at first, hard to hear. Hard to credit too. On and off. But emerging, upwelling just like that whiteness. What I can only describe. As a moaning.'

'Haffa. I have to just—narf, no.'

'A kinda rolling throated moan, pitched between pain and dumbness. Between expectancy and a kind of innuration.'

'Hm. Innuration.'

'It was hard to tell if it was man or woman. It was—almost bestial.'

'Haffa, sorry.'

'Like one who can see before them the instrument of their torture.'

'I see.'

Jesse looked round the circle, nose over his cup. It was a mixed expression, mirthful but intent. 'I just remember this sensation of horror. Just *horror*.' This was one of his favourite words, pronounced with maximum leverage on the *r*. As if taking a slow hit, he reeled back, beatifically smiling, somewhere between *anagnorisis* and *catharsis*. 'What could I do? I peeled back from the window and ran. I'm not kidding, I ran like I don't think I've ever ran before. I know it was a forest, I know there was snow on the ground, and I had a rucksack and a flashlight and everything—hiking boots on my feet—but I could *swear* I've never run so fast in my life. I was flying through those firs for about five minutes—flat out. Then I kind of carried on at a jog, with my heart still pounding in my head and—I *swear*—these—instant—flares of adrenaline, released through the body, pressing the mind's eye, so you feel like you could map your own veins from memory. And, in another five minutes, I crashed up a bank, through a ditch of fern and I was out on the original junction. The one I'd been seeking all along. I could not believe it. More than that, the moon was shining out, coming over the mountains. I didn't even need the flashlight. I just strolled—and, by the way, I *was* strolling now, totally relaxed, *transformed*, you could say, by the advent of the open road—through the lines of trees, up the road, round the hillside to the hostel and the houses there. Honestly, that was the worst couple of hours, followed by the best hour, of hiking I've ever done. By the time I got up to the hostel, I felt like I could walk all night. I only realised how tired I was when I polished off a couple plates of soup with meatballs, took my book to the fire and fell asleep beside it.'

There was a silence. A movement of feet, a touching of cups. But a silence. That which horror requires of its votaries.

'Crumbs,' said Bjørn. You've been TEN THOUSAND MILES in the MOUTH of a GRAVEYARD!'

This was a kind of cue. A murmur went through

the company. A murmur like applause.

'That is quite eery, isn't it, to say the least. Lace, you say.' Tomas drew on a cigarette. 'Hmm.'

'Really elaborate stuff. Masses of it. As if it were clogging up the room.'

'It should actually be legal. It shouldn't—*actually*—be *legal.*'

'Ff-ff, what shouldn't be legal?' asked Tomas, with that patter-like voice, very pleasant. The waiter slid two open bottles on the table.

'Living alone in the woods, collecting lace and moaning. At the very least there should be a curfew on such things.'

'What about living in the woods and *nott* collecting lace, or moaning?

'Held in high-suspicion. Subject to regular checks, not to say *raids*, not to say *purges*, by the relevant authorities.'

'Nn, what about HENRY! DAVID! THOREAU?! Whatt would you have said to WALDEN POND?!'

'The checks, the raids, the purges.'

'Actually you know,' said Jesse, who was in a narrative groove, 'you put me in mind of one of my favourite Sherlock Holmes' observations, from the story, "The Copper Beeches". Holmes and Watson are on the train, going through the countryside. Watson remarks that the farms are beautiful and Holmes replies:—' and, pink-faced and enspirited, he assumed his best British accent: '"They always fill me with a certain *horror*."' At this word, like a tent-fabric suddenly stanchioned, the soft British accent got American strengths. He collapsed it again though, like one who enjoys being covered in cloth: '"It is my belief, Watson, founded upon my experience, that the lowest and vilest alleys in London do not present a more dreadful record of sin than does the smiling and beautiful countryside." Jesse bunched his shoulders, leaned into the table-edge. '"It is the five miles of country,"' he pronounced, '"which makes the danger."' He ended, blushing and satisfied, wondering where his wine had gone. With invisible grace, Tomas reminded him.

'Exactly so. Exactly so,' said Jude, accepting Tomas' proffered cigarette. He leaned in to Pilar. '*Hast Du Feuer?*'

'I was about to ask you the same question.'

Jude raised an eyebrow. He placed Saint's lighter, like a bribe, precisely on the table, and tapped the lid with a forefinger. It was an outrageous gesture: a quotation; covert and overt at the same time.

'Exactly so.'

Pilar lit up, both tobacco and grin, and pocketed the lighter. There was some coming and going at the next table. Through the press, stopping and starting like the stages of an intellectual problem, came Frau Hawelka with the cakes. She stopped, opened her mouth as if to say something, then shook her head and was gone behind the hatstand.

'Sherlock Holmes,' mused Tomas, as if connecting trains of thought. 'I'm curious, what did you do about it? After all, that was a somewhat *suspicious* situation there. It's not every day you hear tortured moans in the woods.' Tomas' words were ornate chess-pieces. They emerged in rank and file from that precise, if oblong, mouth. It was like an inside-out chess-box, that mouth, with the velvet padding of lips and the wood case of teeth and jaw. Bjørn had once been distracted by it. Deep down he resented it. A Swede loved to muscle-in on your terrain.

'I did nothin'. You know I've been wondering if I should have, but, by the time I'd gotten back the whole thing already seemed exaggerated. Not a figment of the imagination exactly, but aided and abetted thereby.' Not unlike the Spectre, Jesse had a certain archaic, if playful, turn of phrase, at once inspired and intimidated by the presence of Old Worlders. 'Even the next day I didn't make much of it. I was just glad the sun was shining. It was only over the succeeding couple days, back in the populous metropoli, in Ljubljana and now here, I started wondering about that; if I hadn't actually been right first time; if my first instincts were not my best. I'd told myself that the moan wasn't that long, or that fearful. That it could have been anything: someone stubbing their toe, or walking into a door.'

'Which would have been *terrifying*, sir. Not to say suspicious. And well worth reporting to the authorities.'

'Hee-hee. Ah. But actually I think I was right. It *was* a suspicious situation. It *was* a moan of fear.'

'Though it could, as you say, have been a lace-loving Slovenian's legitimate fear at seeing a mad, shaggy American at their window.'

'Hee-hee. There's always that. I didn't shave while I was away so I was fairly shaggy. But I started thinking I maybe should have reported it. You know, it could be I was too freaked out. Or perhaps I just couldn't be bothered. I was too tired to think about it.'

'This was a few days ago, I take it. I suppose there's still time.'

'I suppose there is.'

Jesse looked intently at the table. Bjørn tapped his teeth. Tomas squinted dreamily through smoke. Jude was looking at the Lizard looking round at him in the window.

'Don't all rush at once!' cried the Lizard. 'Haff-haff-haff.'

'Ha-ha-ha,' said Jude, turning from the reflection.

'Though if it comes to that, I suppose I'm as guilty as anyone. Haff-haff-haff, oh no, not like that.'

'Ff-ff-ff.'

'Well, that too of course, haff-haff, but for reasons more related to Jesse's "moral dilemma".' The Lizard underscored these two words, *moral* and *dilemma*, as if he were placing on the table a suitcase full of bank-notes. A cliché, but a persuasive one. The Lizard liked a good cliché, enclosed by the inverted commas of his teeth. He liked innuendo too. It was almost a speech-defect.

'Oh, I see!' said Jude, overturning the metaphorical table. 'His *moral dilemma!*' The bank-notes went all over the floor.

'Well, it's like this you see. In fact, I have a bit of a spine-chiller of my own to tell. Somethin' to "freeze the marrow", so to speak. Haff-haff, no not Sarah Kent, that's a different story. Haff-haff-haff. No, it was back in the Glum, see, early last month. I haven't told you this, have I Jude?'

'Ha! I don't know! It wouldn't surprise me.'

'Haff-haff. Leastwise, I don't think I have.'

'Let's see shall we?'

'I suppose we might as well.'

'WE haven't heard it ANYhow,' said Bjørn, including the rest in the circle of his finger.

'It was Magnus you see. He sort of "coerced" me into helping him, you might say, on account of you and Harper were exiled more or less, weren't you?' The Lizard sounded surprised. 'As I say, first it was just a few errands. I had time on my hands. And I had a car, look. I still have it actually, haff, that's ridickalous, isn't it, the "narrative" past simple, in that particular situation, haff-a, you could say I'm gettin' above myself there, aren't I. Ah dear, I'll become an "omniscient narrator" if I'm not careful. Grrr, I know where I'd be omniscient if I had half a chance, haff-a-haff haff! Ah dear, I'll give them "omniscience" in a minute! Haff-a-haff! Right up the you-know-where! Haff-a-haff-a-haff! Haff-a-haff!' Jude roared with laughter. The Lizard leaned in. Everyone noticed he had barely touched his drink. 'That was at first, look. But pretty soon, he began asking other favours. Naaoh, no. No, Magnus wanted me to protest against the Bullish expansion. He got me to lobby the local council, but I'm not the best lobbier to be honest. Although I can lob Jude easily enough, on the rare occasion he goes in goal. Haff haff. Let's be fair, though, it's not difficult is it?—it only needs a dink, doesn't it, haff-a-haff haff haff! No, I did write them a letter but I got a bit slack about it. "Lackadaisical" you might say. I went to your Dad, though, to see if he could help but there was nothing he could do.' The Lizard looked resigned to the world's doom. 'So Magnus resorted to Plan B.'

'What was that?' said Tomas, intrigued.

'It's probably not what you're expecting, to be fair.'

'I don't doubt it.'

'You haven't heard it yet, to be fair. Haff-a—well

he hasn't has he? He wanted me to go up to town, up to the library, look, and read about the history of Ossly, and Bullish, and the building of the reservoirs. How they were built, designs and so forth. All kinds of local history, he had me investigating. He even had me digging about in the genealogy section. Let's face it. I don't need a lot of encouragement do I? Ohhhh no, nooo! It was just sitting up for me, wasn't it? Begging to be hit, as they say. Like someone around here.' The Lie assumed a puzzled expression, wondering if he could chance a joke, opting for a cryptic: 'Hm, who could that be?' He touched his nose. 'I didn't mind, to be honest, 'cause it gave me a chance to "indulge" my interest in etymology. Anyway, he had me in there, researching Hole and Nemmins' family history. And the Freely-Lowe's. You know, above Meal Common there?'

'*I* do. *I do* know,' said Jude, but he didn't look as though he did. He was making eyes at Laura Barbosa and Bjørn was quietly chuckling. Even Pilar snorted. Olivia stayed quiet, holding a cigarette away from the conversation. It was questionable, which she would have untouched by which.

'And, though it's a bit of a digression—but let's face it, when is genealogy anything more than a digression, haff-a—who do you think I see in the genealogy section, doing his own bit of "research"?

Ah dear, they call it "research" don't they, but it looks like diggin' dirt to me. Haff-a-haff! Plain old-fashioned dirt-diggin'. Moagh, they've got some fancy terms, haven't they? So there I am, trying to trace Nemmins' family history—it goes way back, look, to the seventeenth century—and who's sitting at the table, leafing through the very book I wanted, calm as you like, but Hole himself. In a pair of reading glasses. I'm not bein' funny! Ridickalous, isn't it? And where was he the second time I saw him? Would you believe in the urban geography? Fighting over a book with some angry old Scot. Although "sot" might be the better term. Ah dear, it was hilarious. There was that Scot, effing and blinding, waving his library card, saying he had a right to the book, that he'd seen it first, and so on, and there was Hole, lookin' like Oliver Cromwell, just fixing his blue eyes on 'im, still as a pool. Arrrgh, dear. "Still as a pool", that's an awful one isn't it? I'd better research in the "simile" section next time. Could be hard to find, though, couldn't it? Probably looks the same as the other sections, haff-a-haff! Argh, no. In the end, the Scot reached the end of his tether and flounced off to the film section, saying, in no uncertain terms, that he would "bide his time, like Raving Wood," or somesuch. Don't ask me what he meant. "Bide his time" indeed. That sounds like an uncertain term to me. Argh, dear, "in no uncertain terms". People do talk a lot of rot, don't they?'

'What was the book about, do you know?'

'Well,' and the finger went back to the nose. 'It's funny you should say that. Because I did sneak a look actually, from behind the shelves. That's one thing I can do, isn't it, sneak a look. I've had a lot of practise, haven't I, over the years. Behind the shelves, in front of them, I'm not fussy, haff-a-haff. Neeaaargh. But I sidled behind him, look, pretending to interest myself in a book about "regeneration" and "modern urban planning". Is there anything else you can do with a book like that? Ah dear, he should have seen through that, shouldn't he? "Modern urban planning," I don't believe it. How boring can you get? Not boring enough actually—oh no, that's a terrible "segue", if you will—"segue", ah dear, I'm getting far above my station, aren't I?—because the real "boring" so to speak took place almost two hundred years ago, when Wilson built his famous—and pointless, if we're going to be honest, haff-a-haff—network of tunnels under the town. Which, it turns out,'—his forefinger jabbed the table like a woodpecker—'is what Hole was reading about.'

'Wilson's tunnels.' Tomas dwelt on that one.

'And that's not all. Finally—to round off a series of coincidences, if you like—with a few prompts from Magnus, my research took me to the field of heraldry. And a sable field it is too. And what should I see, when I take open up a book on local heraldic symbology? Only Hole's name, printed in capitals, right there on the library card. He'd taken it out a few weeks before me! Seriously! Ah dear, the plot grows thicker, doesn't it? Either he's very well read, or he's up to no good. Or possibly both! Haff-a-haff, you can't rule out that possibility can you? Haff-a-haff!'

'Hee hee. Sounds like Magnus had rumbled him!'

'What was Magnus' theory, if I may?'

'Well that's the thing you see. Magnus—'. The Lie struggled for the right words, hands hovering. 'Magnus is someone who plays his cards very close to his chest. A bit like me.' He stuck out his lips, daring his audience. 'Not really, do I? I'm too busy playing them close to other people's chests, aren't I. Ohhhh, nooo! Raaagh, haff-a-haff! Sarah Kent's to name but one! Ah dear, is it any wonder Magnus plays his cards close to his chest, with me around. Fat lot of good I do him, don't I? There's him, playing his cards close to his chest, and there's me, spilling mine all over the table. If this was bridge, we'd be losing hand over over fist, wouldn't we? Not that I know how to play bridge. The only card game you can see me playing is poker, isn't it? I'd "poker" with pleasure! Ohhh noooo, I've gone too far haven't I? Texas Hold 'Em? Alright, if you insist! Where shall I put them now? Haff-a-haff! Arrrgh, noooo. That's enough. That's enough.'

The hands outspread, as if making shadows on the wall. 'No, in all honesty, see, Magnus doesn't let me into very much. I'm the dogsbody, if you like. The water carrier. He couldn't do it, see, because he was rather "*persona non grata*", as they say. I don't know what it means, but it sounds fancy enough, doesn't it? "*Persona non grata*", arrgh no. What will I come out with next?'

'Ha! A spine-chiller, apparently.'

'Ah. Yes. I'm getting to that.' The Lie upped his game. 'That was soon before I came here actually, end of November. I didn't manage to find out that much about Nemmins. How could I? Hole had all the books out! So Magnus cooked up this plan to break into Fourpoints Farm. He had a theory, see, so far as I could grasp it, about Nemmins' father. He thought the farm held secrets. Only he needed my help on that one, on account of the house was so well-alarmed and protected, and the Water Board watchmen were always down the road. So one night, we met at midnight, at that ring of hawthorn trees on top of that hill—I suppose it would be Meal Hill—you know, between Meal Common and the lake?'

'*I* do. *I do* know,' said Jude again, touching Barbosa's foot under the table. Bjørn was red in the face, folded in on himself with a bright, clenched grin. He was looking down, elbow on the table, hand sampling the air.

'Above the Police Station, above where they hold the Harvest Fair, look. Near Pete Packer's Repair Yard?'

'Oh yes—Pete Packer's notorious *Repair Yard.*' Again the foot sought its target, applied a subtle pressure. Barbosa looked shifty. There was no way of knowing whose foot that was, bar an open challenge. This was unnerving. On the other hand, this was also its saving grace. She studied her wine as if mulling it herself. What was a foot between friends? She adopted a sullen expression, sought somewhere to fix it on, chanced upon Benjamin Keppery-*Algo* and sunk into a slough of despond.

'That was the "specified location".'

'The hawthorn ring?'

'I suppose it was, wasn't it?'

'Well was it?'

'Weeell, sometimes I wonder—ahaff-ahaff-ahaff!'

'Ha-ha-ha-ha-ha!' Jude's laugh, like his football, was a joyous mixture of abandon and control.

'Huh-huh, CRUMBS!' interjected Bjørn, still laughing but returned from his sojourns. 'This is, ah, a classic example of the UNRELIABLE NARRATOR!' He nodded emphatically.

'Perhaps,' said Tomas, 'we should hear out the story before we judge of that.'

'Not necessarily,' said Jude, who had finished laughing. 'That's the thing about your unreliable narrator. At a certain point he becomes *entirely* reliable. The devil's greatest trick was to convince the world that his stupid lie was actually his greatest trick. Except that after a small inquiry, everyone realised that it was in fact a stupid lie and went home, disappointed with the devil. No, give me a reliable narrator, strapped with facts to the wheel. Wherever it roll, he rolleth too. Except in the crags, obviously. A King with crown of thorn, is your reliable narrator.'

'Nnn, may be some alto clumulus in there somewhere, rolling away.'

'What are they goin' on about?' said the Lizard flashing a look at Tomas beside him. 'I don't know about narrators but that's an unreliable audience right there.'

'I'm not altogether sure. I should continue with your narrative.'

'I probably should, shouldn't I? So, as I say, we met at the ring of hawthorns. But he hadn't told me, as yet, what it was we were going to do. All he'd told me was to wear dark clothes. Arrgh, no, bet he was delighted when I turned up in my Juventus top. Well, I got it half right, didn't I? I always do, don't I—that's just the trouble, haff-a-haff! No, all I knew was that we were going to be driving to some "unspecified location".'

'Ha!'

'Haff-haff, ohohno, we know what "unspecified

location" you'd like to be driven to. It's gettin' more specific by the minute, haff-a-haff haff! Seriously though. We went over to Pete Packer's yard, where I'd parked the car, look, and drove up Cleave Hill, in the direction of Dimly, Magnus directing. Eventually we drift down toward Bullish Lake and park the car in a field, a little way above Fourpoints Farm. He thought he'd identified a weakness in the bathroom window, which was often open. For reasons which I won't go into, haff-a-haff-a-haff! But it faced the side, see—the yard—over this lower roof. He thought the window wouldn't be alarmed. It was too small for him, but he thought I could do it. So we waited, watching the house. Nemmins was out on his nightwatch, wasn't he, and the house was quiet. No lights at all. We crept in up through the fields, round the back, comin' from Bullish lake. It was so sloppy in those fields, you couldn't believe it. The floods, look. The fields were all underwater, and that was just from rain. There's rumours it'll all be underwater soon—'cause they want to extend Bullish. Glum Lake's not working, you see. Too many flaws and leaks. It's cheaper to extend Bullish, apparently, than mend all that's wrong with the Glum. Anyway, we slopped up through those fields, falling in the water a good few times, I can tell you—at least I did. Magnus had already seen to the dogs, look. He'd found some sort of hole in the ground, under the road, near the main gate. "Scoped it out" you might say.'

Something—a sense of injury—bristled in Jude. 'Ha!' he said, and refrained from explanation.

The Lie was sidetracked. He eyed Jude warily, and continued. 'Anyway, he'd crawled in there with some steaming meat. Drugged, wasn't it; sleeping pills, I suppose. Even then, he thought it might be watched. So we went via the fields, then round into the yard and he helped me onto this covered-way I suppose you'd call it, and from there onto the roof. I watched him trip along the apex of the roof, all erect (ohohono), with his fingers branching from his waist. He really is a scarecrow, isn't he. They call him Crow don't they? Rawk! Haff-a-haff. He is like a bit like a crow, at the end of the day.'

'Nnn, the CROW is aspechaRYNchus!'

'Well, the crow is a permanent resident throughout its range.' Jude put his arm around Pilar. Bjørn was well away now, chuckling again and again, like a man hearing voices, in a mental hospital, on the edge of the Bergen fjords.

'Haff,' said the Lie, perplexed. 'Aspecharynchus or not, I followed him, look, stirred by his example, as it were. And we got down from the main roof, to the lower roof, from which the bathroom window becomes accessible. It's complicated isn't it? Needless to say, we did all this as silent as possible, and did a pretty good job of it though I say so myself. So there we are, on this roof, pressed against the wall, inching up under the window. Magnus is going to wait here, to cover eventualities, and I'm going to worm my way inside. Oh no, I'm always worming my way inside, aren't I? Ohohono.'

'Hee-hee.'

'So he makes a step with his hands and, you know, levers me up to the sill.' The Lie made a heave-ho motion. 'It was one of those old, bobbled-glass affairs, with the narrow, rectangular window at the top, which, as I say, was open. No sooner had I grabbed hold of the opening, I heard a thump. Two, actually, because my heart jumped into my mouth. I just hung there, staring into the dark opening. Naooogh, naooo. There wasn't much I could do at that point, was there. I was pretty red-handed so to speak. It would have been hard to talk my way out of that one. Eventually it seemed all quiet, so I just poked my head through the hole. Magnus was right, of course. No alarm. There was a funny smell, though, but I wasn't paying much attention to that. It was a toilet after all, wasn't it! Haff-a-haff!' His jaw wagged mechanically. He couldn't take his spine-chiller seriously. 'But it was all dark inside. I could barely see anything, and I didn't have Magnus' torch yet. He was going to hand it through, look. So I squeezed through the tiny window—and I'm not as slim as I used to be, look—head first, so I had to put my hands on the toilet and kind of shuffle my legs through. But of course that was very difficult to do, wasn't it, so I fell, didn't I?'

'I expect you did.' Jude looked like someone trying to keep his cool.

'Right on top of someone, didn't I?'

'Did you?'

'I did, didn't I? Imagine my horror.' He nodded at Jesse. 'I had to stifle a bit of a scream I can tell you. I probably sort of sobbed instead. It was dark in there. Only Magnus' torch to see by, on the bobbled glass, look. But I could tell by the soft landing that it was a person. I'd know that old human flesh anywhere, wouldn't I, haff-o-haff!'

'Yes, *especially* old human flesh.'

'Ah dear, but it was a still person, wasn't it. A person who didn't move when I landed on it. And remember, I'm not as slim as I once was.'

'I'll remember.'

'So of course, I pounced to my feet, tripping over the body again as I did so. Again I sprung to my feet and stood on the toilet and got hold of the torch through the window. I almost dropped it on the ground, I was that scared. But I fumbled it in my hands—a bit like Quentin trying to catch one of my cover drives, haff-haff—and managed to train it on the person.' He was solemn again, using expensive language. 'It was a body, like I said, a woman's body, by all reckoning. But really strangely dressed.' He folded his lips, as if mourning. 'She wore big plastic rings, look, laden with plastic fruit. She had these big nails, honestly like ship's chimneys, and this crinkly burnt-wheat wig. Then, unfortunately, there was the upturned skirt, look, with meadowgrass designs. A scar on the belly, comin' up from under. It was pretty sexless to be honest.'

'Hmm!' said Tomas. Jude had turned white.

'The only way I can describe it—it was like her sex was turned inside-out. There it was, visible in ornaments. It was horrible. Horrible, look. What I can only describe—if you'll pardon the expression—as a woman dressed as a man dressed as a woman.'

There was a silence.

'The mind boggles, doesn't it?'

It really did. Another silence followed, filled with adjusting and settling. Then came Jude's more-metallic voice:

'The horror.' He sounded as if he were swallowing a truth, as if what he knew all along were confirmed. 'The horror.' He pushed away his cup with a forefinger. 'You see, women have got to realise: it's not their bodies—their absences and abysses, nay nor abeyances—we're afraid of. It's their *clothes*. Their trails and trappings, skimp and gauze, lace and largesse flowing. All that extraneous appendage. Repulsive. Repulsive. I'm heterosexual *already*. Give me the nude woman, give me her tits and *arse*.' He patted his derriere. 'Cease to make apology for them. For what is seduction but *apology?*'

Bjørn demurred. 'Uh, you're a bit of a misOGYNIST!'

'No, I just don't like women.'

Jude regarded Bjørn with disdain. An uneasy titter went through the booth. When it was gone, he looked aside. 'Cleopatra always excepted.'

'Nnn, BIRDS are not aggressive creatures,' said Bjørn, knowingly. He seemed relieved. 'They bring BEAUTY into the world. It is MANKIND who insists upon making it difficult for life to exist on this planet.'

'It's the *End of the World!*' cried Jude.

Bjørn chuckled, propped a pincered hand on its elbow, and got comfortable. He also got serious again, as if the two were related. 'Ah, but—er—I TOO am heteroSEXUAL. But I have to say, that doesn't STOP me liking a bit of—er—lace and LINGERIE!' He sipped some wine, expounded on different styles and traditions. 'Mmm,' he said, 'that is the MYSTERY of the FEMININE!'

But, like Byron, Jude hated an air of mystery. 'No this is the problem sir.' And he gazed through, or at, the window, depending on the angle. 'This well-worn coin—vagina if you will—of feminine *mystery*. An apology if ever I saw one, by which men hide their repulsion.'

'Er, NOW, you sound like a FEMINIST!'

Jude resumed his hauteur. 'You need to introduce more play—*jouissance*, if you will'—he nodded to the sniggering Lie—'into your vocabulary. Language that drives you into a *camp*—and I use the word *advisedly*—' (advising the Lie) 'take it any way you will (for it means the same)—is bad language. Just look at the Spectre. The fact is, language is a *medias res* (if you will), halfway along the road we have to go.'

'A kind of BIsexuality?'

Jude had turned back to the window, with its array of faces. 'Male and female, sir, is all very well. But it's not everything. Look at the angels.' In the window, Bjørn was staring at his wine, Tomas fiddling with a cigarette, Olivia glaring at Jude; all of them, complacent with metaphor.

'Well look at them!' roared Jude, turning and returning.

'Haff-a-haff-a-haff!'

'Mm, na, perhaps you're right,' said Bjørn reflectively, rejoining fast: 'How would I KNOW? And what would it MATTER anyway?'

'Besides, the fact that men are delusional doesn't elevate women. It just dooms the race.' Jude could see the Lie in reflection, leaning in on the other side of Tomas.

'So you're a misANTHROPIST!'

In the window, where Jude was still gazing, the Lie was gazing too, over at Jude's reflection in fact. 'You couldn't accuse The Man Who Would Be King of that, could you?' he pursued. 'He's always got people's best interests at heart. Haff-a-haff.' He was leaning in close now. His reflected beady eye was fixed on Jude's.

'He is transparent,' said Jude, coldly. He turned back to the company. 'He has divided himself into layers, much like the Karst Plateau. Let's number 'em.' And he put up his thumb. 'The jolly, handshaking gimp you see first up; the pathological tyrant you perceive immediately afterward' (up thundered the index); 'third' (lastly came the middle) 'the despairing Johnny-Come-Lately whom from pillar to post you habitually bandy. His layers are the secrets he pathologically spreads; hence the redundancy of his name—an overlap if ever I saw one.'

He turned back to the window. There was the Lie in it, saying, 'I hope you didn't! Oh no, oh noo. It wouldn't surprise me though! Haff-a-haff.'

Tomas leaned in, though not as far as the Lie. They looked like a fenced crowd, pressing, expectant. The window was the aisle at a wedding, or coronation. 'We're back to escaping names, I see. Only rather than predetermining it, here the name dilutes the object. Overdetermines it, so to speak.'

'Like being shut in a BATHROOM with a CORPSE.'

'Hee-hee. That's so *horrible!* What did you do?'

'I scarpered, didn't I. Haff-a-haff! I wasn't goin' to take a shower, was I? Haff, haffa? (Though God knows I needed it.) No, I got out. Right out the window where I came in. Got a little bit stuck, look, but I managed to squeeze my way out. I always do, don't I, ohh noo, haff-a-haff! Ahh, it beggars belief.'

'*Noch eine Flasche!*'

'But that's not all. The strangest thing of all was, lying beside her, as if it had fallen from her hand, was a video camera. Magnus was peeking through the window, with his torch, and he made me take it, look. So I did, and back at my house, running it through the computer, what did that camera reveal?' The Lie was reaching the end of his narrative far more convinced than he had started it. He chopped slowly but weightily at the table. 'Not much at first, to be fair. Mmnao.' The finger scratched the side of his head. 'Too dark, look. Just pitch black and scratchy, like the old silents. Then there's these three lines across the screen—metallic looking, like railings—and, with them, this sound: a distorted sound; a murmur, to be fair. A sort of torture-murmur if that makes any sense.' He nodded to Jesse, respectfully. '"Who's there?", it says, if you can credit that. "Who's there?"' he repeated. 'Then deadness again: a gloomy silence, really, like night fishing. A bit like that, haff.' The Lie spread his hands. 'Suddenly a figure flaps on! Just for a second, mind, but, unless my eye deceives me—and it is at a distance, in profile, in silhouette almost—it's Magnus bloody Kroner! dressed as a woman, in a wig and shawl!' The hands sank. 'Or is he a King? A Beggar-King you might say. A-haff.' The Lie's was a forced laugh, short-lived. It was hard to tell which impressed him more: the apparition or Magnus himself. 'Of course, it's gone as quick as it came. Almost a trick of the eye—un "*trompe l'oeil*" as they say. After that, more dark. It goes on a while. Briefly, you see shadows—a tree, a car, long drips of water—or are they scratches? Could be. Then—hardly visible, as if ghosts themselves, two dark shapes roam like wolves over a field. Then nothing again. A big black square, if you can imagine that. Let's face it, it's not very difficult is it? Ah dear! In the "realm" of the imagination, that particular image is one of the easier ones to summon, isn't it. You can hardly avoid it, can you? Haff-a-haff. Deary me, a big black square indeed. You can tell I'm not much of a film buff, can't you? Ah dear, I wouldn't know the difference between the new wave and the old wave, to be honest. Haff-a-haff! Let's be fair, one wave is pretty much like the last, isn't it? When all's said and done.' Sensing that Bjørn was about to fill him in on the distinction, the Lie channelled his energies into finishing his tale. 'No, anyway, that old black square continues about half a minute. Then you hear a thump, and a crunching sound. Could it be footsteps? Hard to tell. You see nothin'. Just one of them long drips again. All is quiet. Until. Suddenly.' The Lie planted his hands, as if playing an imaginary piano. 'Leapin' into the foreground of the screen, all white and sweaty, what did I see but—' The hands trembled in readiness. '—"Yours bloody truly"?!'

The hands rose, as if borne upon the chord.

There was an awful pause.

'Good God.'

The silence of digestion.

'It was like a horror film. She was filming us breaking in, look. She must have been scared witless. She was probably wondering where we'd got to. Then, just like that, who appears at the window but old Benjamin McCormack Kepperley Lie. In all my glory, so to speak. It's enough to give anyone the willies, isn't it? It was me, anyway.'

Tomas' voice was cold. 'I can imagine that would be—discomforting—all round.'

'But, honestly, I think I'll always remember that white face looking up at me.'

'Which one?'

'Haff-a-haff, it's hard to tell isn't it? Haff-a-haff!'

The Lie was still leaning in. There was no limit to how far he could lean. He saw Jude, Jude saw him, jiggered if they didn't terrify each other. That hideous gap between the mirror and nature. A cliché, but, like all clichés, a fatal one. 'It will haunt my dreams, so to speak. The lipsticked lips. The plastered eyes. Just like a doll.'

'But enough of Sarah Kent.' Jude's lips were moving, but his eyes were fixed. 'What about the corpse?'

'Here it is!' said the Lie, lunging toward the window.

They laughed and laughed and laughed and suddenly tried to scare each other with a sudden movement.

Printed in Great Britain
by Amazon

84852355R00366